Feel the love for

The characters are charming and believable, and the teen soap drama is well-paced; it all adds up to a solid coming-of-age romance.

Publishers Weekly

The long-form style of the storytelling, along with Vieceli's striking visual style, really helps to create a deep investment in these fictional characters. While readers going through similar situations with their feelings and attractions will likely find certain moments resonating more powerfully, even casual readers will find themselves drawn into the story, likely willing the two leads to find a way to remove all the complications in their lives and simply be happy.

Big Comic Page

No heroes [are] here to jump in and save the day, just ordinary people with ordinary problems that we are all likely to face... Breaks seems like an appropriate name for the series, because the characters seem to be on the verge of breaking point. And unsurprising, we want to read the series further because we want to find out which characters actually will break.

A Place to Hang Your Cape

Breaks has all of the good juicy drama stuff: hurt people hurting people, sizzling sexual tension, mysterious violent back stories, a multi-ethnic cast to a T... The relationships in all directions are relatable and believable both within and beyond high school or Yaoi tropes. Worth picking up.

Broken Frontier

"So where is the love?!" I hear you cry... It's in every line: both those written... and those drawn.

There is ever so much mischief and tenderness evidenced by and in both. There is a vulnerability to the art and an uncertainty in the dialogue whose speakers (in Ian and occasionally Cortland) seek to cover their tentative tracks.

Page 45

...[A]s the boys posture and threaten and circle each other...[t]he expressions are terrific... and the dialogue authentic.

Comics Worth Reading

EMMA VIECELI ~ MALIN RYDÉN

BREAKS

2: TRUTH AND DARE

Cover coloured by Triona Farrell

SOARING PENGUIN
PRESS

UK & CANADA

BREAKS

By Emma Vieceli and Malin Rydén

Published by Soaring Penguin Press
Flat 2
42 Highcroft Villas
Brighton
East Sussex
BM 5PS

www.soaringpenguinpress.com

ISBN 978-1-908030-33-7

Printed in Latvia

To love,

and whoever you choose to share

the adventure with.

- Emma

To Aleph and CJ for making me a better writer.

To Elle and the DAH crew

for sparking these shenanigans.

- Malin

BREAKS

THE STORY SO FAR...

Cortland and Ian had been rivals since Cortland and his best friend, Irena Chrona, transferred into Queen Anne's school & sixth form college three years ago.

KISS ME I'M A TWAT

CHRIST...

Cortland's failure to fall in line and bow down to Ian's friend and school alpha-male, Spencer, lead to a brutal and very public fight at a school dance; suggesting some truth behind the rumours surrounding Cortland's mysterious transfer.

When Spencer enacted a violent revenge against Cortland, Ian failed to step in; unable to choose a side between his bully best friend and the boy he had growing feelings for. The results were...not good.

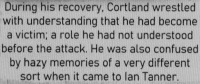

Wracked with guilt, Ian visited the unconscious Cortland in hospital and surprised even himself by planting a tender, but stolen, kiss...

...UH

During his recovery, Cortland wrestled with understanding that he had become a victim; a role he had not understood before the attack. He was also confused by hazy memories of a very different sort when it came to Ian Tanner.

At a party, and promted by Amilah's decision to reveal Ian's part in the attack, Cortland pieced together his memories from the hospital...and any hope of romance felt lost.

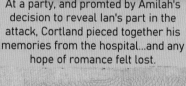

But when Ian went to Spencer to finally speak his mind, regardless of Cortland's anger toward him, he was redeemed. Together, Ian and Cortland overturned Spencer's reign, and finally turned their thoughts toward how they should handle a blatant mutual attraction that neither of them had been ready for.

BREAKS CHARACTERS

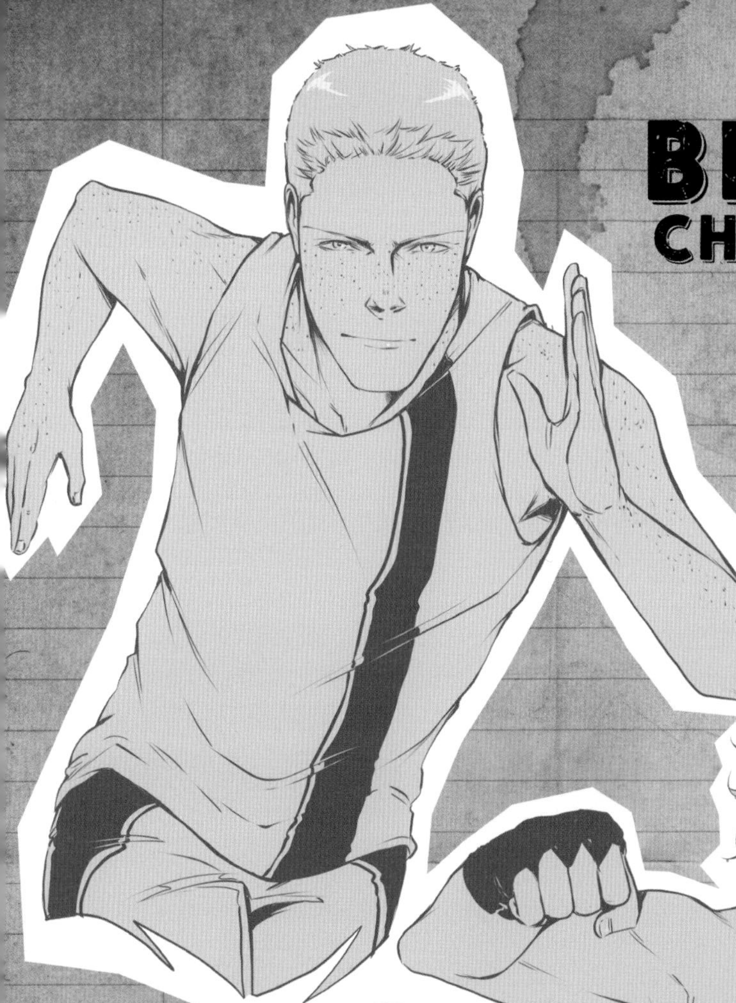

IAN TANNER

Runner. Joker.
Just accepted he's bisexual.

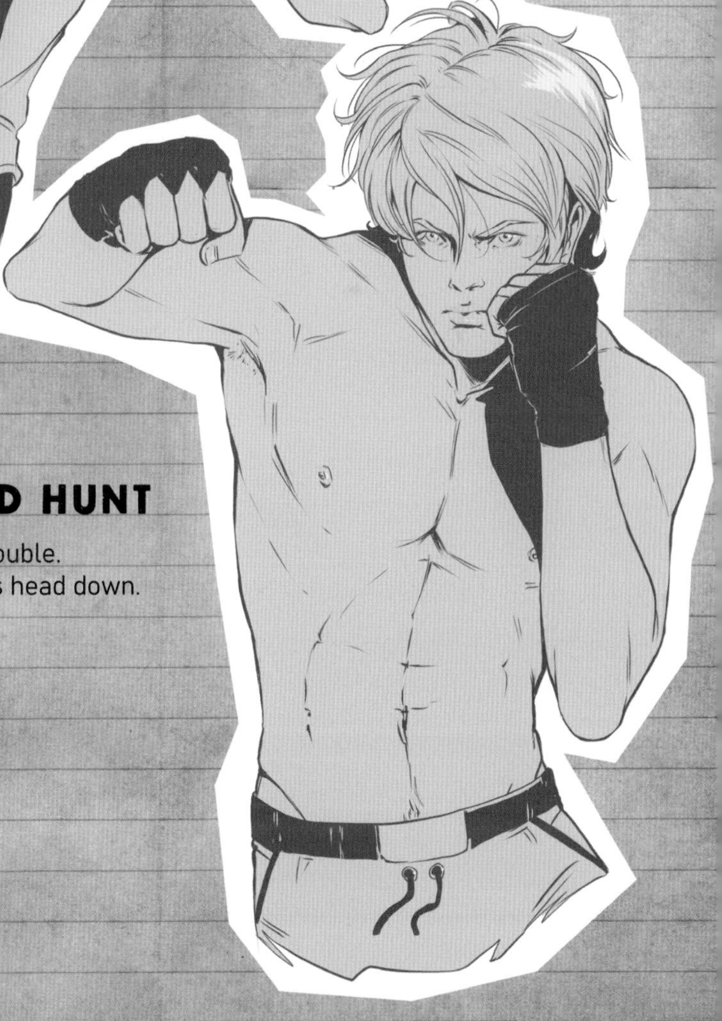

CORTLAND HUNT

Boxer. Trouble.
Trying to keep his head down.

BREAKS
CHARACTERS

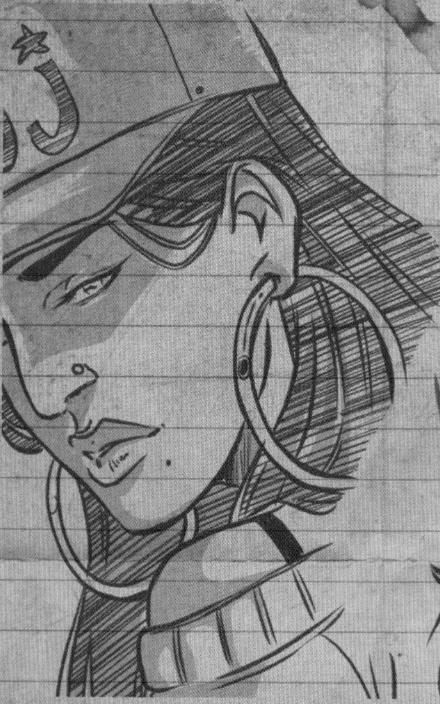
DJ★
MILLY

AMILAH PATEL

DJ and budding music star. Best friend and girlfriend (for now) to Ian. Smart. Ambitious. Amilah sees all. Amilah is wise.

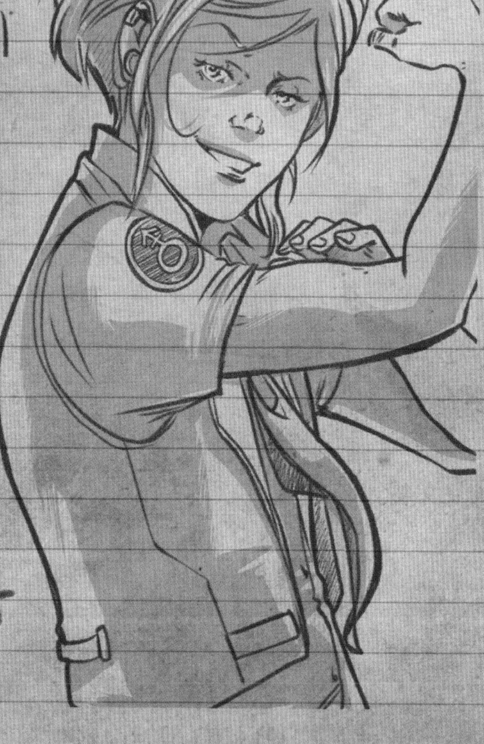
ACE
Pilot

IRENA CHRONA

Polish immigrant artist warrior. Best friend and ally to Cortland. Fierce. Often angry at Cortland's brother, Harvey.

yeah, but... girls smell... really good.

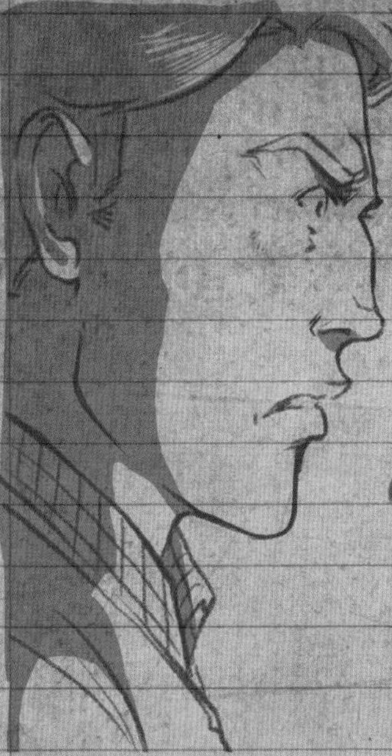

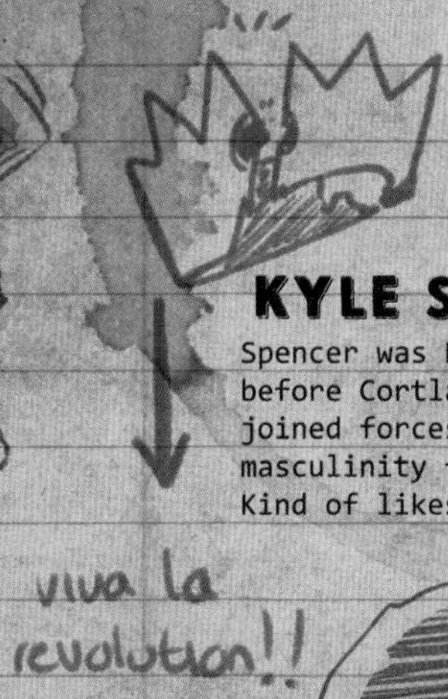
viva la
revolution!!

KYLE SPENCER

Spencer was King on campus
before Cortland and Ian
joined forces. Drinks toxic
masculinity for breakfast.
Kind of likes Milly.

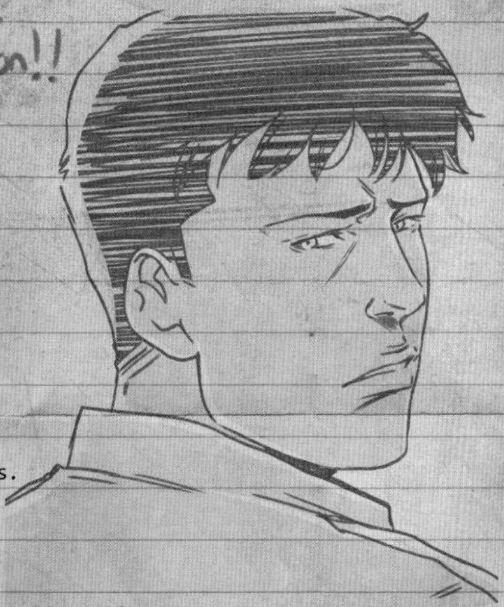

HARVEY HUNT

Cortland's big brother.
Legal guardian since their
Mother was hospitalised.
Has his own secrets. Harvey
doesn't fight. Harvey survives.

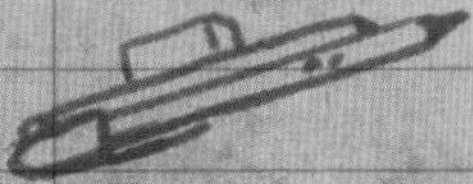

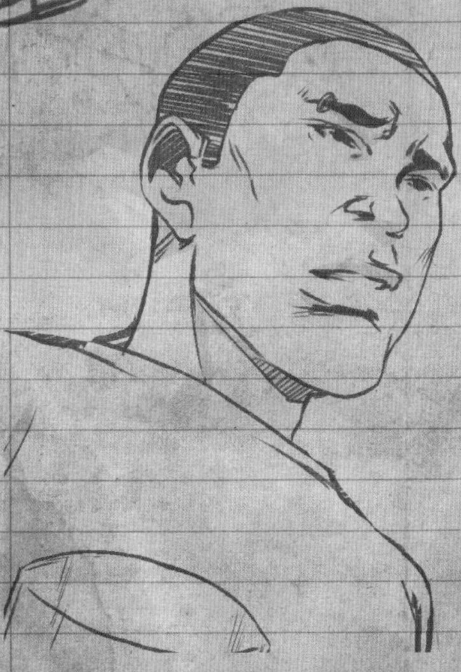

MIKE RUSSELL

Mates with Spence, Ian
and Milly.
Cortland broke his jaw
once. Not quite over it.
Grounded. Sensible. Cares.

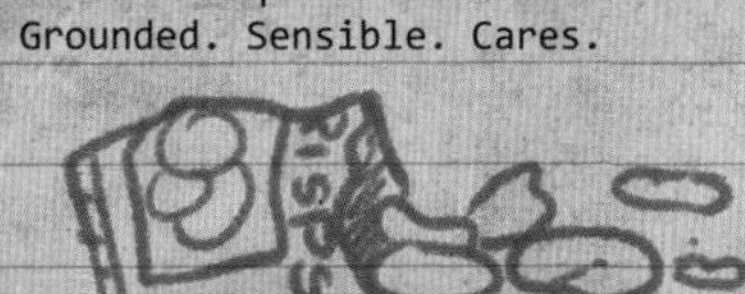

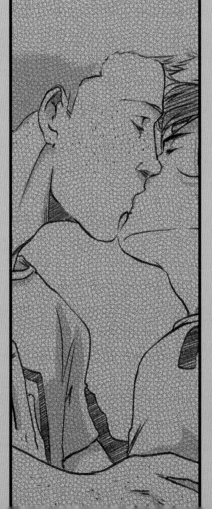

ISSUE 7

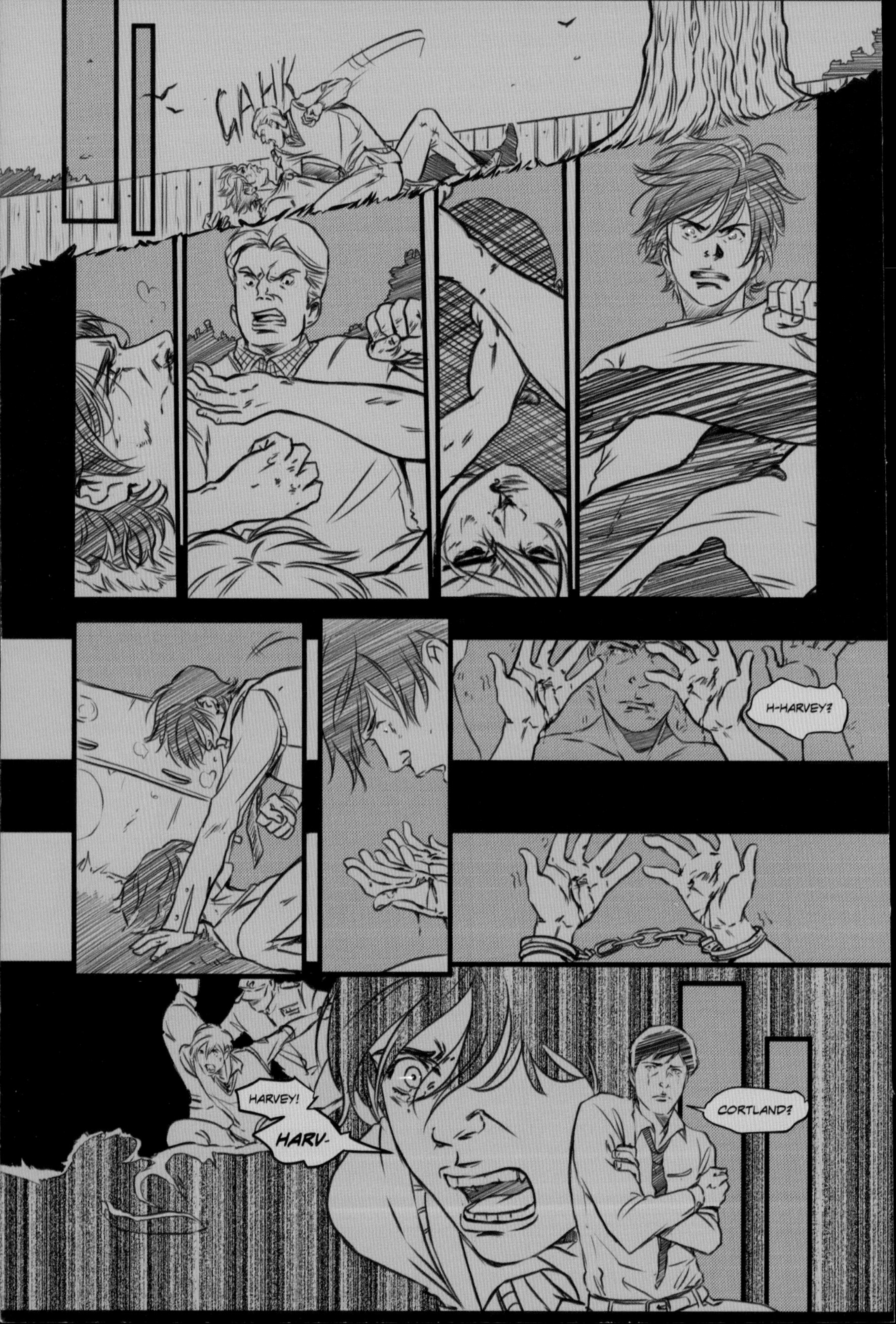
GAHK
H-HARVEY?
HARVEY!
HARV-
CORTLAND?

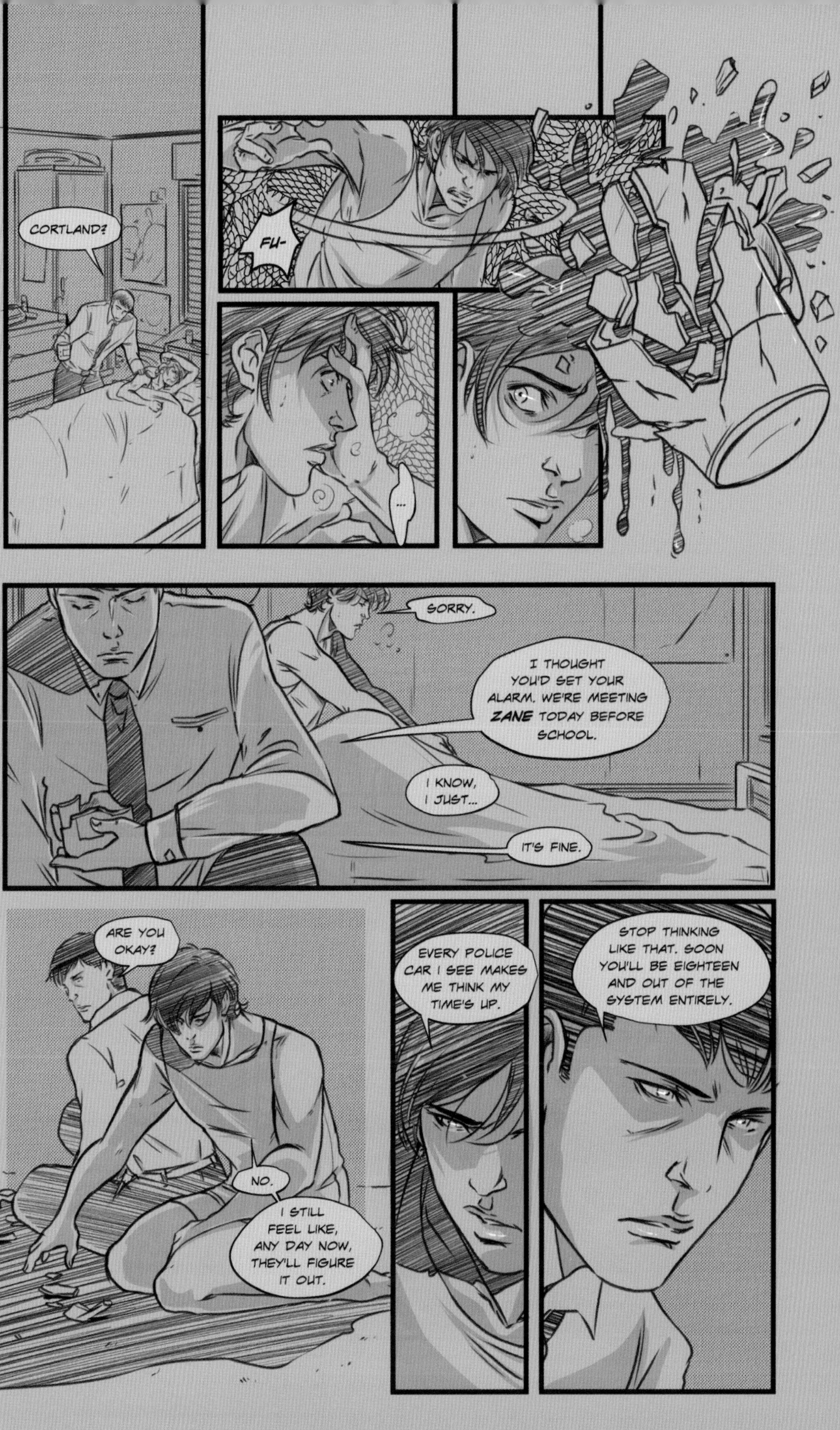
CORTLAND?
FU-
...
SORRY.
I THOUGHT YOU'D SET YOUR ALARM. WE'RE MEETING ZANE TODAY BEFORE SCHOOL.
I KNOW, I JUST...
IT'S FINE.
ARE YOU OKAY?
NO.
I STILL FEEL LIKE, ANY DAY NOW, THEY'LL FIGURE IT OUT.
EVERY POLICE CAR I SEE MAKES ME THINK MY TIME'S UP.
STOP THINKING LIKE THAT. SOON YOU'LL BE EIGHTEEN AND OUT OF THE SYSTEM ENTIRELY.

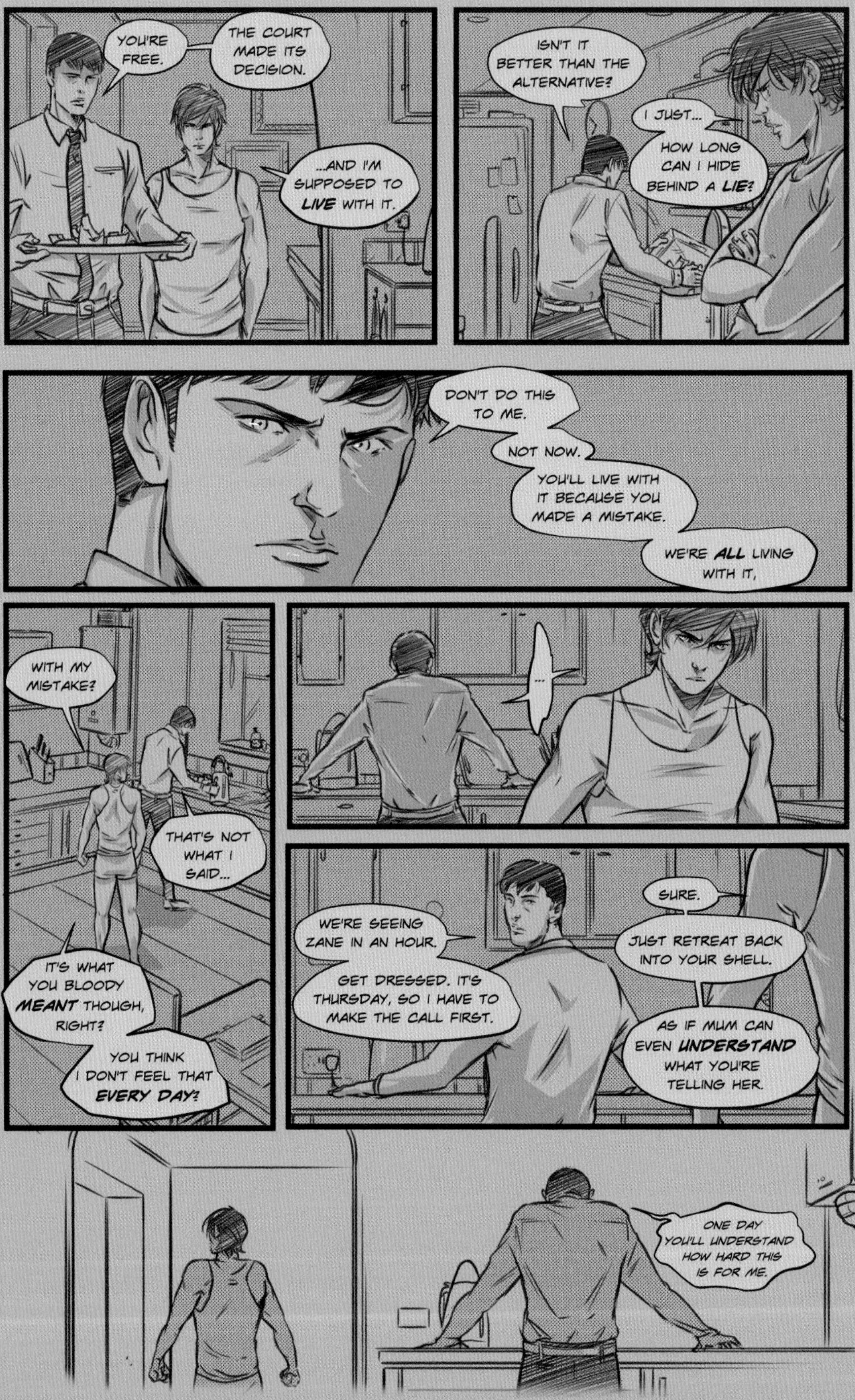
YOU'RE FREE.
THE COURT MADE ITS DECISION.
...AND I'M SUPPOSED TO LIVE WITH IT.
ISN'T IT BETTER THAN THE ALTERNATIVE?
I JUST...
HOW LONG CAN I HIDE BEHIND A LIE?
DON'T DO THIS TO ME.
NOT NOW.
YOU'LL LIVE WITH IT BECAUSE YOU MADE A MISTAKE.
WE'RE ALL LIVING WITH IT,
WITH MY MISTAKE?
THAT'S NOT WHAT I SAID...
IT'S WHAT YOU BLOODY MEANT THOUGH, RIGHT?
YOU THINK I DON'T FEEL THAT EVERY DAY?
...
WE'RE SEEING ZANE IN AN HOUR.
GET DRESSED. IT'S THURSDAY, SO I HAVE TO MAKE THE CALL FIRST.
SURE.
JUST RETREAT BACK INTO YOUR SHELL.
AS IF MUM CAN EVEN UNDERSTAND WHAT YOU'RE TELLING HER.
ONE DAY YOU'LL UNDERSTAND HOW HARD THIS IS FOR ME.

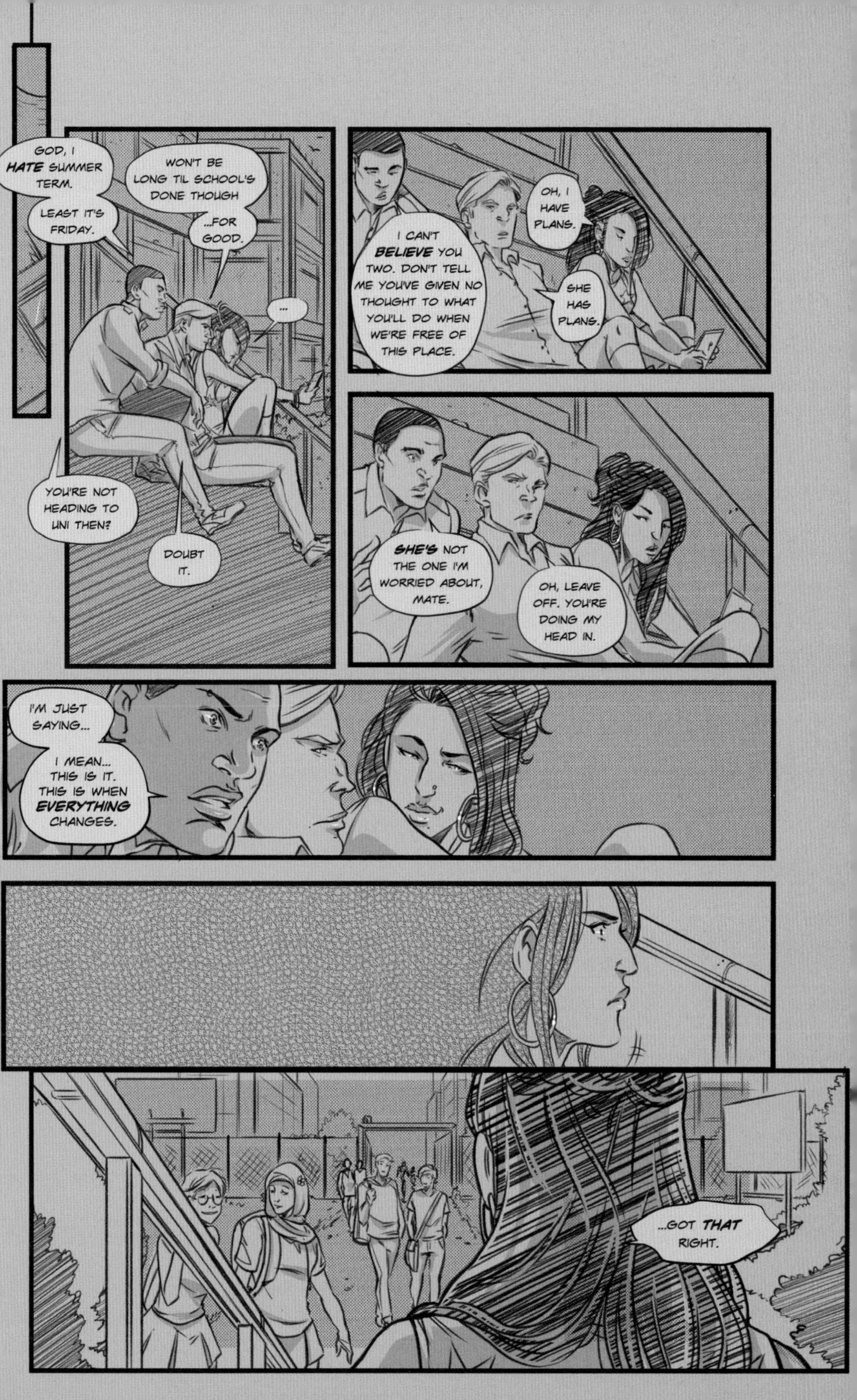
GOD, I HATE SUMMER TERM.
LEAST IT'S FRIDAY.
WON'T BE LONG TIL SCHOOL'S DONE THOUGH
...FOR GOOD.
...
YOU'RE NOT HEADING TO UNI THEN?
DOUBT IT.
OH, I HAVE PLANS.
I CAN'T BELIEVE YOU TWO. DON'T TELL ME YOU'VE GIVEN NO THOUGHT TO WHAT YOU'LL DO WHEN WE'RE FREE OF THIS PLACE.
SHE HAS PLANS.
SHE'S NOT THE ONE I'M WORRIED ABOUT, MATE.
OH, LEAVE OFF. YOU'RE DOING MY HEAD IN.
I'M JUST SAYING...
I MEAN... THIS IS IT. THIS IS WHEN EVERYTHING CHANGES.
...GOT THAT RIGHT.

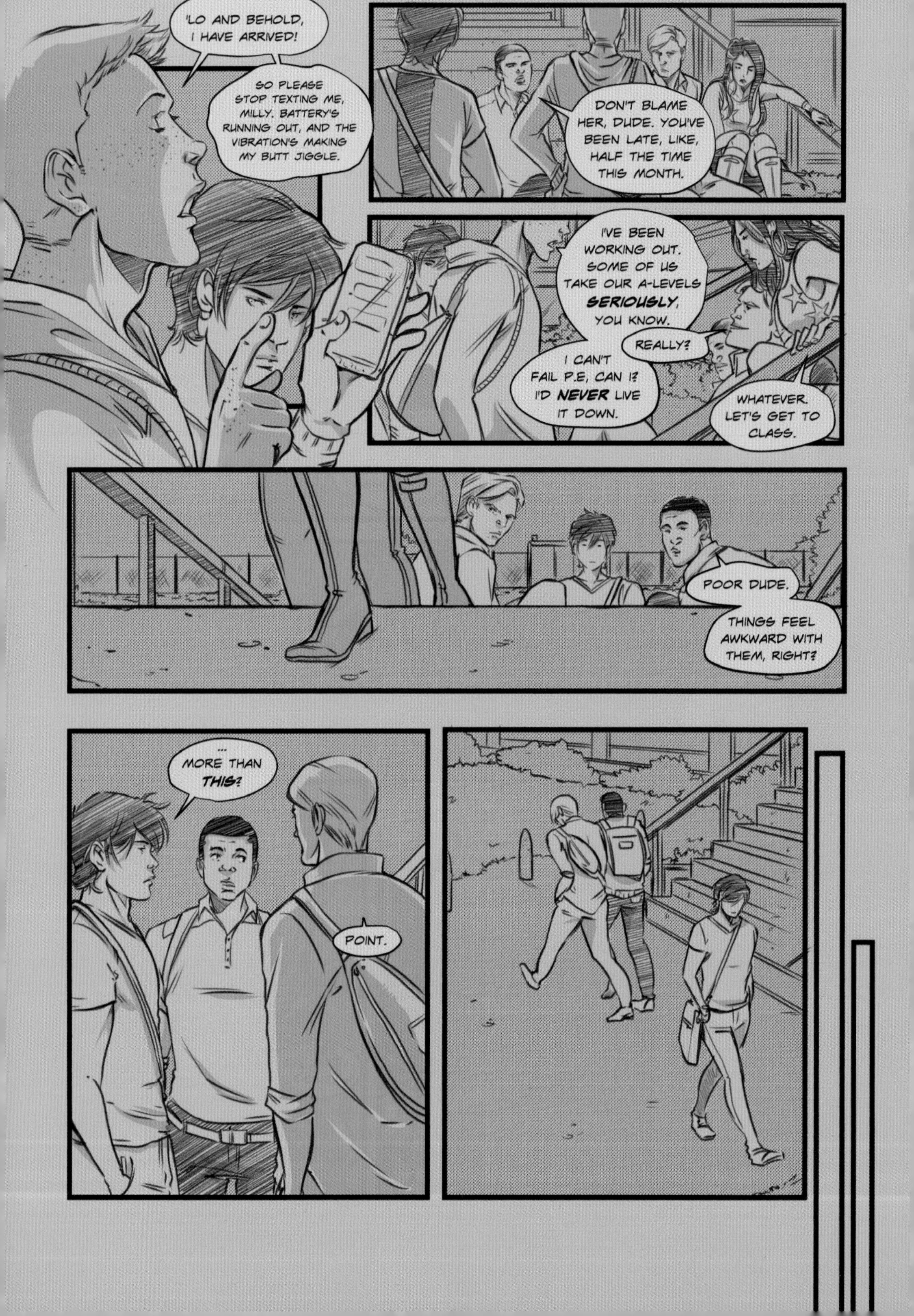
'LO AND BEHOLD, I HAVE ARRIVED!
SO PLEASE STOP TEXTING ME, MILLY. BATTERY'S RUNNING OUT, AND THE VIBRATION'S MAKING MY BUTT JIGGLE.
DON'T BLAME HER, DUDE. YOU'VE BEEN LATE, LIKE, HALF THE TIME THIS MONTH.
I'VE BEEN WORKING OUT. SOME OF US TAKE OUR A-LEVELS **SERIOUSLY**, YOU KNOW.
REALLY?
I CAN'T FAIL P.E, CAN I? I'D **NEVER** LIVE IT DOWN.
WHATEVER. LET'S GET TO CLASS.
POOR DUDE.
THINGS FEEL AWKWARD WITH THEM, RIGHT?
... MORE THAN **THIS**?
POINT.

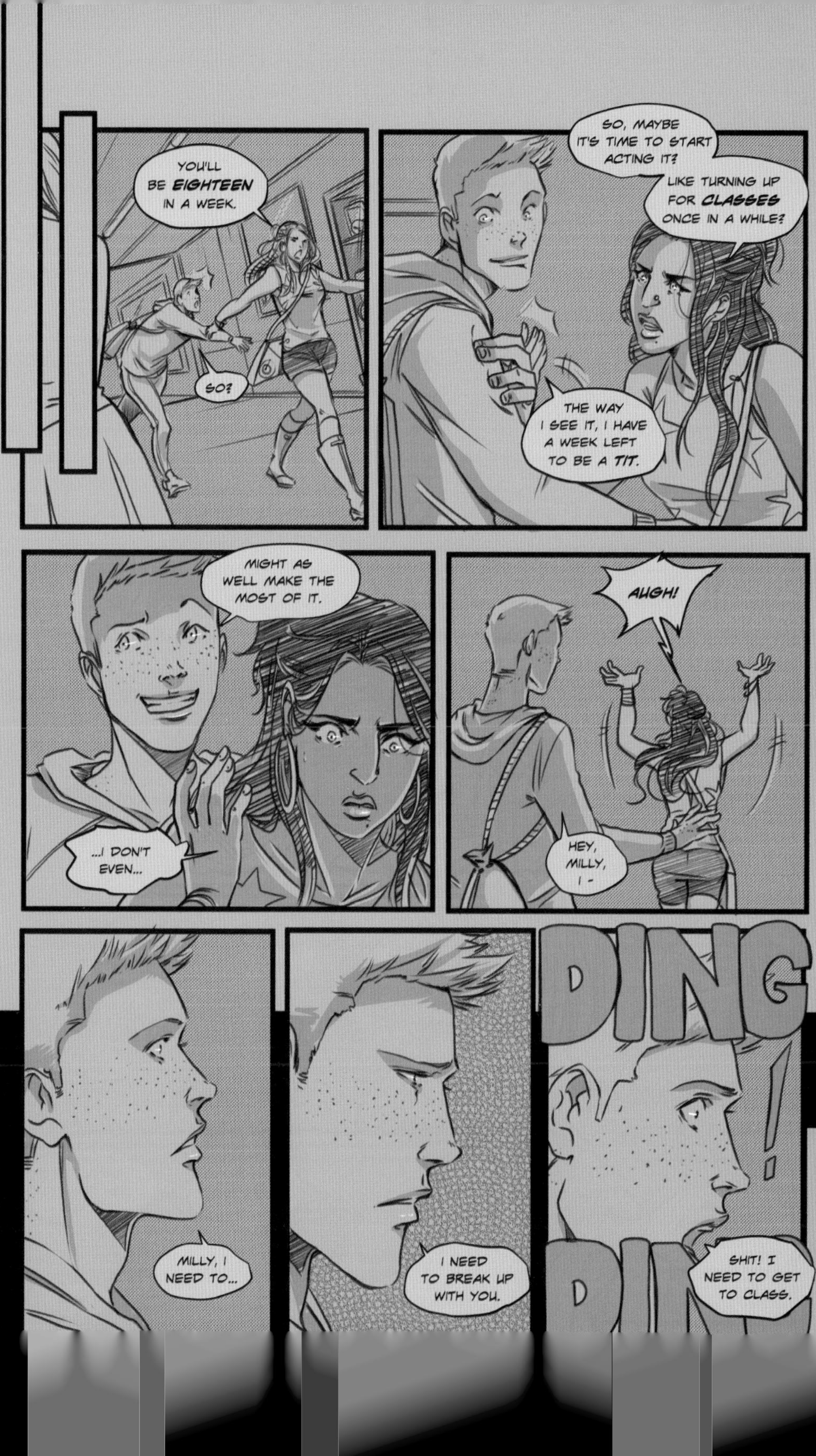
YOU'LL BE EIGHTEEN IN A WEEK.
SO?
SO, MAYBE IT'S TIME TO START ACTING IT?
LIKE TURNING UP FOR CLASSES ONCE IN A WHILE?
THE WAY I SEE IT, I HAVE A WEEK LEFT TO BE A TIT.
MIGHT AS WELL MAKE THE MOST OF IT.
...I DON'T EVEN...
AUGH!
HEY, MILLY, I -
MILLY, I NEED TO...
I NEED TO BREAK UP WITH YOU.
DING
!
SHIT! I NEED TO GET TO CLASS.

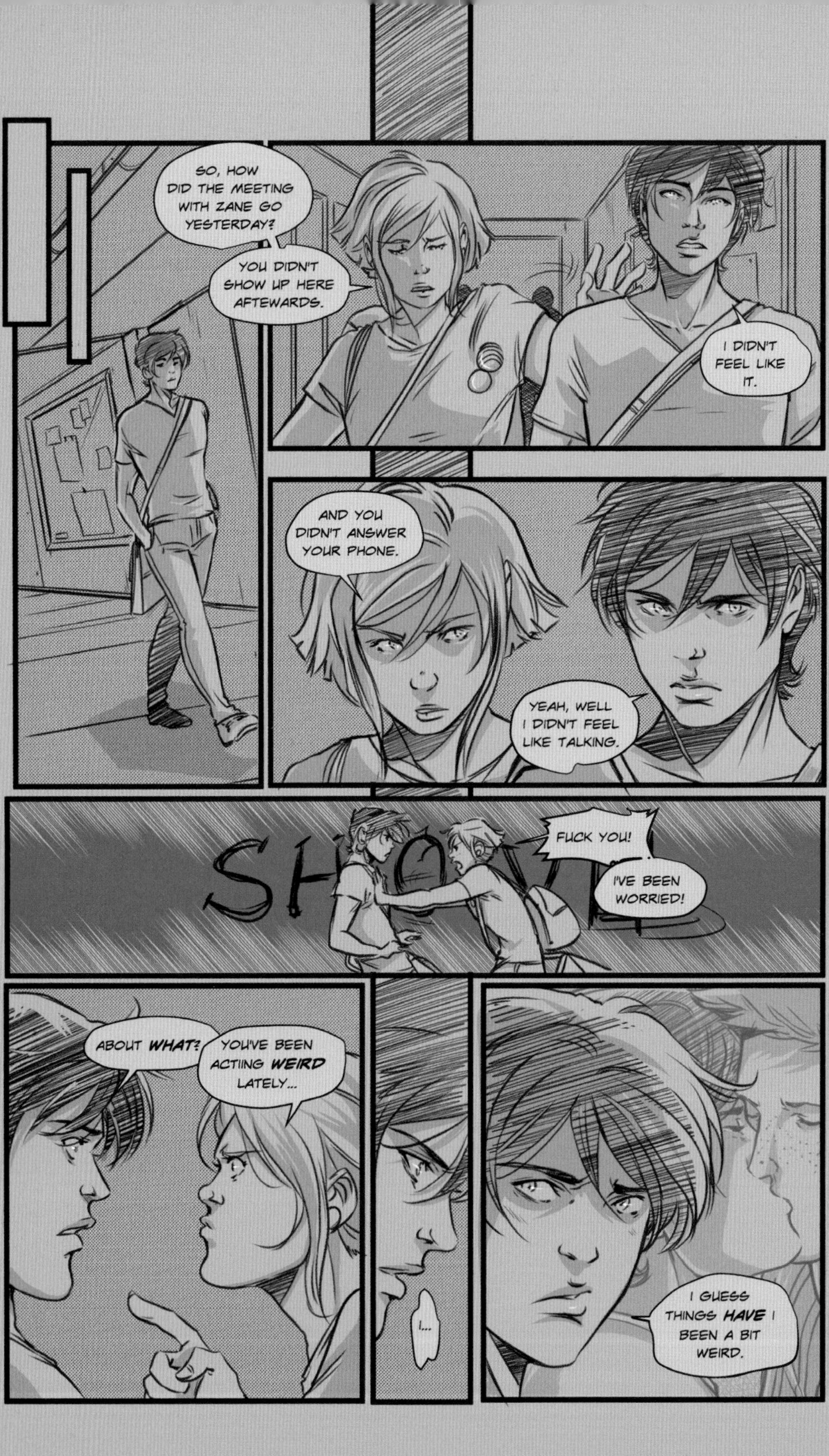
SO, HOW DID THE MEETING WITH ZANE GO YESTERDAY?
YOU DIDN'T SHOW UP HERE AFTEWARDS.
I DIDN'T FEEL LIKE IT.
AND YOU DIDN'T ANSWER YOUR PHONE.
YEAH, WELL I DIDN'T FEEL LIKE TALKING.
SHOVE
FUCK YOU!
I'VE BEEN WORRIED!
ABOUT **WHAT**?
YOU'VE BEEN ACTIING **WEIRD** LATELY...
I...
I GUESS THINGS **HAVE** BEEN A BIT WEIRD.

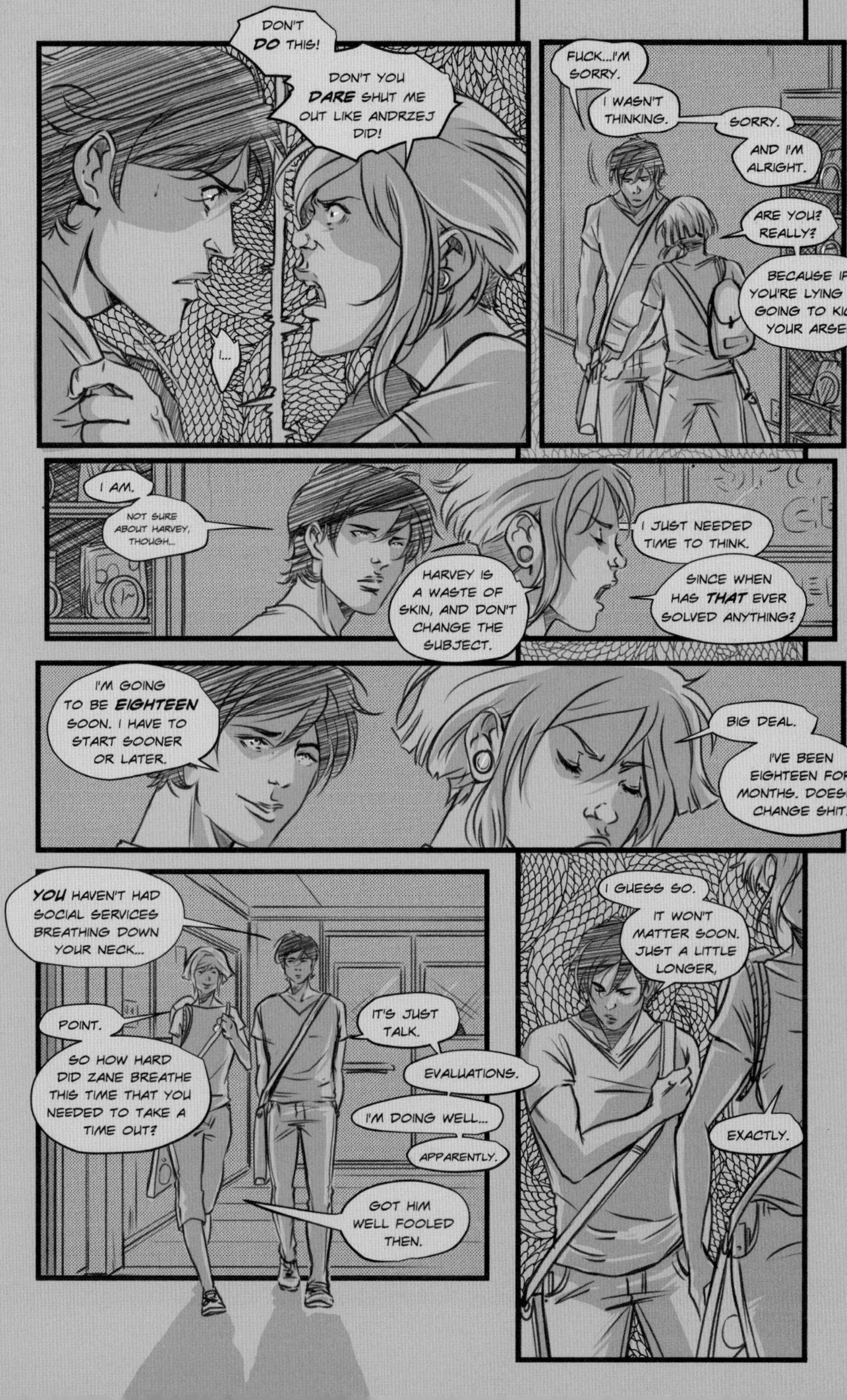
DON'T DO THIS!
DON'T YOU DARE SHUT ME OUT LIKE ANDRZEJ DID!
I...
FUCK...I'M SORRY.
I WASN'T THINKING.
SORRY.
AND I'M ALRIGHT.
ARE YOU? REALLY?
BECAUSE IF YOU'RE LYING I'M GOING TO KICK YOUR ARSE!
I AM.
NOT SURE ABOUT HARVEY, THOUGH...
I JUST NEEDED TIME TO THINK.
HARVEY IS A WASTE OF SKIN, AND DON'T CHANGE THE SUBJECT.
SINCE WHEN HAS THAT EVER SOLVED ANYTHING?
I'M GOING TO BE EIGHTEEN SOON. I HAVE TO START SOONER OR LATER.
BIG DEAL.
I'VE BEEN EIGHTEEN FOR MONTHS. DOESN'T CHANGE SHIT.
YOU HAVEN'T HAD SOCIAL SERVICES BREATHING DOWN YOUR NECK...
POINT.
SO HOW HARD DID ZANE BREATHE THIS TIME THAT YOU NEEDED TO TAKE A TIME OUT?
IT'S JUST TALK.
EVALUATIONS.
I'M DOING WELL...
APPARENTLY.
GOT HIM WELL FOOLED THEN.
I GUESS SO.
IT WON'T MATTER SOON. JUST A LITTLE LONGER,
EXACTLY.

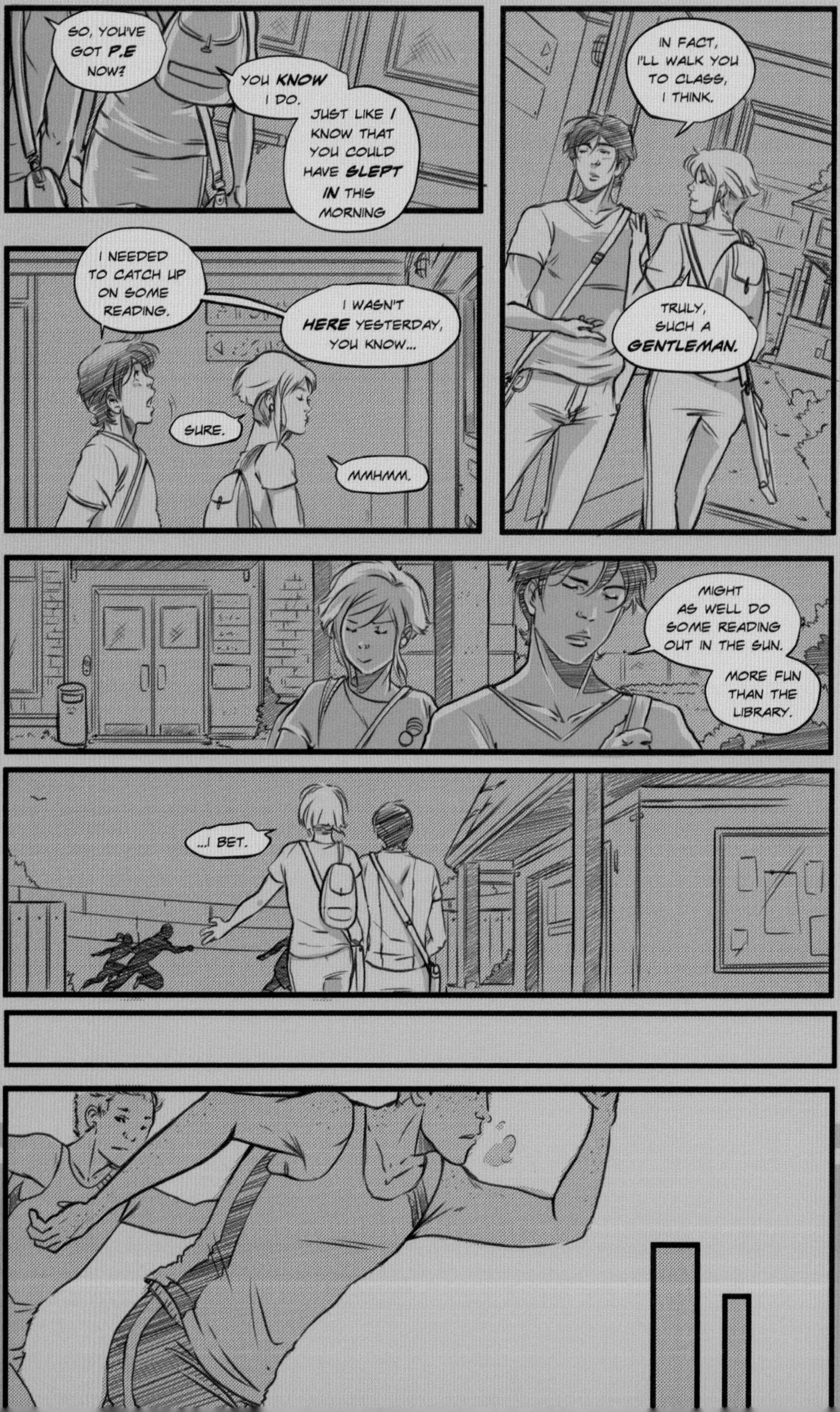
SO, YOU'VE GOT P.E NOW?
YOU KNOW I DO.
JUST LIKE I KNOW THAT YOU COULD HAVE SLEPT IN THIS MORNING
I NEEDED TO CATCH UP ON SOME READING.
I WASN'T HERE YESTERDAY, YOU KNOW...
SURE.
MMHMM.
IN FACT, I'LL WALK YOU TO CLASS, I THINK.
TRULY, SUCH A GENTLEMAN.
MIGHT AS WELL DO SOME READING OUT IN THE SUN.
MORE FUN THAN THE LIBRARY.
...I BET.

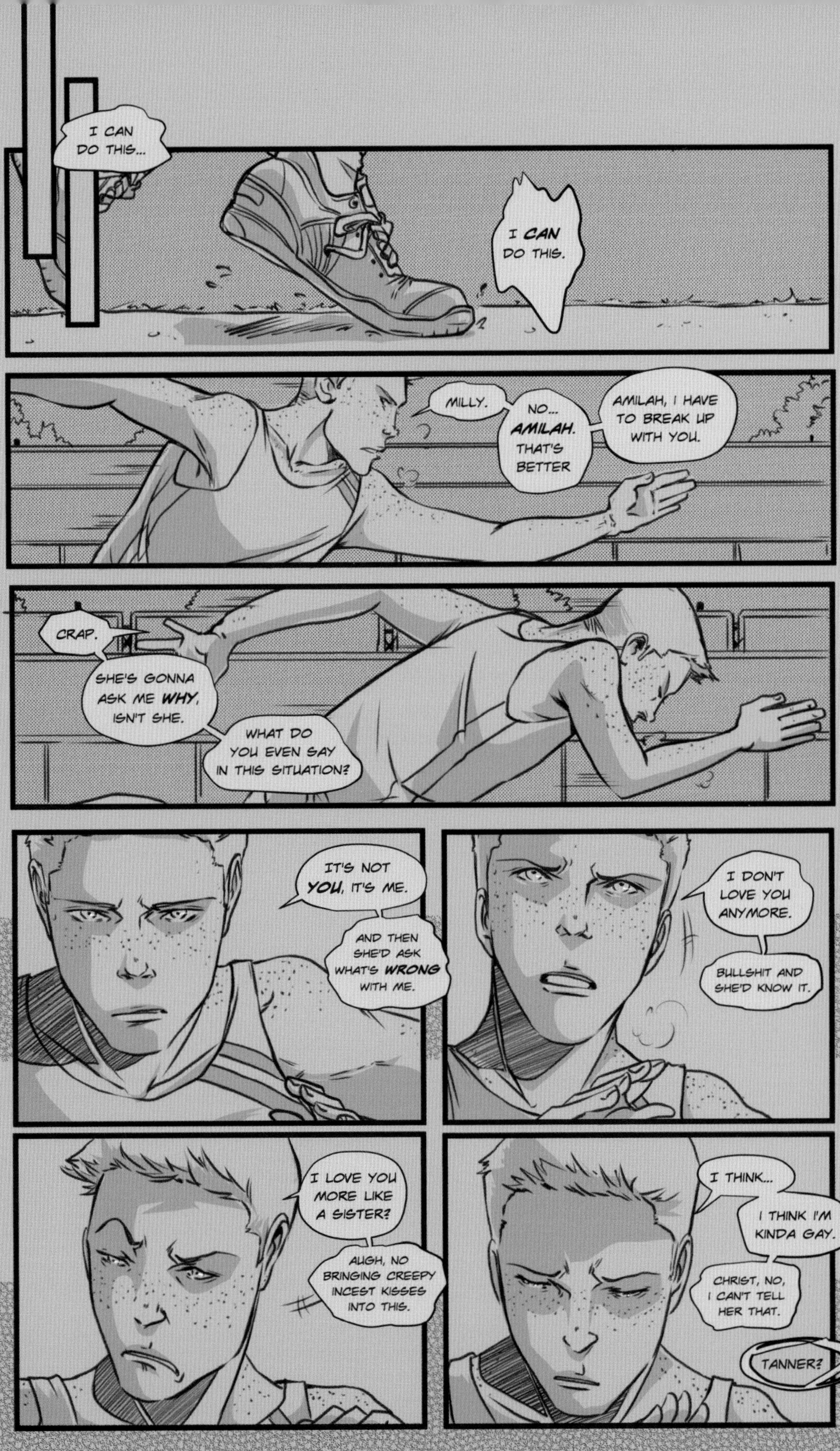

I CAN DO THIS...
I CAN DO THIS.
MILLY.
NO... AMILAH. THAT'S BETTER
AMILAH, I HAVE TO BREAK UP WITH YOU.
CRAP.
SHE'S GONNA ASK ME WHY, ISN'T SHE.
WHAT DO YOU EVEN SAY IN THIS SITUATION?
IT'S NOT YOU, IT'S ME.
AND THEN SHE'D ASK WHAT'S WRONG WITH ME.
I DON'T LOVE YOU ANYMORE.
BULLSHIT AND SHE'D KNOW IT.
I LOVE YOU MORE LIKE A SISTER?
AUGH, NO BRINGING CREEPY INCEST KISSES INTO THIS.
I THINK...
I THINK I'M KINDA GAY.
CHRIST, NO, I CAN'T TELL HER THAT.
TANNER?

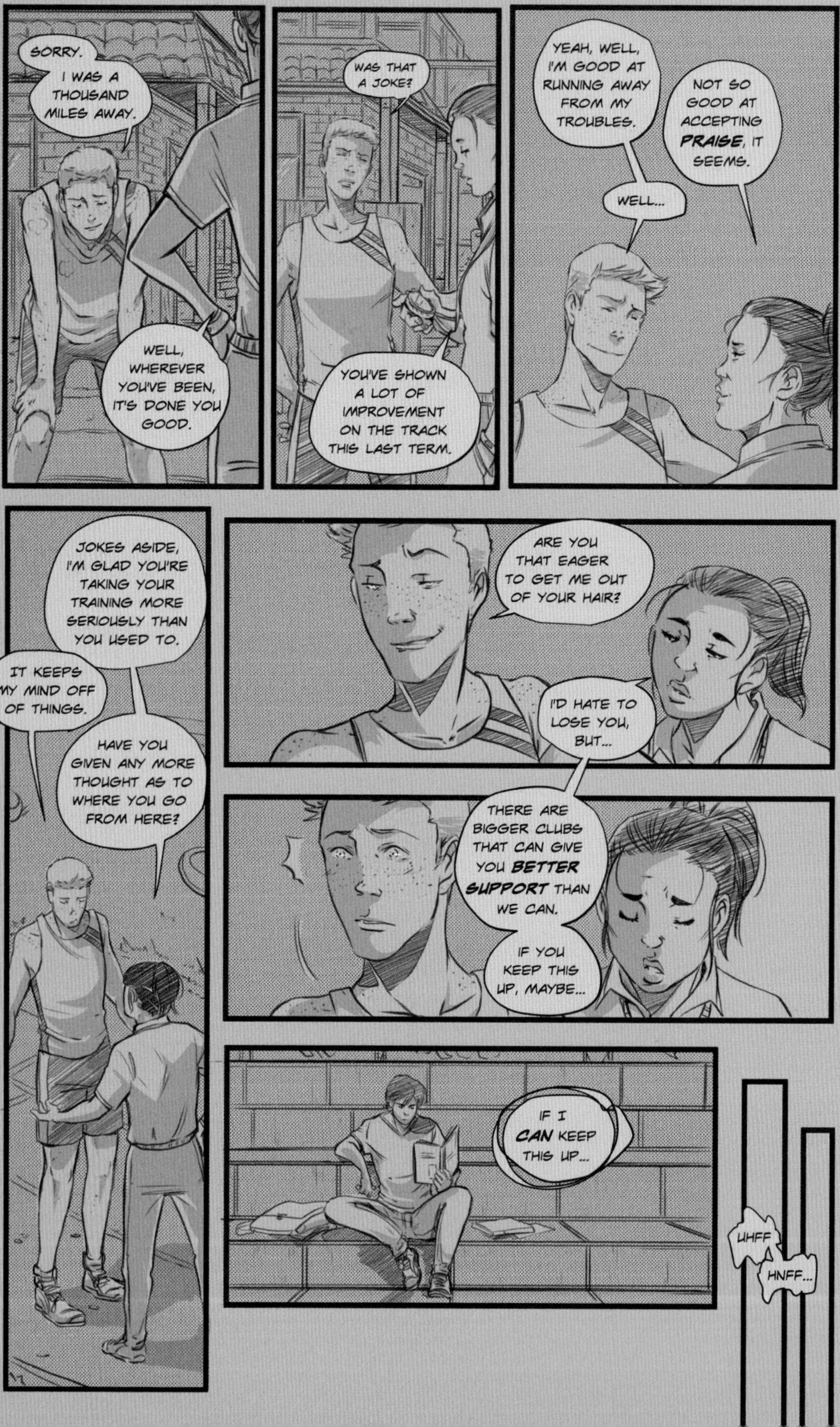
SORRY.
I WAS A THOUSAND MILES AWAY.
WELL, WHEREVER YOU'VE BEEN, IT'S DONE YOU GOOD.
WAS THAT A JOKE?
YOU'VE SHOWN A LOT OF IMPROVEMENT ON THE TRACK THIS LAST TERM.
YEAH, WELL, I'M GOOD AT RUNNING AWAY FROM MY TROUBLES.
NOT SO GOOD AT ACCEPTING PRAISE, IT SEEMS.
WELL...
JOKES ASIDE, I'M GLAD YOU'RE TAKING YOUR TRAINING MORE SERIOUSLY THAN YOU USED TO.
IT KEEPS MY MIND OFF OF THINGS.
HAVE YOU GIVEN ANY MORE THOUGHT AS TO WHERE YOU GO FROM HERE?
ARE YOU THAT EAGER TO GET ME OUT OF YOUR HAIR?
I'D HATE TO LOSE YOU, BUT...
THERE ARE BIGGER CLUBS THAT CAN GIVE YOU BETTER SUPPORT THAN WE CAN.
IF YOU KEEP THIS UP, MAYBE...
IF I CAN KEEP THIS UP...
UHFF
HNFF...

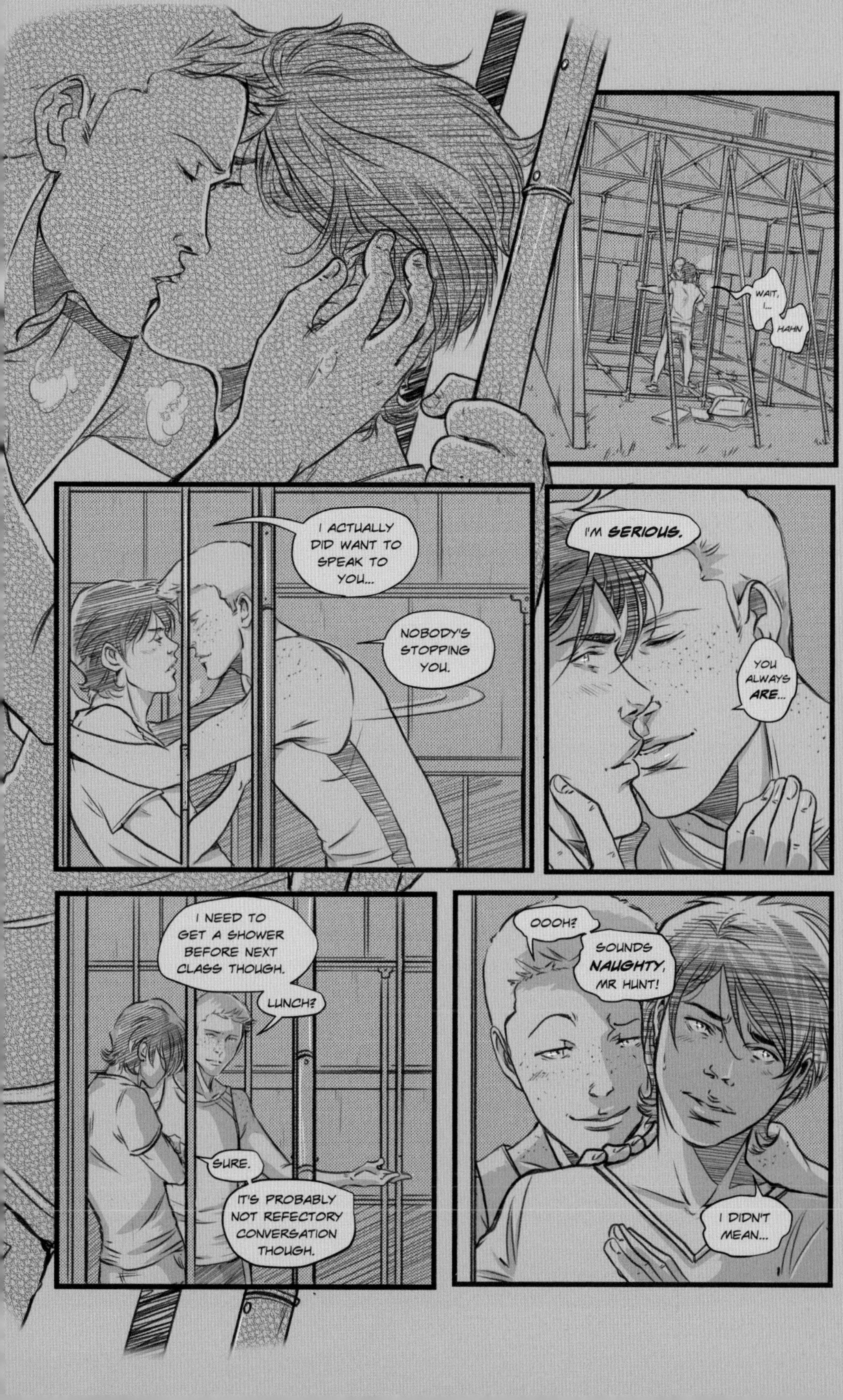
WAIT, I...
HAHN
I ACTUALLY DID WANT TO SPEAK TO YOU...
NOBODY'S STOPPING YOU.
I'M **SERIOUS.**
YOU ALWAYS **ARE...**
I NEED TO GET A SHOWER BEFORE NEXT CLASS THOUGH.
LUNCH?
SURE.
IT'S PROBABLY NOT REFECTORY CONVERSATION THOUGH.
OOOH?
SOUNDS **NAUGHTY**, MR HUNT!
I DIDN'T MEAN...

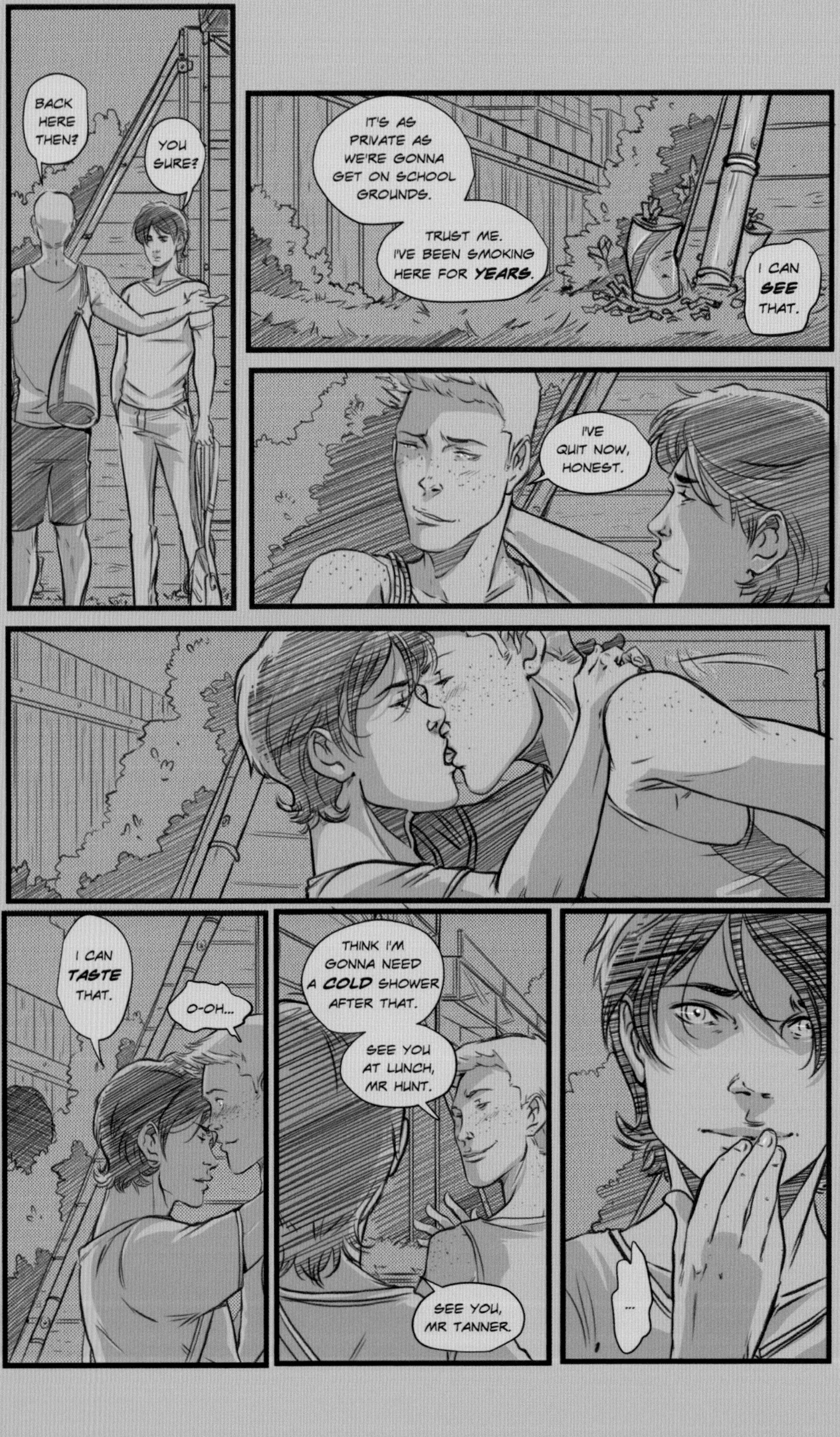
BACK HERE THEN?
YOU SURE?
IT'S AS PRIVATE AS WE'RE GONNA GET ON SCHOOL GROUNDS.
TRUST ME. I'VE BEEN SMOKING HERE FOR **YEARS**.
I CAN **SEE** THAT.
I'VE QUIT NOW, HONEST.
I CAN **TASTE** THAT.
O-OH...
THINK I'M GONNA NEED A **COLD** SHOWER AFTER THAT.
SEE YOU AT LUNCH, MR HUNT.
SEE YOU, MR TANNER.
...

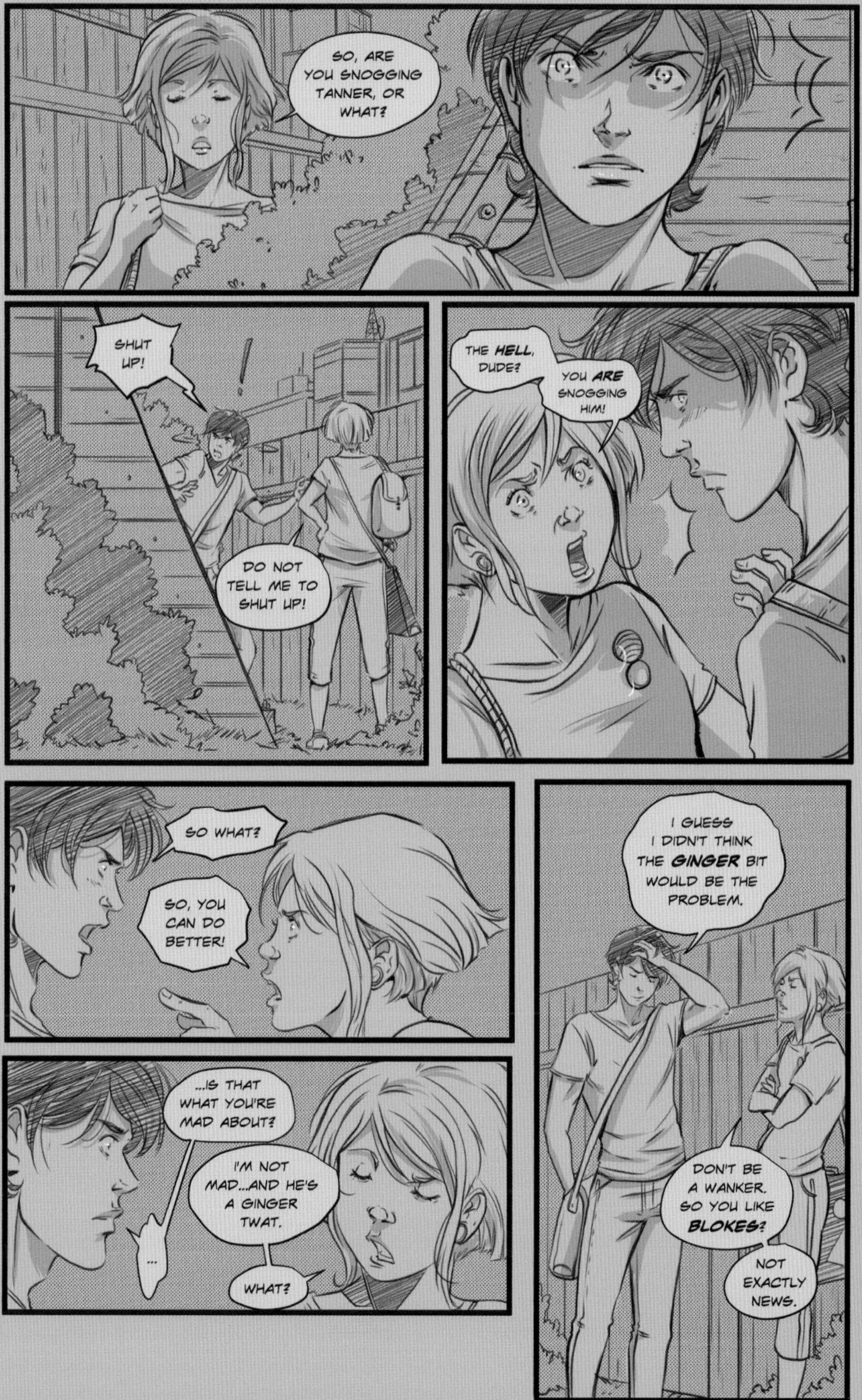
SO, ARE YOU SNOGGING TANNER, OR WHAT?
SHUT UP!
DO NOT TELL ME TO SHUT UP!
THE **HELL**, DUDE?
YOU **ARE** SNOGGING HIM!
SO WHAT?
SO, YOU CAN DO BETTER!
...IS THAT WHAT YOU'RE MAD ABOUT?
I'M NOT MAD...AND HE'S A GINGER TWAT.
...
WHAT?
I GUESS I DIDN'T THINK THE **GINGER** BIT WOULD BE THE PROBLEM.
DON'T BE A WANKER. SO YOU LIKE **BLOKES**?
NOT EXACTLY NEWS.

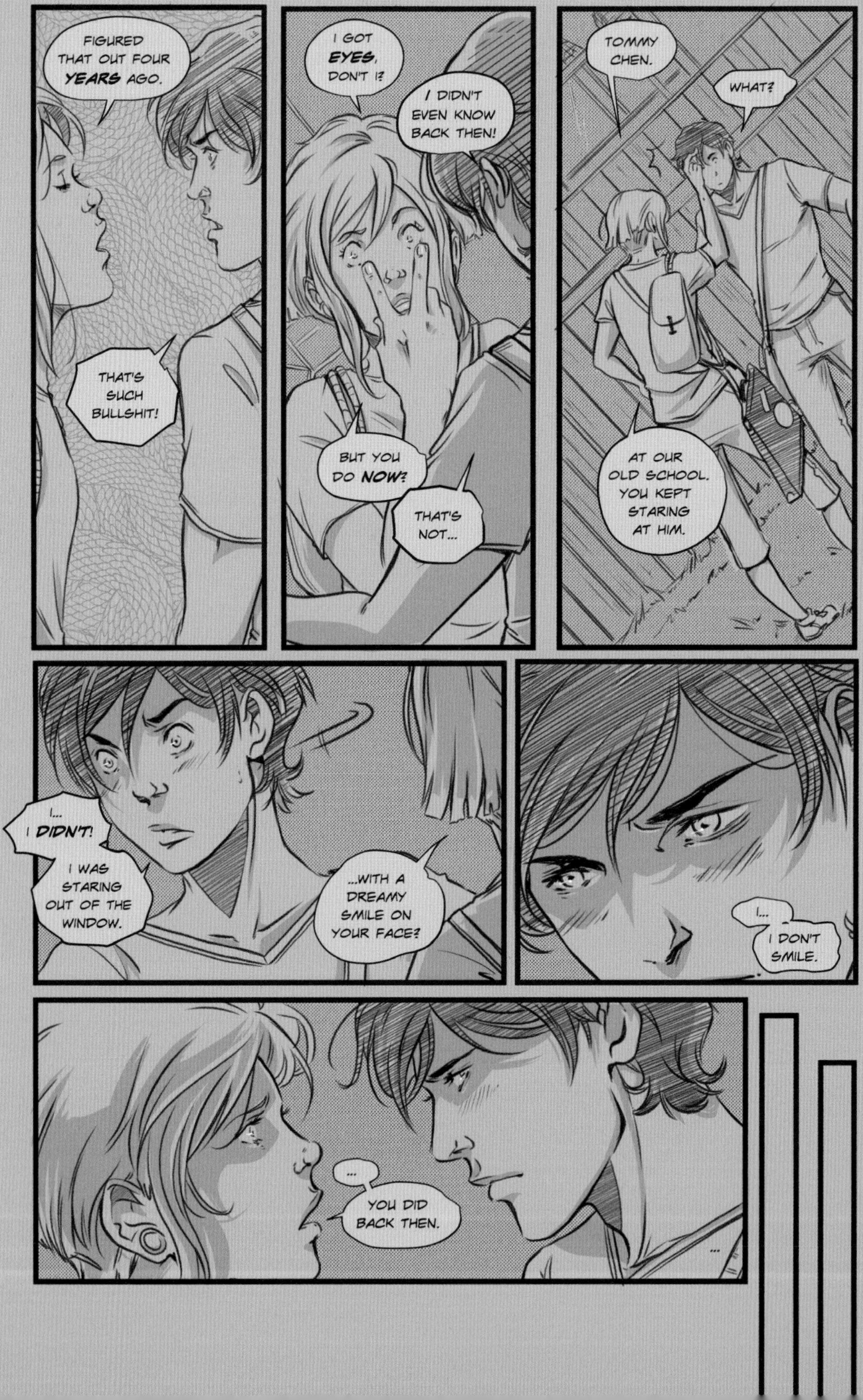

FIGURED THAT OUT FOUR YEARS AGO.
THAT'S SUCH BULLSHIT!
I GOT EYES, DON'T I?
I DIDN'T EVEN KNOW BACK THEN!
BUT YOU DO NOW?
THAT'S NOT...
TOMMY CHEN.
WHAT?
AT OUR OLD SCHOOL. YOU KEPT STARING AT HIM.
I... I DIDN'T! I WAS STARING OUT OF THE WINDOW.
...WITH A DREAMY SMILE ON YOUR FACE?
I... I DON'T SMILE.
...
YOU DID BACK THEN.
...

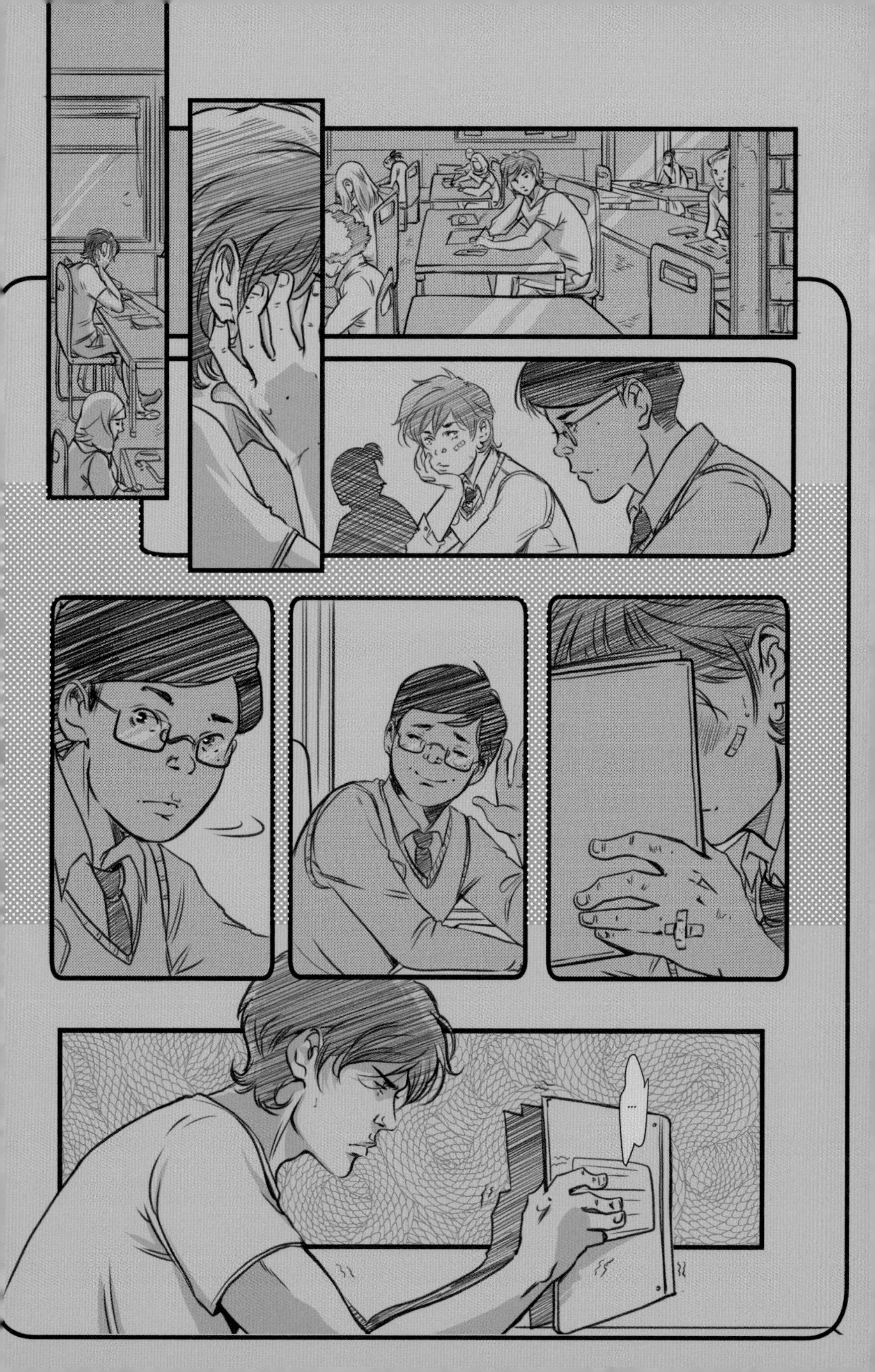
...

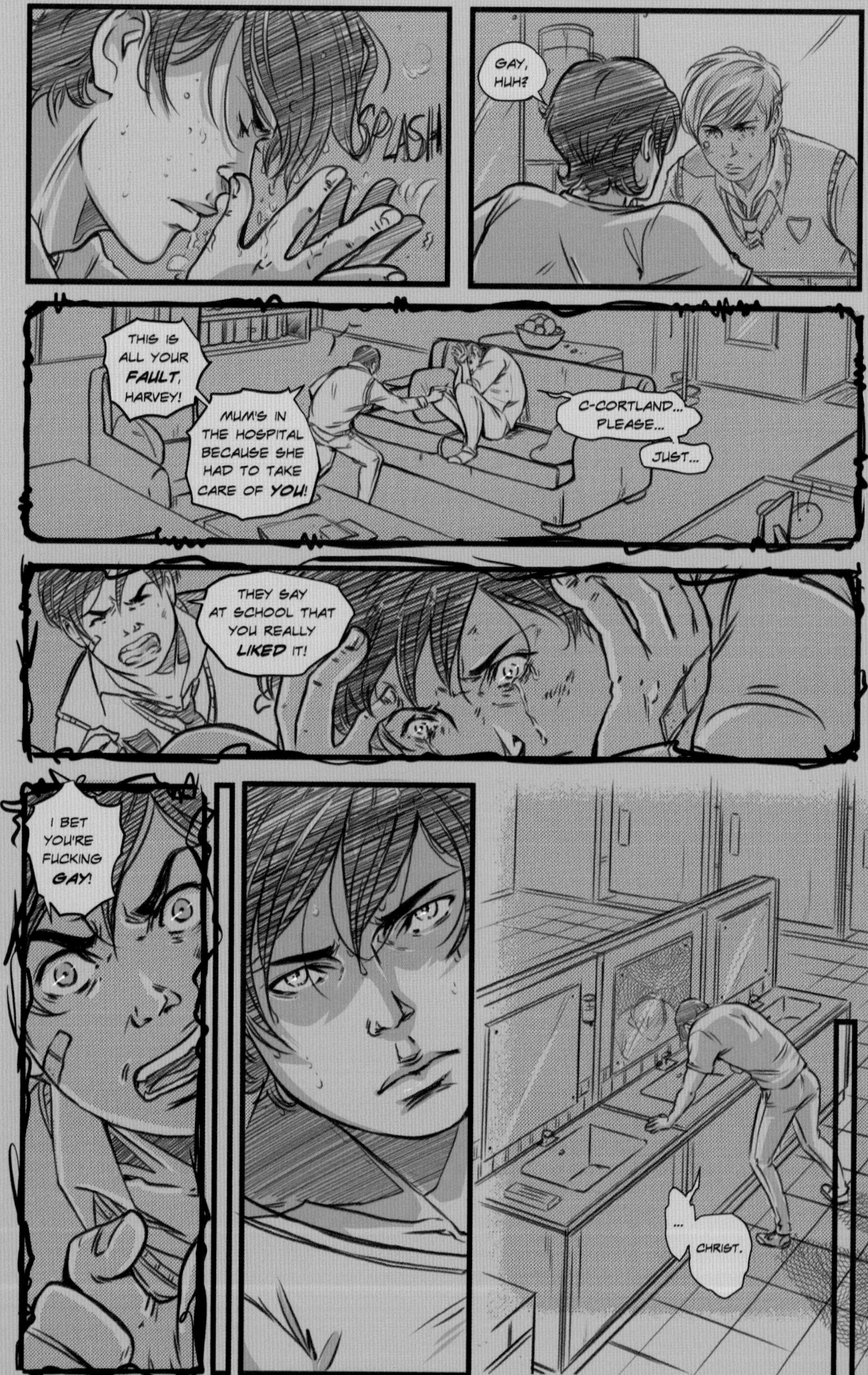
SPLASH
GAY, HUH?
THIS IS ALL YOUR FAULT, HARVEY!
MUM'S IN THE HOSPITAL BECAUSE SHE HAD TO TAKE CARE OF YOU!
C-CORTLAND... PLEASE...
JUST...
THEY SAY AT SCHOOL THAT YOU REALLY LIKED IT!
I BET YOU'RE FUCKING GAY!
...
CHRIST.

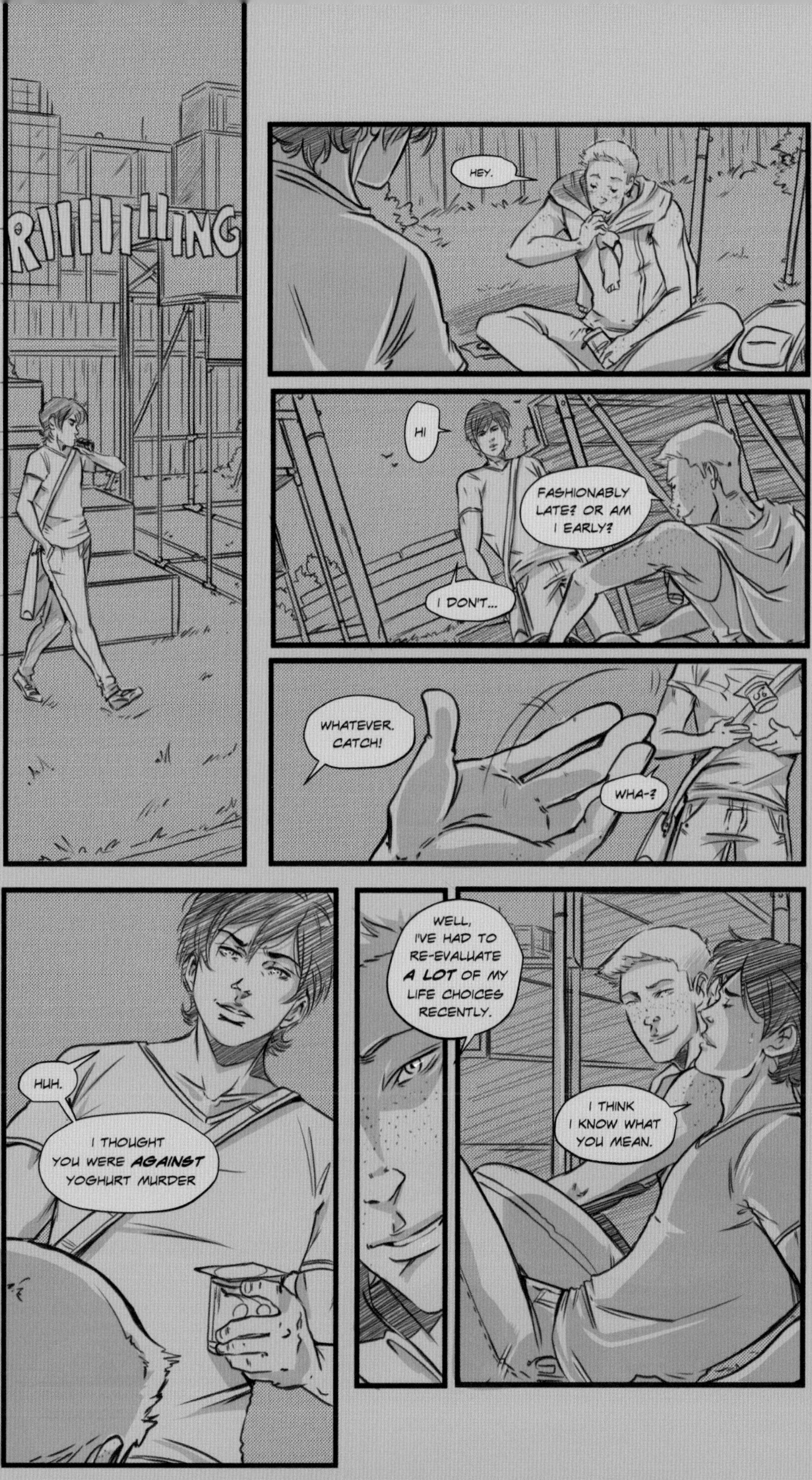
RIIIIIIING
HEY.
HI
FASHIONABLY LATE? OR AM I EARLY?
I DON'T...
WHATEVER. CATCH!
WHA-?
HUH.
I THOUGHT YOU WERE AGAINST YOGHURT MURDER
WELL, I'VE HAD TO RE-EVALUATE A LOT OF MY LIFE CHOICES RECENTLY.
I THINK I KNOW WHAT YOU MEAN.

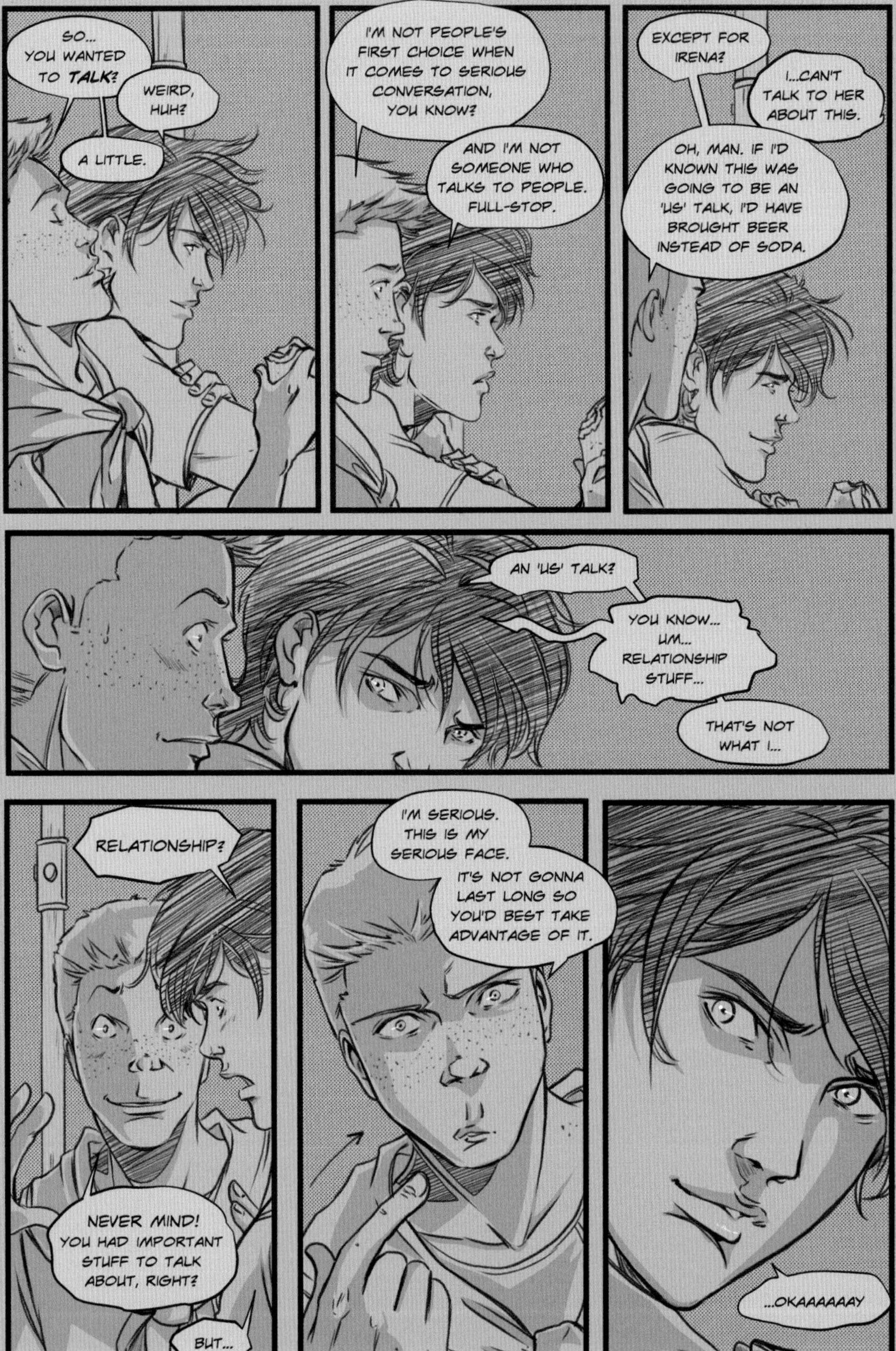
SO... YOU WANTED TO TALK?
WEIRD, HUH?
A LITTLE.
I'M NOT PEOPLE'S FIRST CHOICE WHEN IT COMES TO SERIOUS CONVERSATION, YOU KNOW?
AND I'M NOT SOMEONE WHO TALKS TO PEOPLE. FULL-STOP.
EXCEPT FOR IRENA?
I...CAN'T TALK TO HER ABOUT THIS.
OH, MAN. IF I'D KNOWN THIS WAS GOING TO BE AN 'US' TALK, I'D HAVE BROUGHT BEER INSTEAD OF SODA.
AN 'US' TALK?
YOU KNOW... UM... RELATIONSHIP STUFF...
THAT'S NOT WHAT I...
RELATIONSHIP?
NEVER MIND! YOU HAD IMPORTANT STUFF TO TALK ABOUT, RIGHT?
BUT...
I'M SERIOUS. THIS IS MY SERIOUS FACE.
IT'S NOT GONNA LAST LONG SO YOU'D BEST TAKE ADVANTAGE OF IT.
...OKAAAAAAY

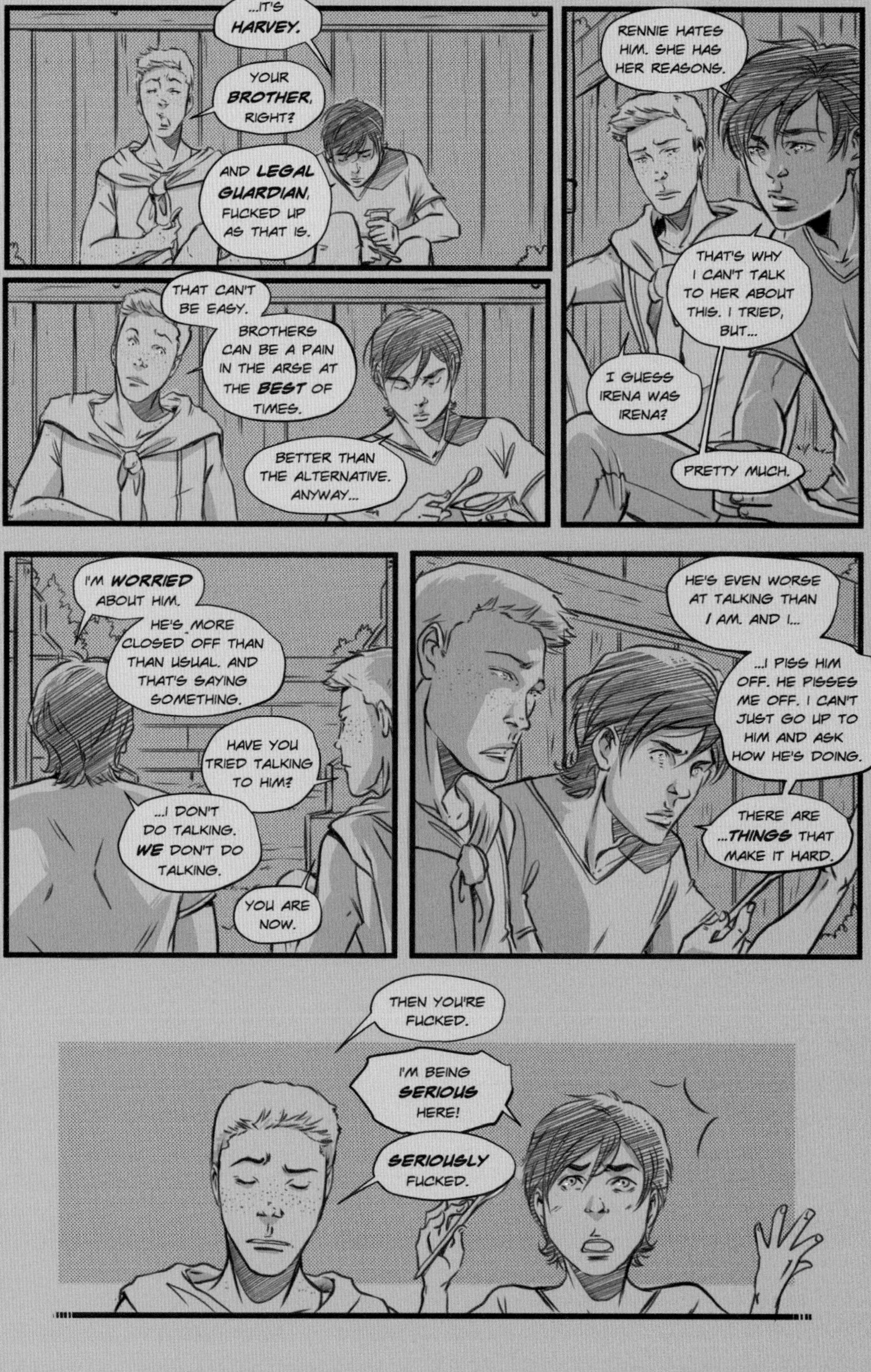
...IT'S HARVEY.
YOUR BROTHER, RIGHT?
AND LEGAL GUARDIAN, FUCKED UP AS THAT IS.
THAT CAN'T BE EASY.
BROTHERS CAN BE A PAIN IN THE ARSE AT THE BEST OF TIMES.
BETTER THAN THE ALTERNATIVE. ANYWAY...
RENNIE HATES HIM. SHE HAS HER REASONS.
THAT'S WHY I CAN'T TALK TO HER ABOUT THIS. I TRIED, BUT...
I GUESS IRENA WAS IRENA?
PRETTY MUCH.
I'M WORRIED ABOUT HIM.
HE'S MORE CLOSED OFF THAN THAN USUAL. AND THAT'S SAYING SOMETHING.
HAVE YOU TRIED TALKING TO HIM?
...I DON'T DO TALKING. WE DON'T DO TALKING.
YOU ARE NOW.
HE'S EVEN WORSE AT TALKING THAN I AM. AND I...
...I PISS HIM OFF. HE PISSES ME OFF. I CAN'T JUST GO UP TO HIM AND ASK HOW HE'S DOING.
THERE ARE ...THINGS THAT MAKE IT HARD.
THEN YOU'RE FUCKED.
I'M BEING SERIOUS HERE!
SERIOUSLY FUCKED.

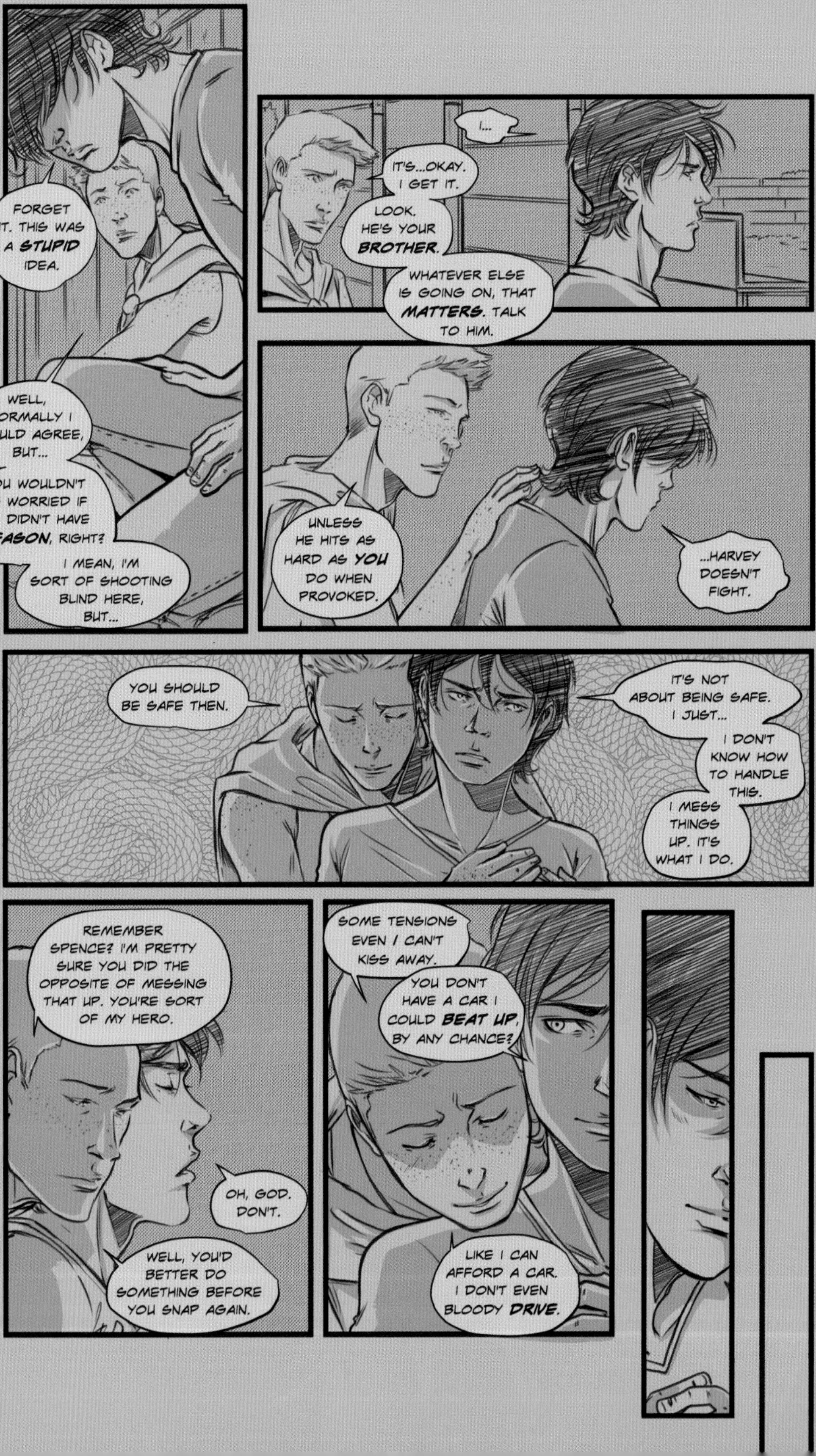
FORGET IT. THIS WAS A STUPID IDEA.
I...
IT'S...OKAY. I GET IT.
LOOK. HE'S YOUR BROTHER.
WHATEVER ELSE IS GOING ON, THAT MATTERS. TALK TO HIM.
WELL, NORMALLY I WOULD AGREE, BUT...
YOU WOULDN'T BE WORRIED IF YOU DIDN'T HAVE A REASON, RIGHT?
I MEAN, I'M SORT OF SHOOTING BLIND HERE, BUT...
...HARVEY DOESN'T FIGHT.
UNLESS HE HITS AS HARD AS YOU DO WHEN PROVOKED.
YOU SHOULD BE SAFE THEN.
IT'S NOT ABOUT BEING SAFE. I JUST...
I DON'T KNOW HOW TO HANDLE THIS.
I MESS THINGS UP. IT'S WHAT I DO.
REMEMBER SPENCE? I'M PRETTY SURE YOU DID THE OPPOSITE OF MESSING THAT UP. YOU'RE SORT OF MY HERO.
OH, GOD. DON'T.
WELL, YOU'D BETTER DO SOMETHING BEFORE YOU SNAP AGAIN.
SOME TENSIONS EVEN I CAN'T KISS AWAY.
YOU DON'T HAVE A CAR I COULD BEAT UP, BY ANY CHANCE?
LIKE I CAN AFFORD A CAR. I DON'T EVEN BLOODY DRIVE.

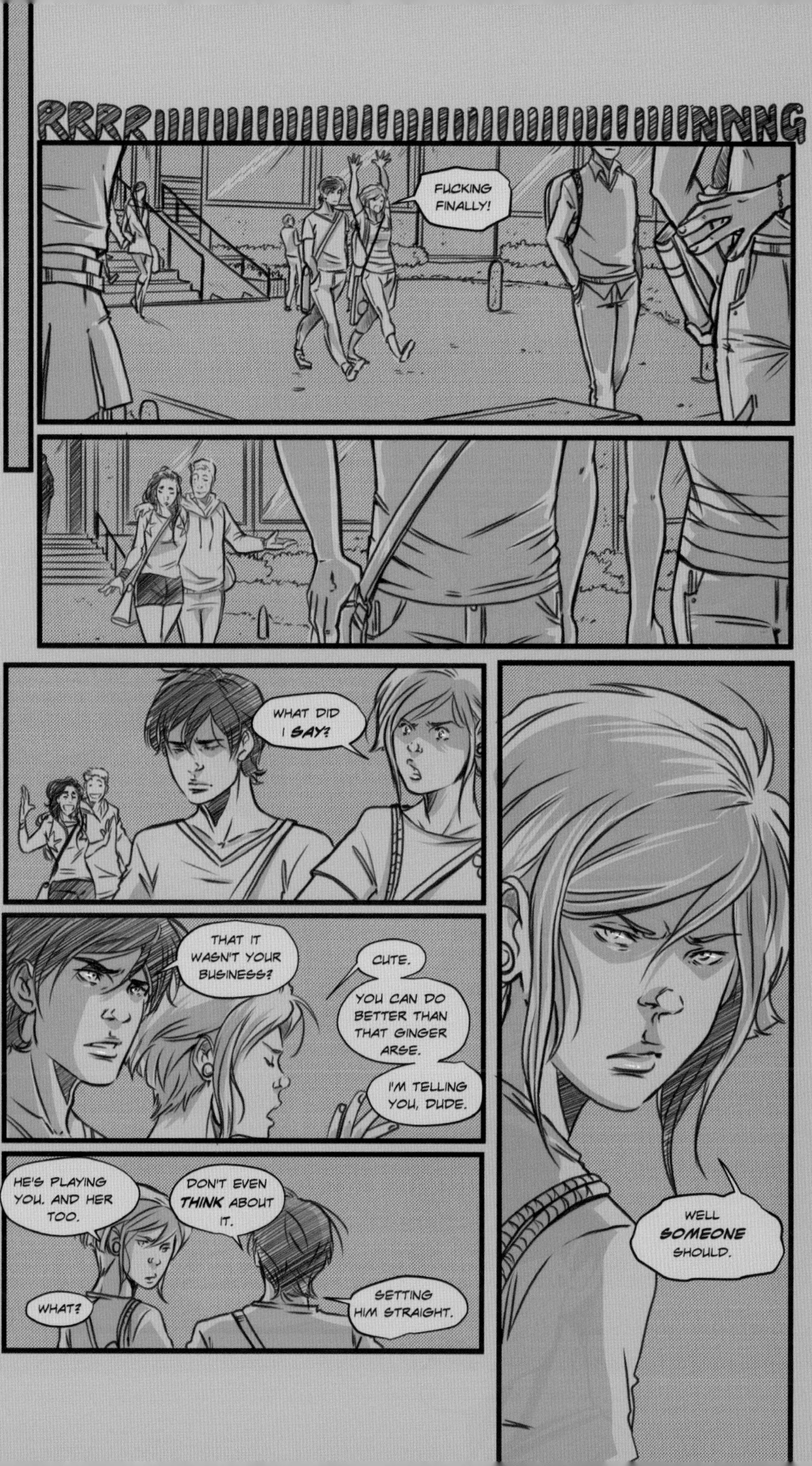
RRRRIIIIIIIIIIIIIIIIIIIIIIIIIIIIIIIIIIIIIIIIINNNNG
FUCKING FINALLY!
WHAT DID I SAY?
WELL SOMEONE SHOULD.
THAT IT WASN'T YOUR BUSINESS?
CUTE.
YOU CAN DO BETTER THAN THAT GINGER ARSE.
I'M TELLING YOU, DUDE.
HE'S PLAYING YOU. AND HER TOO.
DON'T EVEN THINK ABOUT IT.
WHAT?
SETTING HIM STRAIGHT.

ISSUE 8

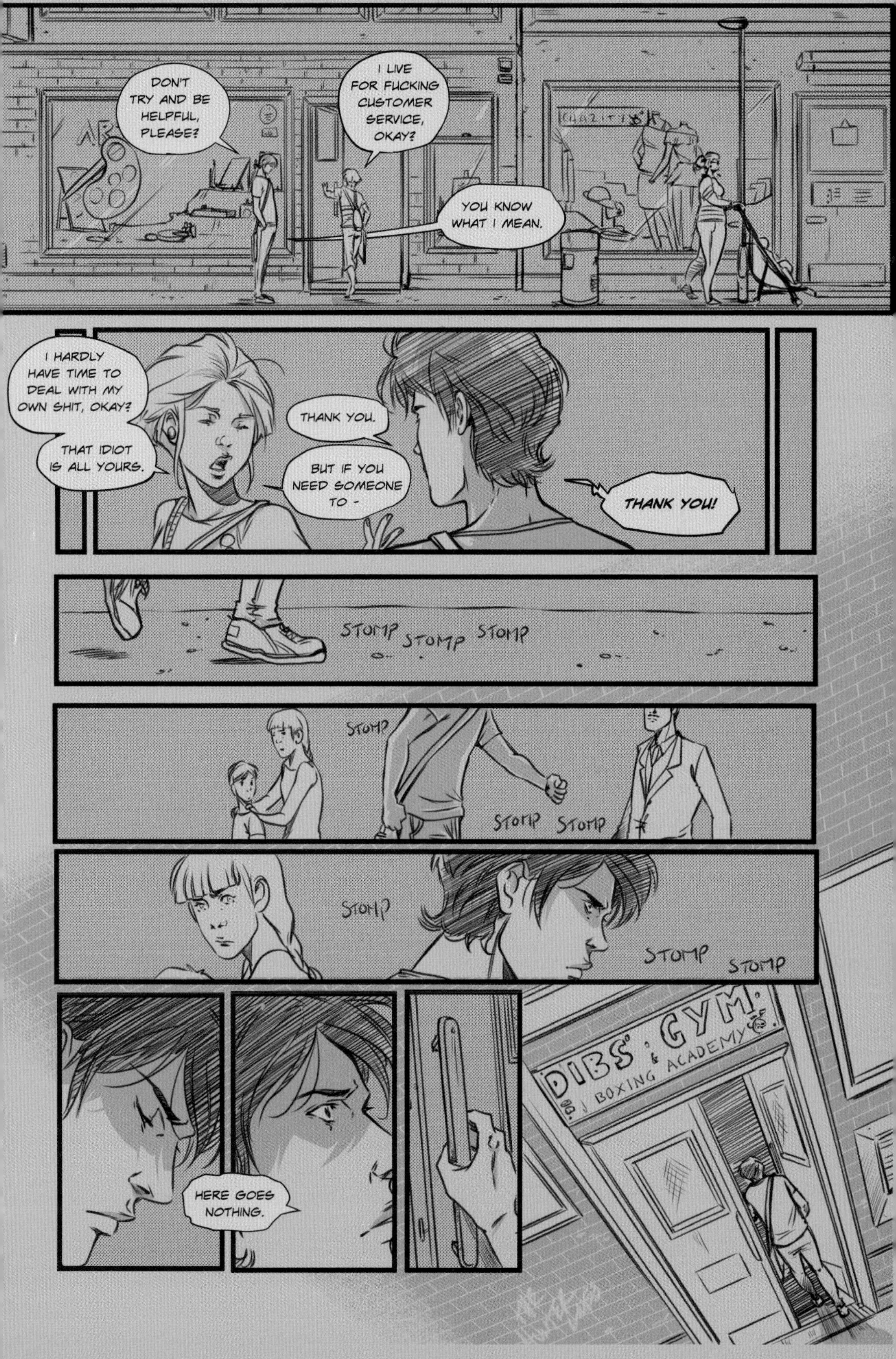
DON'T TRY AND BE HELPFUL, PLEASE?
I LIVE FOR FUCKING CUSTOMER SERVICE, OKAY?
YOU KNOW WHAT I MEAN.
I HARDLY HAVE TIME TO DEAL WITH MY OWN SHIT, OKAY?
THAT IDIOT IS ALL YOURS.
THANK YOU.
BUT IF YOU NEED SOMEONE TO -
THANK YOU!
STOMP STOMP STOMP
STOMP
STOMP STOMP
STOMP
STOMP STOMP
HERE GOES NOTHING.
DIBS' GYM & BOXING ACADEMY

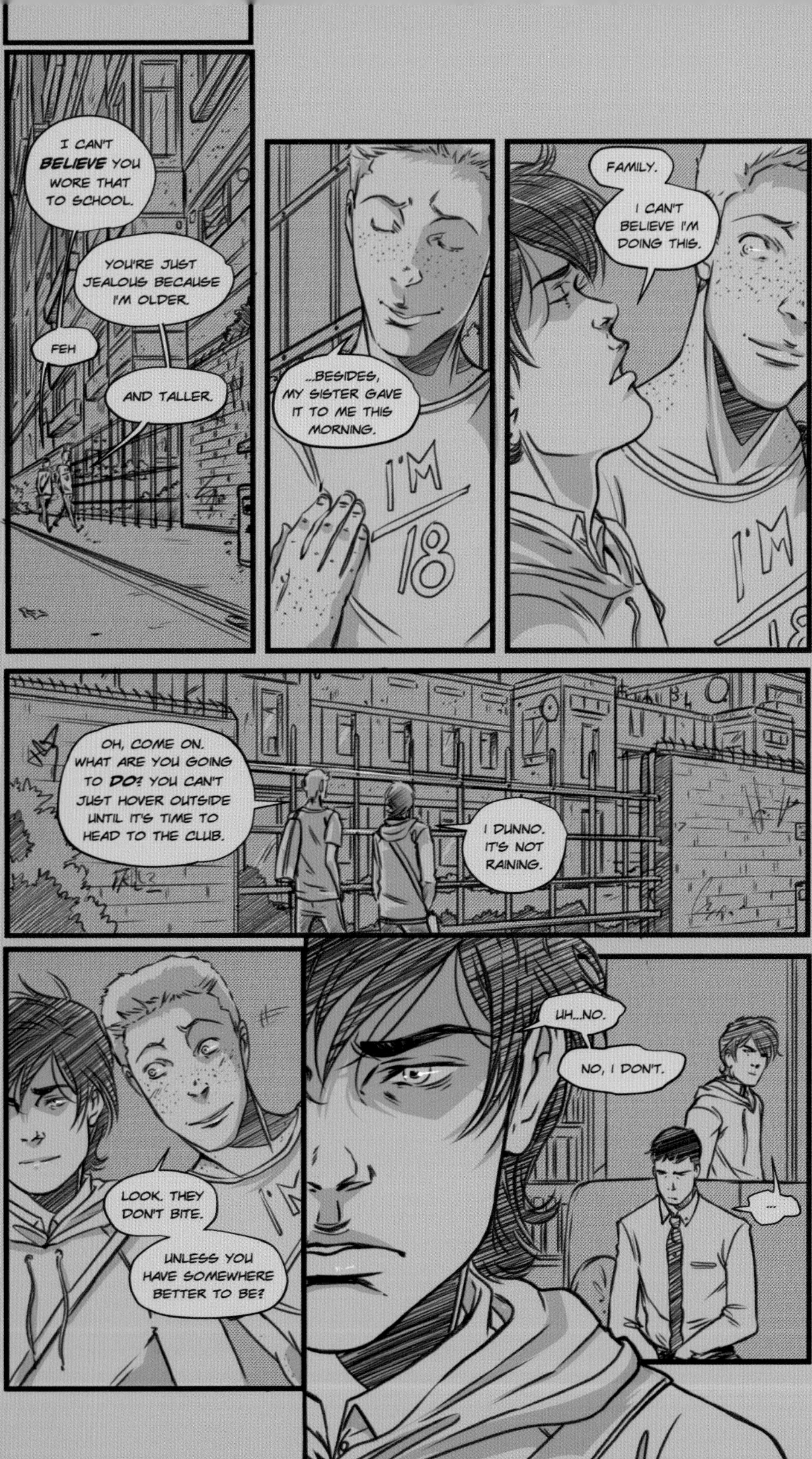
I CAN'T BELIEVE YOU WORE THAT TO SCHOOL.
YOU'RE JUST JEALOUS BECAUSE I'M OLDER.
FEH
AND TALLER.
...BESIDES, MY SISTER GAVE IT TO ME THIS MORNING.
I'M 18
FAMILY.
I CAN'T BELIEVE I'M DOING THIS.
OH, COME ON. WHAT ARE YOU GOING TO DO? YOU CAN'T JUST HOVER OUTSIDE UNTIL IT'S TIME TO HEAD TO THE CLUB.
I DUNNO. IT'S NOT RAINING.
LOOK. THEY DON'T BITE.
UNLESS YOU HAVE SOMEWHERE BETTER TO BE?
UH...NO.
NO, I DON'T.
...

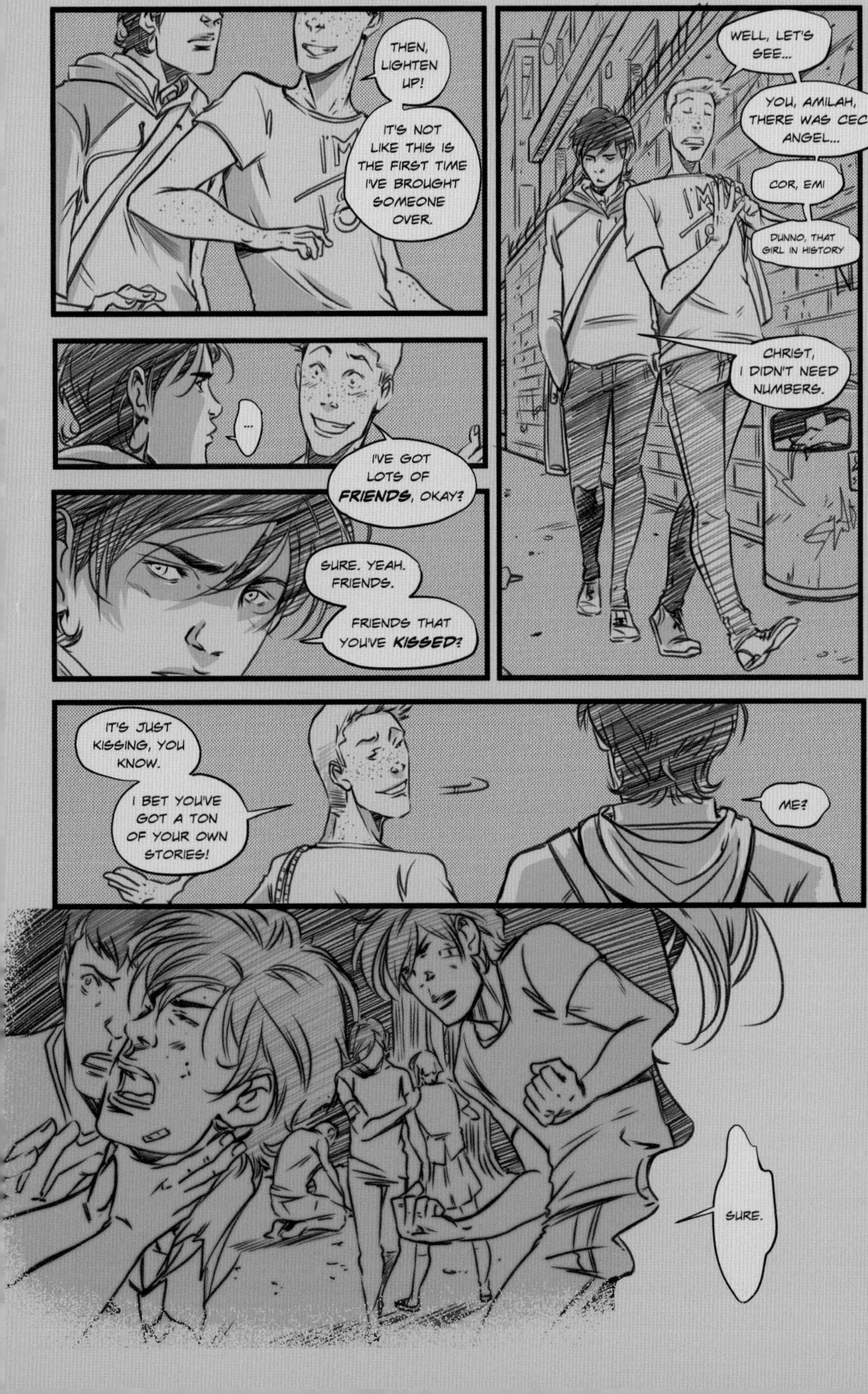
THEN, LIGHTEN UP!
IT'S NOT LIKE THIS IS THE FIRST TIME I'VE BROUGHT SOMEONE OVER.
WELL, LET'S SEE...
YOU, AMILAH, THERE WAS CECI, ANGEL...
COR, EMI
DUNNO, THAT GIRL IN HISTORY
CHRIST, I DIDN'T NEED NUMBERS.
...
I'VE GOT LOTS OF FRIENDS, OKAY?
SURE. YEAH. FRIENDS.
FRIENDS THAT YOU'VE KISSED?
IT'S JUST KISSING, YOU KNOW.
I BET YOU'VE GOT A TON OF YOUR OWN STORIES!
ME?
SURE.

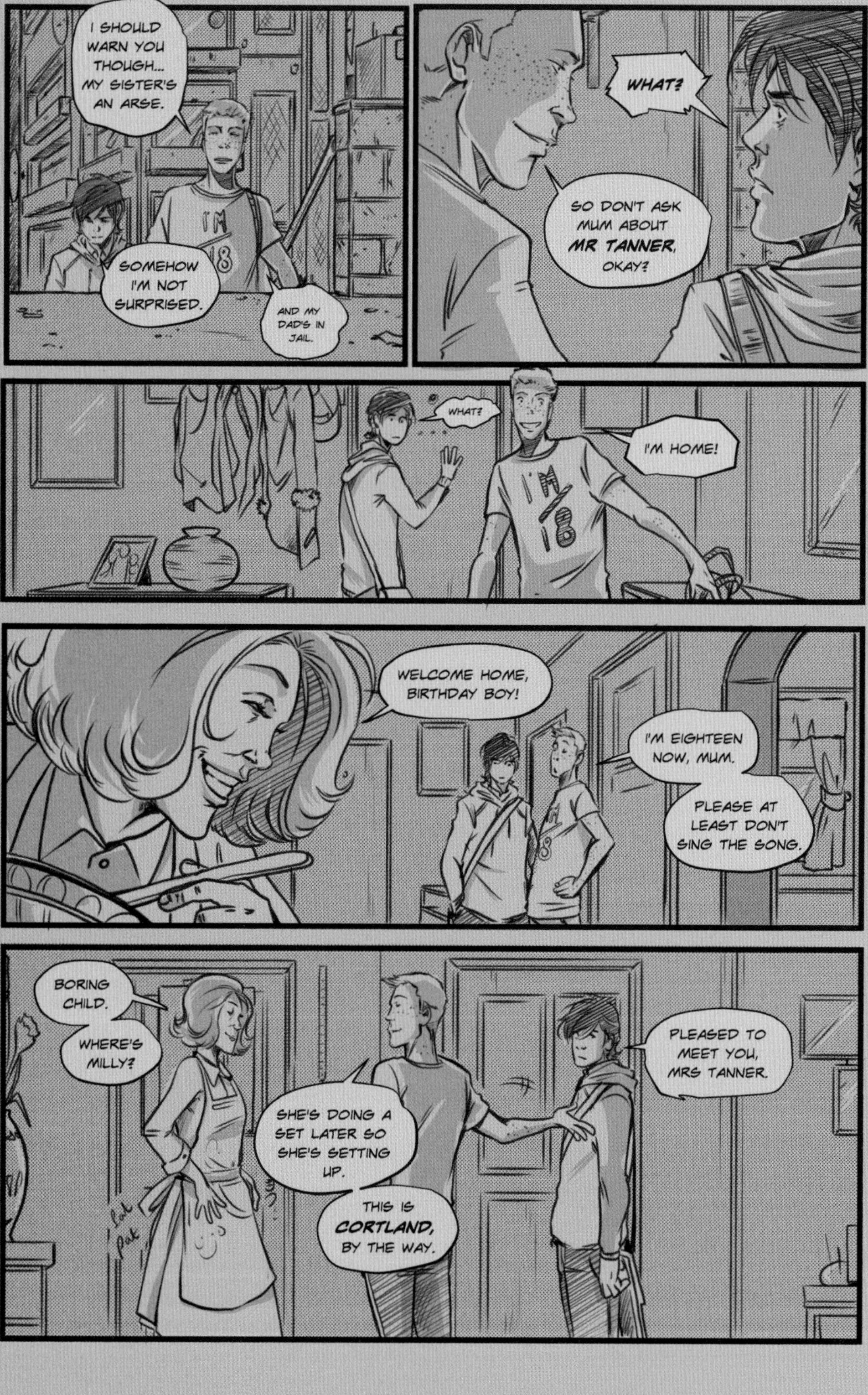

I SHOULD WARN YOU THOUGH... MY SISTER'S AN ARSE.
SOMEHOW I'M NOT SURPRISED.
AND MY DAD'S IN JAIL.
WHAT?
SO DON'T ASK MUM ABOUT **MR TANNER**, OKAY?
WHAT?
I'M HOME!
WELCOME HOME, BIRTHDAY BOY!
I'M EIGHTEEN NOW, MUM.
PLEASE AT LEAST DON'T SING THE SONG.
BORING CHILD.
WHERE'S MILLY?
SHE'S DOING A SET LATER SO SHE'S SETTING UP.
THIS IS **CORTLAND,** BY THE WAY.
PLEASED TO MEET YOU, MRS TANNER.

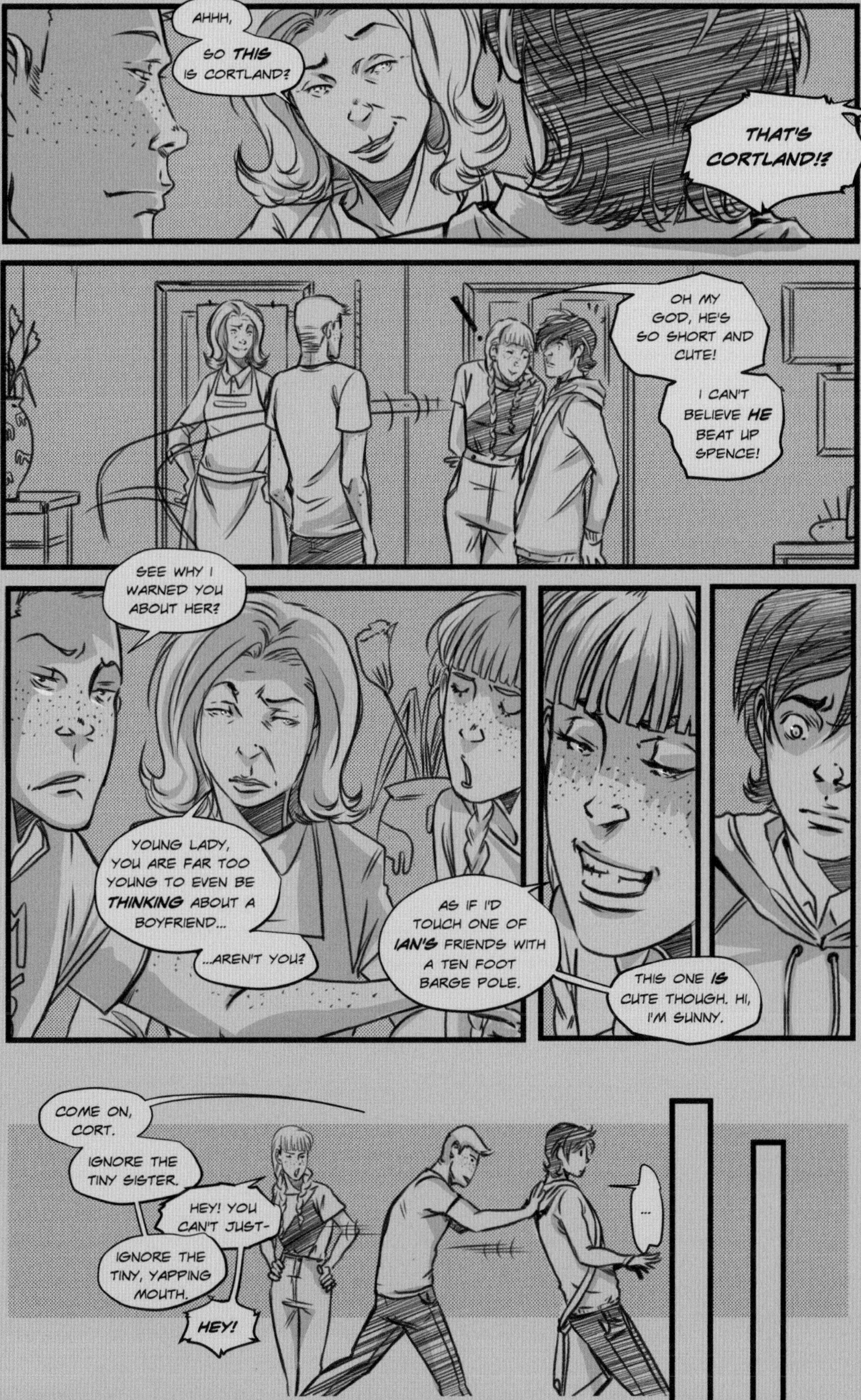
AHHH,
SO THIS IS CORTLAND?
THAT'S CORTLAND!?
OH MY GOD, HE'S SO SHORT AND CUTE!
I CAN'T BELIEVE HE BEAT UP SPENCE!
SEE WHY I WARNED YOU ABOUT HER?
YOUNG LADY, YOU ARE FAR TOO YOUNG TO EVEN BE THINKING ABOUT A BOYFRIEND...
...AREN'T YOU?
AS IF I'D TOUCH ONE OF IAN'S FRIENDS WITH A TEN FOOT BARGE POLE.
THIS ONE IS CUTE THOUGH. HI, I'M SUNNY.
COME ON, CORT.
IGNORE THE TINY SISTER.
HEY! YOU CAN'T JUST-
IGNORE THE TINY, YAPPING MOUTH.
HEY!
...

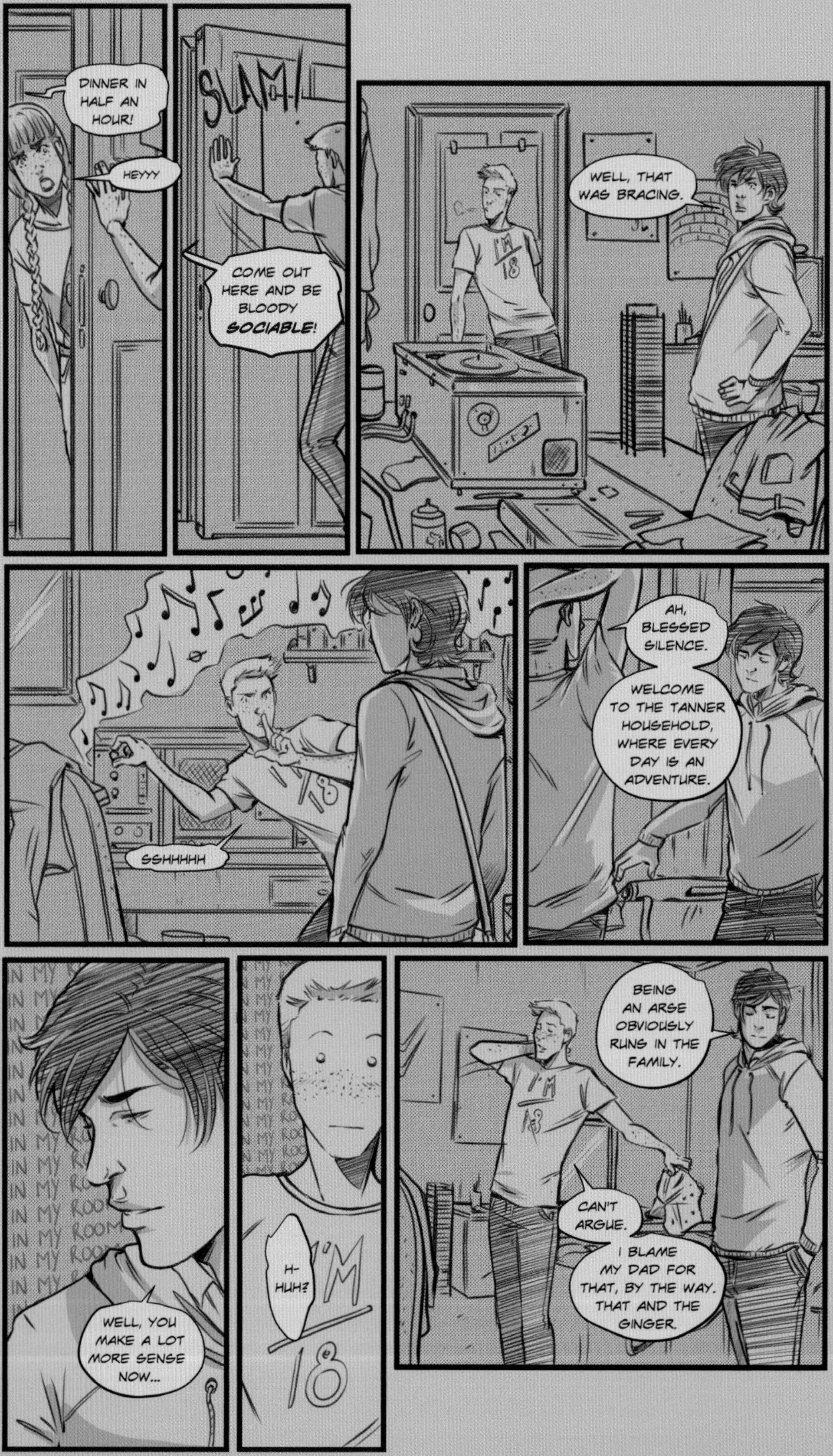
DINNER IN HALF AN HOUR!
HEYYY
SLAM!
COME OUT HERE AND BE BLOODY **SOCIABLE**!
WELL, THAT WAS BRACING.
SSHHHHH
AH, BLESSED SILENCE.
WELCOME TO THE TANNER HOUSEHOLD, WHERE EVERY DAY IS AN ADVENTURE.
IN MY ROOM
WELL, YOU MAKE A LOT MORE SENSE NOW...
H-HUH?
I'M 18
BEING AN ARSE OBVIOUSLY RUNS IN THE FAMILY.
CAN'T ARGUE.
I BLAME MY DAD FOR THAT, BY THE WAY. THAT AND THE GINGER.

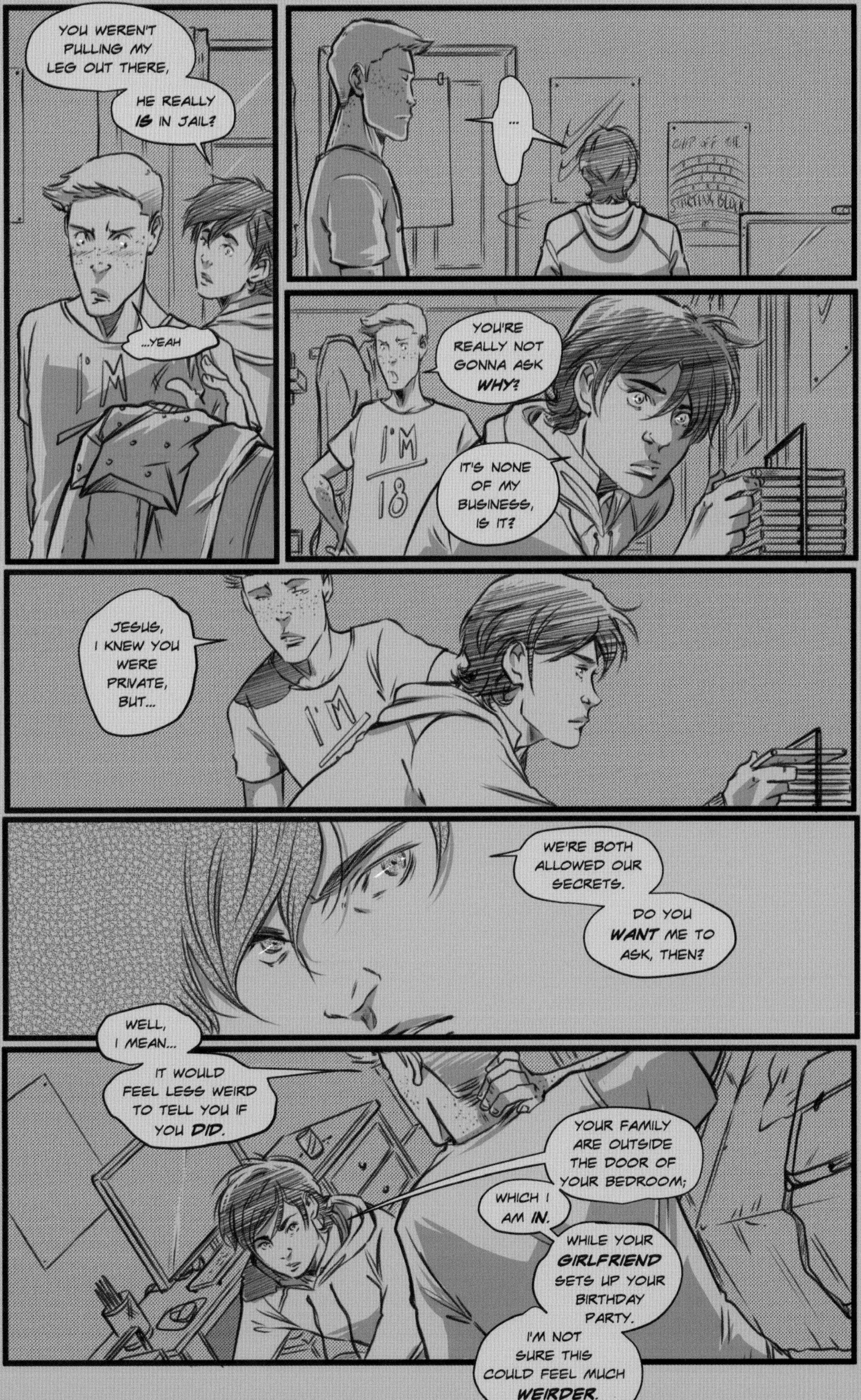
YOU WEREN'T PULLING MY LEG OUT THERE,
HE REALLY **IS** IN JAIL?
...YEAH
...
YOU'RE REALLY NOT GONNA ASK **WHY?**
IT'S NONE OF MY BUSINESS, IS IT?
JESUS, I KNEW YOU WERE PRIVATE, BUT...
WE'RE BOTH ALLOWED OUR SECRETS.
DO YOU **WANT** ME TO ASK, THEN?
WELL, I MEAN...
IT WOULD FEEL LESS WEIRD TO TELL YOU IF YOU **DID**.
YOUR FAMILY ARE OUTSIDE THE DOOR OF YOUR BEDROOM;
WHICH I AM **IN**.
WHILE YOUR **GIRLFRIEND** SETS UP YOUR BIRTHDAY PARTY.
I'M NOT SURE THIS COULD FEEL MUCH **WEIRDER**.

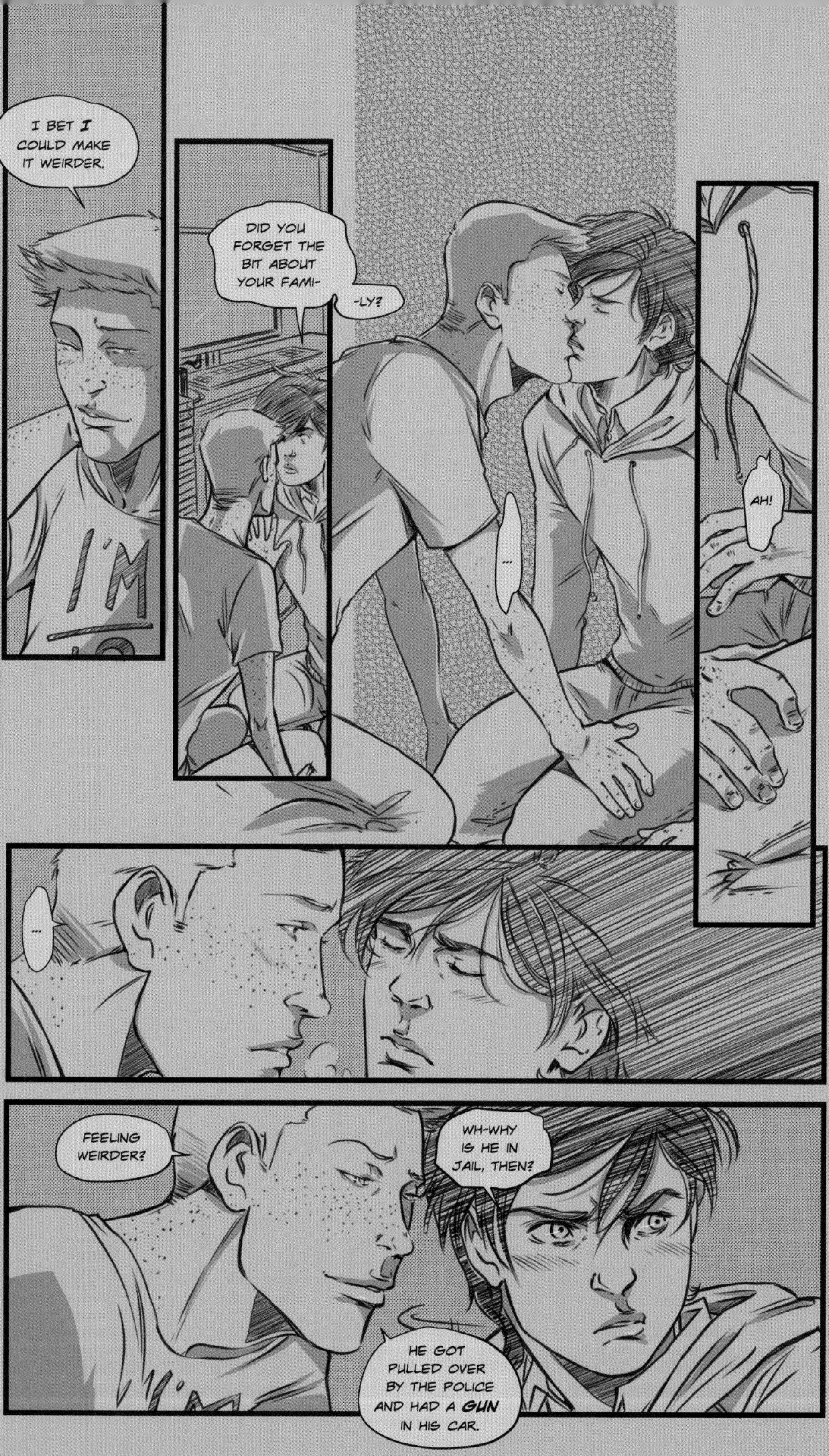
I BET I COULD MAKE IT WEIRDER.
DID YOU FORGET THE BIT ABOUT YOUR FAMI-
-LY?
...
AH!
...
FEELING WEIRDER?
WH-WHY IS HE IN JAIL, THEN?
HE GOT PULLED OVER BY THE POLICE AND HAD A GUN IN HIS CAR.

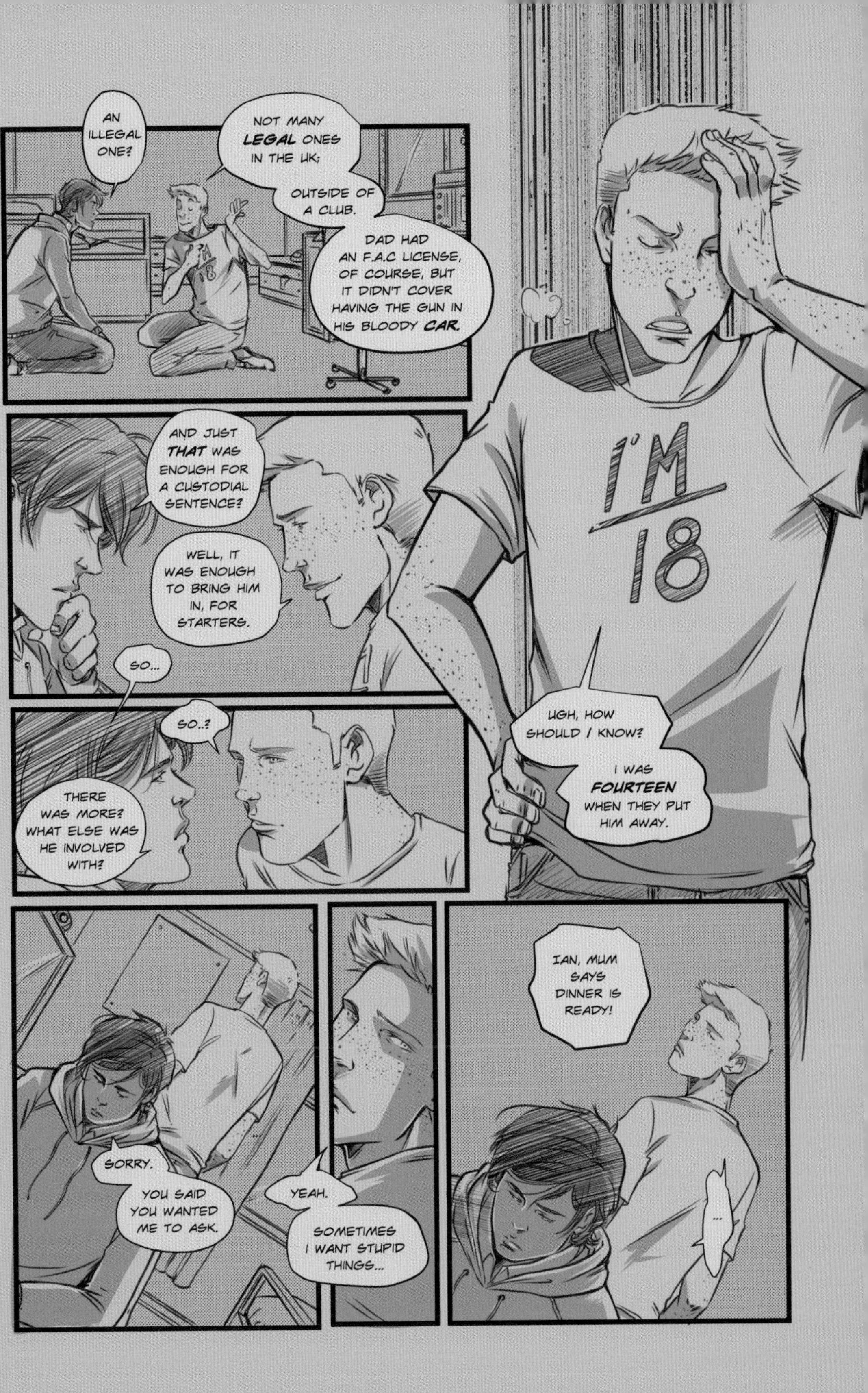
AN ILLEGAL ONE?
NOT MANY LEGAL ONES IN THE UK;
OUTSIDE OF A CLUB.
DAD HAD AN F.A.C LICENSE, OF COURSE, BUT IT DIDN'T COVER HAVING THE GUN IN HIS BLOODY CAR.
AND JUST THAT WAS ENOUGH FOR A CUSTODIAL SENTENCE?
WELL, IT WAS ENOUGH TO BRING HIM IN, FOR STARTERS.
SO...
SO..?
THERE WAS MORE? WHAT ELSE WAS HE INVOLVED WITH?
I'M 18
UGH, HOW SHOULD I KNOW?
I WAS FOURTEEN WHEN THEY PUT HIM AWAY.
SORRY.
YOU SAID YOU WANTED ME TO ASK.
YEAH.
SOMETIMES I WANT STUPID THINGS...
IAN, MUM SAYS DINNER IS READY!
...

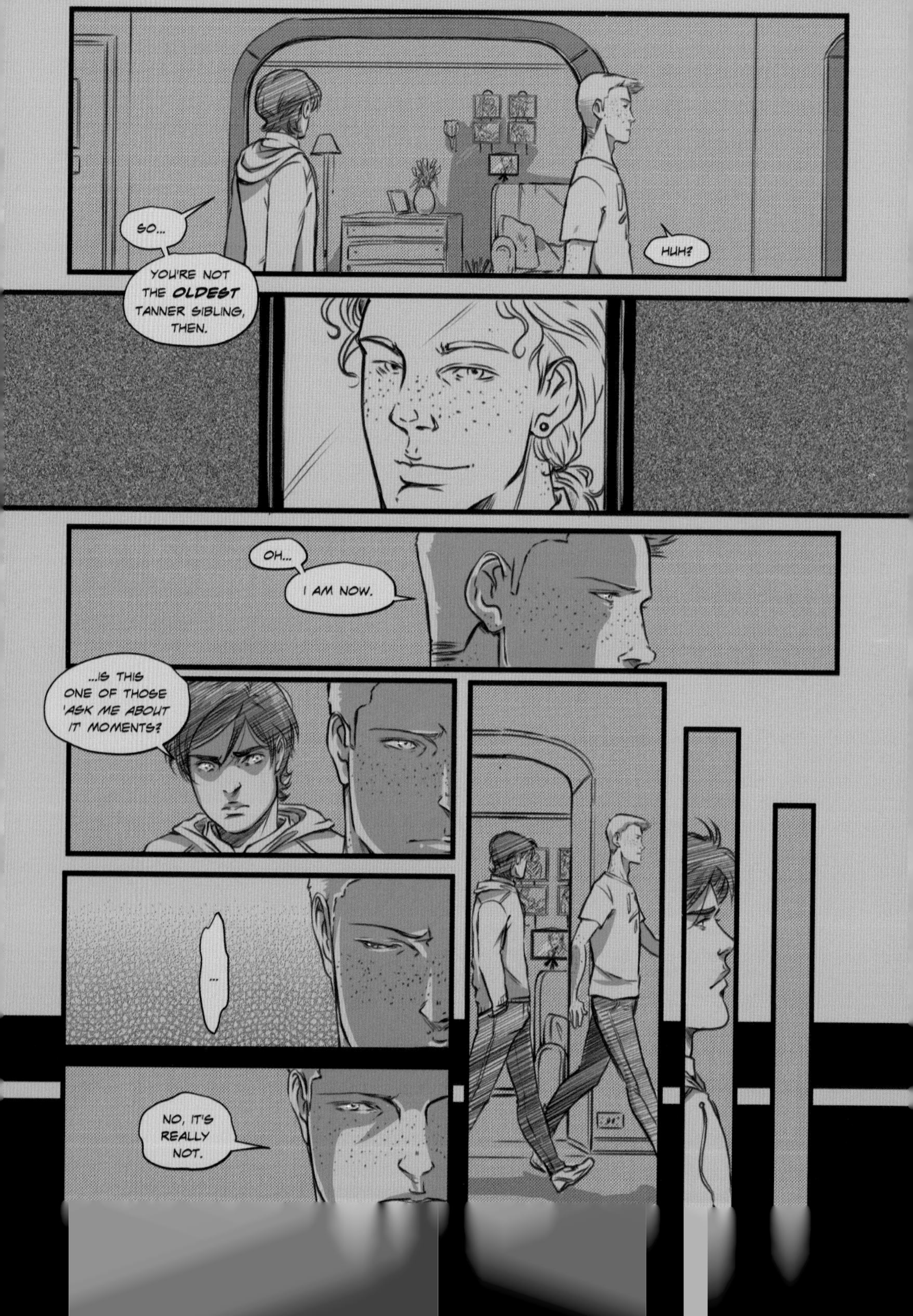
SO...
HUH?
YOU'RE NOT THE OLDEST TANNER SIBLING, THEN.
OH...
I AM NOW.
...IS THIS ONE OF THOSE 'ASK ME ABOUT IT' MOMENTS?
...
NO, IT'S REALLY NOT.

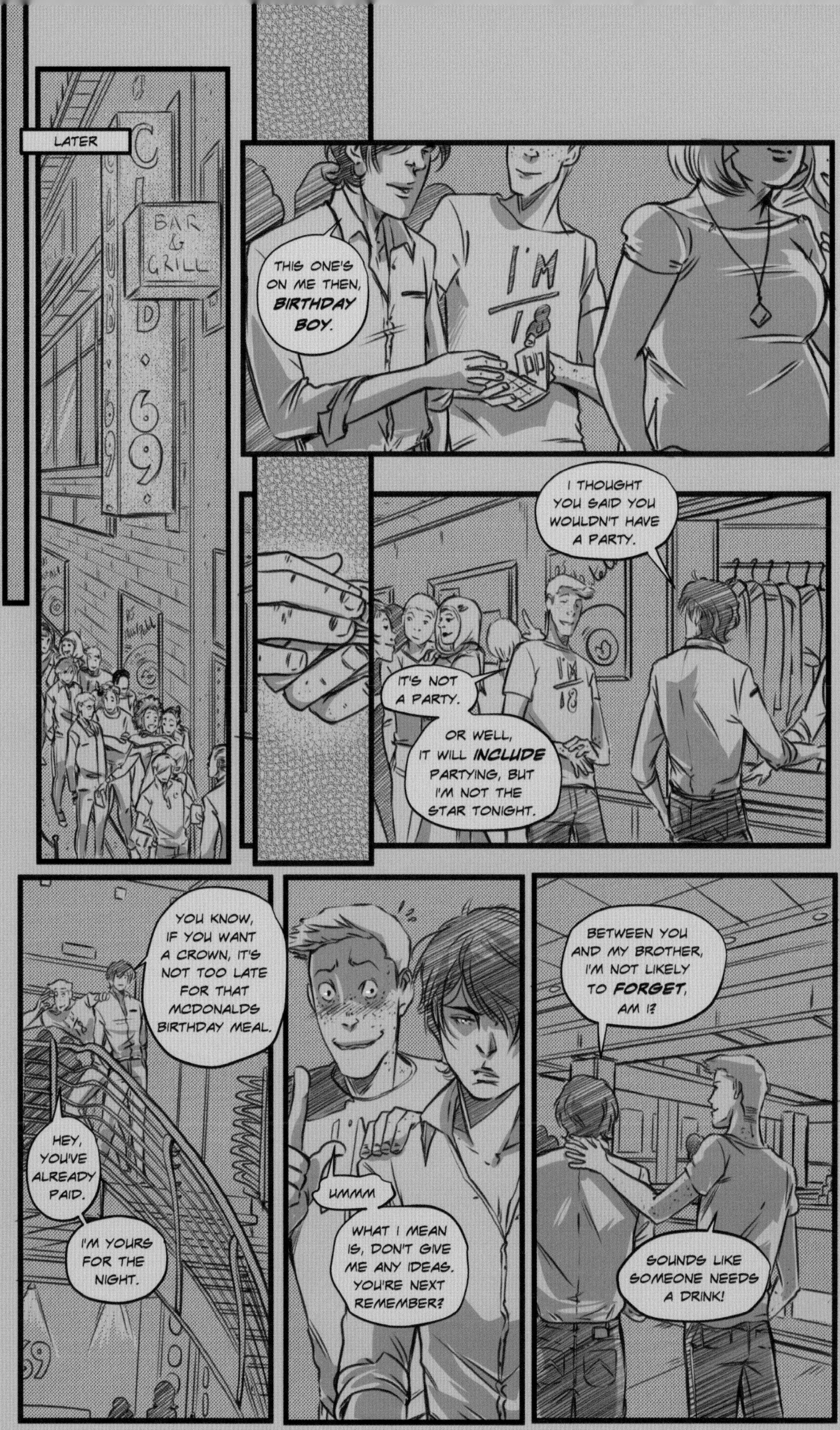
LATER
BAR & GRILL
CLUB 69
THIS ONE'S ON ME THEN, BIRTHDAY BOY.
I'M 18
I THOUGHT YOU SAID YOU WOULDN'T HAVE A PARTY.
IT'S NOT A PARTY.
OR WELL, IT WILL INCLUDE PARTYING, BUT I'M NOT THE STAR TONIGHT.
YOU KNOW, IF YOU WANT A CROWN, IT'S NOT TOO LATE FOR THAT MCDONALDS BIRTHDAY MEAL.
HEY, YOU'VE ALREADY PAID.
I'M YOURS FOR THE NIGHT.
UMMM
WHAT I MEAN IS, DON'T GIVE ME ANY IDEAS. YOU'RE NEXT REMEMBER?
BETWEEN YOU AND MY BROTHER, I'M NOT LIKELY TO FORGET, AM I?
SOUNDS LIKE SOMEONE NEEDS A DRINK!

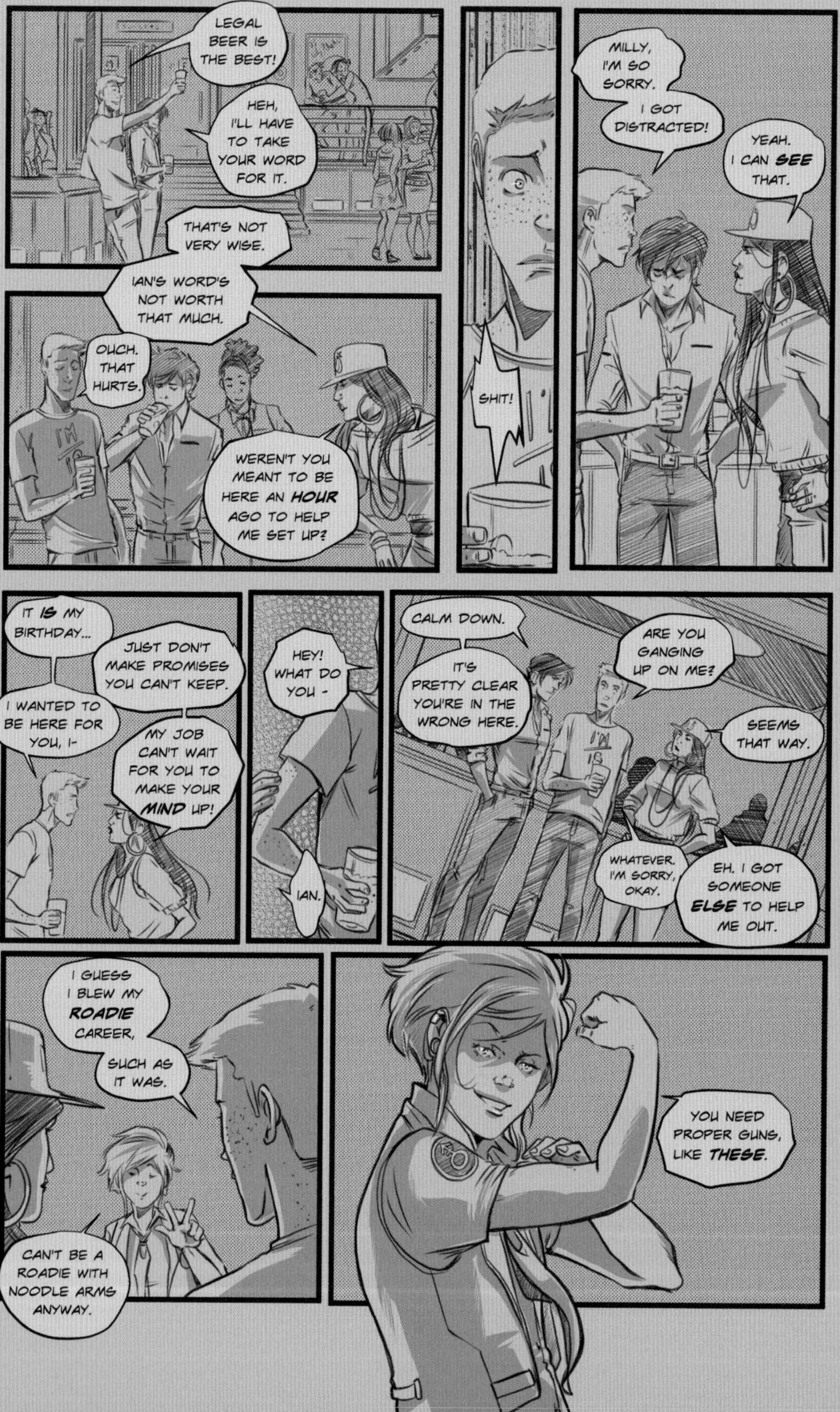
LEGAL BEER IS THE BEST!
HEH, I'LL HAVE TO TAKE YOUR WORD FOR IT.
THAT'S NOT VERY WISE.
IAN'S WORD'S NOT WORTH THAT MUCH.
OUCH. THAT HURTS.
WEREN'T YOU MEANT TO BE HERE AN HOUR AGO TO HELP ME SET UP?
SHIT!
MILLY, I'M SO SORRY.
I GOT DISTRACTED!
YEAH. I CAN SEE THAT.
IT IS MY BIRTHDAY...
JUST DON'T MAKE PROMISES YOU CAN'T KEEP.
I WANTED TO BE HERE FOR YOU, I-
MY JOB CAN'T WAIT FOR YOU TO MAKE YOUR MIND UP!
HEY! WHAT DO YOU -
IAN.
CALM DOWN.
IT'S PRETTY CLEAR YOU'RE IN THE WRONG HERE.
ARE YOU GANGING UP ON ME?
SEEMS THAT WAY.
WHATEVER. I'M SORRY, OKAY.
EH. I GOT SOMEONE ELSE TO HELP ME OUT.
I GUESS I BLEW MY ROADIE CAREER,
SUCH AS IT WAS.
CAN'T BE A ROADIE WITH NOODLE ARMS ANYWAY.
YOU NEED PROPER GUNS, LIKE THESE.

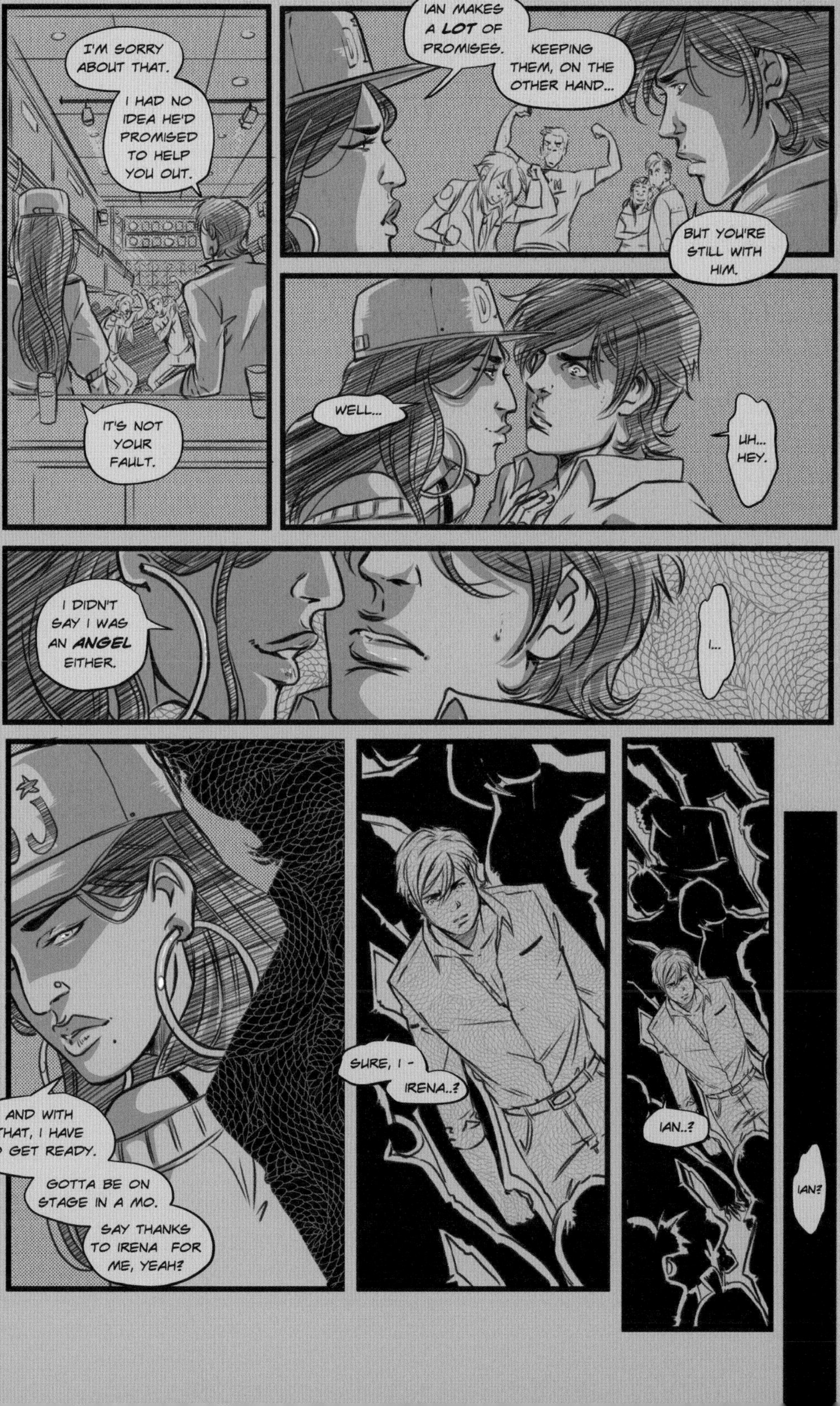
I'M SORRY ABOUT THAT.
I HAD NO IDEA HE'D PROMISED TO HELP YOU OUT.
IT'S NOT YOUR FAULT.
IAN MAKES A **LOT** OF PROMISES.
KEEPING THEM, ON THE OTHER HAND...
BUT YOU'RE STILL WITH HIM.
WELL...
UH... HEY.
I DIDN'T SAY I WAS AN ***ANGEL*** EITHER.
I...
AND WITH THAT, I HAVE TO GET READY.
GOTTA BE ON STAGE IN A MO.
SAY THANKS TO IRENA FOR ME, YEAH?
SURE, I -
IRENA..?
IAN..?
IAN?

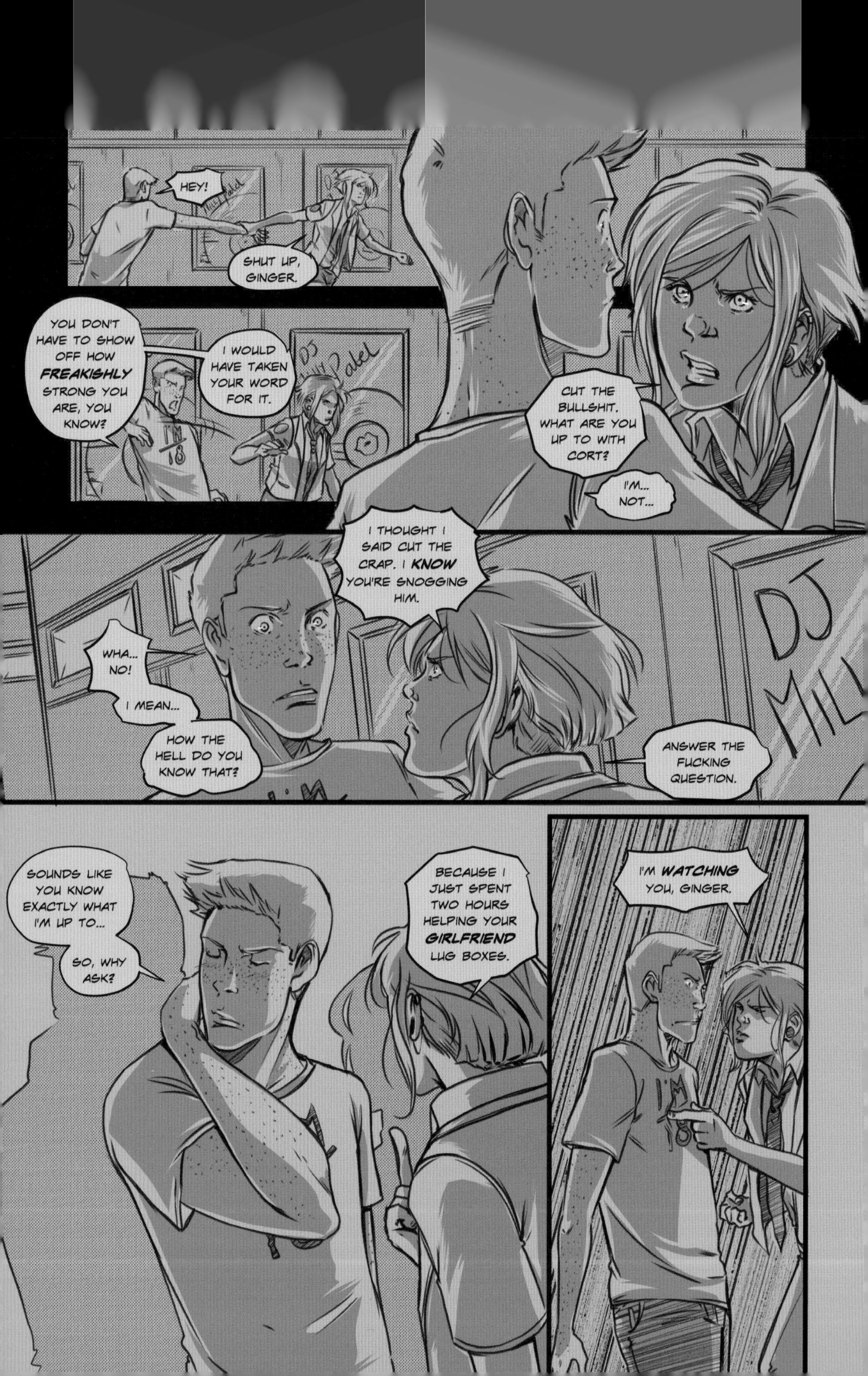
HEY!
SHUT UP, GINGER.
YOU DON'T HAVE TO SHOW OFF HOW **FREAKISHLY** STRONG YOU ARE, YOU KNOW?
I WOULD HAVE TAKEN YOUR WORD FOR IT.
CUT THE BULLSHIT. WHAT ARE YOU UP TO WITH CORT?
I'M... NOT...
I THOUGHT I SAID CUT THE CRAP. I **KNOW** YOU'RE SNOGGING HIM.
WHA... NO!
I MEAN...
HOW THE HELL DO YOU KNOW THAT?
ANSWER THE FUCKING QUESTION.
SOUNDS LIKE YOU KNOW EXACTLY WHAT I'M UP TO...
SO, WHY ASK?
BECAUSE I JUST SPENT TWO HOURS HELPING YOUR **GIRLFRIEND** LUG BOXES.
I'M **WATCHING** YOU, GINGER.

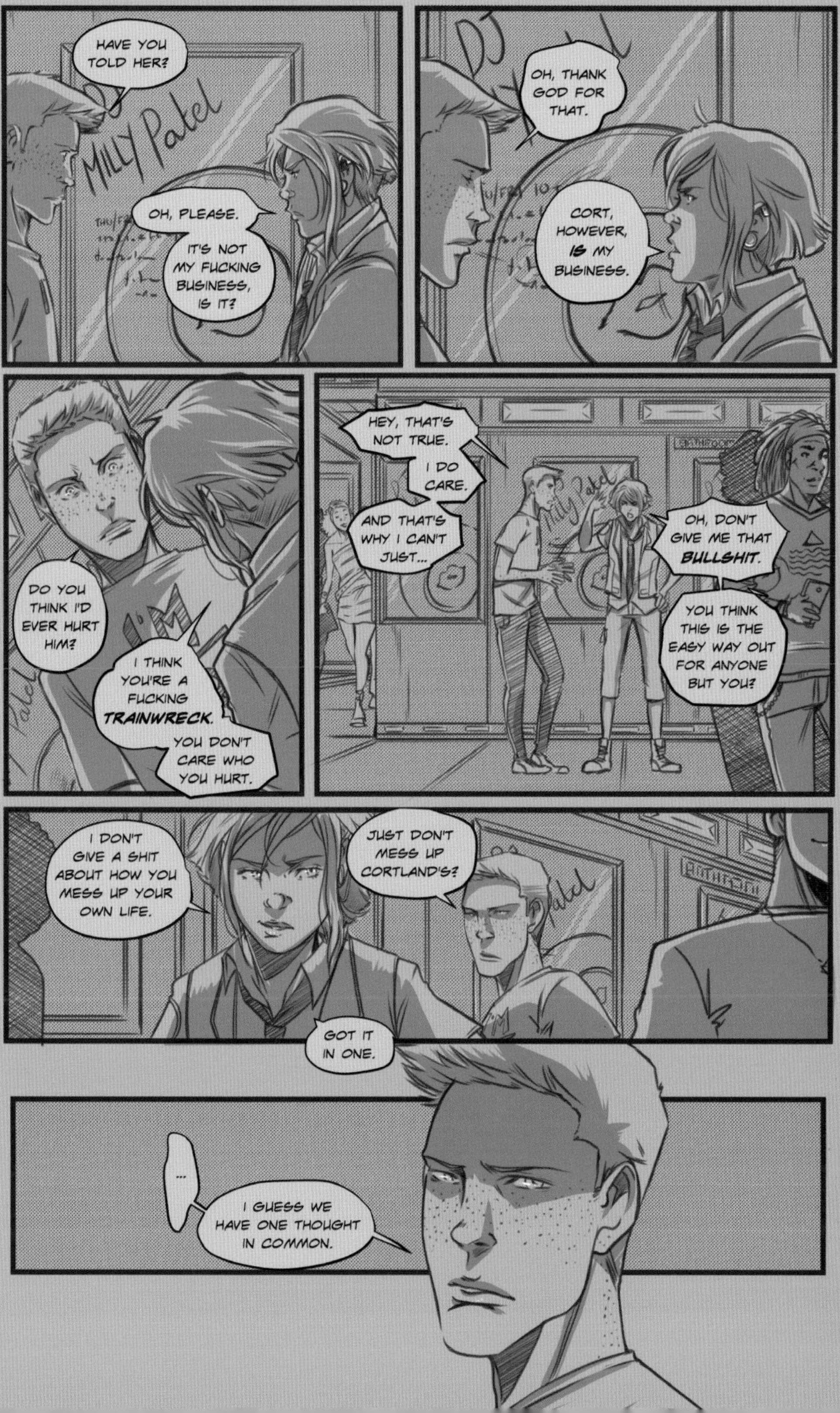
MILLY Patel
HAVE YOU TOLD HER?
OH, PLEASE.
IT'S NOT MY FUCKING BUSINESS, IS IT?
OH, THANK GOD FOR THAT.
CORT, HOWEVER, ***IS*** MY BUSINESS.
DO YOU THINK I'D EVER HURT HIM?
I THINK YOU'RE A FUCKING ***TRAINWRECK***.
YOU DON'T CARE WHO YOU HURT.
HEY, THAT'S NOT TRUE.
I DO CARE.
AND THAT'S WHY I CAN'T JUST...
OH, DON'T GIVE ME THAT ***BULLSHIT***.
YOU THINK THIS IS THE EASY WAY OUT FOR ANYONE BUT YOU?
I DON'T GIVE A SHIT ABOUT HOW YOU MESS UP YOUR OWN LIFE.
JUST DON'T MESS UP CORTLAND'S?
GOT IT IN ONE.
...
I GUESS WE HAVE ONE THOUGHT IN COMMON.

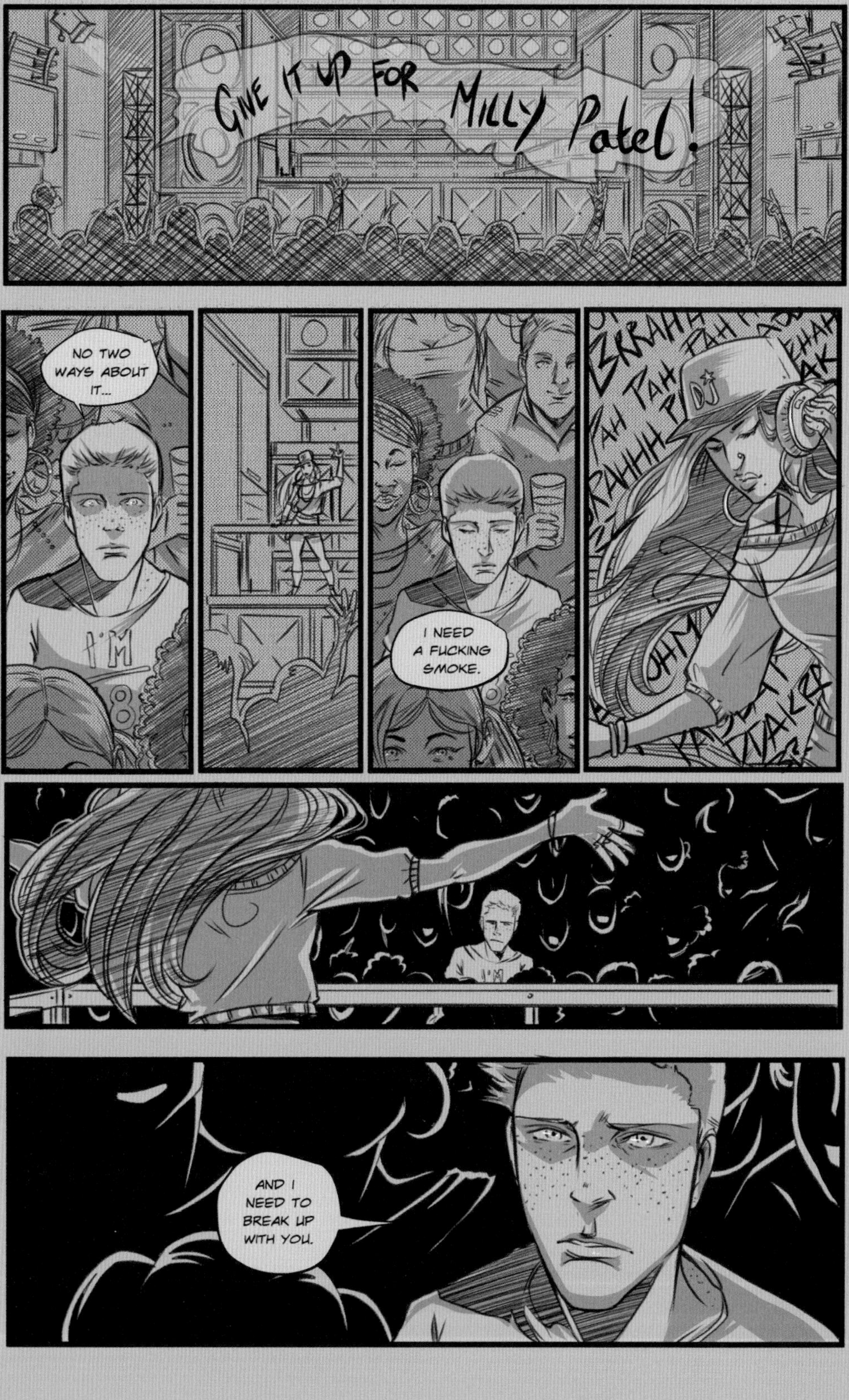
GIVE IT UP FOR MILLY PATEL!
NO TWO WAYS ABOUT IT...
I NEED A FUCKING SMOKE.
AND I NEED TO BREAK UP WITH YOU.

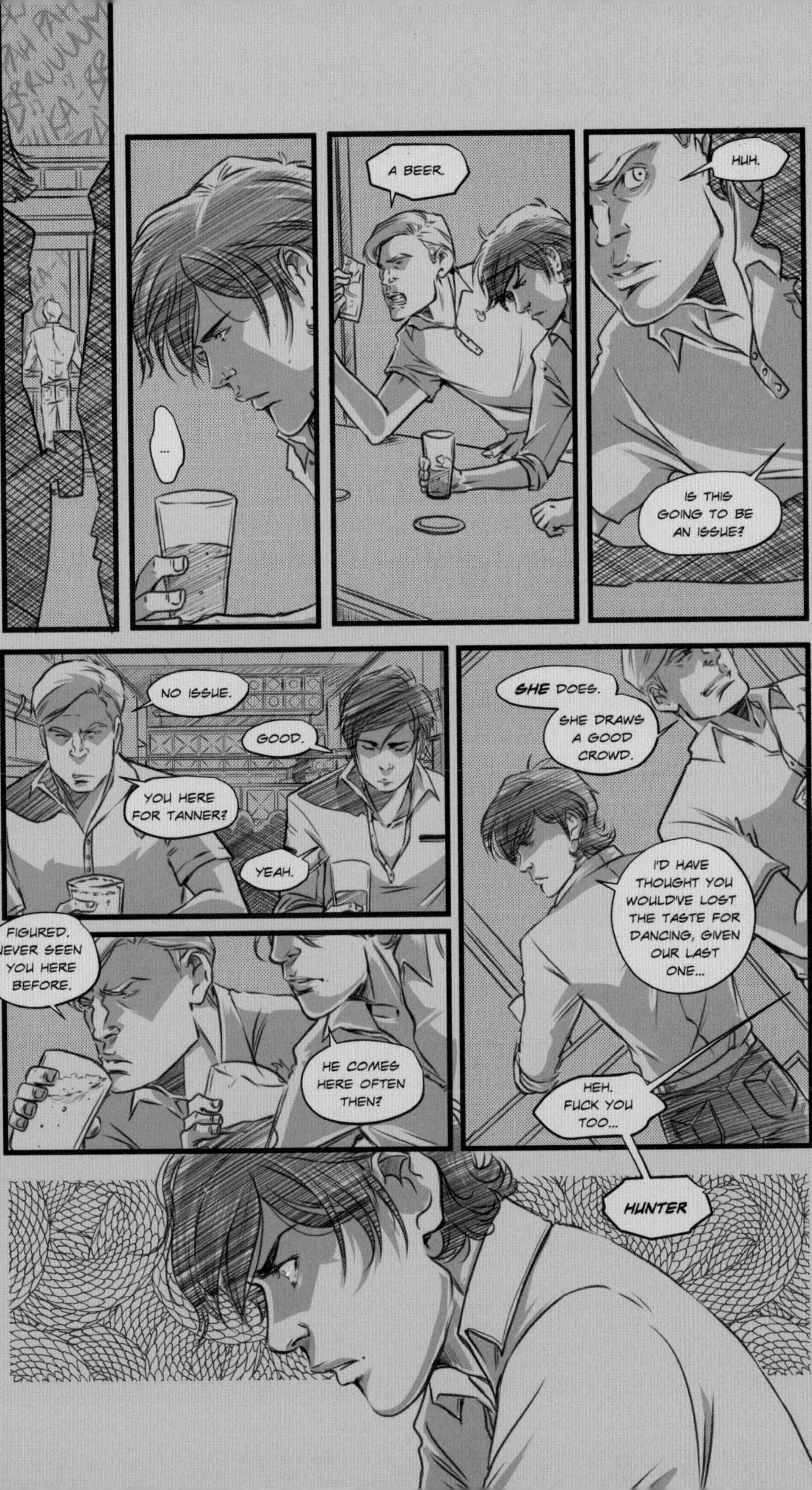
...
A BEER.
HUH.
IS THIS GOING TO BE AN ISSUE?
NO ISSUE.
GOOD.
YOU HERE FOR TANNER?
YEAH.
FIGURED. NEVER SEEN YOU HERE BEFORE.
HE COMES HERE OFTEN THEN?
SHE DOES.
SHE DRAWS A GOOD CROWD.
I'D HAVE THOUGHT YOU WOULD'VE LOST THE TASTE FOR DANCING, GIVEN OUR LAST ONE...
HEH. FUCK YOU TOO...
HUNTER

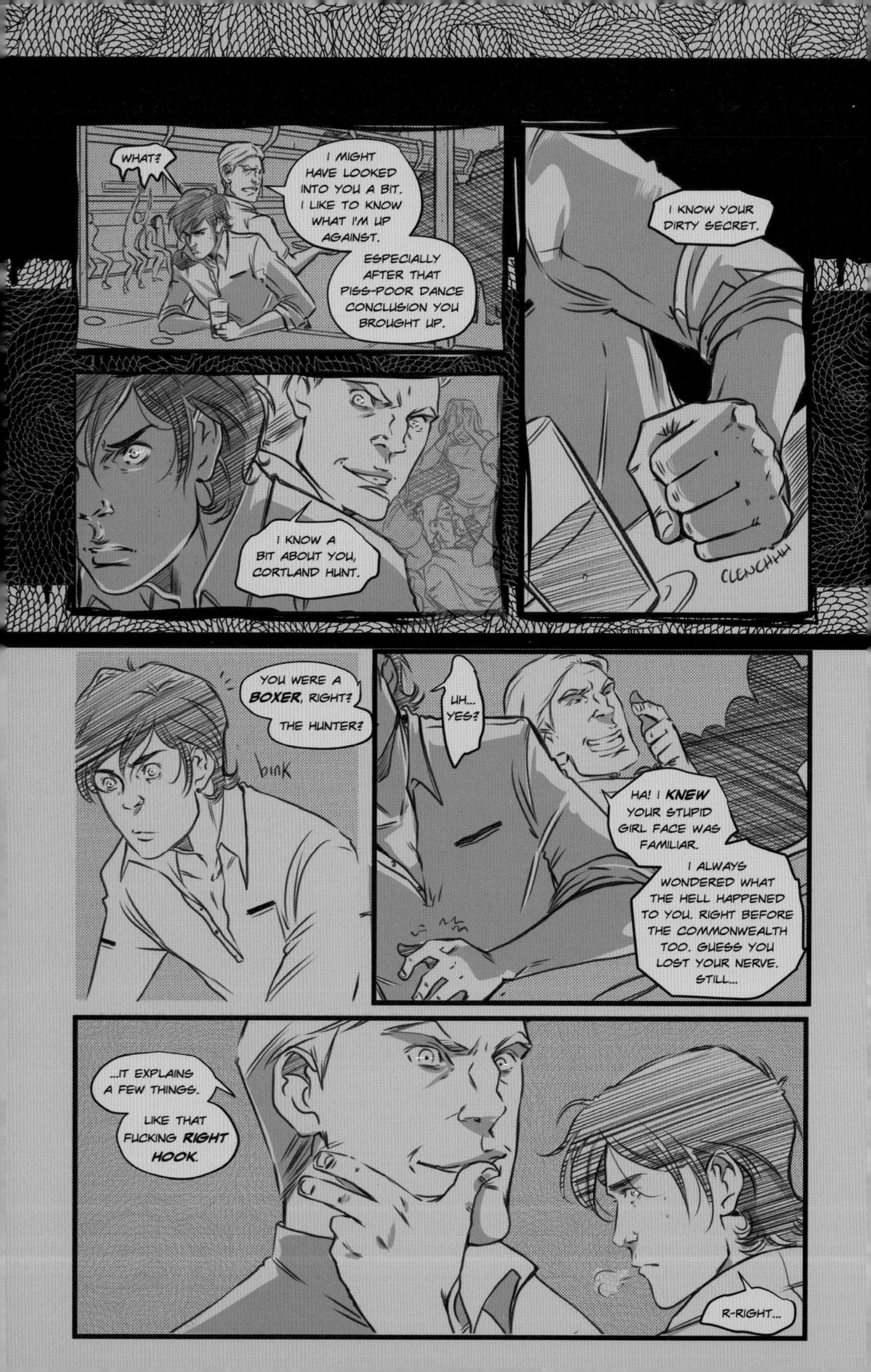
WHAT?
I MIGHT HAVE LOOKED INTO YOU A BIT. I LIKE TO KNOW WHAT I'M UP AGAINST.
ESPECIALLY AFTER THAT PISS-POOR DANCE CONCLUSION YOU BROUGHT UP.
I KNOW A BIT ABOUT YOU, CORTLAND HUNT.
I KNOW YOUR DIRTY SECRET.
CLENCHHH
YOU WERE A BOXER, RIGHT?
THE HUNTER?
bink
UH... YES?
HA! I KNEW YOUR STUPID GIRL FACE WAS FAMILIAR.
I ALWAYS WONDERED WHAT THE HELL HAPPENED TO YOU. RIGHT BEFORE THE COMMONWEALTH TOO. GUESS YOU LOST YOUR NERVE. STILL...
...IT EXPLAINS A FEW THINGS.
LIKE THAT FUCKING RIGHT HOOK.
R-RIGHT...

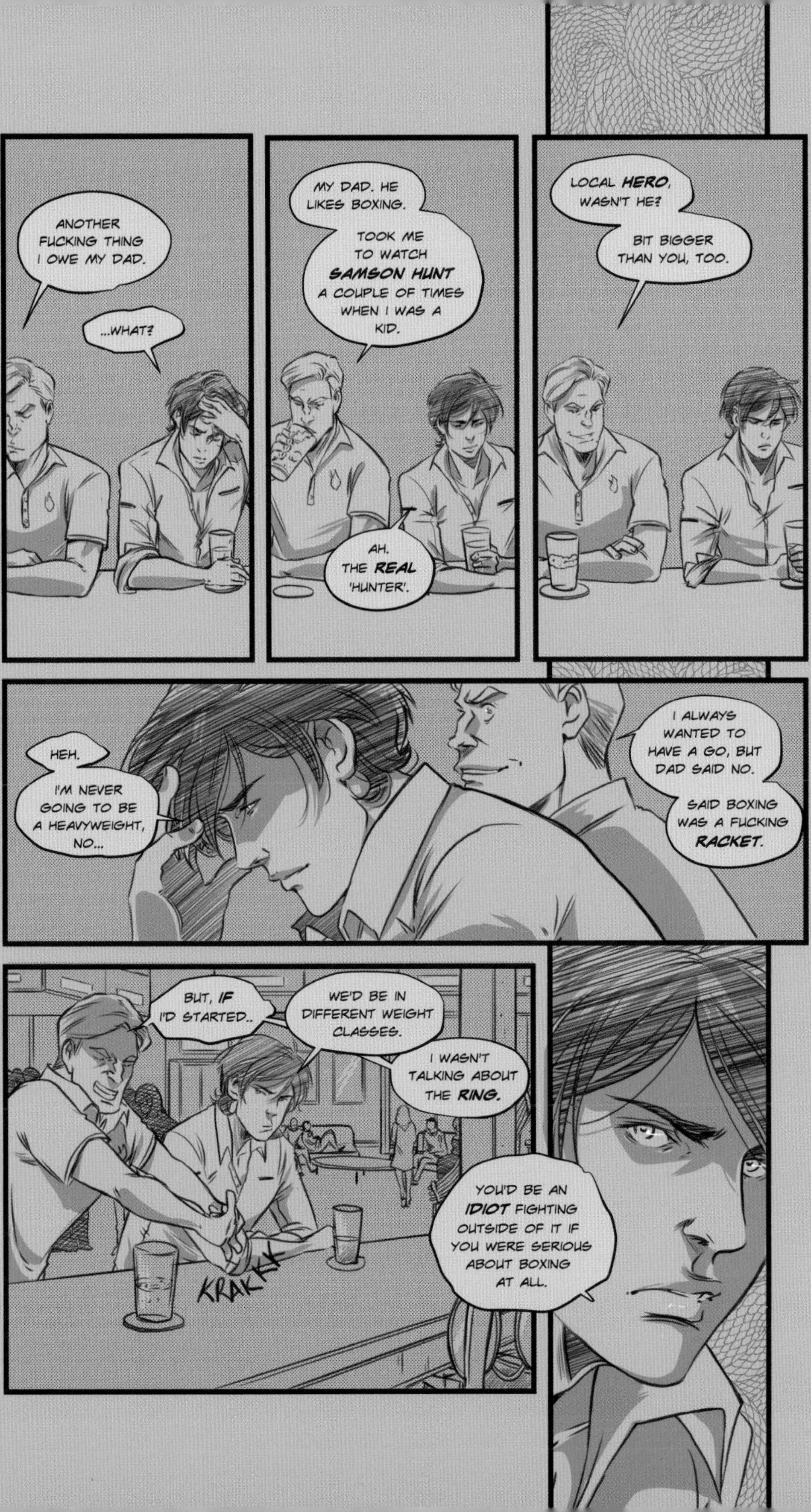
ANOTHER FUCKING THING I OWE MY DAD.
...WHAT?
MY DAD. HE LIKES BOXING.
TOOK ME TO WATCH SAMSON HUNT A COUPLE OF TIMES WHEN I WAS A KID.
AH. THE REAL 'HUNTER'.
LOCAL HERO, WASN'T HE?
BIT BIGGER THAN YOU, TOO.
HEH.
I'M NEVER GOING TO BE A HEAVYWEIGHT, NO...
I ALWAYS WANTED TO HAVE A GO, BUT DAD SAID NO.
SAID BOXING WAS A FUCKING RACKET.
BUT, IF I'D STARTED..
WE'D BE IN DIFFERENT WEIGHT CLASSES.
I WASN'T TALKING ABOUT THE RING.
KRAKKK
YOU'D BE AN IDIOT FIGHTING OUTSIDE OF IT IF YOU WERE SERIOUS ABOUT BOXING AT ALL.

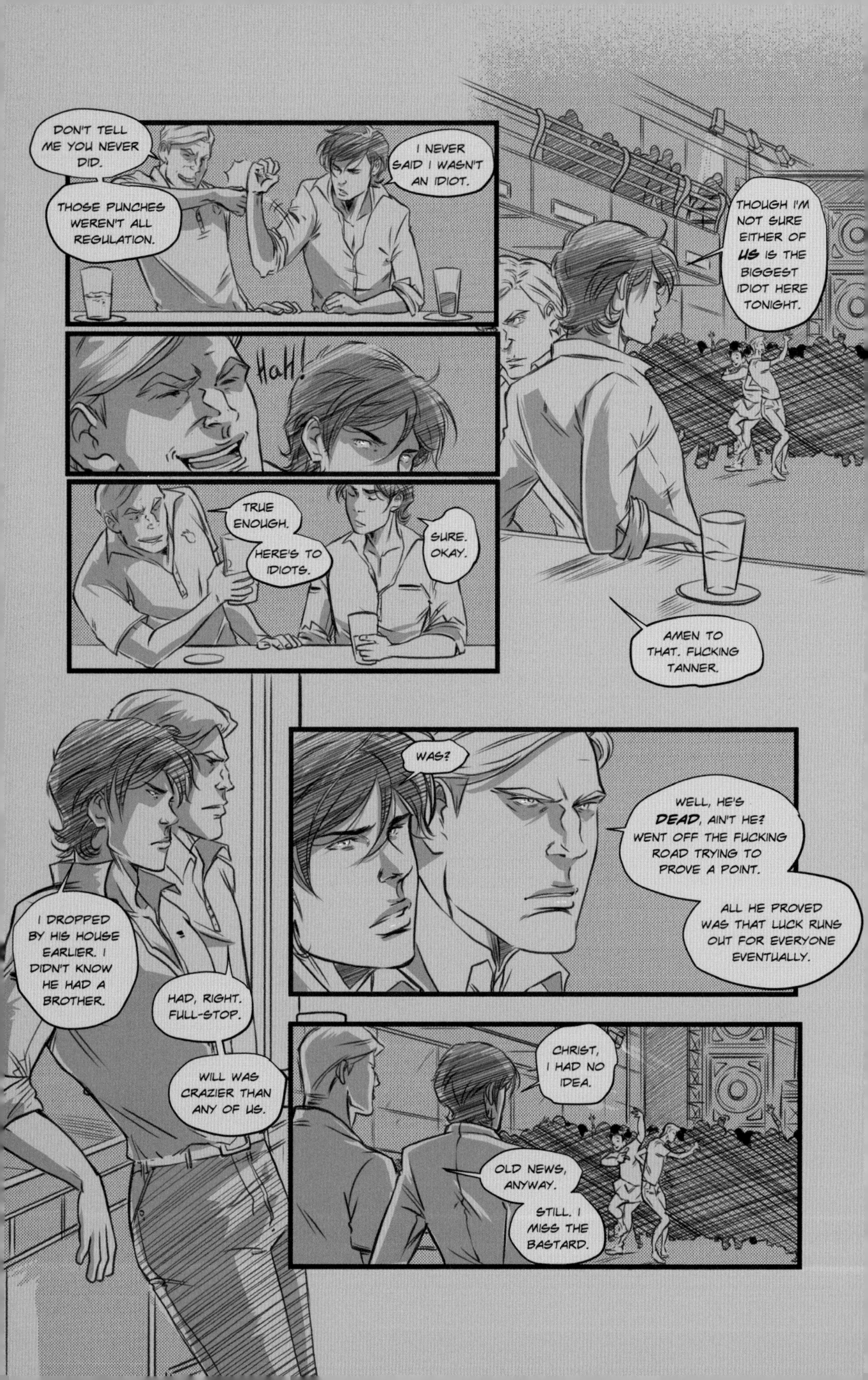
DON'T TELL ME YOU NEVER DID.
THOSE PUNCHES WEREN'T ALL REGULATION.
I NEVER SAID I WASN'T AN IDIOT.
HAH!
TRUE ENOUGH.
HERE'S TO IDIOTS.
SURE. OKAY.
THOUGH I'M NOT SURE EITHER OF US IS THE BIGGEST IDIOT HERE TONIGHT.
AMEN TO THAT. FUCKING TANNER.
WAS?
WELL, HE'S DEAD, AIN'T HE? WENT OFF THE FUCKING ROAD TRYING TO PROVE A POINT.
ALL HE PROVED WAS THAT LUCK RUNS OUT FOR EVERYONE EVENTUALLY.
I DROPPED BY HIS HOUSE EARLIER. I DIDN'T KNOW HE HAD A BROTHER.
HAD, RIGHT. FULL-STOP.
WILL WAS CRAZIER THAN ANY OF US.
CHRIST, I HAD NO IDEA.
OLD NEWS, ANYWAY.
STILL. I MISS THE BASTARD.

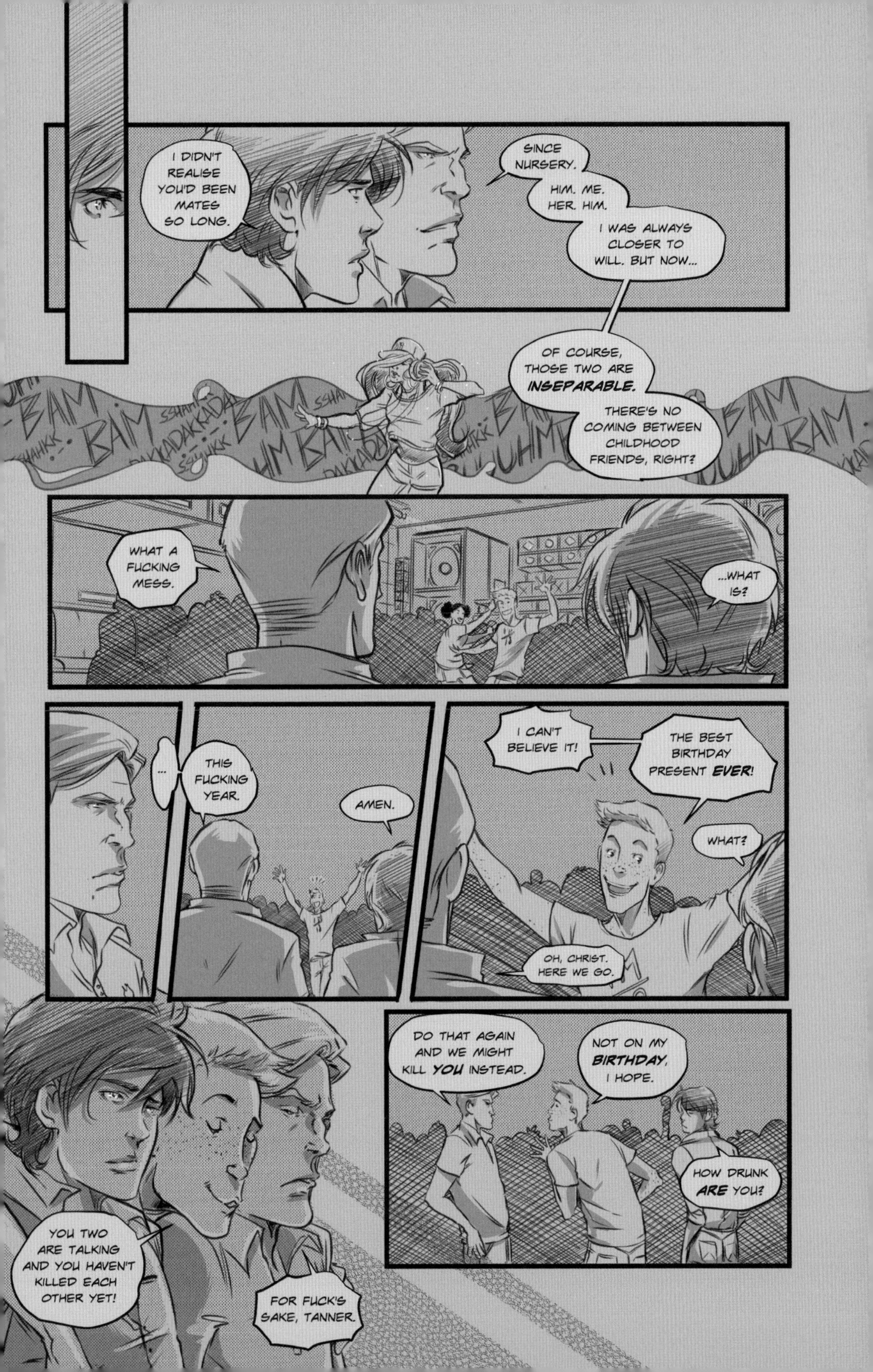
I DIDN'T REALISE YOU'D BEEN MATES SO LONG.
SINCE NURSERY.
HIM. ME. HER. HIM.
I WAS ALWAYS CLOSER TO WILL. BUT NOW...
OF COURSE, THOSE TWO ARE INSEPARABLE.
THERE'S NO COMING BETWEEN CHILDHOOD FRIENDS, RIGHT?
BAM
BAM
BAM
WHAT A FUCKING MESS.
...WHAT IS?
...
THIS FUCKING YEAR.
AMEN.
I CAN'T BELIEVE IT!
THE BEST BIRTHDAY PRESENT EVER!
WHAT?
OH, CHRIST. HERE WE GO.
YOU TWO ARE TALKING AND YOU HAVEN'T KILLED EACH OTHER YET!
FOR FUCK'S SAKE, TANNER.
DO THAT AGAIN AND WE MIGHT KILL YOU INSTEAD.
NOT ON MY BIRTHDAY, I HOPE.
HOW DRUNK ARE YOU?

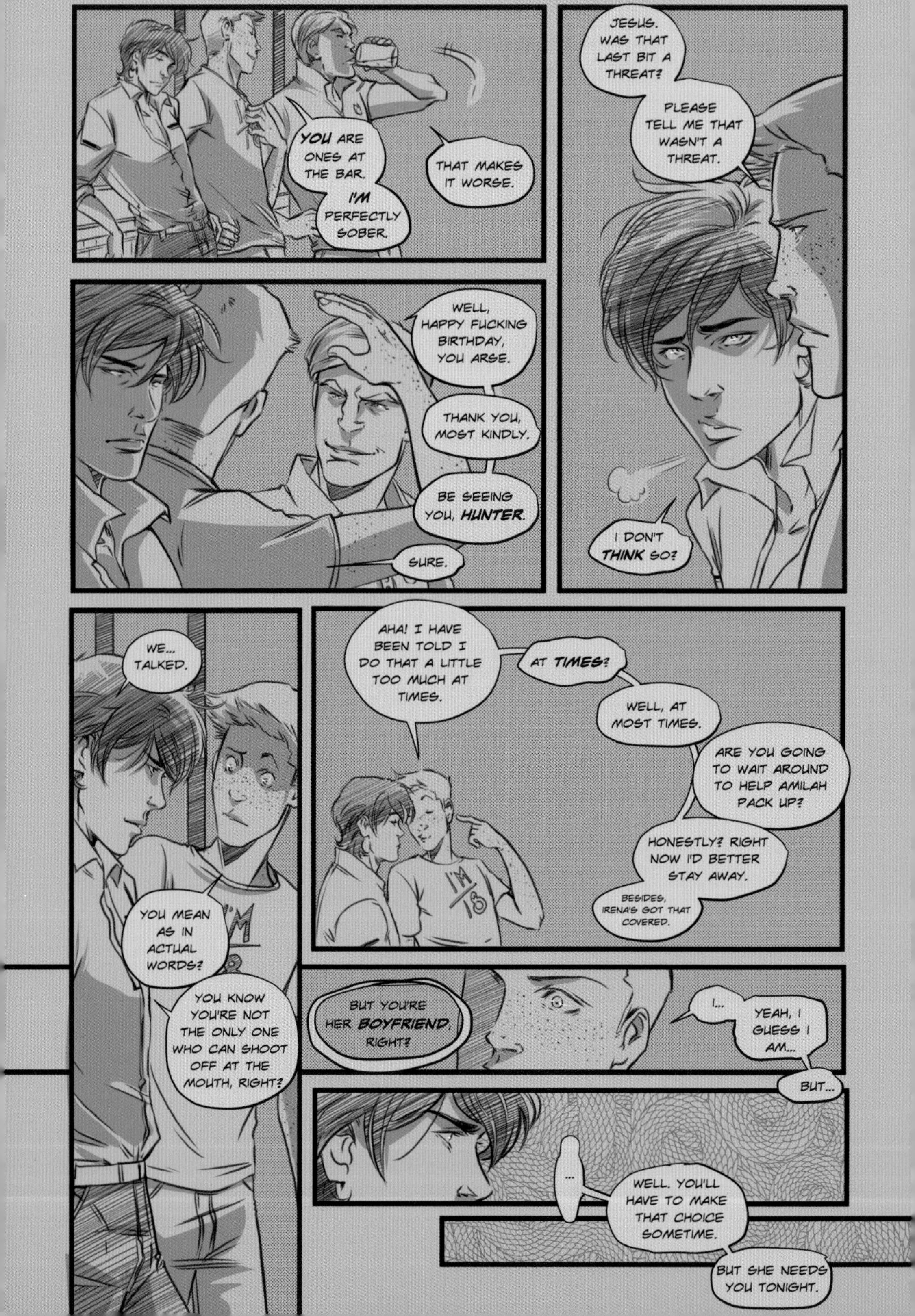
YOU ARE ONES AT THE BAR. I'M PERFECTLY SOBER.
THAT MAKES IT WORSE.
JESUS. WAS THAT LAST BIT A THREAT?
PLEASE TELL ME THAT WASN'T A THREAT.
WELL, HAPPY FUCKING BIRTHDAY, YOU ARSE.
THANK YOU, MOST KINDLY.
BE SEEING YOU, HUNTER.
SURE.
I DON'T THINK SO?
WE... TALKED.
YOU MEAN AS IN ACTUAL WORDS?
YOU KNOW YOU'RE NOT THE ONLY ONE WHO CAN SHOOT OFF AT THE MOUTH, RIGHT?
AHA! I HAVE BEEN TOLD I DO THAT A LITTLE TOO MUCH AT TIMES.
AT TIMES?
WELL, AT MOST TIMES.
ARE YOU GOING TO WAIT AROUND TO HELP AMILAH PACK UP?
HONESTLY? RIGHT NOW I'D BETTER STAY AWAY.
BESIDES, IRENA'S GOT THAT COVERED.
I'M 18
BUT YOU'RE HER BOYFRIEND, RIGHT?
I...
YEAH, I GUESS I AM...
BUT...
...
WELL. YOU'LL HAVE TO MAKE THAT CHOICE SOMETIME.
BUT SHE NEEDS YOU TONIGHT.

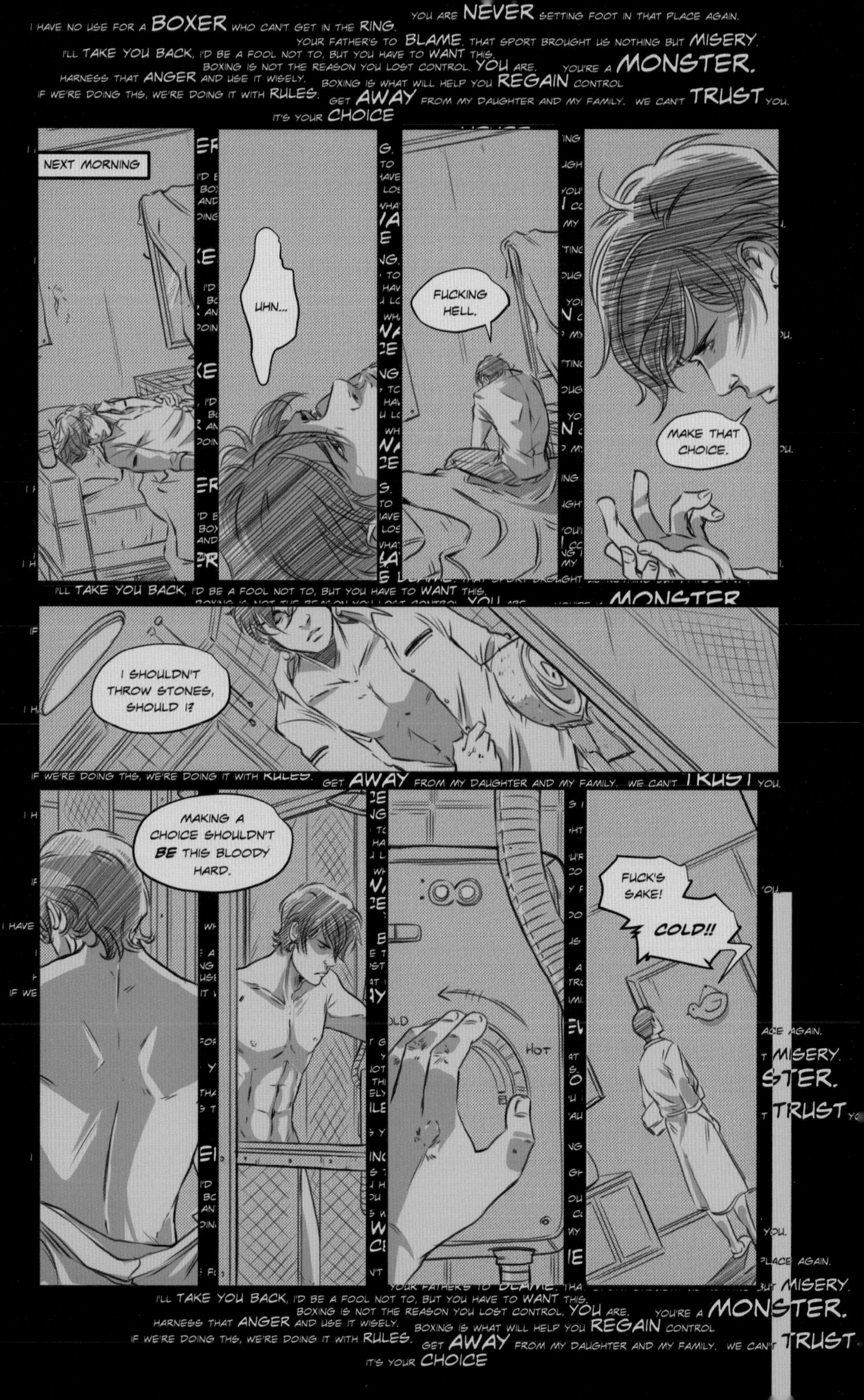
YOU ARE NEVER SETTING FOOT IN THAT PLACE AGAIN.
I HAVE NO USE FOR A BOXER WHO CAN'T GET IN THE RING.
YOUR FATHER'S TO BLAME. THAT SPORT BROUGHT US NOTHING BUT MISERY.
I'LL TAKE YOU BACK, I'D BE A FOOL NOT TO, BUT YOU HAVE TO WANT THIS.
BOXING IS NOT THE REASON YOU LOST CONTROL. YOU ARE. YOU'RE A MONSTER.
HARNESS THAT ANGER AND USE IT WISELY.
BOXING IS WHAT WILL HELP YOU REGAIN CONTROL
IF WE'RE DOING THIS, WE'RE DOING IT WITH RULES.
GET AWAY FROM MY DAUGHTER AND MY FAMILY. WE CAN'T TRUST YOU.
IT'S YOUR CHOICE
NEXT MORNING
UHN...
FUCKING HELL.
MAKE THAT CHOICE.
I SHOULDN'T THROW STONES, SHOULD I?
MAKING A CHOICE SHOULDN'T BE THIS BLOODY HARD.
COLD
HOT
FUCK'S SAKE!
COLD!!

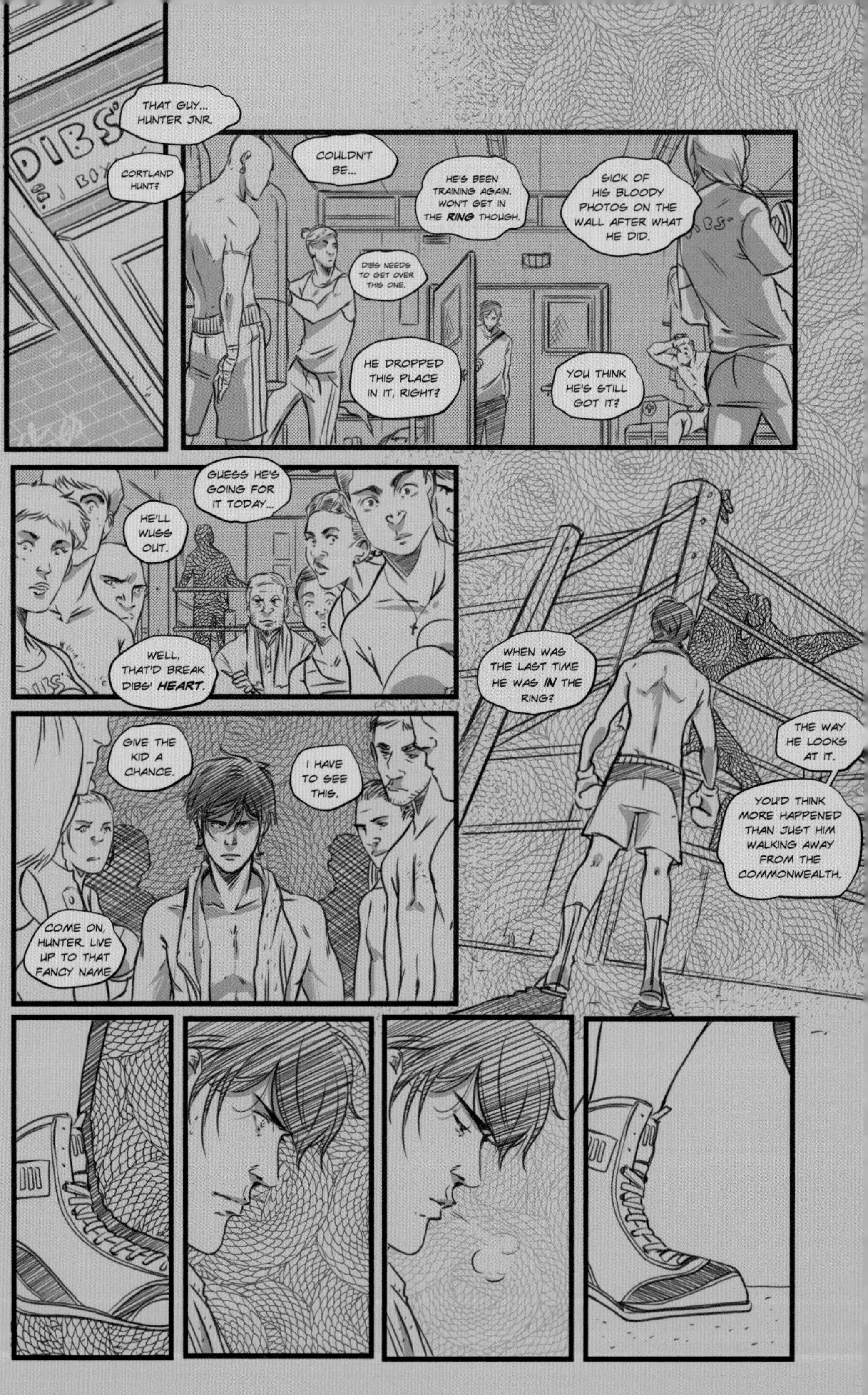
THAT GUY... HUNTER JNR.
CORTLAND HUNT?
COULDN'T BE...
HE'S BEEN TRAINING AGAIN. WON'T GET IN THE RING THOUGH.
SICK OF HIS BLOODY PHOTOS ON THE WALL AFTER WHAT HE DID.
DIBS NEEDS TO GET OVER THIS ONE.
HE DROPPED THIS PLACE IN IT, RIGHT?
YOU THINK HE'S STILL GOT IT?
GUESS HE'S GOING FOR IT TODAY...
HE'LL WUSS OUT.
WELL, THAT'D BREAK DIBS' HEART.
WHEN WAS THE LAST TIME HE WAS IN THE RING?
THE WAY HE LOOKS AT IT.
YOU'D THINK MORE HAPPENED THAN JUST HIM WALKING AWAY FROM THE COMMONWEALTH.
GIVE THE KID A CHANCE.
I HAVE TO SEE THIS.
COME ON, HUNTER. LIVE UP TO THAT FANCY NAME

ISSUE 9

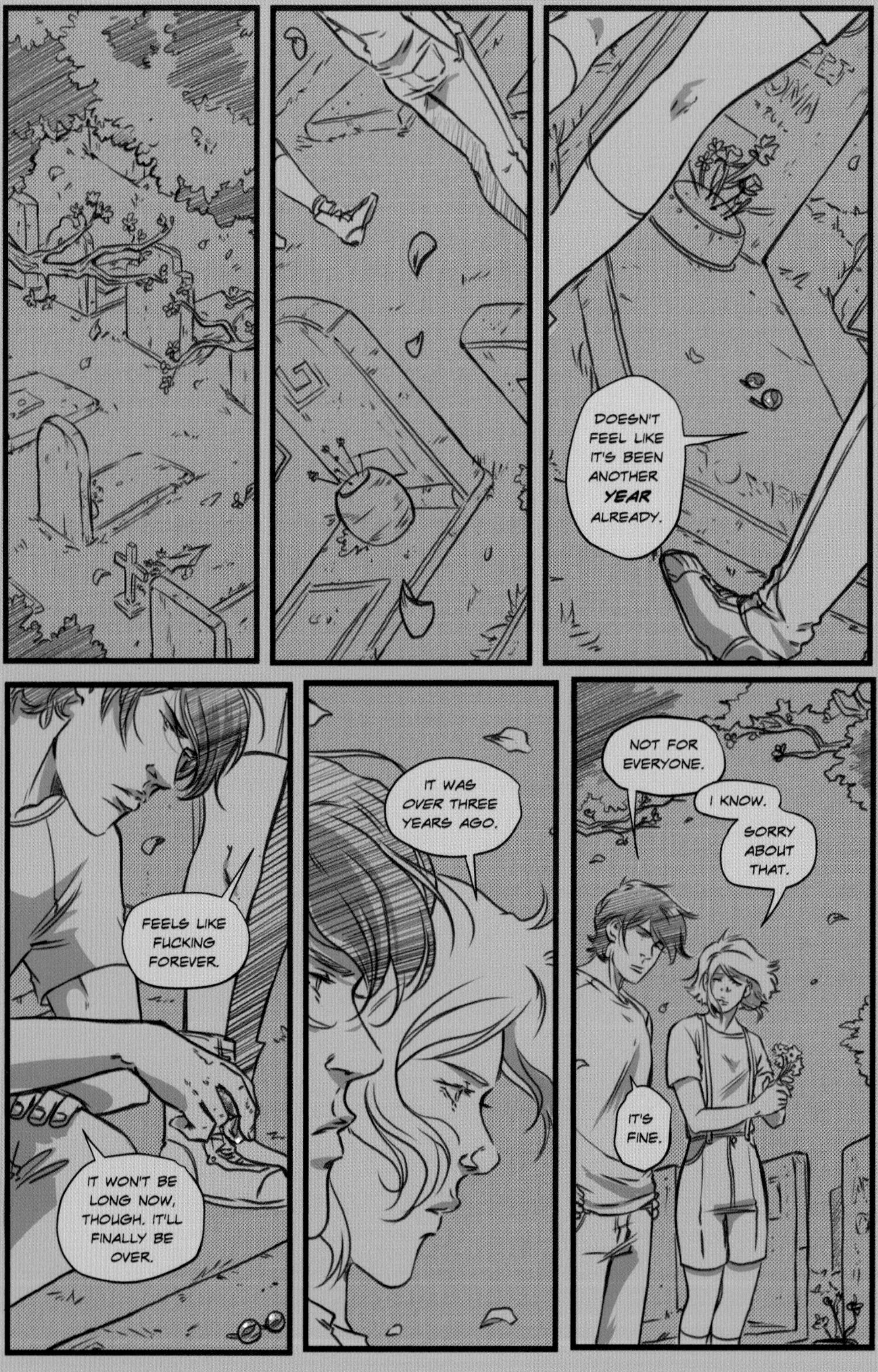
DOESN'T FEEL LIKE IT'S BEEN ANOTHER **YEAR** ALREADY.
FEELS LIKE FUCKING FOREVER.
IT WON'T BE LONG NOW, THOUGH. IT'LL FINALLY BE OVER.
IT WAS OVER THREE YEARS AGO.
NOT FOR EVERYONE.
I KNOW.
SORRY ABOUT THAT.
IT'S FINE.

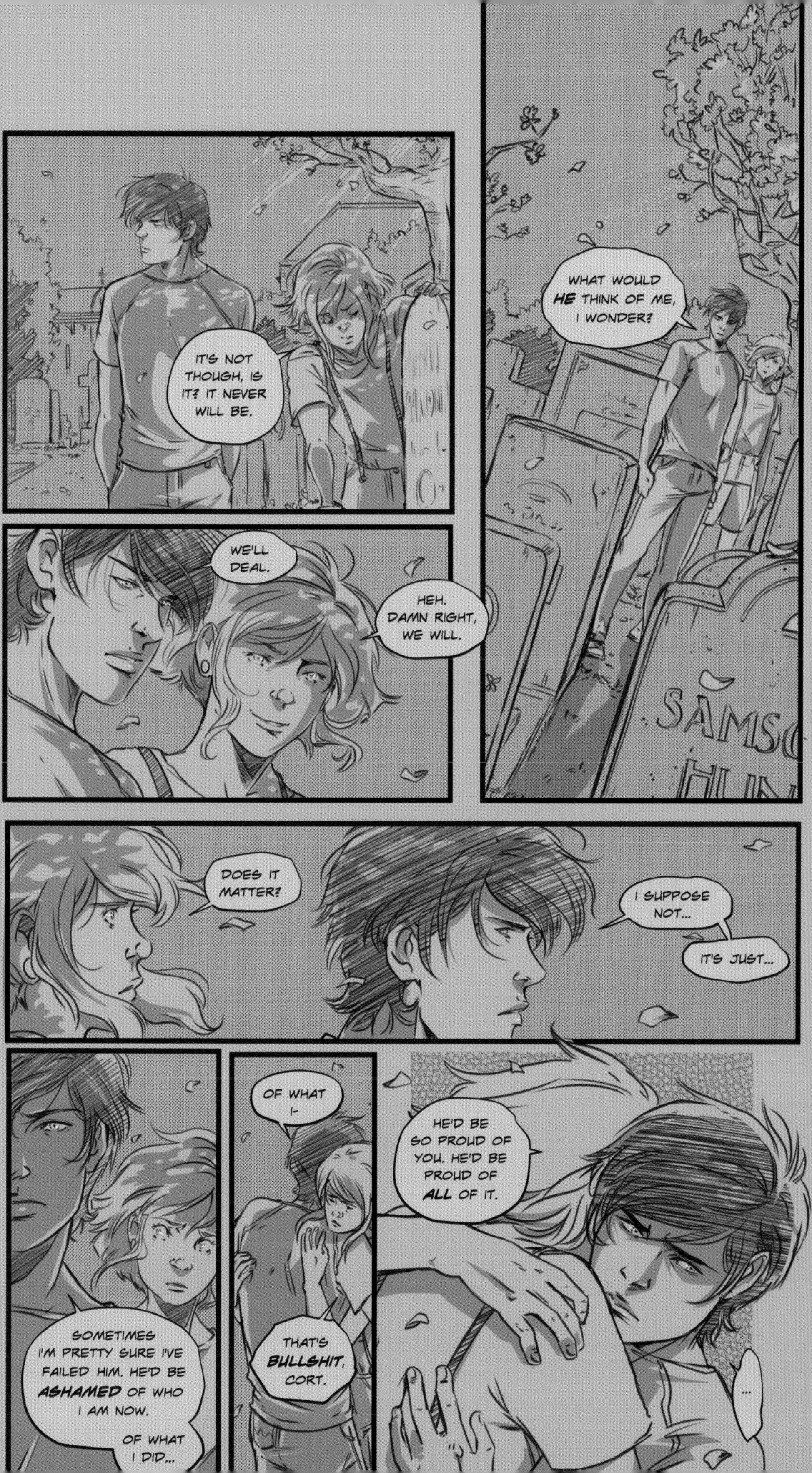
IT'S NOT THOUGH, IS IT? IT NEVER WILL BE.
WE'LL DEAL.
HEH. DAMN RIGHT, WE WILL.
WHAT WOULD **HE** THINK OF ME, I WONDER?
DOES IT MATTER?
I SUPPOSE NOT...
IT'S JUST...
SOMETIMES I'M PRETTY SURE I'VE FAILED HIM. HE'D BE **ASHAMED** OF WHO I AM NOW.
OF WHAT I DID...
OF WHAT I-
THAT'S **BULLSHIT**, CORT.
HE'D BE SO PROUD OF YOU. HE'D BE PROUD OF **ALL** OF IT.
...

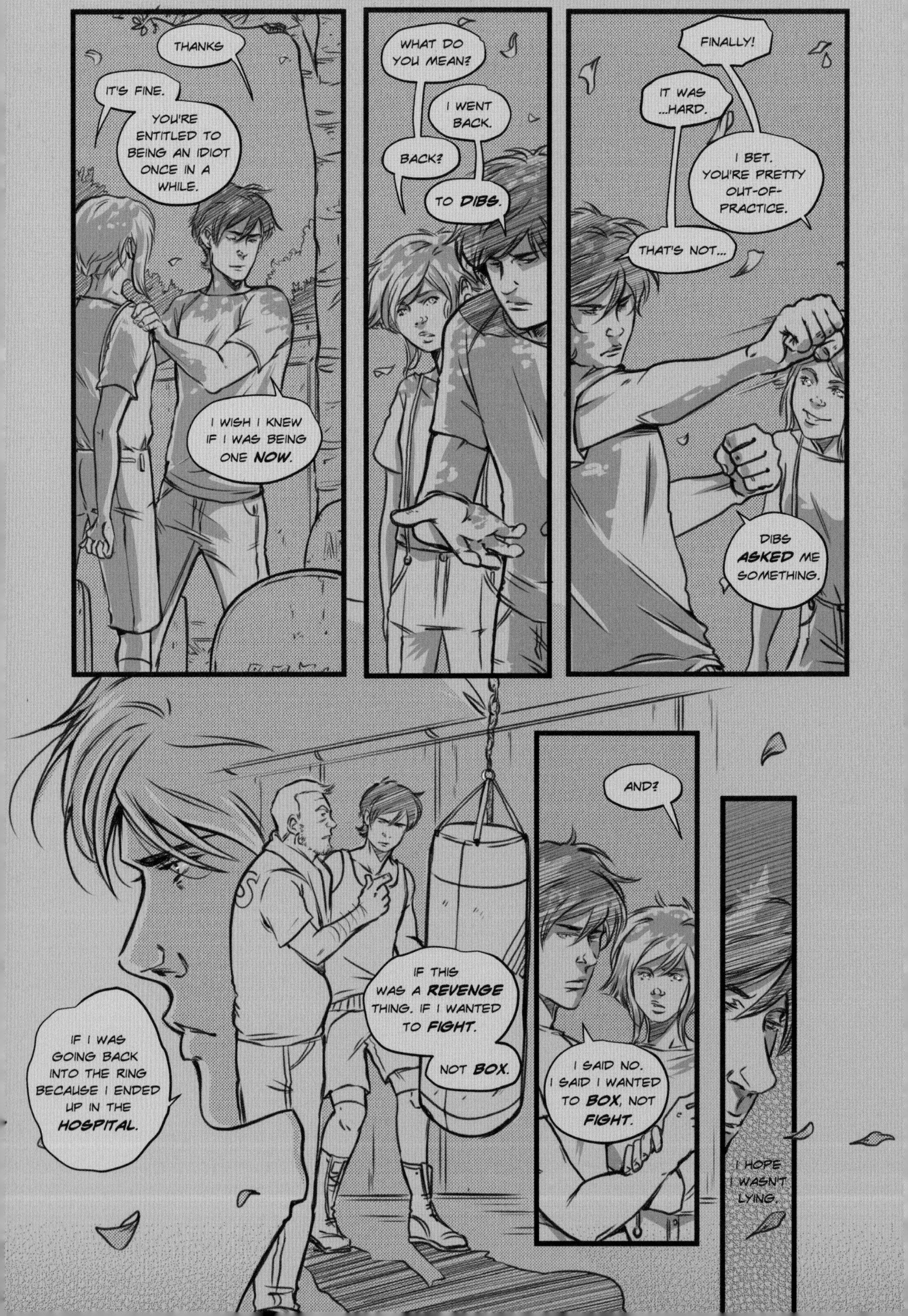
THANKS
IT'S FINE.
YOU'RE ENTITLED TO BEING AN IDIOT ONCE IN A WHILE.
I WISH I KNEW IF I WAS BEING ONE NOW.
WHAT DO YOU MEAN?
I WENT BACK.
BACK?
TO DIBS.
FINALLY!
IT WAS ...HARD.
I BET. YOU'RE PRETTY OUT-OF-PRACTICE.
THAT'S NOT...
DIBS ASKED ME SOMETHING.
IF I WAS GOING BACK INTO THE RING BECAUSE I ENDED UP IN THE HOSPITAL.
IF THIS WAS A REVENGE THING. IF I WANTED TO FIGHT.
NOT BOX.
AND?
I SAID NO. I SAID I WANTED TO BOX, NOT FIGHT.
I HOPE I WASN'T LYING.

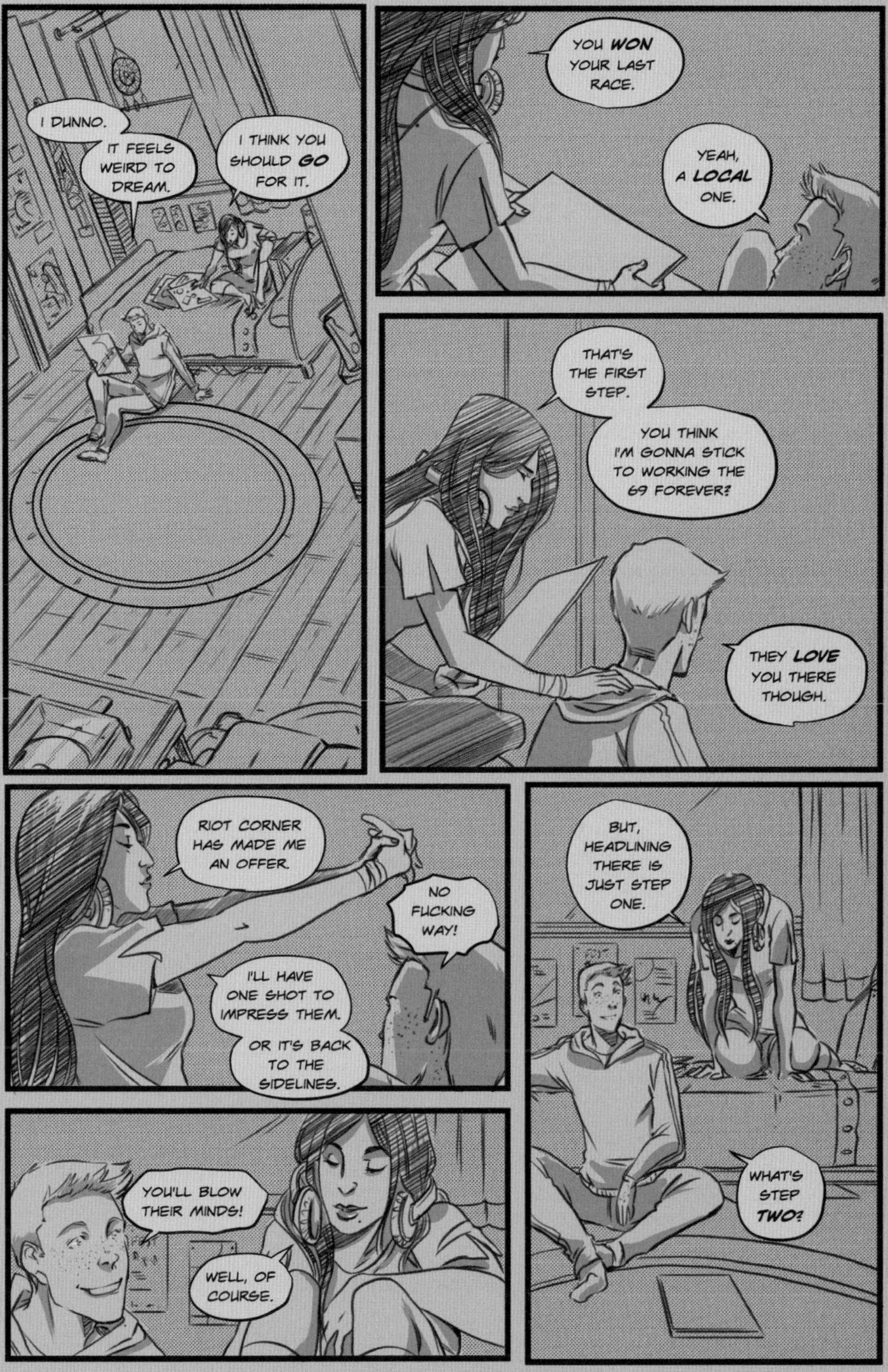
I DUNNO.
IT FEELS WEIRD TO DREAM.
I THINK YOU SHOULD GO FOR IT.
YOU WON YOUR LAST RACE.
YEAH, A LOCAL ONE.
THAT'S THE FIRST STEP.
YOU THINK I'M GONNA STICK TO WORKING THE 69 FOREVER?
THEY LOVE YOU THERE THOUGH.
RIOT CORNER HAS MADE ME AN OFFER.
NO FUCKING WAY!
I'LL HAVE ONE SHOT TO IMPRESS THEM.
OR IT'S BACK TO THE SIDELINES.
YOU'LL BLOW THEIR MINDS!
WELL, OF COURSE.
BUT, HEADLINING THERE IS JUST STEP ONE.
WHAT'S STEP TWO?

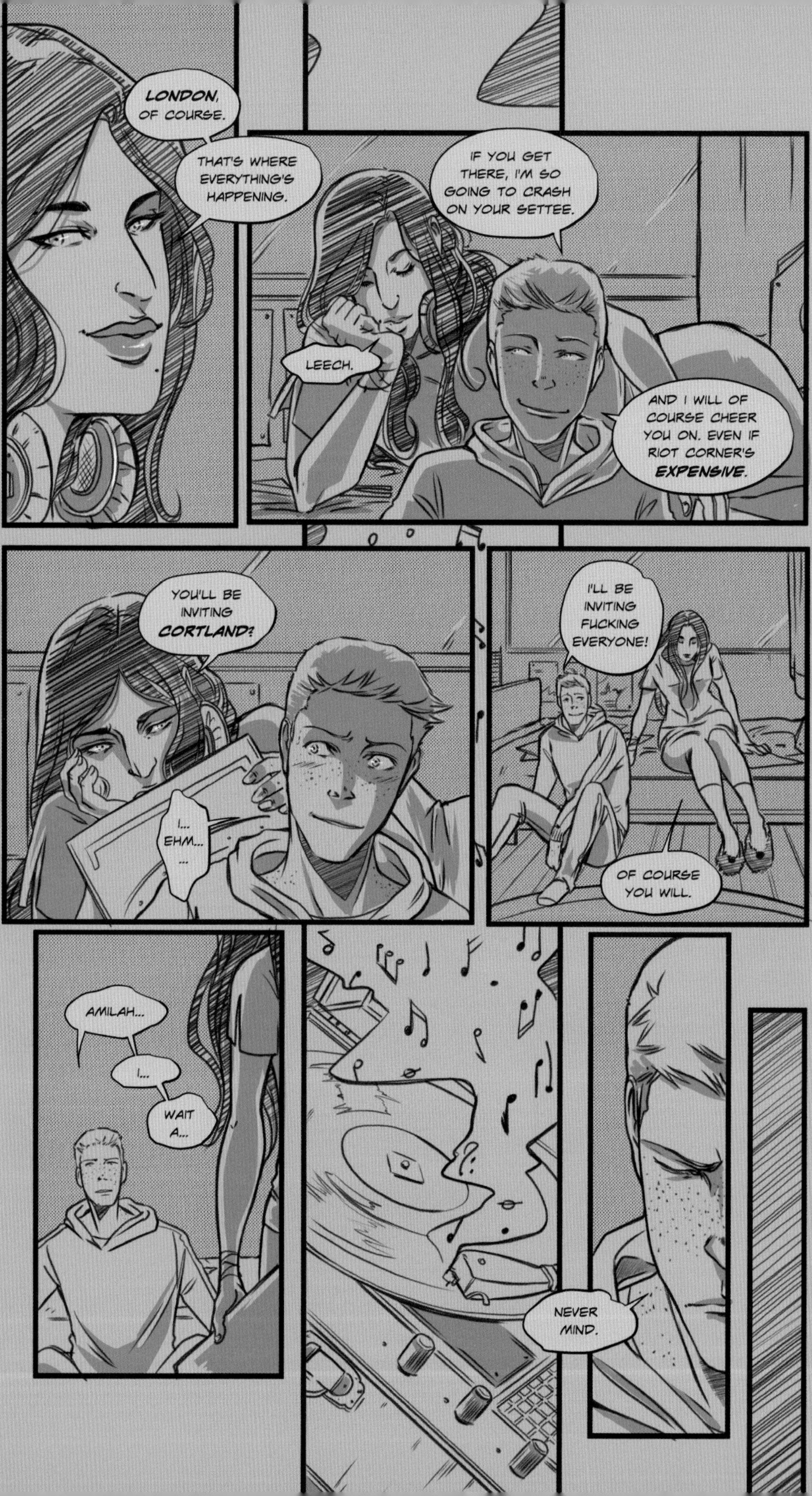
LONDON, OF COURSE.
THAT'S WHERE EVERYTHING'S HAPPENING.
IF YOU GET THERE, I'M SO GOING TO CRASH ON YOUR SETTEE.
LEECH.
AND I WILL OF COURSE CHEER YOU ON. EVEN IF RIOT CORNER'S EXPENSIVE.
YOU'LL BE INVITING CORTLAND?
I... EHM... ...
I'LL BE INVITING FUCKING EVERYONE!
OF COURSE YOU WILL.
AMILAH...
I...
WAIT A...
NEVER MIND.

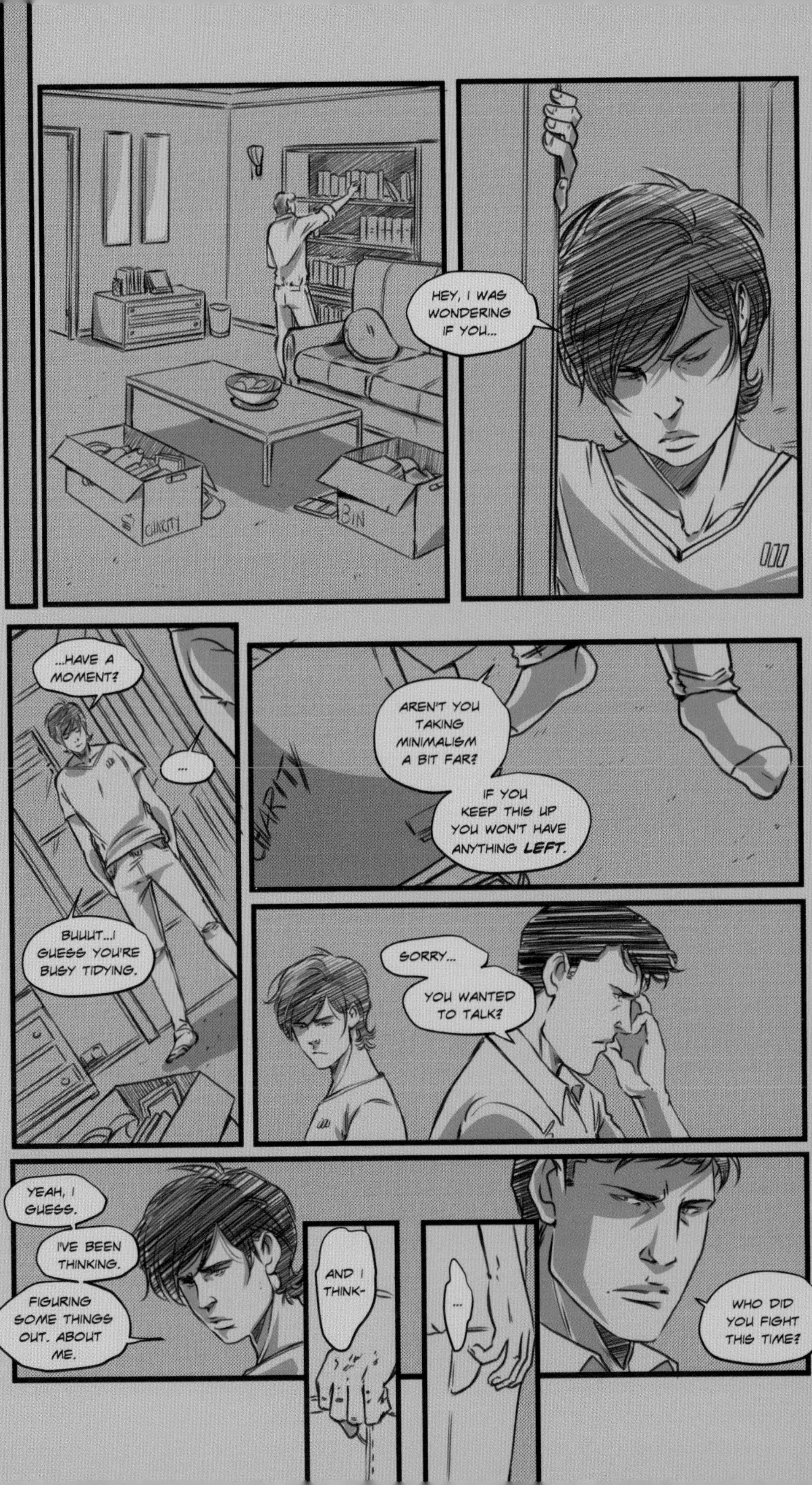
HEY, I WAS WONDERING IF YOU...
...HAVE A MOMENT?
...
ARE'NT YOU TAKING MINIMALISM A BIT FAR?
IF YOU KEEP THIS UP YOU WON'T HAVE ANYTHING LEFT.
BUUUT...I GUESS YOU'RE BUSY TIDYING.
SORRY...
YOU WANTED TO TALK?
YEAH, I GUESS.
I'VE BEEN THINKING.
FIGURING SOME THINGS OUT. ABOUT ME.
AND I THINK-
...
WHO DID YOU FIGHT THIS TIME?

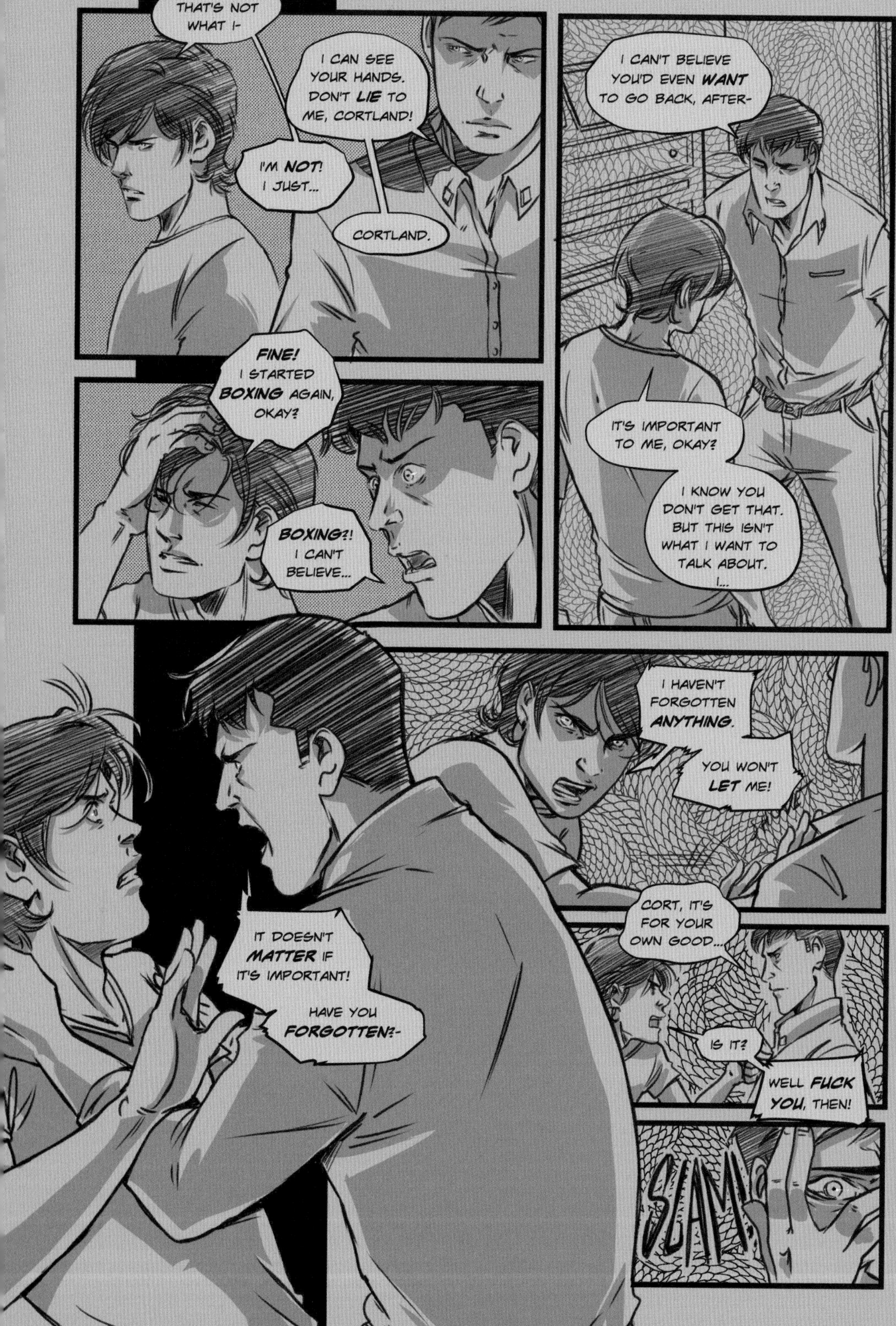
THAT'S NOT WHAT I-
I CAN SEE YOUR HANDS. DON'T LIE TO ME, CORTLAND!
I'M NOT! I JUST...
CORTLAND.
I CAN'T BELIEVE YOU'D EVEN WANT TO GO BACK, AFTER-
FINE! I STARTED BOXING AGAIN, OKAY?
BOXING?! I CAN'T BELIEVE...
IT'S IMPORTANT TO ME, OKAY?
I KNOW YOU DON'T GET THAT. BUT THIS ISN'T WHAT I WANT TO TALK ABOUT. I...
IT DOESN'T MATTER IF IT'S IMPORTANT!
HAVE YOU FORGOTTEN?-
I HAVEN'T FORGOTTEN ANYTHING.
YOU WON'T LET ME!
CORT, IT'S FOR YOUR OWN GOOD...
IS IT?
WELL FUCK YOU, THEN!
SLAM!

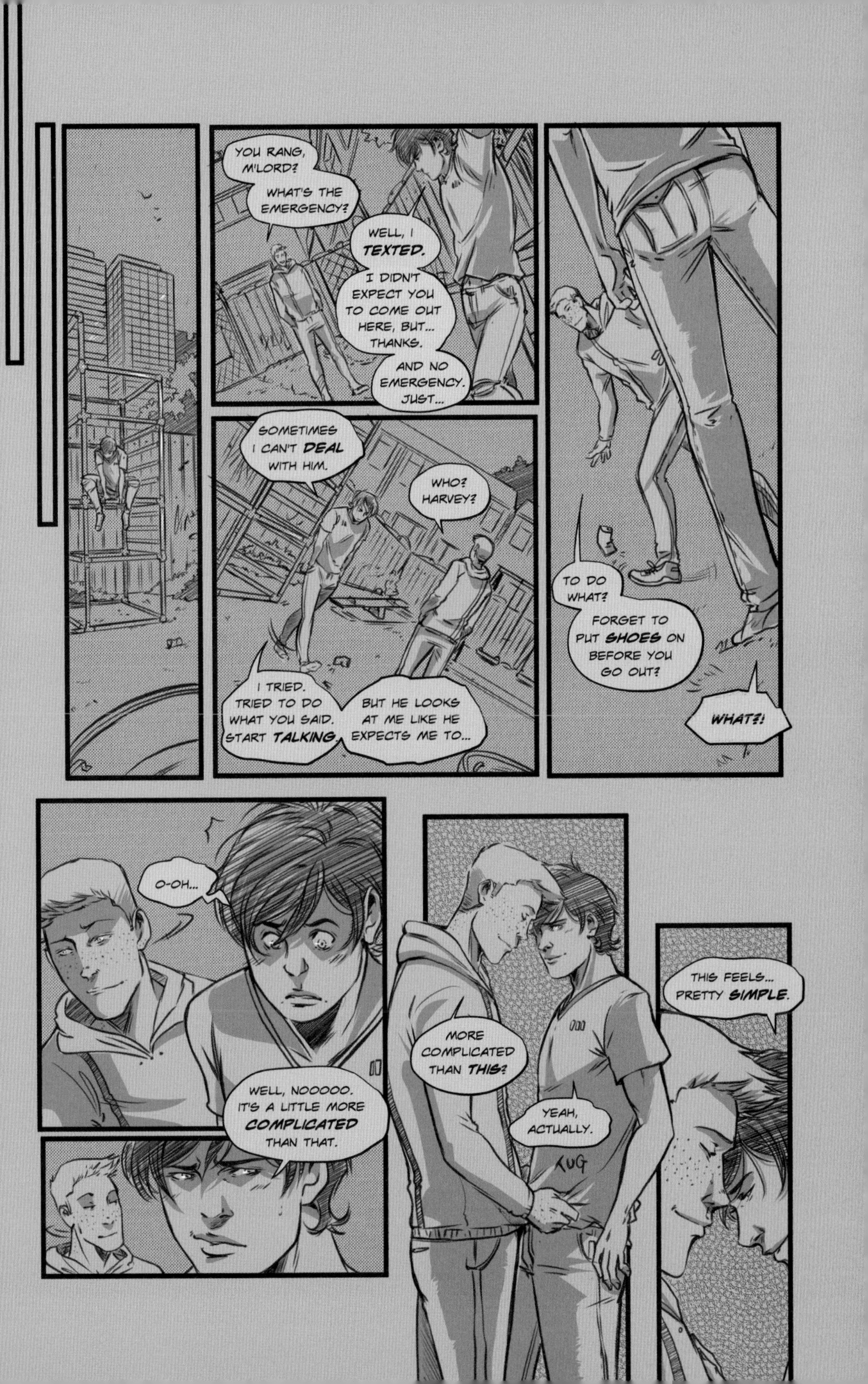

YOU RANG, M'LORD?
WHAT'S THE EMERGENCY?
WELL, I TEXTED.
I DIDN'T EXPECT YOU TO COME OUT HERE, BUT... THANKS.
AND NO EMERGENCY. JUST...
SOMETIMES I CAN'T DEAL WITH HIM.
WHO? HARVEY?
I TRIED. TRIED TO DO WHAT YOU SAID. START TALKING.
BUT HE LOOKS AT ME LIKE HE EXPECTS ME TO...
TO DO WHAT?
FORGET TO PUT SHOES ON BEFORE YOU GO OUT?
WHAT?!
O-OH...
WELL, NOOOOO. IT'S A LITTLE MORE COMPLICATED THAN THAT.
MORE COMPLICATED THAN THIS?
YEAH, ACTUALLY.
TUG
THIS FEELS... PRETTY SIMPLE.

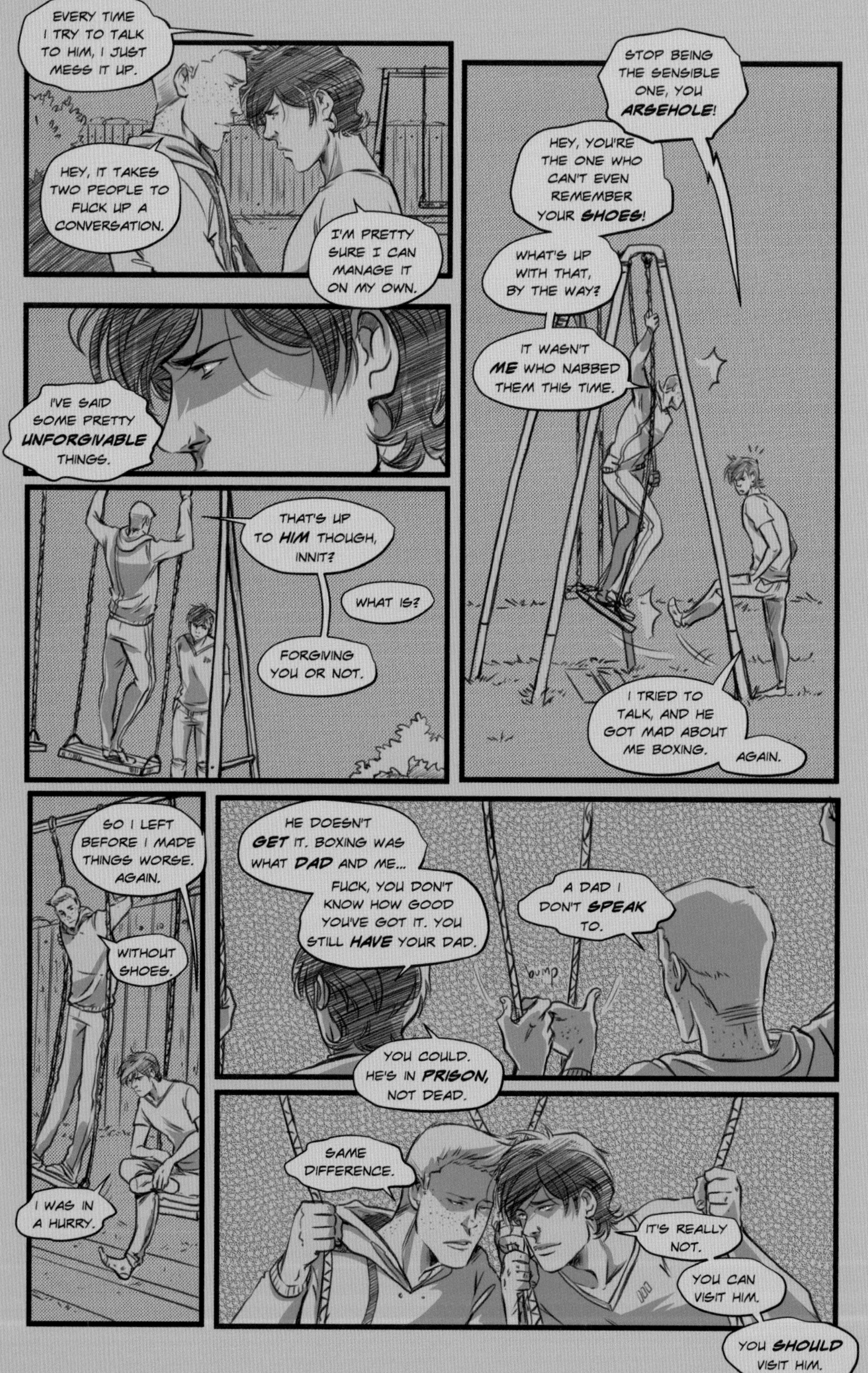

EVERY TIME I TRY TO TALK TO HIM, I JUST MESS IT UP.
HEY, IT TAKES TWO PEOPLE TO FUCK UP A CONVERSATION.
I'M PRETTY SURE I CAN MANAGE IT ON MY OWN.
I'VE SAID SOME PRETTY UNFORGIVABLE THINGS.
THAT'S UP TO HIM THOUGH, INNIT?
WHAT IS?
FORGIVING YOU OR NOT.
STOP BEING THE SENSIBLE ONE, YOU ARSEHOLE!
HEY, YOU'RE THE ONE WHO CAN'T EVEN REMEMBER YOUR SHOES!
WHAT'S UP WITH THAT, BY THE WAY?
IT WASN'T ME WHO NABBED THEM THIS TIME.
I TRIED TO TALK, AND HE GOT MAD ABOUT ME BOXING.
AGAIN.
SO I LEFT BEFORE I MADE THINGS WORSE. AGAIN.
WITHOUT SHOES.
I WAS IN A HURRY.
HE DOESN'T GET IT. BOXING WAS WHAT DAD AND ME...
FUCK, YOU DON'T KNOW HOW GOOD YOU'VE GOT IT. YOU STILL HAVE YOUR DAD.
A DAD I DON'T SPEAK TO.
bump
YOU COULD. HE'S IN PRISON, NOT DEAD.
SAME DIFFERENCE.
IT'S REALLY NOT.
YOU CAN VISIT HIM.
YOU SHOULD VISIT HIM.

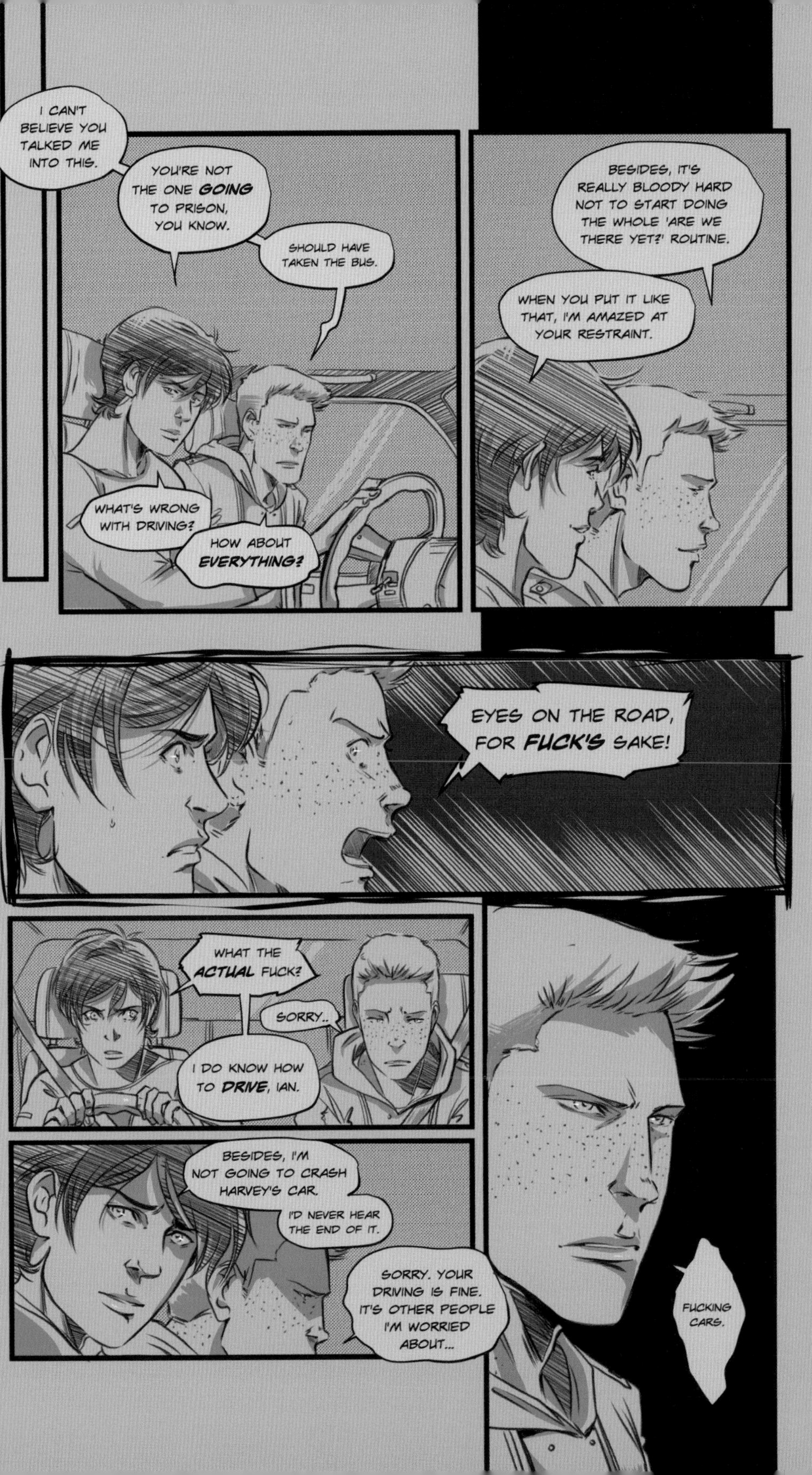
I CAN'T BELIEVE YOU TALKED ME INTO THIS.
YOU'RE NOT THE ONE GOING TO PRISON, YOU KNOW.
SHOULD HAVE TAKEN THE BUS.
WHAT'S WRONG WITH DRIVING?
HOW ABOUT EVERYTHING?
BESIDES, IT'S REALLY BLOODY HARD NOT TO START DOING THE WHOLE 'ARE WE THERE YET?' ROUTINE.
WHEN YOU PUT IT LIKE THAT, I'M AMAZED AT YOUR RESTRAINT.
EYES ON THE ROAD, FOR FUCK'S SAKE!
WHAT THE ACTUAL FUCK?
SORRY..
I DO KNOW HOW TO DRIVE, IAN.
BESIDES, I'M NOT GOING TO CRASH HARVEY'S CAR.
I'D NEVER HEAR THE END OF IT.
SORRY. YOUR DRIVING IS FINE. IT'S OTHER PEOPLE I'M WORRIED ABOUT...
FUCKING CARS.

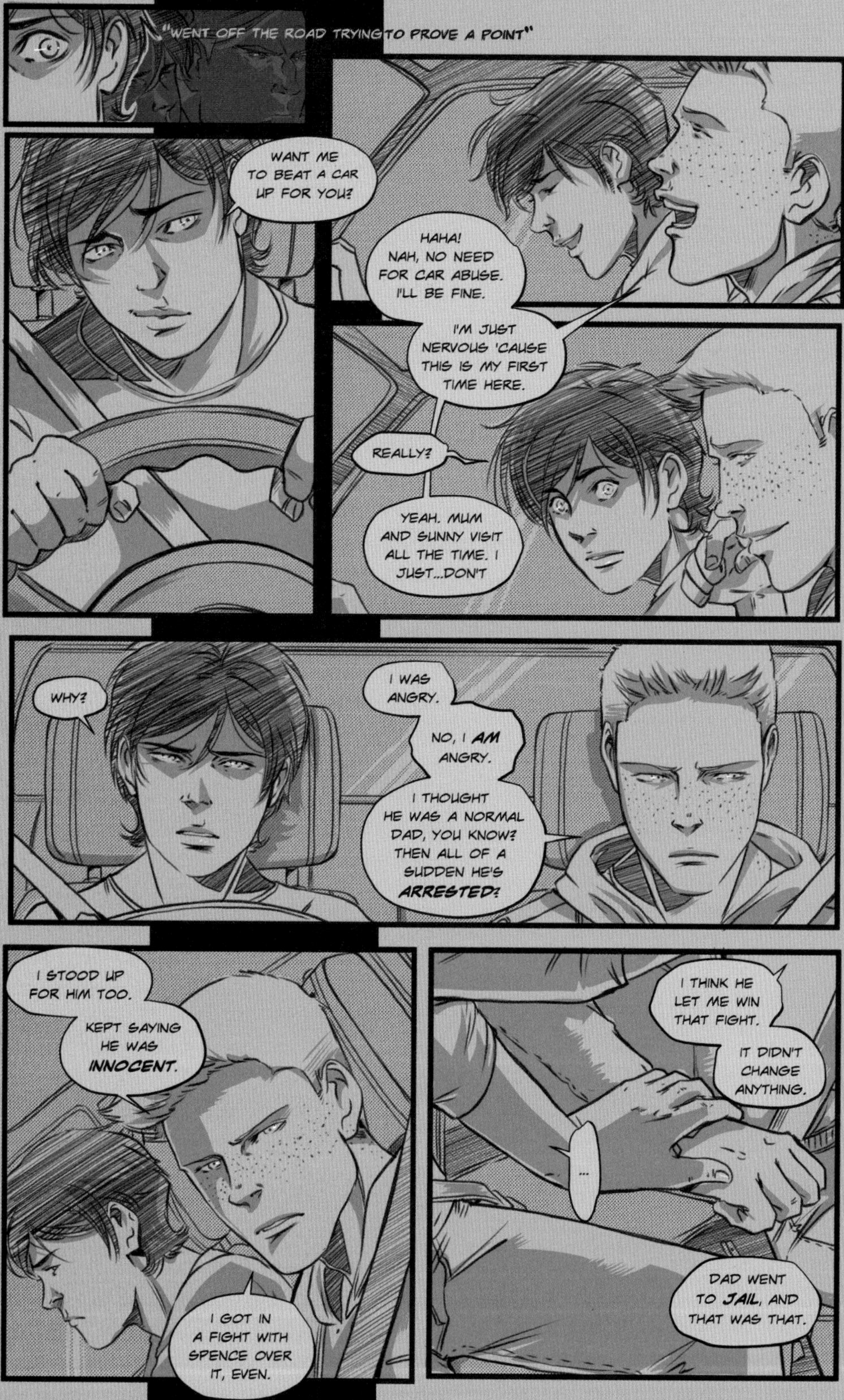
"WENT OFF THE ROAD TRYING TO PROVE A POINT"
WANT ME TO BEAT A CAR UP FOR YOU?
HAHA! NAH, NO NEED FOR CAR ABUSE. I'LL BE FINE.
I'M JUST NERVOUS 'CAUSE THIS IS MY FIRST TIME HERE.
REALLY?
YEAH. MUM AND SUNNY VISIT ALL THE TIME. I JUST...DON'T
WHY?
I WAS ANGRY.
NO, I AM ANGRY.
I THOUGHT HE WAS A NORMAL DAD, YOU KNOW? THEN ALL OF A SUDDEN HE'S ARRESTED?
I STOOD UP FOR HIM TOO.
KEPT SAYING HE WAS INNOCENT.
I GOT IN A FIGHT WITH SPENCE OVER IT, EVEN.
I THINK HE LET ME WIN THAT FIGHT.
IT DIDN'T CHANGE ANYTHING.
...
DAD WENT TO JAIL, AND THAT WAS THAT.

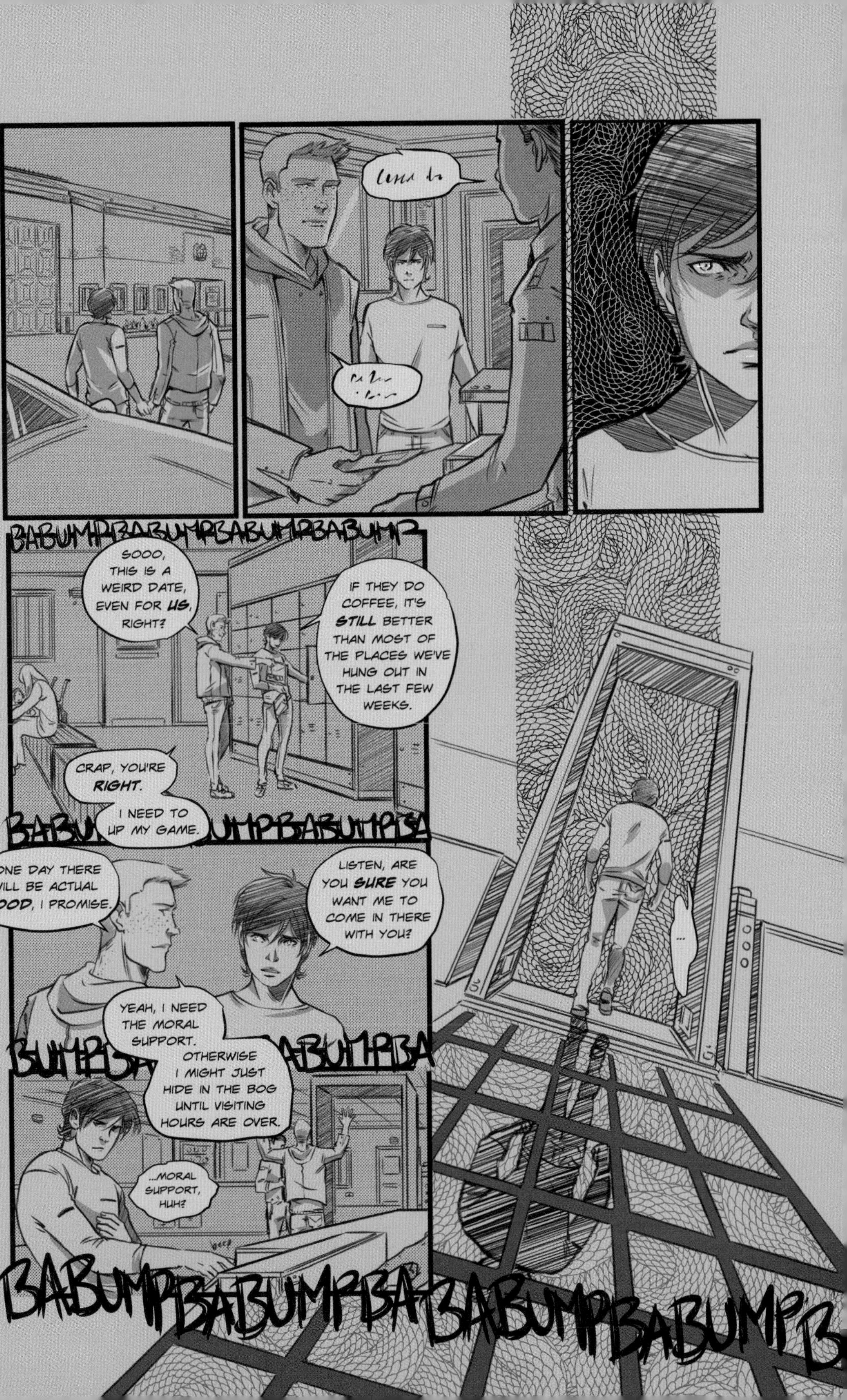

BABUMPBABUMPBABUMPBABUMPB
SOOO, THIS IS A WEIRD DATE, EVEN FOR **US**, RIGHT?
IF THEY DO COFFEE, IT'S **STILL** BETTER THAN MOST OF THE PLACES WE'VE HUNG OUT IN THE LAST FEW WEEKS.
CRAP, YOU'RE **RIGHT**.
I NEED TO UP MY GAME.
ONE DAY THERE WILL BE ACTUAL **FOOD**, I PROMISE.
LISTEN, ARE YOU **SURE** YOU WANT ME TO COME IN THERE WITH YOU?
YEAH, I NEED THE MORAL SUPPORT.
OTHERWISE I MIGHT JUST HIDE IN THE BOG UNTIL VISITING HOURS ARE OVER.
...MORAL SUPPORT, HUH?
...
BABUMPBABUMPBABABUMPBABUMPB

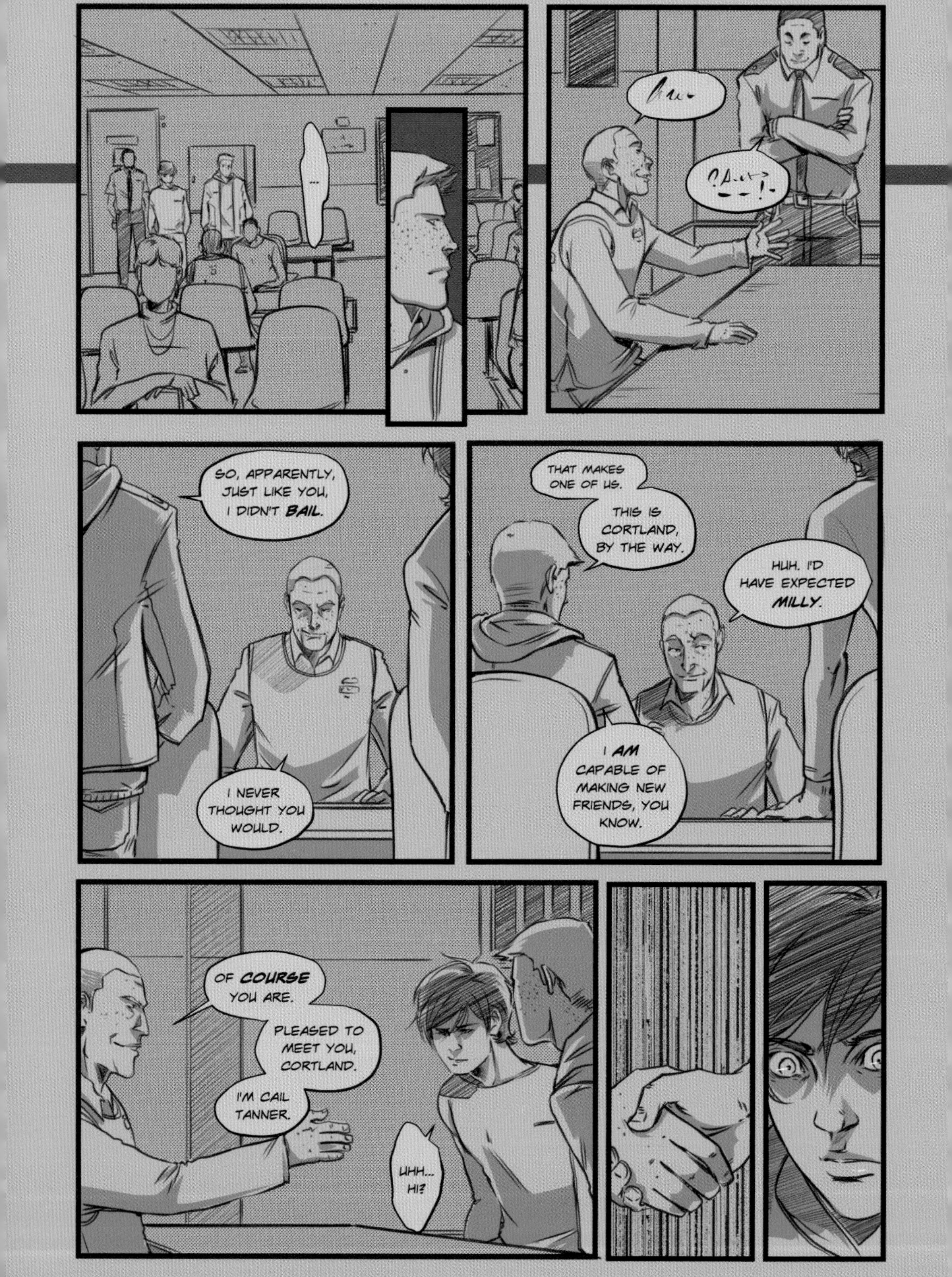
...
SO, APPARENTLY, JUST LIKE YOU, I DIDN'T BAIL.
I NEVER THOUGHT YOU WOULD.
THAT MAKES ONE OF US.
THIS IS CORTLAND, BY THE WAY.
HUH. I'D HAVE EXPECTED MILLY.
I AM CAPABLE OF MAKING NEW FRIENDS, YOU KNOW.
OF COURSE YOU ARE.
PLEASED TO MEET YOU, CORTLAND.
I'M CAIL TANNER.
UHH... HI?

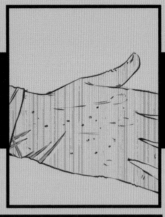

QUITE A **GRIP** YOU'VE GOT THERE.

I COULD SAY THE SAME...

I'M STILL YOUR **DAD**, YOU KNOW.

OF **COURSE** I KNOW WHEN MY SON IS COMING UP EIGHTEEN.

IT'S A **BIG DEAL**, IAN.

SO, WHAT'S THE OCCASION? ARE YOU HERE TO ASK FOR A BELATED BIRTHDAY PRESENT?

NO. NO OCCASION.

AND I'M SURPRISED YOU EVEN **REMEMBERED**.

AT LEAST **ONE** OF US MADE IT, HUH?

...

...DID YOUR MOTHER TELL YOU TO COME?

NO. I... I WANTED TO COME.

I **DECIDED** TO.

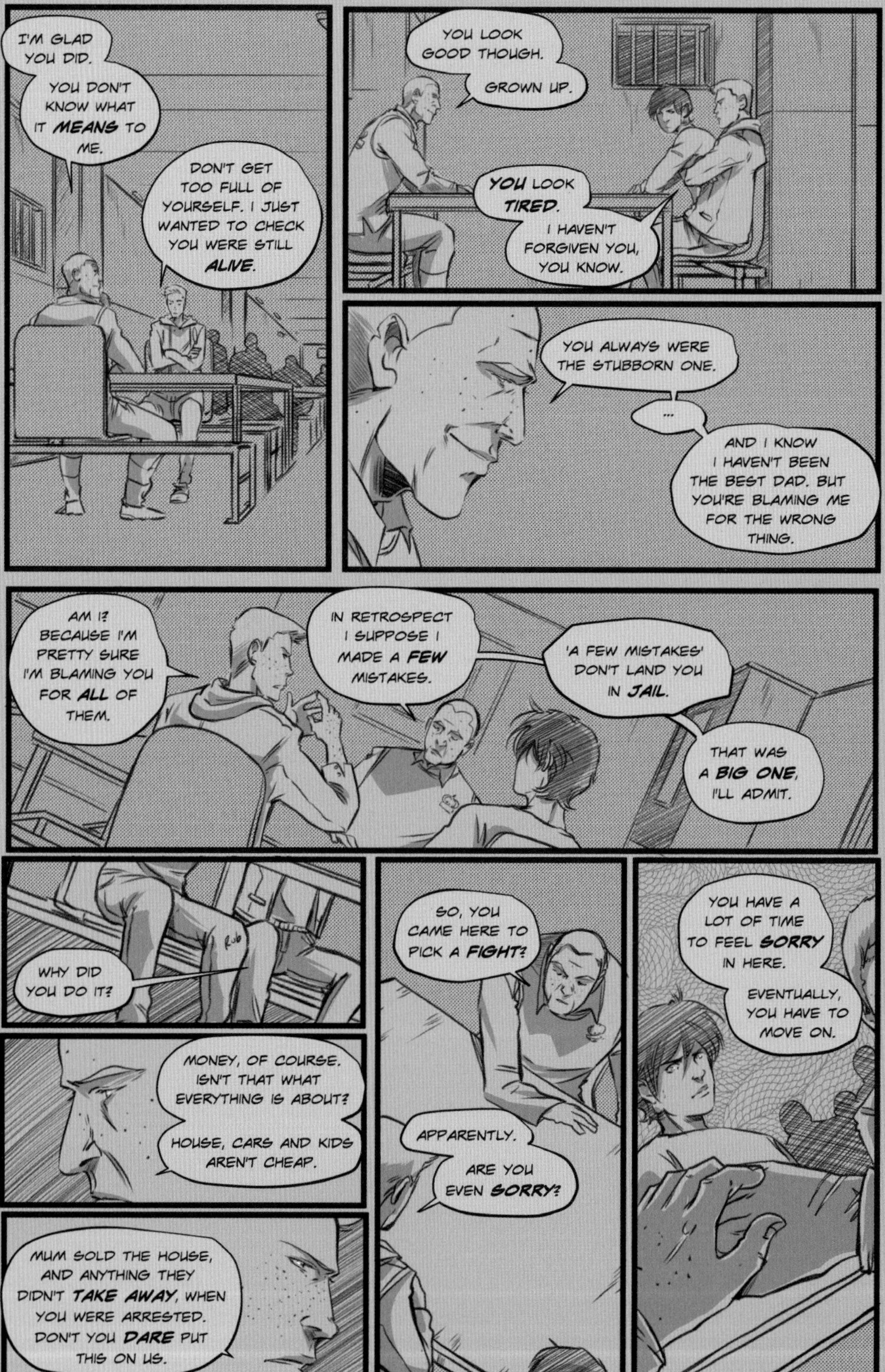

I'M GLAD YOU DID.
YOU DON'T KNOW WHAT IT MEANS TO ME.
DON'T GET TOO FULL OF YOURSELF. I JUST WANTED TO CHECK YOU WERE STILL ALIVE.
YOU LOOK GOOD THOUGH.
GROWN UP.
YOU LOOK TIRED.
I HAVEN'T FORGIVEN YOU, YOU KNOW.
YOU ALWAYS WERE THE STUBBORN ONE.
...
AND I KNOW I HAVEN'T BEEN THE BEST DAD. BUT YOU'RE BLAMING ME FOR THE WRONG THING.
AM I? BECAUSE I'M PRETTY SURE I'M BLAMING YOU FOR ALL OF THEM.
IN RETROSPECT I SUPPOSE I MADE A FEW MISTAKES.
'A FEW MISTAKES' DON'T LAND YOU IN JAIL.
THAT WAS A BIG ONE, I'LL ADMIT.
WHY DID YOU DO IT?
MONEY, OF COURSE. ISN'T THAT WHAT EVERYTHING IS ABOUT?
HOUSE, CARS AND KIDS AREN'T CHEAP.
MUM SOLD THE HOUSE, AND ANYTHING THEY DIDN'T TAKE AWAY, WHEN YOU WERE ARRESTED. DON'T YOU DARE PUT THIS ON US.
SO, YOU CAME HERE TO PICK A FIGHT?
APPARENTLY.
ARE YOU EVEN SORRY?
YOU HAVE A LOT OF TIME TO FEEL SORRY IN HERE.
EVENTUALLY, YOU HAVE TO MOVE ON.

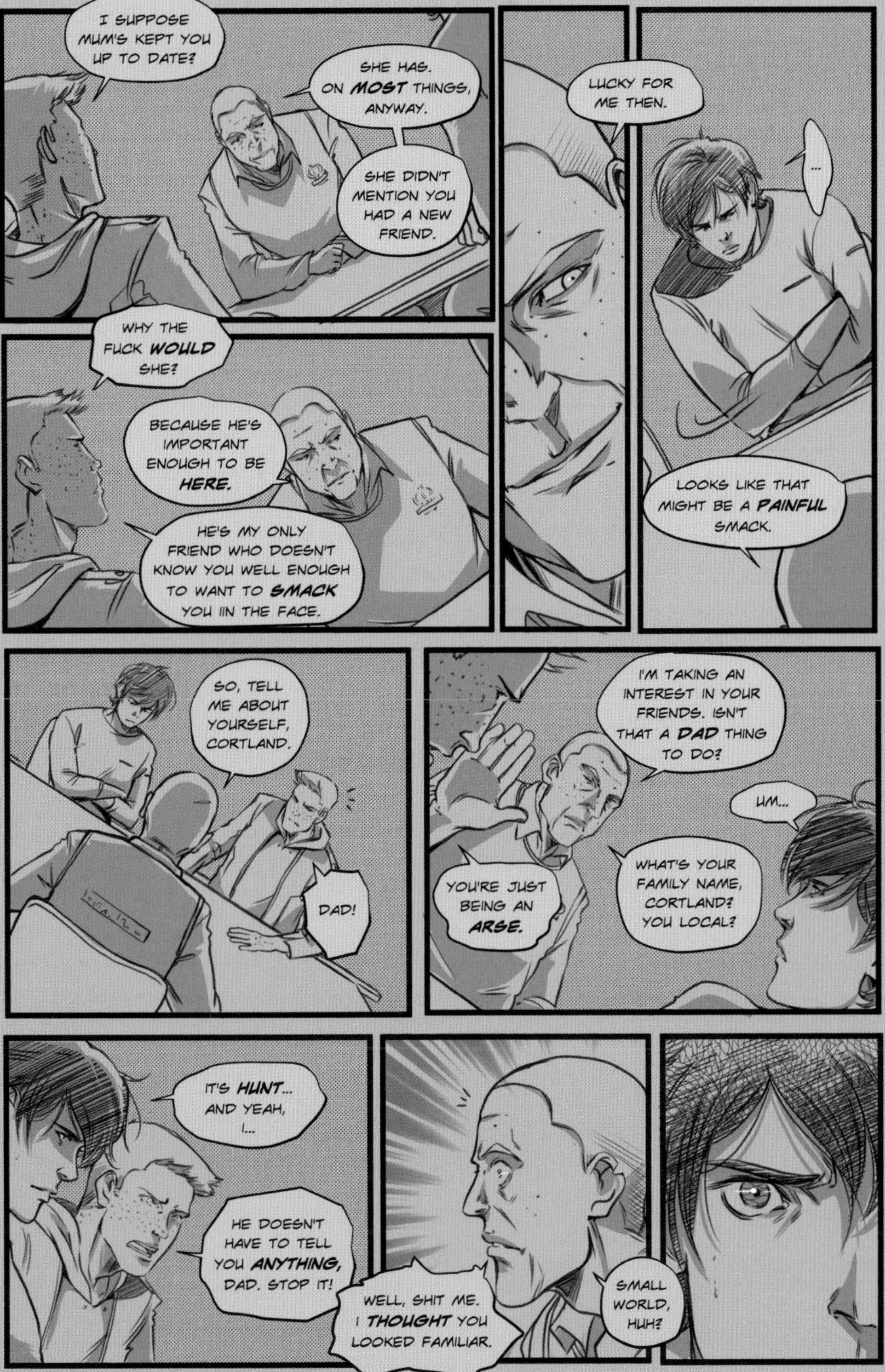
I SUPPOSE MUM'S KEPT YOU UP TO DATE?
SHE HAS. ON MOST THINGS, ANYWAY.
SHE DIDN'T MENTION YOU HAD A NEW FRIEND.
LUCKY FOR ME THEN.
...
WHY THE FUCK WOULD SHE?
BECAUSE HE'S IMPORTANT ENOUGH TO BE HERE.
HE'S MY ONLY FRIEND WHO DOESN'T KNOW YOU WELL ENOUGH TO WANT TO SMACK YOU IIN THE FACE.
LOOKS LIKE THAT MIGHT BE A PAINFUL SMACK.
SO, TELL ME ABOUT YOURSELF, CORTLAND.
DAD!
I'M TAKING AN INTEREST IN YOUR FRIENDS. ISN'T THAT A DAD THING TO DO?
UM...
YOU'RE JUST BEING AN ARSE.
WHAT'S YOUR FAMILY NAME, CORTLAND? YOU LOCAL?
IT'S HUNT... AND YEAH, I...
HE DOESN'T HAVE TO TELL YOU ANYTHING, DAD. STOP IT!
WELL, SHIT ME. I THOUGHT YOU LOOKED FAMILIAR.
SMALL WORLD, HUH?

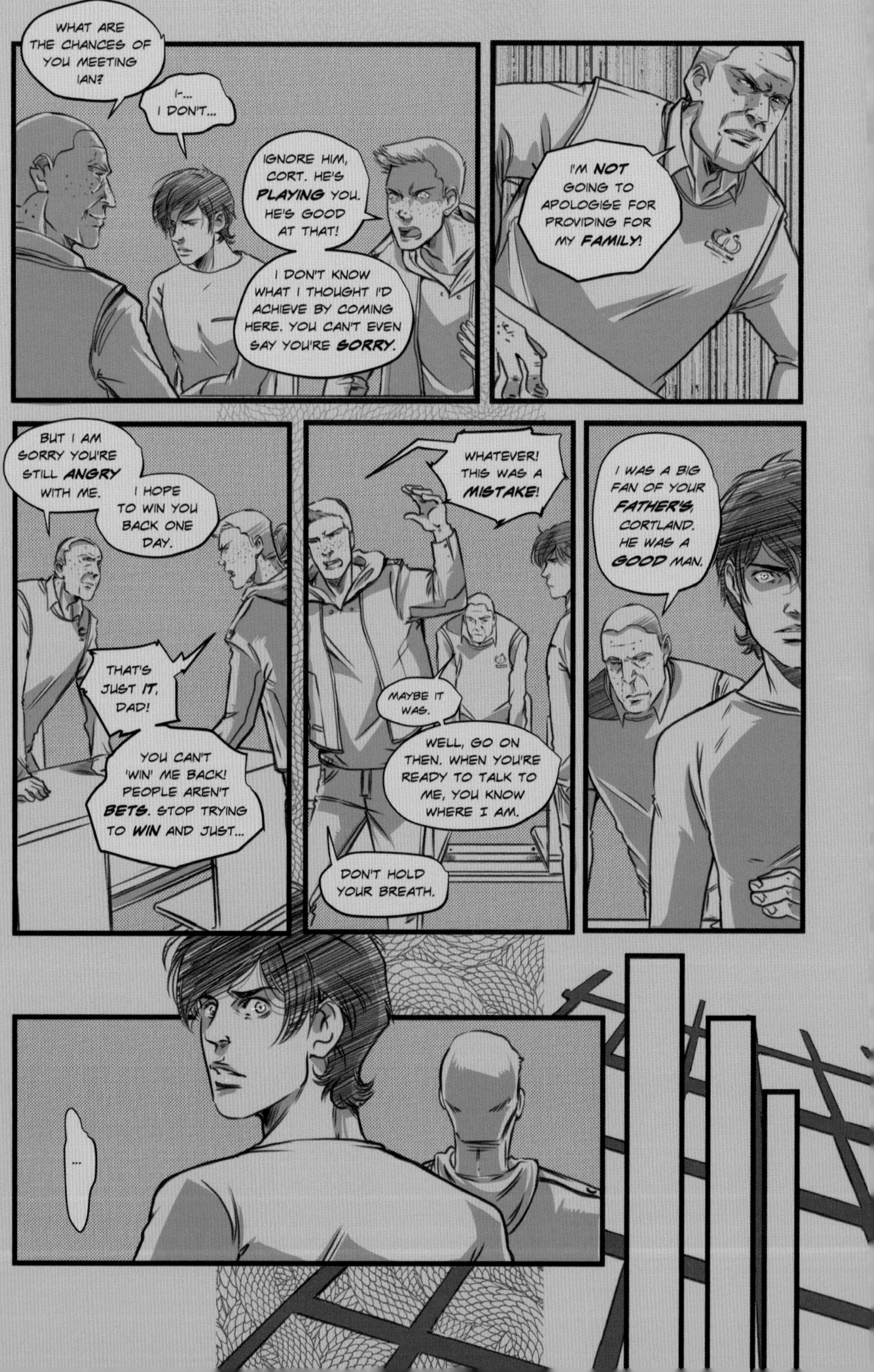
WHAT ARE THE CHANCES OF YOU MEETING IAN?
I-... I DON'T...
IGNORE HIM, CORT. HE'S PLAYING YOU. HE'S GOOD AT THAT!
I DON'T KNOW WHAT I THOUGHT I'D ACHIEVE BY COMING HERE. YOU CAN'T EVEN SAY YOU'RE SORRY.
I'M NOT GOING TO APOLOGISE FOR PROVIDING FOR MY FAMILY!
BUT I AM SORRY YOU'RE STILL ANGRY WITH ME.
I HOPE TO WIN YOU BACK ONE DAY.
THAT'S JUST IT, DAD!
YOU CAN'T 'WIN' ME BACK! PEOPLE AREN'T BETS. STOP TRYING TO WIN AND JUST...
WHATEVER! THIS WAS A MISTAKE!
MAYBE IT WAS.
WELL, GO ON THEN. WHEN YOU'RE READY TO TALK TO ME, YOU KNOW WHERE I AM.
DON'T HOLD YOUR BREATH.
I WAS A BIG FAN OF YOUR FATHER'S, CORTLAND. HE WAS A GOOD MAN.
...

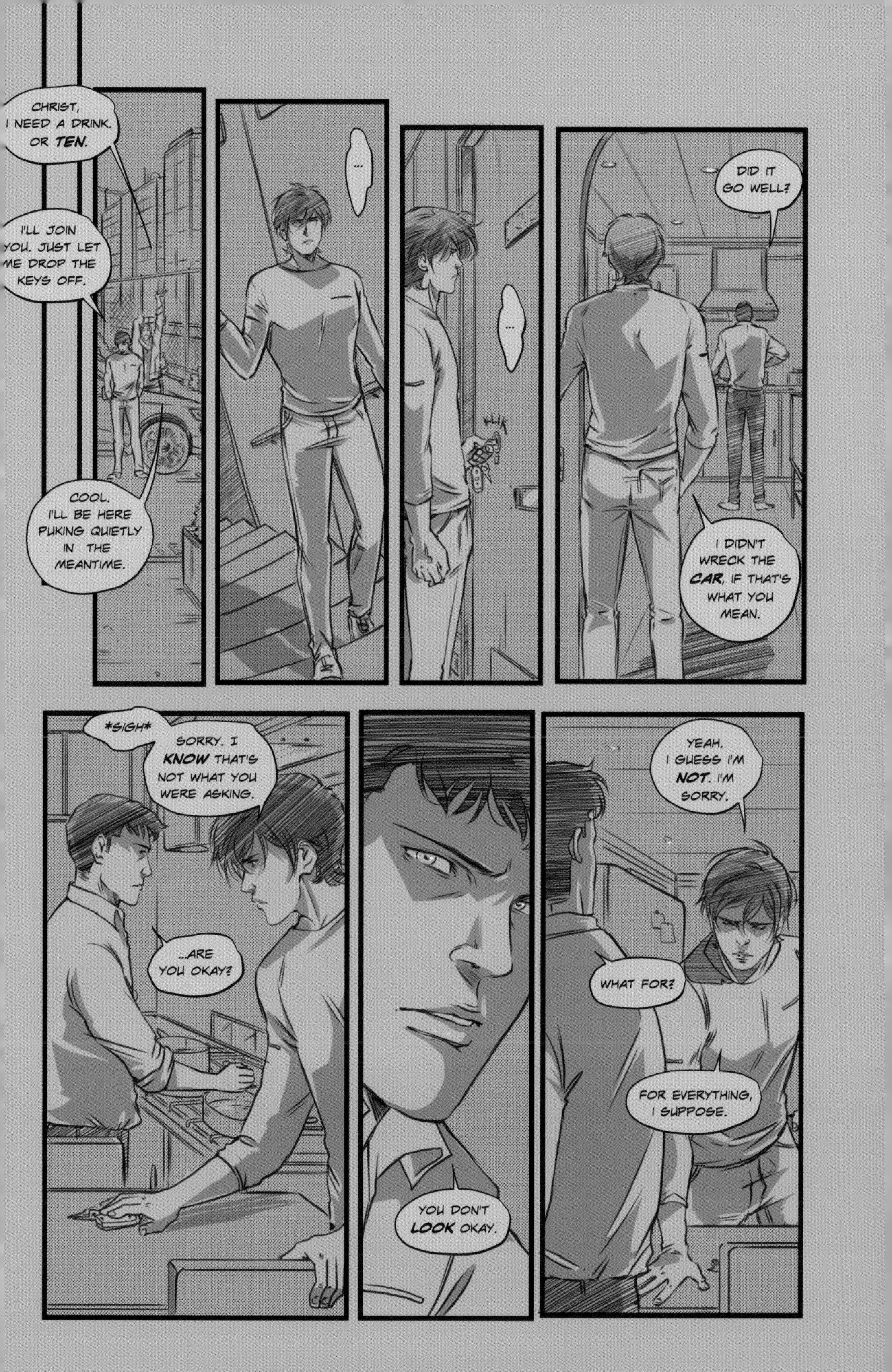
CHRIST, I NEED A DRINK. OR TEN.
I'LL JOIN YOU. JUST LET ME DROP THE KEYS OFF.
COOL. I'LL BE HERE PUKING QUIETLY IN THE MEANTIME.
...
...
KLIK
DID IT GO WELL?
I DIDN'T WRECK THE CAR, IF THAT'S WHAT YOU MEAN.
SIGH
SORRY. I KNOW THAT'S NOT WHAT YOU WERE ASKING.
...ARE YOU OKAY?
YOU DON'T LOOK OKAY.
YEAH. I GUESS I'M NOT. I'M SORRY.
WHAT FOR?
FOR EVERYTHING, I SUPPOSE.

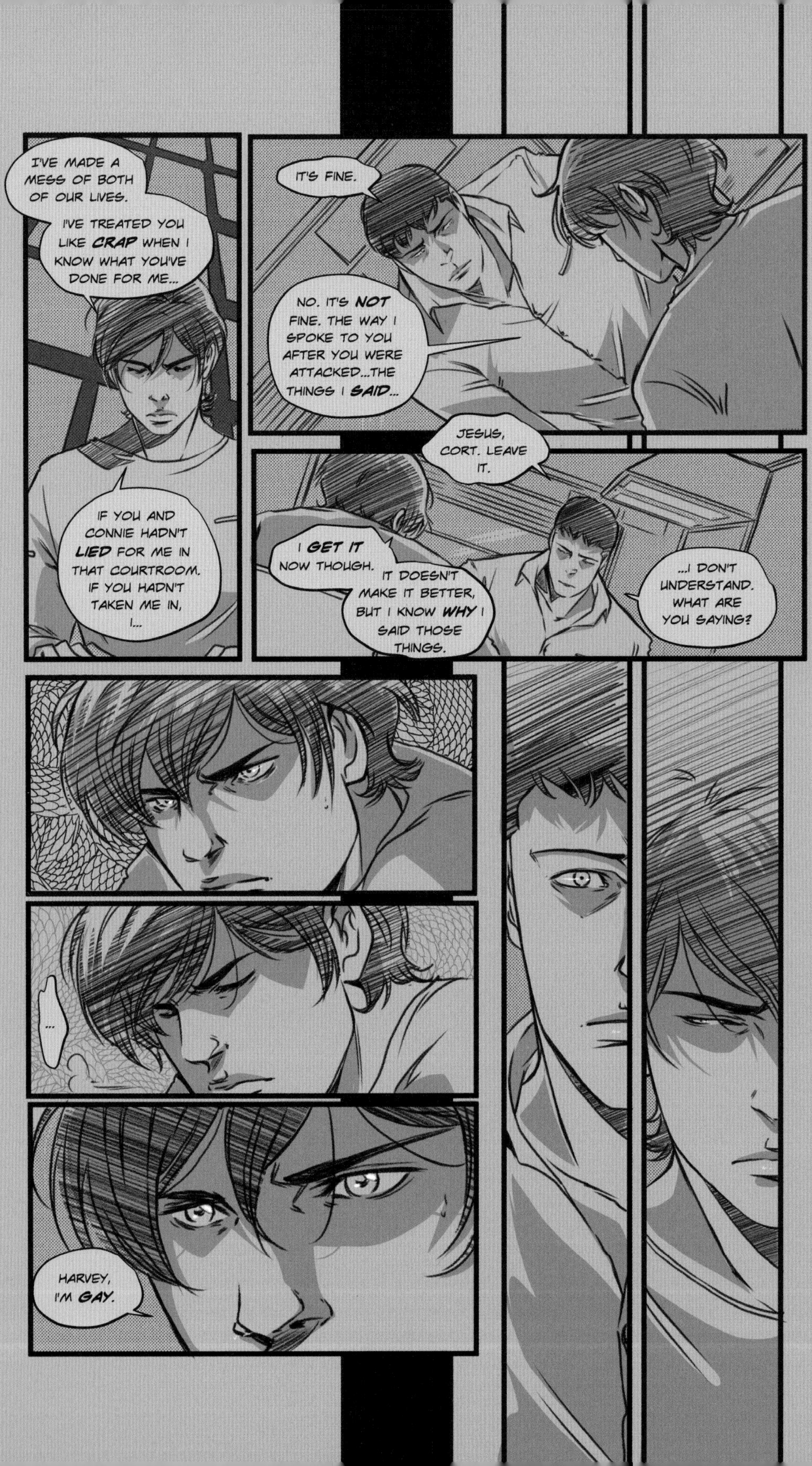
I'VE MADE A MESS OF BOTH OF OUR LIVES.
I'VE TREATED YOU LIKE CRAP WHEN I KNOW WHAT YOU'VE DONE FOR ME...
IF YOU AND CONNIE HADN'T LIED FOR ME IN THAT COURTROOM. IF YOU HADN'T TAKEN ME IN, I...
IT'S FINE.
NO. IT'S NOT FINE. THE WAY I SPOKE TO YOU AFTER YOU WERE ATTACKED...THE THINGS I SAID...
JESUS, CORT. LEAVE IT.
I GET IT NOW THOUGH.
IT DOESN'T MAKE IT BETTER, BUT I KNOW WHY I SAID THOSE THINGS.
...I DON'T UNDERSTAND. WHAT ARE YOU SAYING?
...
HARVEY, I'M GAY.

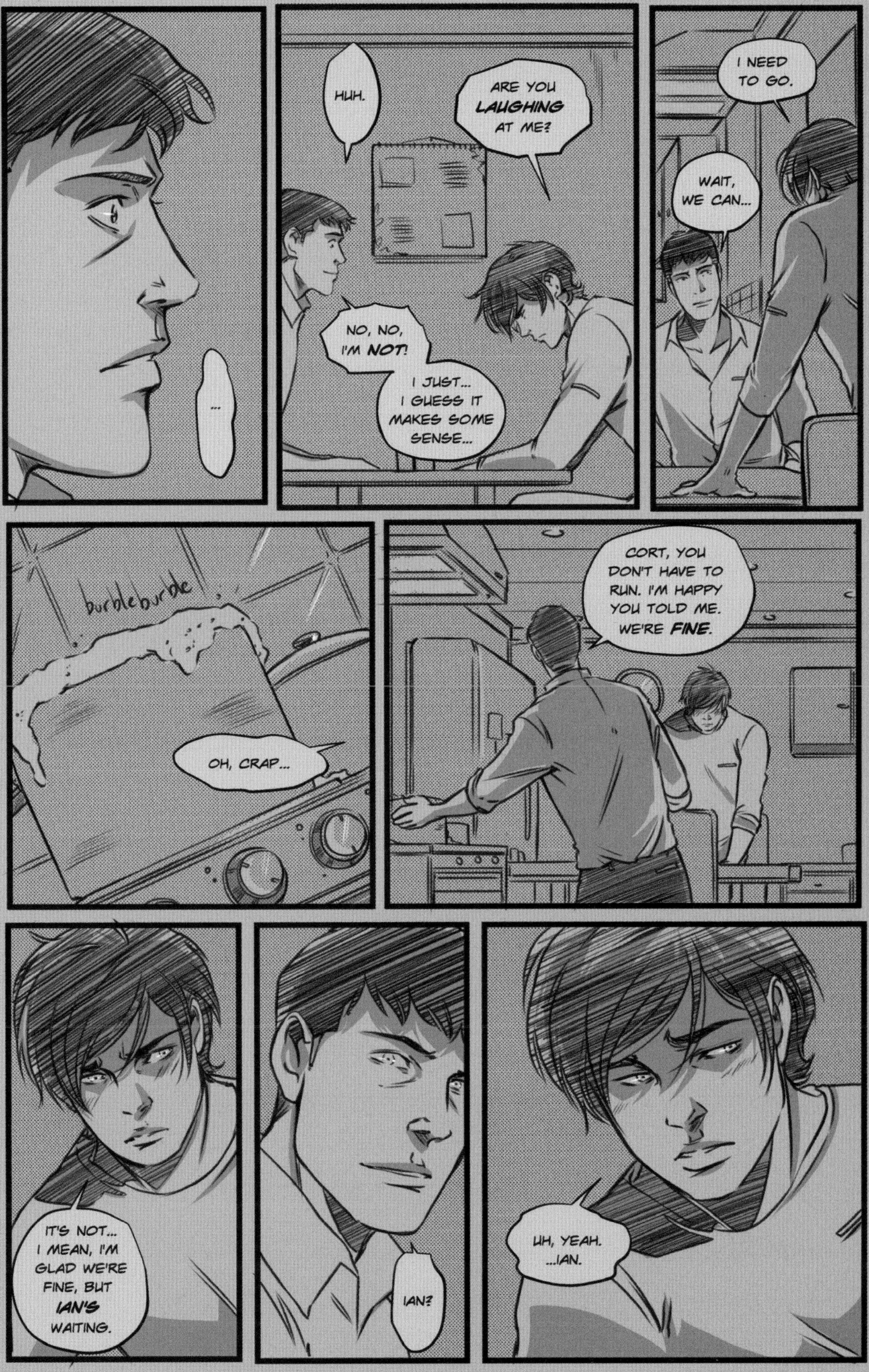
...
HUH.
ARE YOU LAUGHING AT ME?
NO, NO, I'M NOT!
I JUST... I GUESS IT MAKES SOME SENSE...
I NEED TO GO.
WAIT, WE CAN...
burbleburble
OH, CRAP...
CORT, YOU DON'T HAVE TO RUN. I'M HAPPY YOU TOLD ME. WE'RE FINE.
IT'S NOT... I MEAN, I'M GLAD WE'RE FINE, BUT IAN'S WAITING.
IAN?
UH, YEAH. ...IAN.

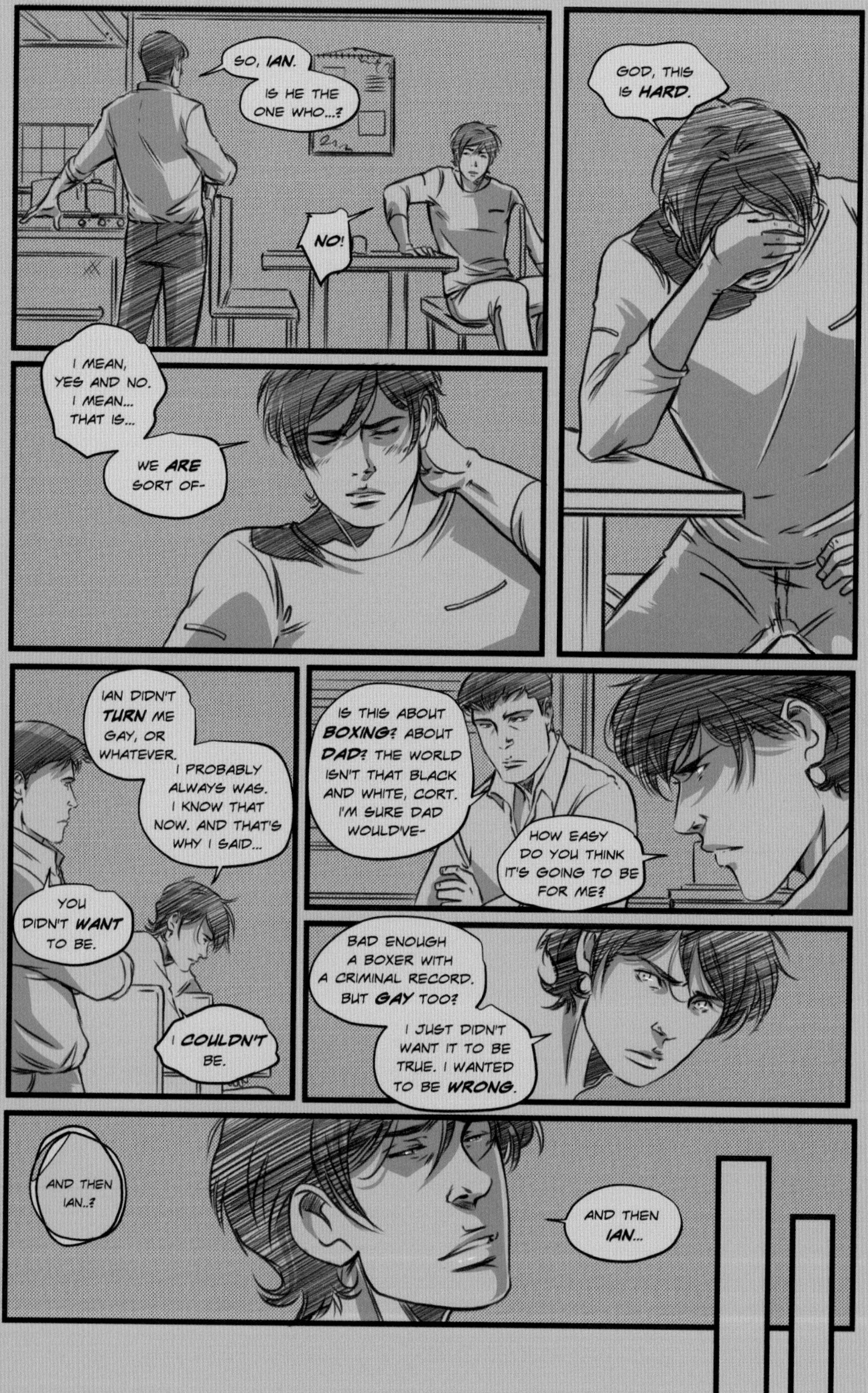
SO, IAN.
IS HE THE ONE WHO...?
NO!
GOD, THIS IS HARD.
I MEAN, YES AND NO. I MEAN... THAT IS...
WE ARE SORT OF-
IAN DIDN'T TURN ME GAY, OR WHATEVER.
I PROBABLY ALWAYS WAS. I KNOW THAT NOW. AND THAT'S WHY I SAID...
YOU DIDN'T WANT TO BE.
I COULDN'T BE.
IS THIS ABOUT BOXING? ABOUT DAD? THE WORLD ISN'T THAT BLACK AND WHITE, CORT. I'M SURE DAD WOULD'VE-
HOW EASY DO YOU THINK IT'S GOING TO BE FOR ME?
BAD ENOUGH A BOXER WITH A CRIMINAL RECORD. BUT GAY TOO?
I JUST DIDN'T WANT IT TO BE TRUE. I WANTED TO BE WRONG.
AND THEN IAN..?
AND THEN IAN...

CLUB BAR & GRILL

YEP. AND THEN HE WANTED TO COME HERE AND GET DRUNK.

HIS *DAD?* YOU WENT TO SEE HIS *DAD?*

IAN WENT TO SEE HIS DAD?

I TAKE IT THE VISIT DIDN'T GO WELL THEN?

THAT'S AN UNDERSTATEMENT ON SO MANY LEVELS.

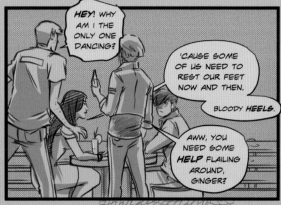

HEY! WHY AM I THE ONLY ONE DANCING?

'CAUSE SOME OF US NEED TO REST OUR FEET NOW AND THEN.

BLOODY *HEELS.*

AWW, YOU NEED SOME *HELP* FLAILING AROUND, GINGER?

WHAT I NEED IS ANOTHER BEER!

HEY, THAT'S *MINE!*

REIN YOUR BOY IN, FOR FUCK'S SAKE!

IAN!

IAN!

WHAAAAT?

YOUR BROKE ARSE ALREADY OWES ME TWO BEERS!

...

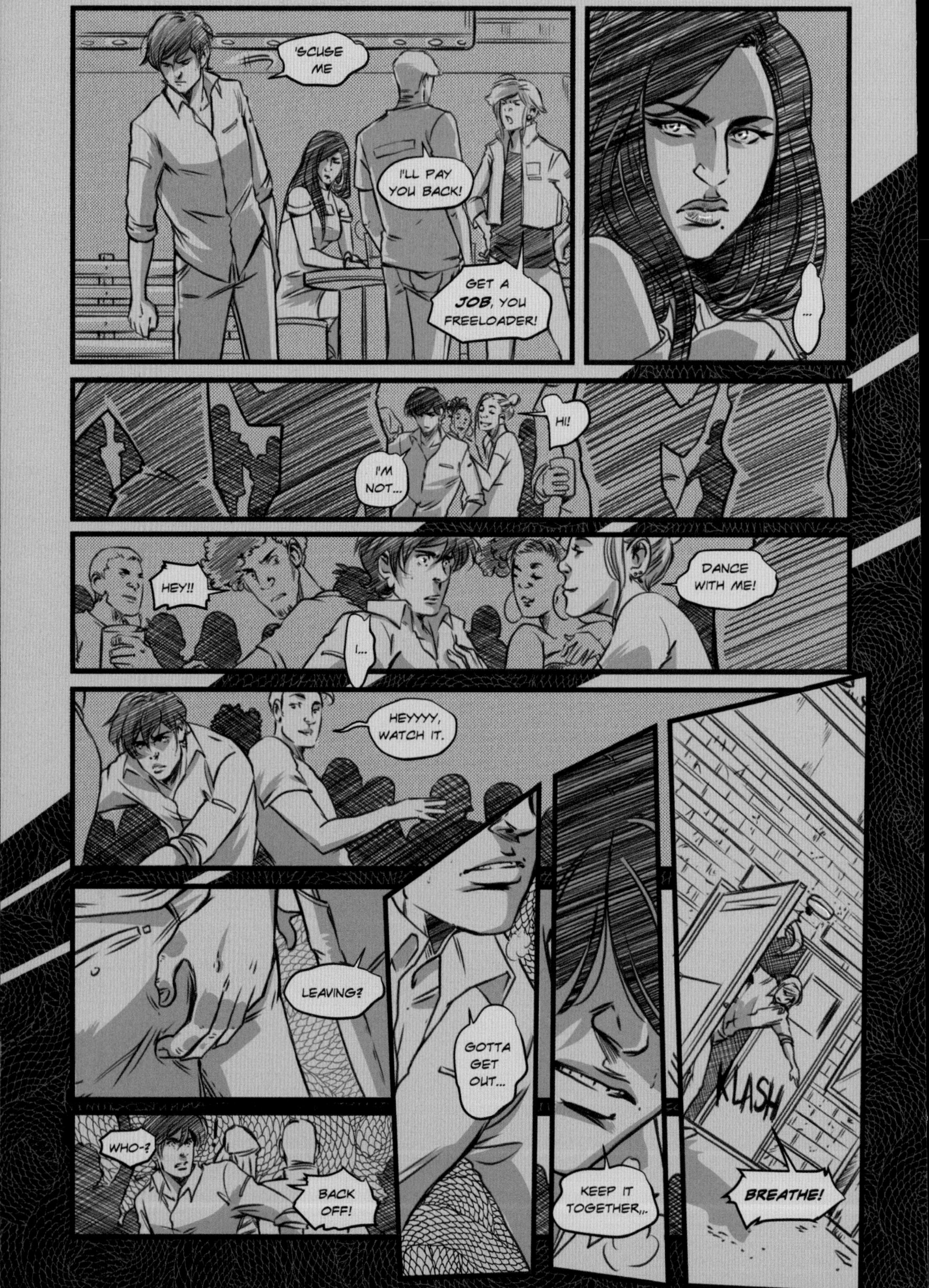
'SCUSE ME
I'LL PAY YOU BACK!
GET A JOB, YOU FREELOADER!
...
HI!
I'M NOT...
HEY!!
DANCE WITH ME!
I...
HEYYYY, WATCH IT.
LEAVING?
GOTTA GET OUT...
KLASH
WHO-?
BACK OFF!
KEEP IT TOGETHER,..
BREATHE!

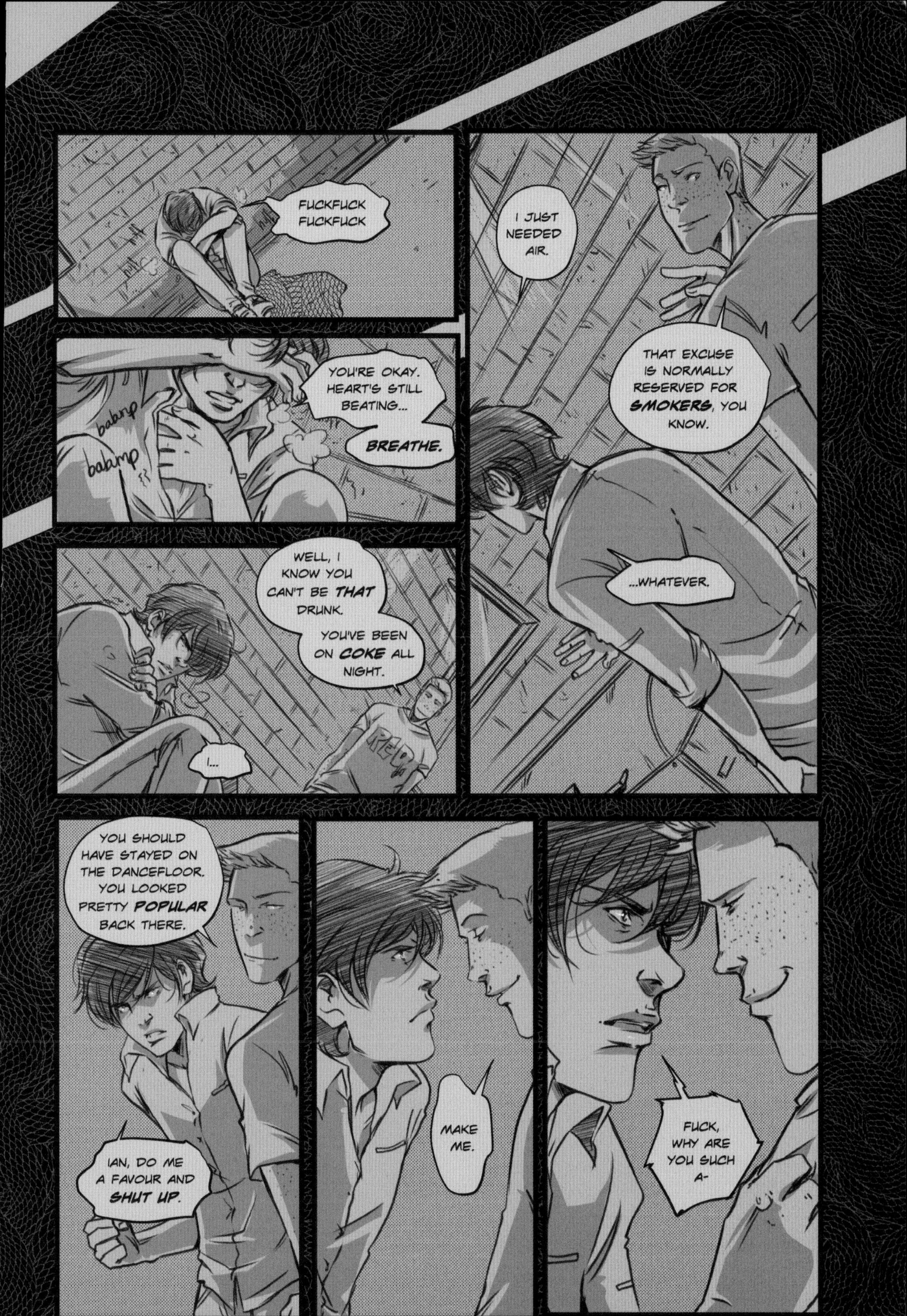
FUCKFUCK FUCKFUCK
YOU'RE OKAY. HEART'S STILL BEATING...
BREATHE.
babmp
babmp
I JUST NEEDED AIR.
THAT EXCUSE IS NORMALLY RESERVED FOR SMOKERS, YOU KNOW.
...WHATEVER.
WELL, I KNOW YOU CAN'T BE THAT DRUNK.
YOU'VE BEEN ON COKE ALL NIGHT.
I...
YOU SHOULD HAVE STAYED ON THE DANCEFLOOR. YOU LOOKED PRETTY POPULAR BACK THERE.
IAN, DO ME A FAVOUR AND SHUT UP.
MAKE ME.
FUCK, WHY ARE YOU SUCH A-

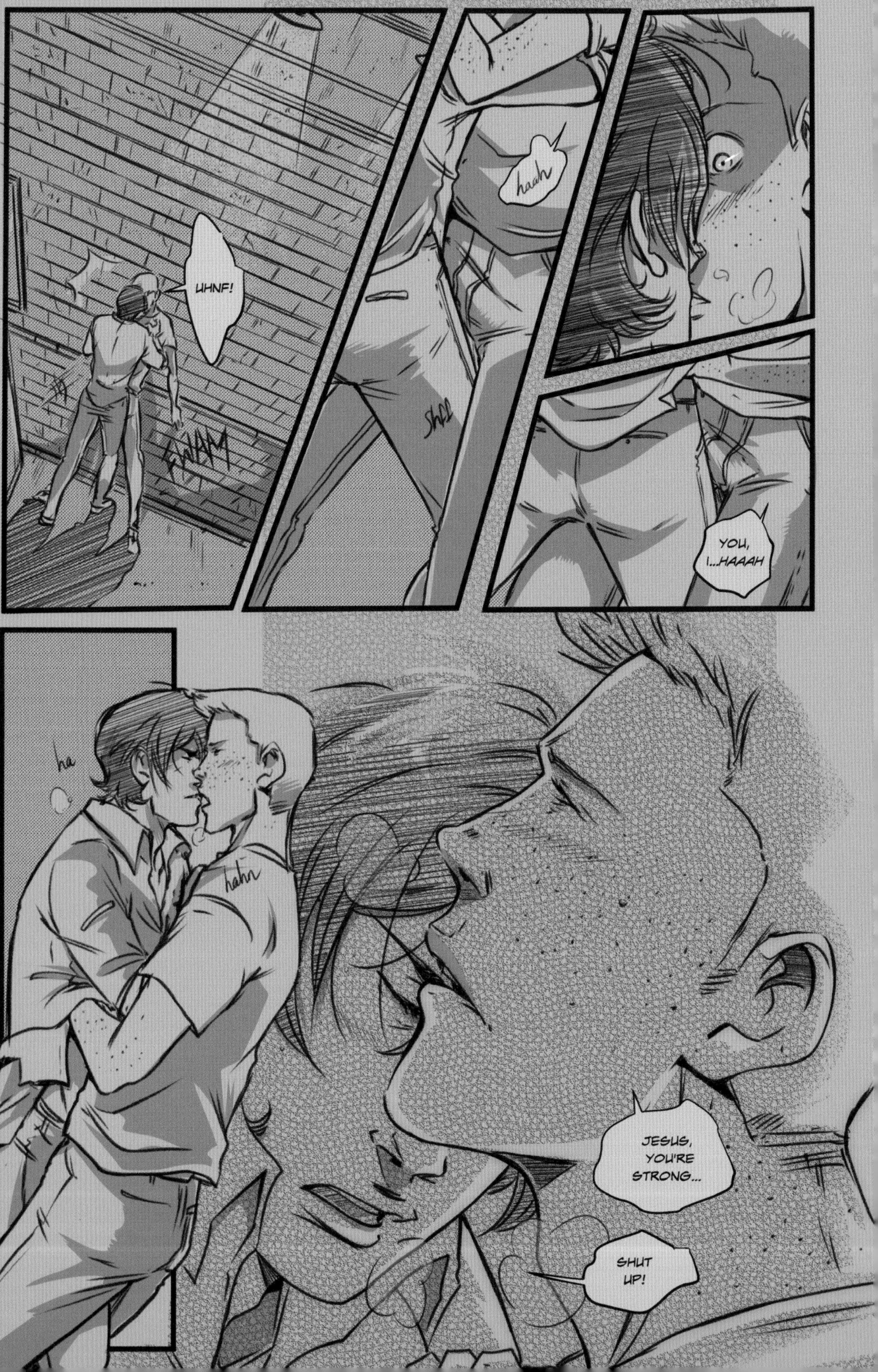
UHNF!
SWAM
haah
YOU, I...HAAAH
ha
hahn
JESUS, YOU'RE STRONG...
SHUT UP!

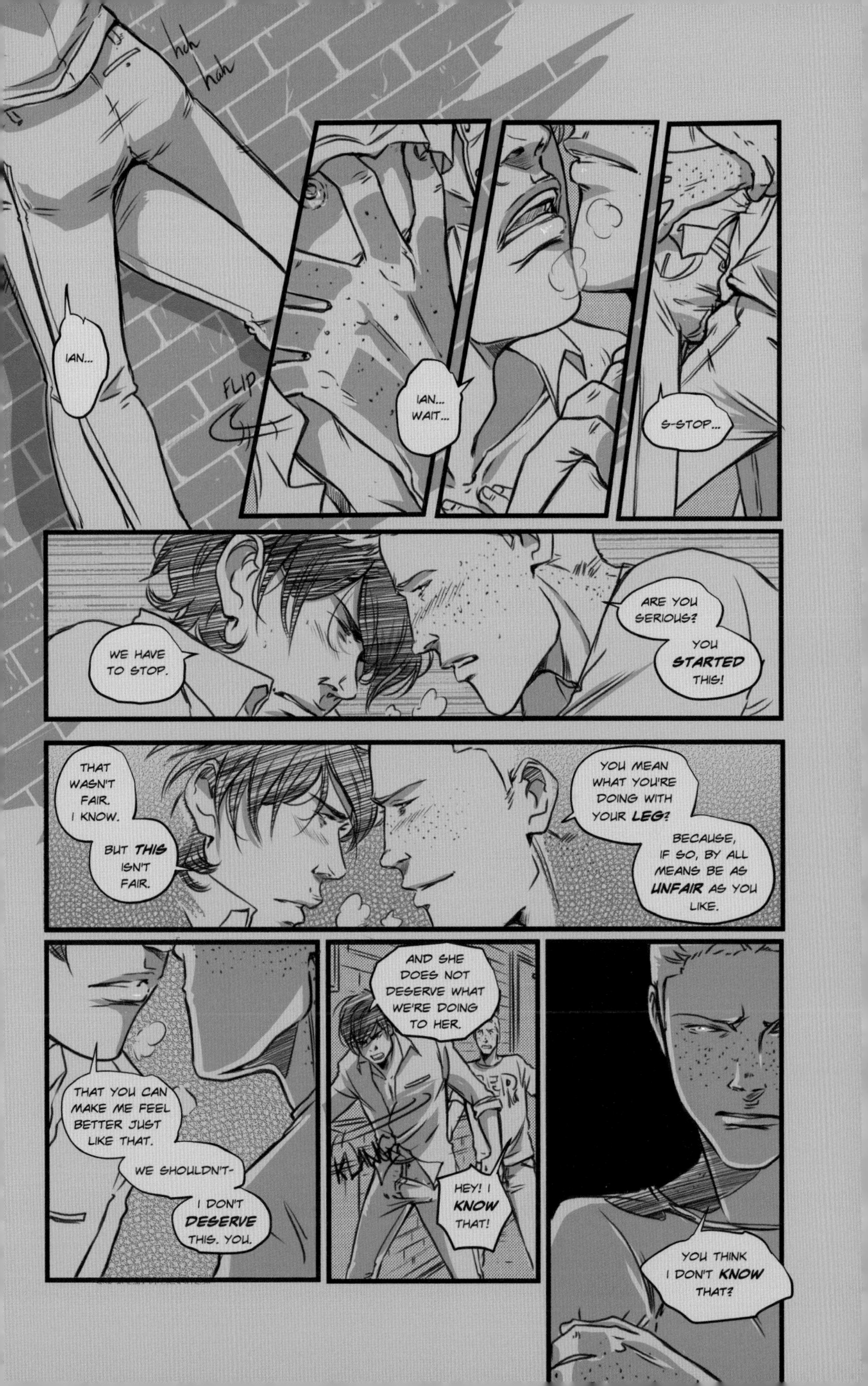
hah
hah
IAN...
FLIP
IAN... WAIT...
S-STOP...
WE HAVE TO STOP.
ARE YOU SERIOUS?
YOU STARTED THIS!
THAT WASN'T FAIR. I KNOW.
BUT THIS ISN'T FAIR.
YOU MEAN WHAT YOU'RE DOING WITH YOUR LEG?
BECAUSE, IF SO, BY ALL MEANS BE AS UNFAIR AS YOU LIKE.
THAT YOU CAN MAKE ME FEEL BETTER JUST LIKE THAT.
WE SHOULDN'T-
I DON'T DESERVE THIS. YOU.
AND SHE DOES NOT DESERVE WHAT WE'RE DOING TO HER.
KLANG
HEY! I KNOW THAT!
YOU THINK I DON'T KNOW THAT?

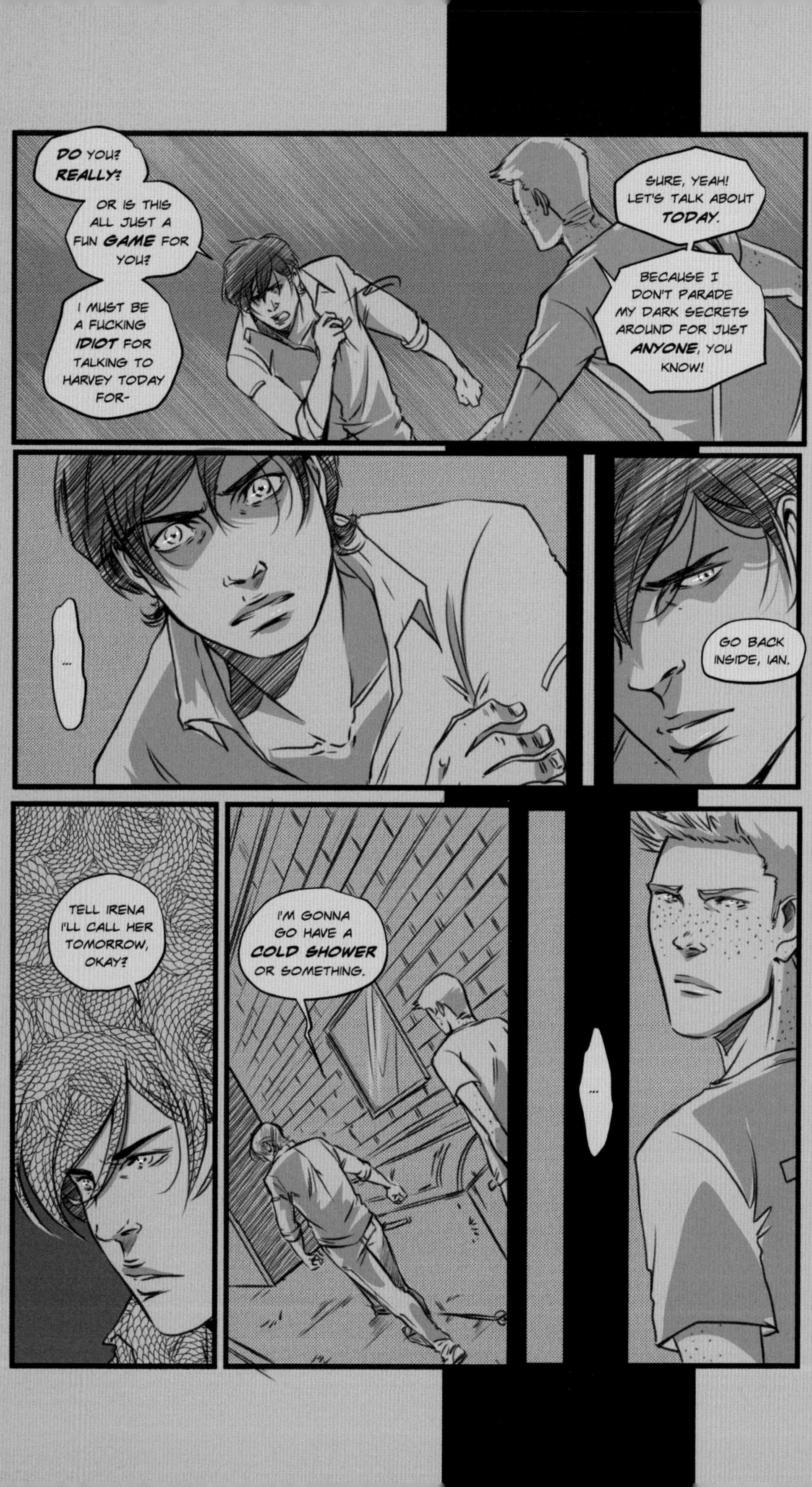
DO YOU? REALLY?
OR IS THIS ALL JUST A FUN GAME FOR YOU?
I MUST BE A FUCKING IDIOT FOR TALKING TO HARVEY TODAY FOR-
SURE, YEAH! LET'S TALK ABOUT TODAY.
BECAUSE I DON'T PARADE MY DARK SECRETS AROUND FOR JUST ANYONE, YOU KNOW!
...
GO BACK INSIDE, IAN.
TELL IRENA I'LL CALL HER TOMORROW, OKAY?
I'M GONNA GO HAVE A COLD SHOWER OR SOMETHING.
...

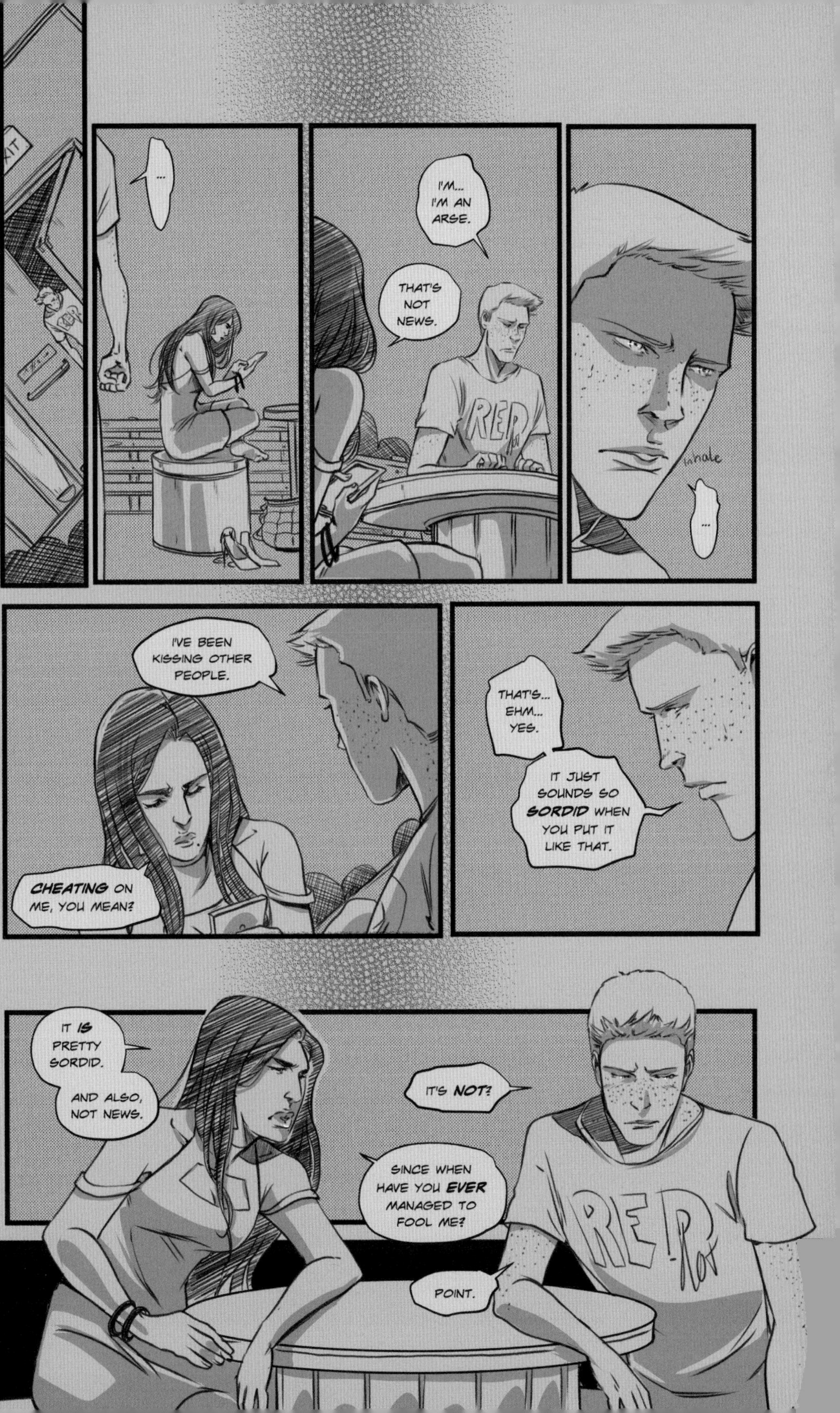
...
I'M... I'M AN ARSE.
THAT'S NOT NEWS.
inhale
...
I'VE BEEN KISSING OTHER PEOPLE.
CHEATING ON ME, YOU MEAN?
THAT'S... EHM... YES.
IT JUST SOUNDS SO SORDID WHEN YOU PUT IT LIKE THAT.
IT IS PRETTY SORDID.
AND ALSO, NOT NEWS.
IT'S NOT?
SINCE WHEN HAVE YOU EVER MANAGED TO FOOL ME?
POINT.

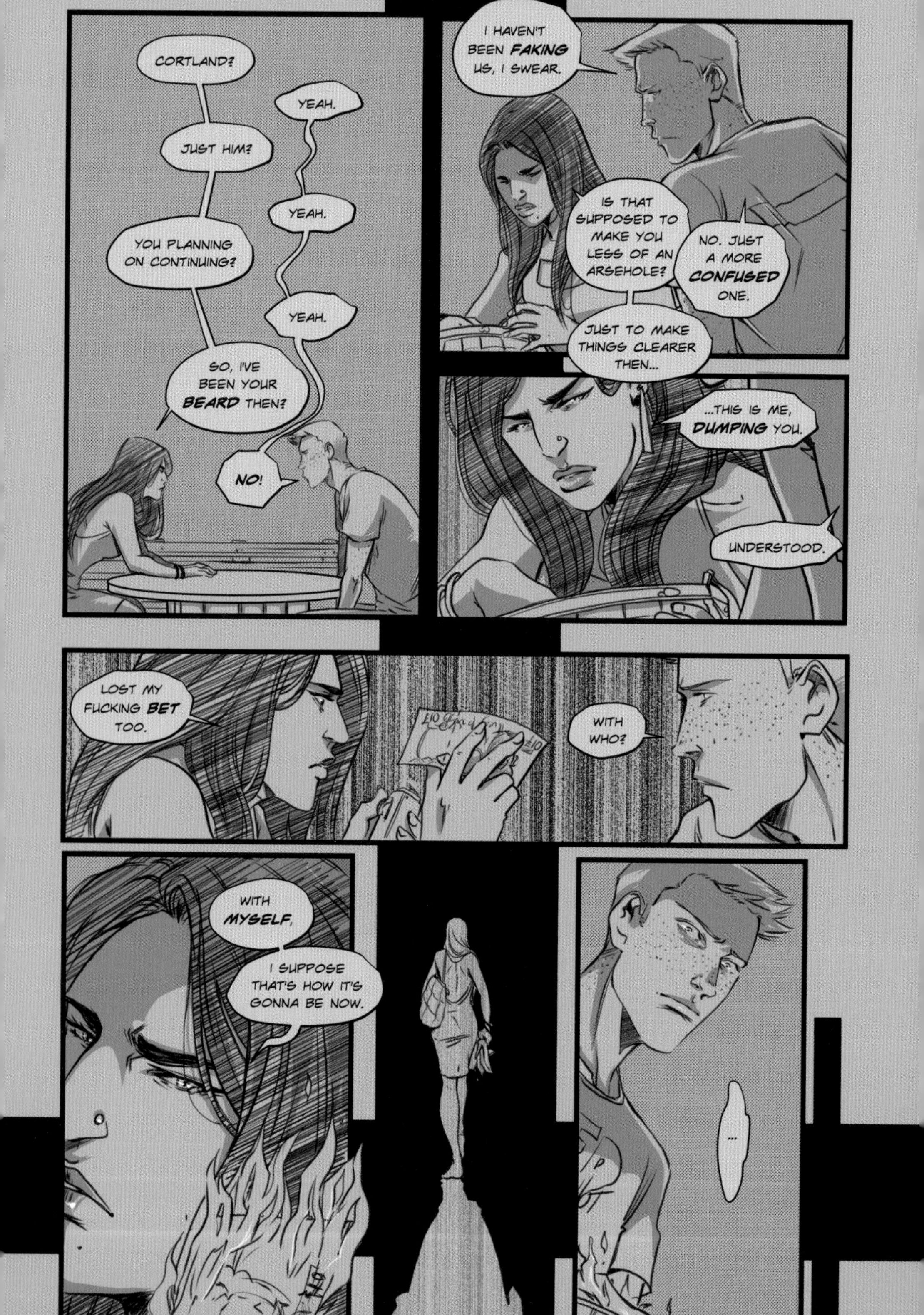
CORTLAND?
YEAH.
JUST HIM?
YEAH.
YOU PLANNING ON CONTINUING?
YEAH.
SO, I'VE BEEN YOUR BEARD THEN?
NO!
I HAVEN'T BEEN FAKING US, I SWEAR.
IS THAT SUPPOSED TO MAKE YOU LESS OF AN ARSEHOLE?
NO. JUST A MORE CONFUSED ONE.
JUST TO MAKE THINGS CLEARER THEN...
...THIS IS ME, DUMPING YOU.
UNDERSTOOD.
LOST MY FUCKING BET TOO.
WITH WHO?
WITH MYSELF,
I SUPPOSE THAT'S HOW IT'S GONNA BE NOW.
...

ISSUE 10

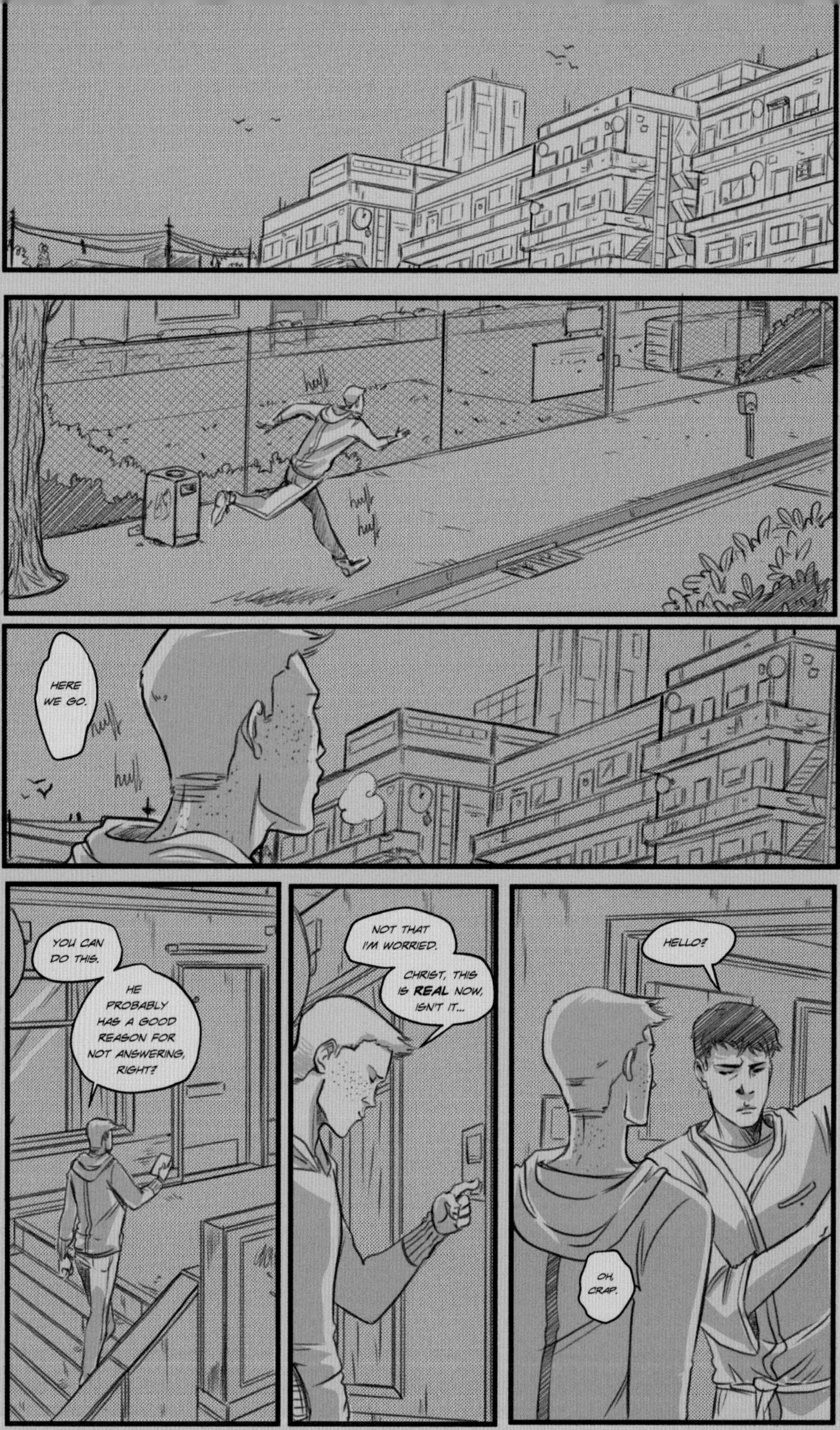
huff
huff
huff
HERE WE GO.
huff
huff
YOU CAN DO THIS.
HE PROBABLY HAS A GOOD REASON FOR NOT ANSWERING, RIGHT?
NOT THAT I'M WORRIED.
CHRIST, THIS IS **REAL** NOW, ISN'T IT...
HELLO?
OH, CRAP.

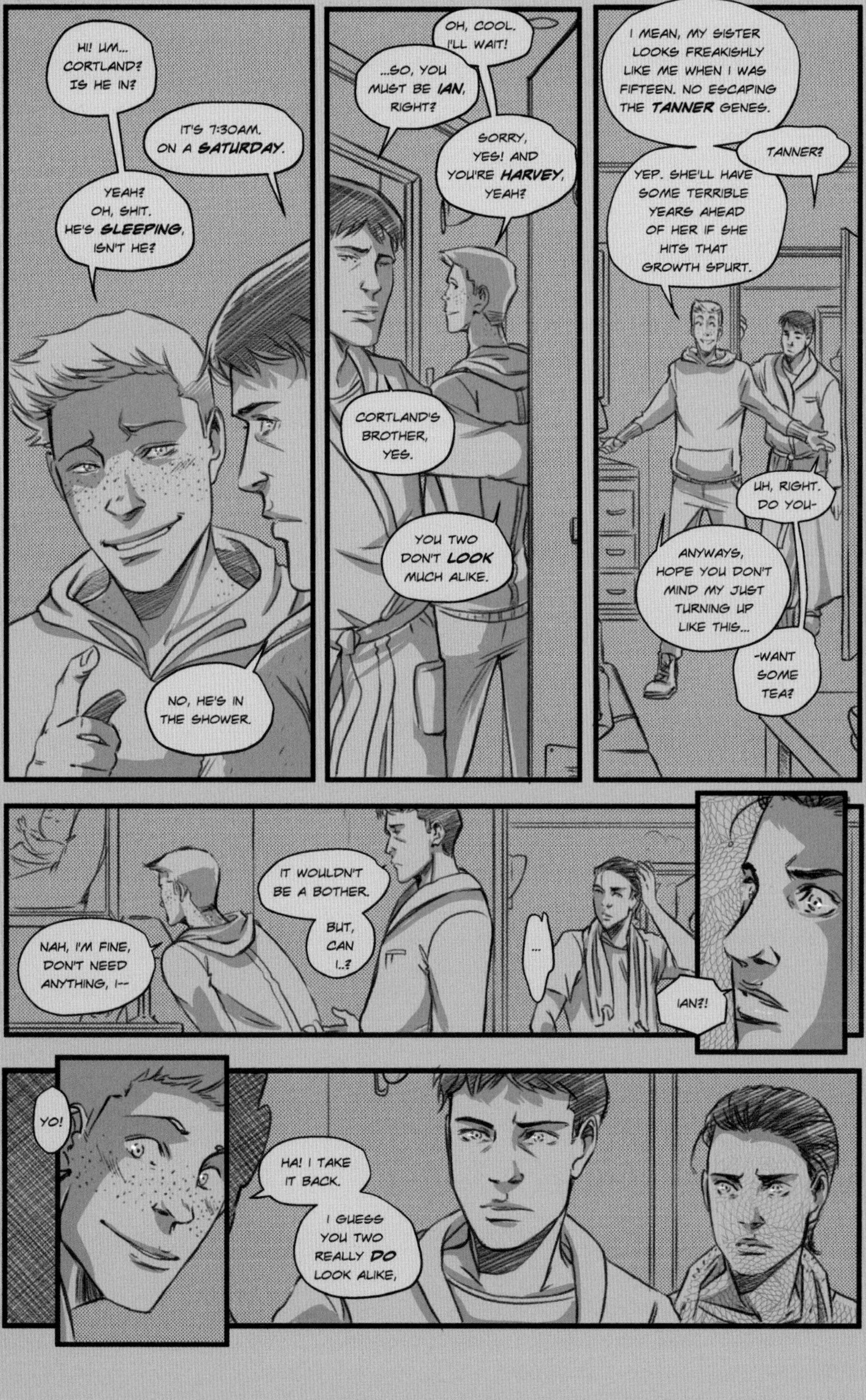
HI! UM... CORTLAND? IS HE IN?
IT'S 7:30AM. ON A SATURDAY.
YEAH? OH, SHIT. HE'S SLEEPING, ISN'T HE?
NO, HE'S IN THE SHOWER.
OH, COOL. I'LL WAIT!
...SO, YOU MUST BE IAN, RIGHT?
SORRY, YES! AND YOU'RE HARVEY, YEAH?
CORTLAND'S BROTHER, YES.
YOU TWO DON'T LOOK MUCH ALIKE.
I MEAN, MY SISTER LOOKS FREAKISHLY LIKE ME WHEN I WAS FIFTEEN. NO ESCAPING THE TANNER GENES.
TANNER?
YEP. SHE'LL HAVE SOME TERRIBLE YEARS AHEAD OF HER IF SHE HITS THAT GROWTH SPURT.
UH, RIGHT. DO YOU-
ANYWAYS, HOPE YOU DON'T MIND MY JUST TURNING UP LIKE THIS...
-WANT SOME TEA?
IT WOULDN'T BE A BOTHER.
NAH, I'M FINE, DON'T NEED ANYTHING, I--
BUT, CAN I..?
...
IAN?!
YO!
HA! I TAKE IT BACK.
I GUESS YOU TWO REALLY DO LOOK ALIKE,

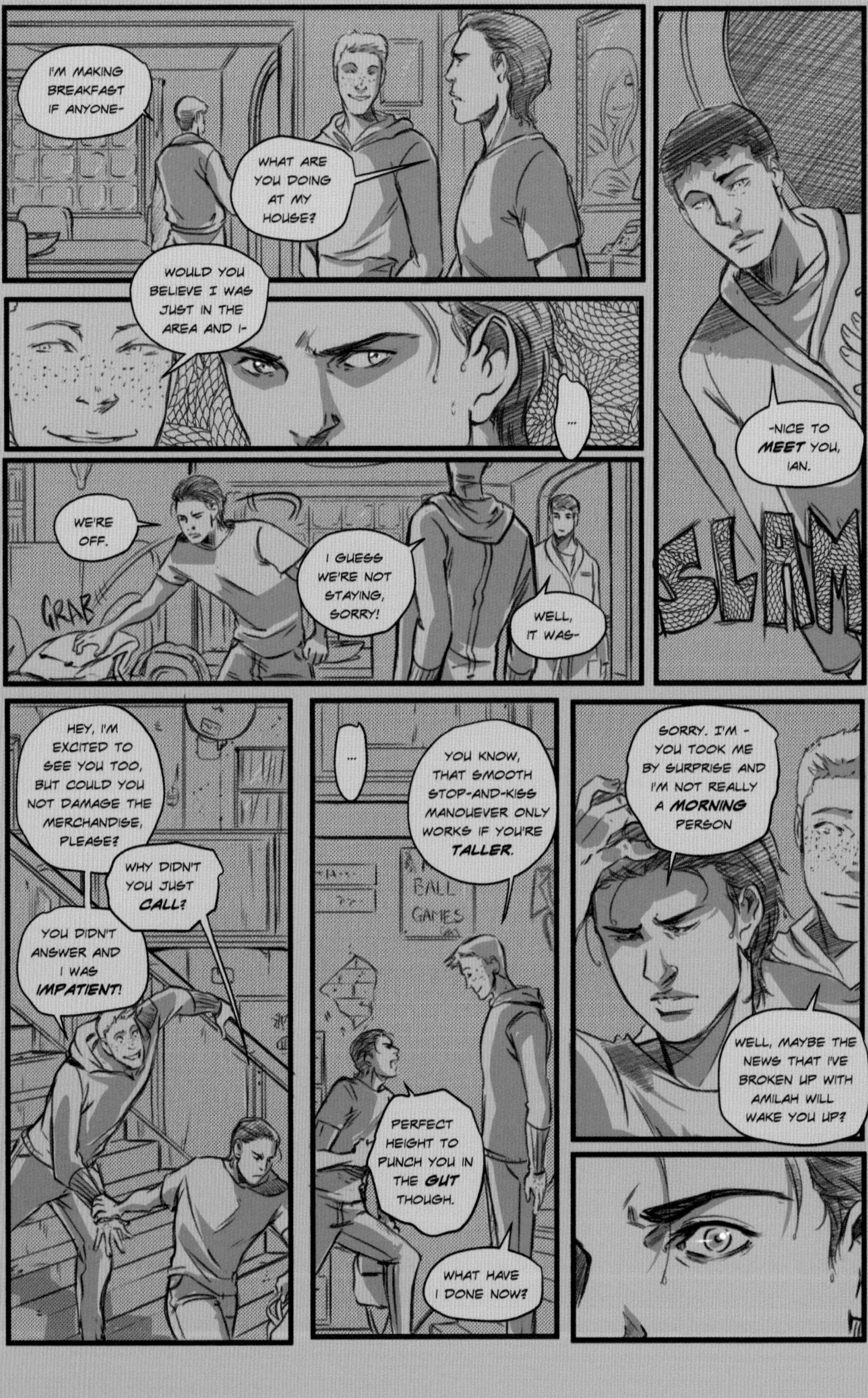
I'M MAKING BREAKFAST IF ANYONE-
WHAT ARE YOU DOING AT MY HOUSE?
WOULD YOU BELIEVE I WAS JUST IN THE AREA AND I-
...
WE'RE OFF.
GRAB
I GUESS WE'RE NOT STAYING, SORRY!
WELL, IT WAS-
-NICE TO **MEET** YOU, IAN.
SLAM
HEY, I'M EXCITED TO SEE YOU TOO, BUT COULD YOU NOT DAMAGE THE MERCHANDISE, PLEASE?
WHY DIDN'T YOU JUST **CALL**?
YOU DIDN'T ANSWER AND I WAS ***IMPATIENT***!
...
YOU KNOW, THAT SMOOTH STOP-AND-KISS MANOUEVER ONLY WORKS IF YOU'RE ***TALLER***.
BALL GAMES
PERFECT HEIGHT TO PUNCH YOU IN THE ***GUT*** THOUGH.
WHAT HAVE I DONE NOW?
SORRY. I'M - YOU TOOK ME BY SURPRISE AND I'M NOT REALLY A ***MORNING*** PERSON
WELL, MAYBE THE NEWS THAT I'VE BROKEN UP WITH AMILAH WILL WAKE YOU UP?

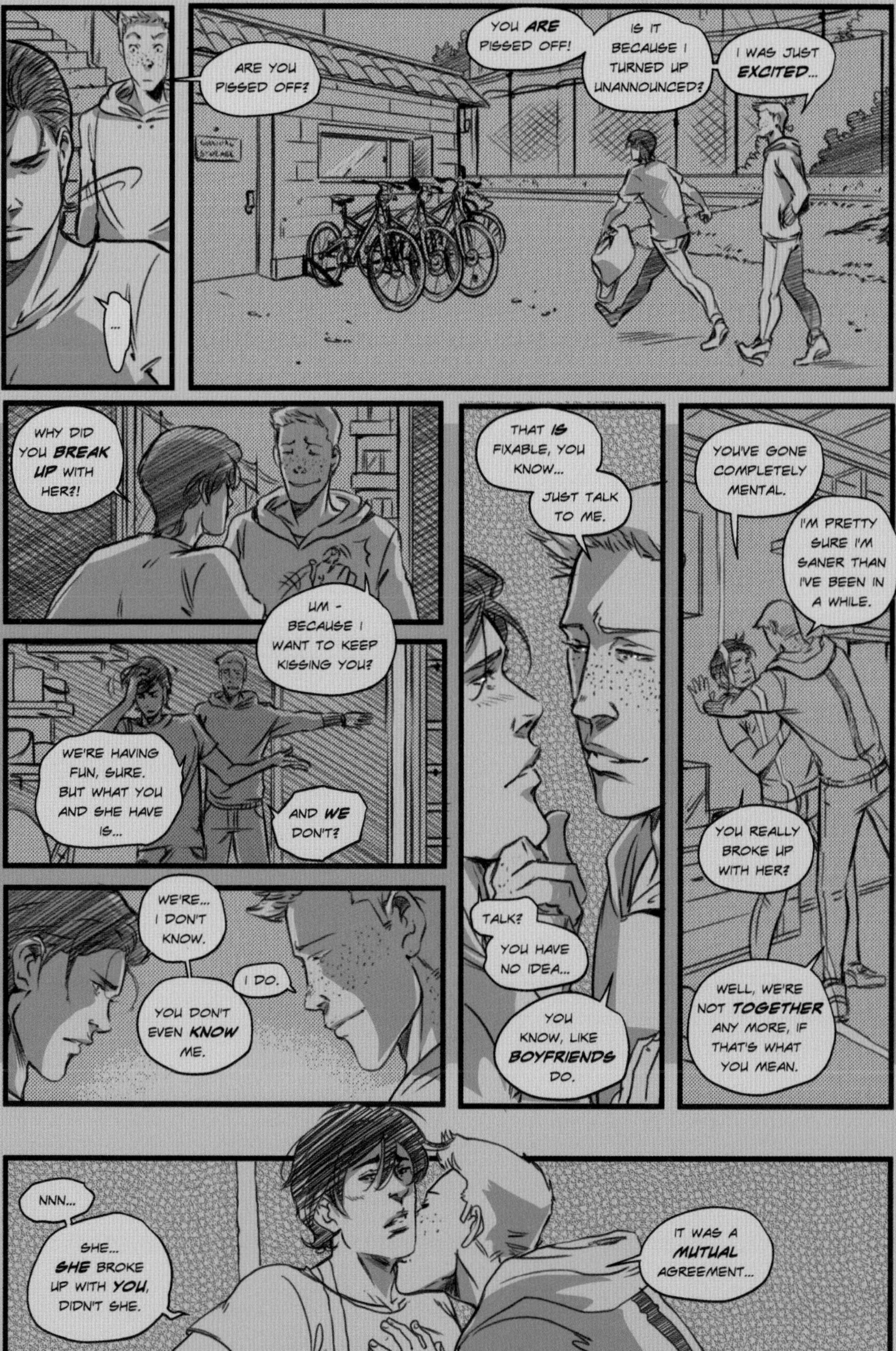
...
ARE YOU PISSED OFF?
YOU ARE PISSED OFF!
IS IT BECAUSE I TURNED UP UNANNOUNCED?
I WAS JUST EXCITED...
WHY DID YOU BREAK UP WITH HER?!
UM - BECAUSE I WANT TO KEEP KISSING YOU?
WE'RE HAVING FUN, SURE. BUT WHAT YOU AND SHE HAVE IS...
AND WE DON'T?
WE'RE... I DON'T KNOW.
I DO.
YOU DON'T EVEN KNOW ME.
THAT IS FIXABLE, YOU KNOW...
JUST TALK TO ME.
TALK?
YOU HAVE NO IDEA...
YOU KNOW, LIKE BOYFRIENDS DO.
YOU'VE GONE COMPLETELY MENTAL.
I'M PRETTY SURE I'M SANER THAN I'VE BEEN IN A WHILE.
YOU REALLY BROKE UP WITH HER?
WELL, WE'RE NOT TOGETHER ANY MORE, IF THAT'S WHAT YOU MEAN.
NNN...
SHE... SHE BROKE UP WITH YOU, DIDN'T SHE.
IT WAS A MUTUAL AGREEMENT...

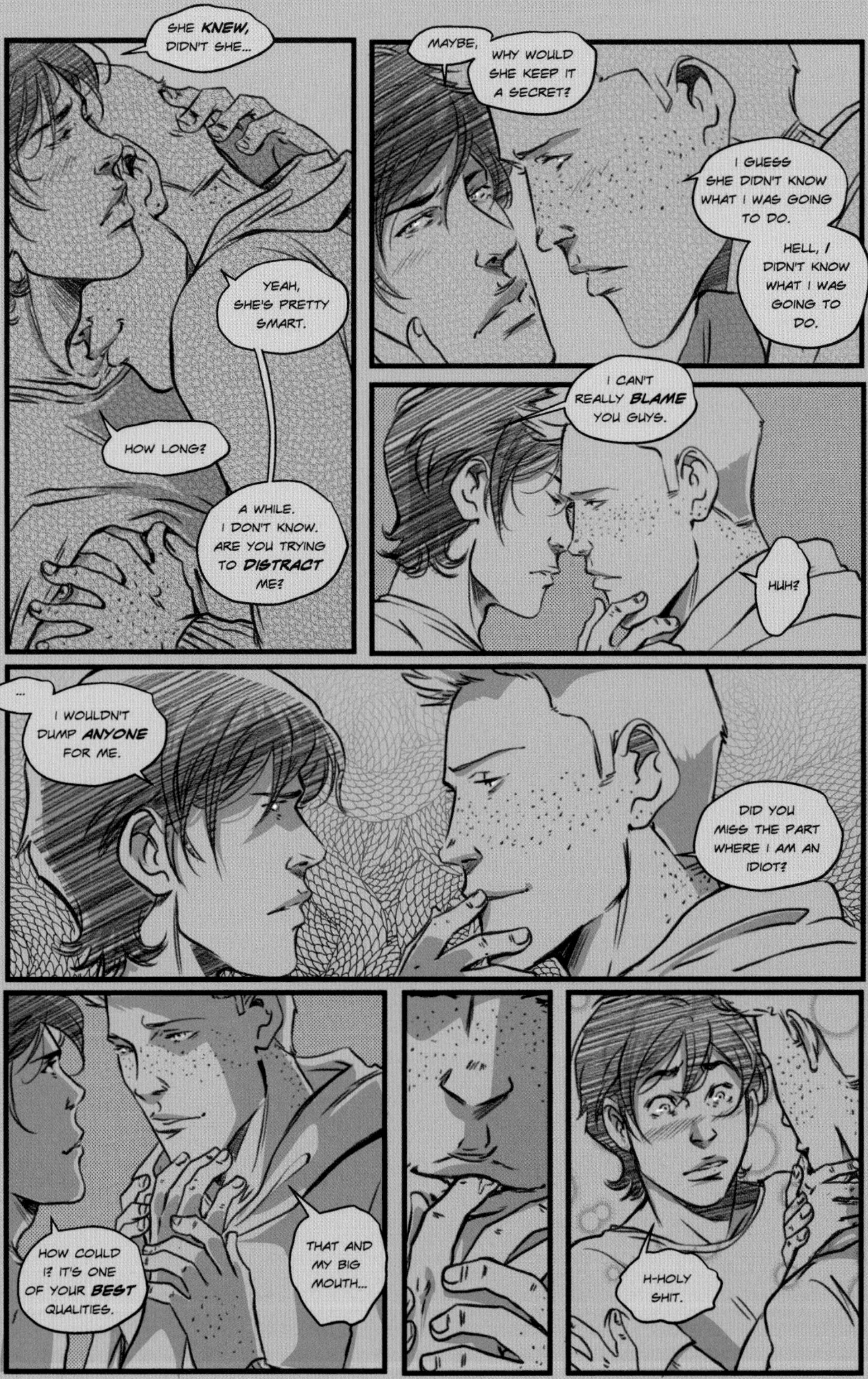
SHE KNEW, DIDN'T SHE...
YEAH, SHE'S PRETTY SMART.
HOW LONG?
A WHILE. I DON'T KNOW. ARE YOU TRYING TO DISTRACT ME?
MAYBE.
WHY WOULD SHE KEEP IT A SECRET?
I GUESS SHE DIDN'T KNOW WHAT I WAS GOING TO DO.
HELL, I DIDN'T KNOW WHAT I WAS GOING TO DO.
I CAN'T REALLY BLAME YOU GUYS.
HUH?
...
I WOULDN'T DUMP ANYONE FOR ME.
DID YOU MISS THE PART WHERE I AM AN IDIOT?
HOW COULD I? IT'S ONE OF YOUR BEST QUALITIES.
THAT AND MY BIG MOUTH...
H-HOLY SHIT.

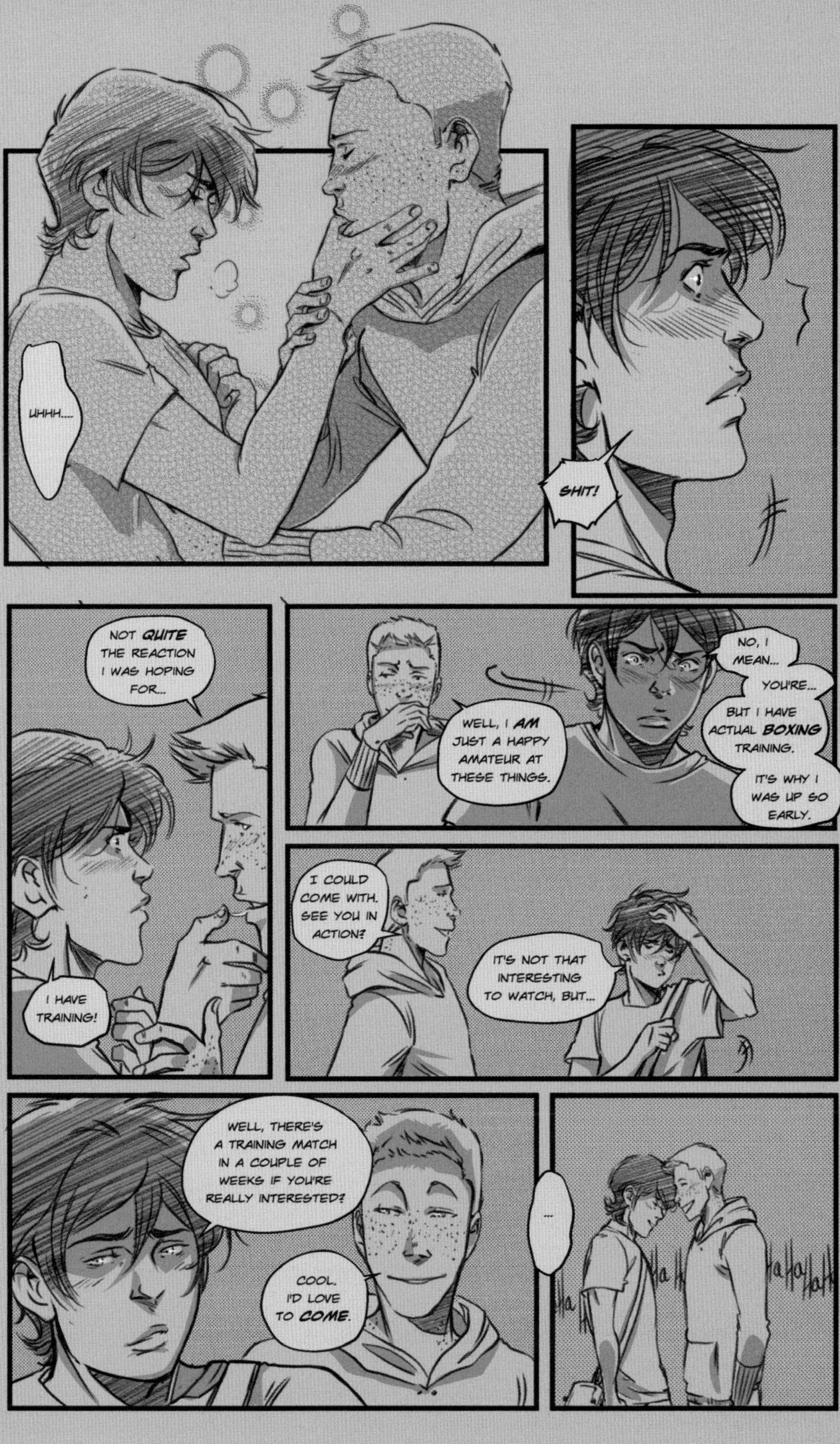
UHHH....
SHIT!
NOT QUITE THE REACTION I WAS HOPING FOR...
I HAVE TRAINING!
WELL, I AM JUST A HAPPY AMATEUR AT THESE THINGS.
NO, I MEAN...
YOU'RE...
BUT I HAVE ACTUAL BOXING TRAINING.
IT'S WHY I WAS UP SO EARLY.
I COULD COME WITH. SEE YOU IN ACTION?
IT'S NOT THAT INTERESTING TO WATCH, BUT...
WELL, THERE'S A TRAINING MATCH IN A COUPLE OF WEEKS IF YOU'RE REALLY INTERESTED?
COOL. I'D LOVE TO COME.
...
Ha Ha Ha Ha Ha Ha

...

...

ARGH ERGH

OH SHIT, OH SHIT, OH SHIT WHAT HAVE I *DONE*?!

HEY, WHY DON'T YOU TELL HIM THAT YOU BROKE UP WITH YOUR GIRLFRIEND?

...GREAT IDEA! *GREAT*!

WON'T FREAK HIM OUT AT *ALL*!

KRASH!

NO...NO. IT *WAS* THE RIGHT IDEA. IT SHOULD HAVE BEEN A GREAT IDEA.

I GUESS I THOUGHT HE'D BE *HAPPY*...

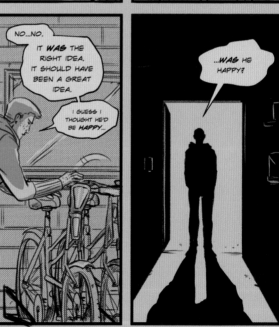

...WAS HE HAPPY?

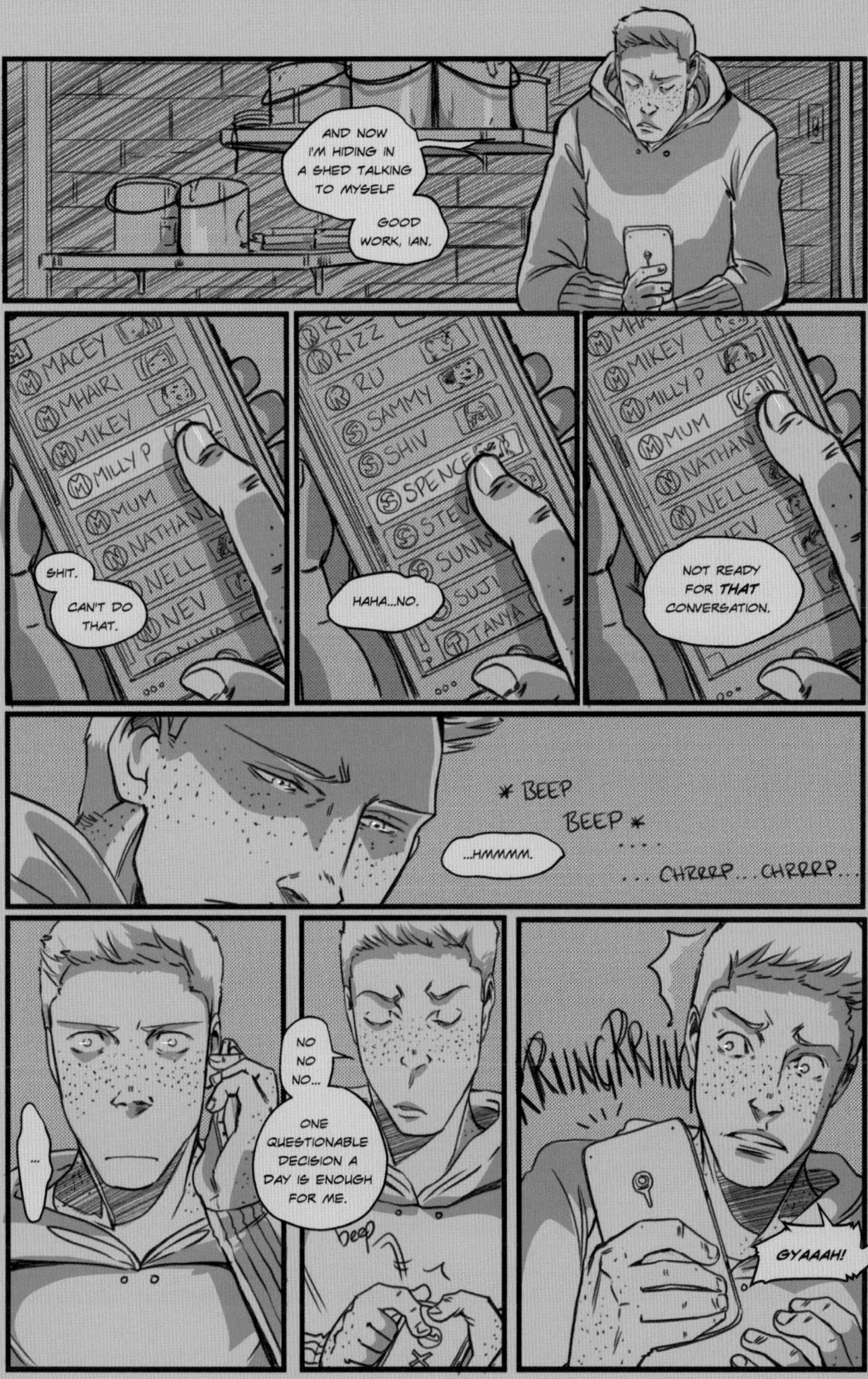
AND NOW I'M HIDING IN A SHED TALKING TO MYSELF
GOOD WORK, IAN.
MACEY
MHAIRI
MIKEY
MILLY P
MUM
NATHAN
NELL
NEV
SHIT.
CAN'T DO THAT.
RIZZ
RU
SAMMY
SHIV
SPENCE
SUNN
TANYA
HAHA...NO.
MIKEY
MILLY P
MUM
NATHAN
NELL
NEV
NOT READY FOR THAT CONVERSATION.
* BEEP
BEEP *
...HMMMM.
... CHRRRP... CHRRRP...
...
NO
NO
NO...
ONE QUESTIONABLE DECISION A DAY IS ENOUGH FOR ME.
beep
RRIINGRRING
GYAAAH!

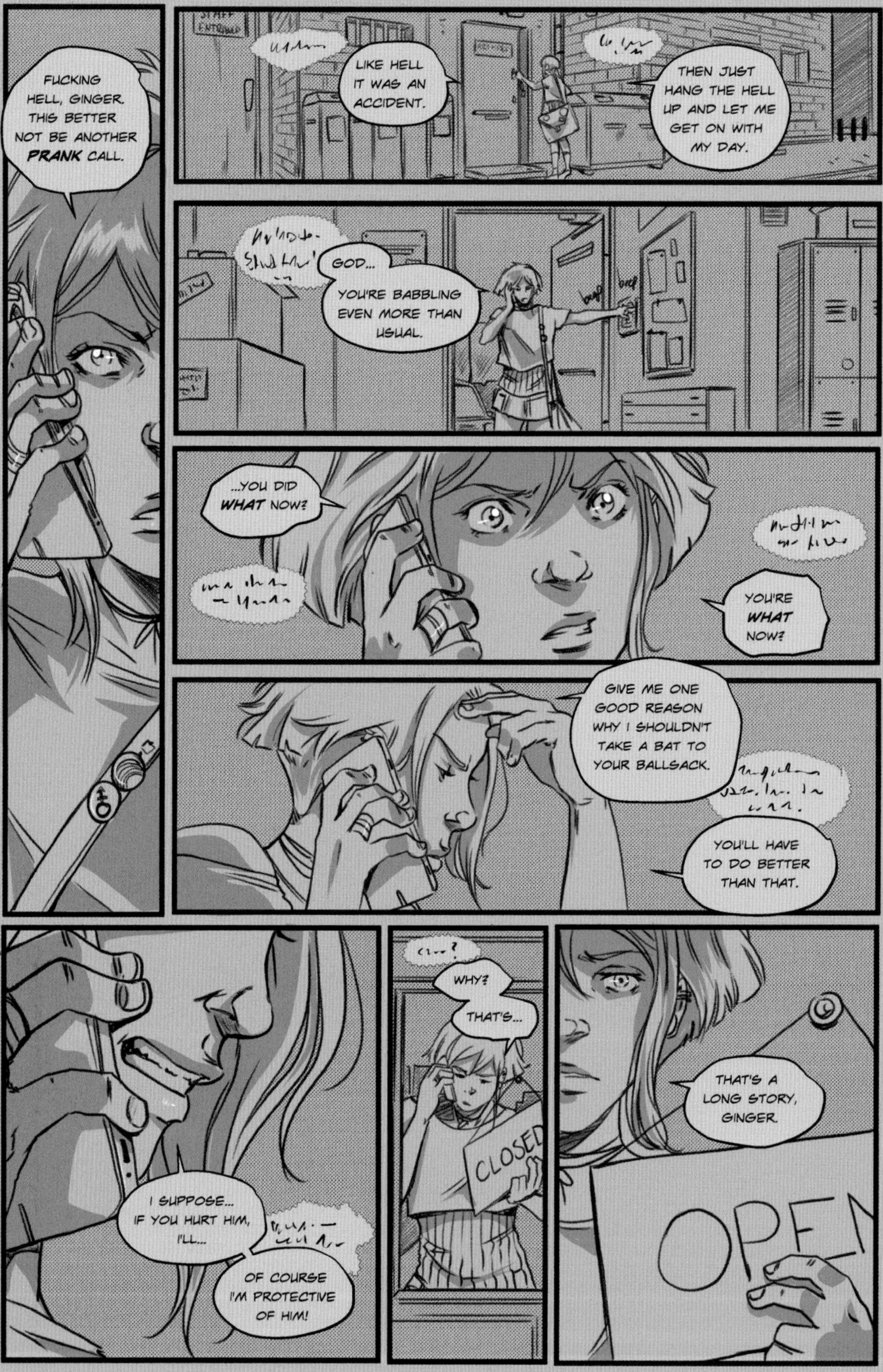
FUCKING HELL, GINGER. THIS BETTER NOT BE ANOTHER PRANK CALL.
LIKE HELL IT WAS AN ACCIDENT.
THEN JUST HANG THE HELL UP AND LET ME GET ON WITH MY DAY.
GOD...
YOU'RE BABBLING EVEN MORE THAN USUAL.
...YOU DID WHAT NOW?
YOU'RE WHAT NOW?
GIVE ME ONE GOOD REASON WHY I SHOULDN'T TAKE A BAT TO YOUR BALLSACK.
YOU'LL HAVE TO DO BETTER THAN THAT.
I SUPPOSE... IF YOU HURT HIM, I'LL...
OF COURSE I'M PROTECTIVE OF HIM!
WHY?
THAT'S...
CLOSED
THAT'S A LONG STORY, GINGER.
OPEN

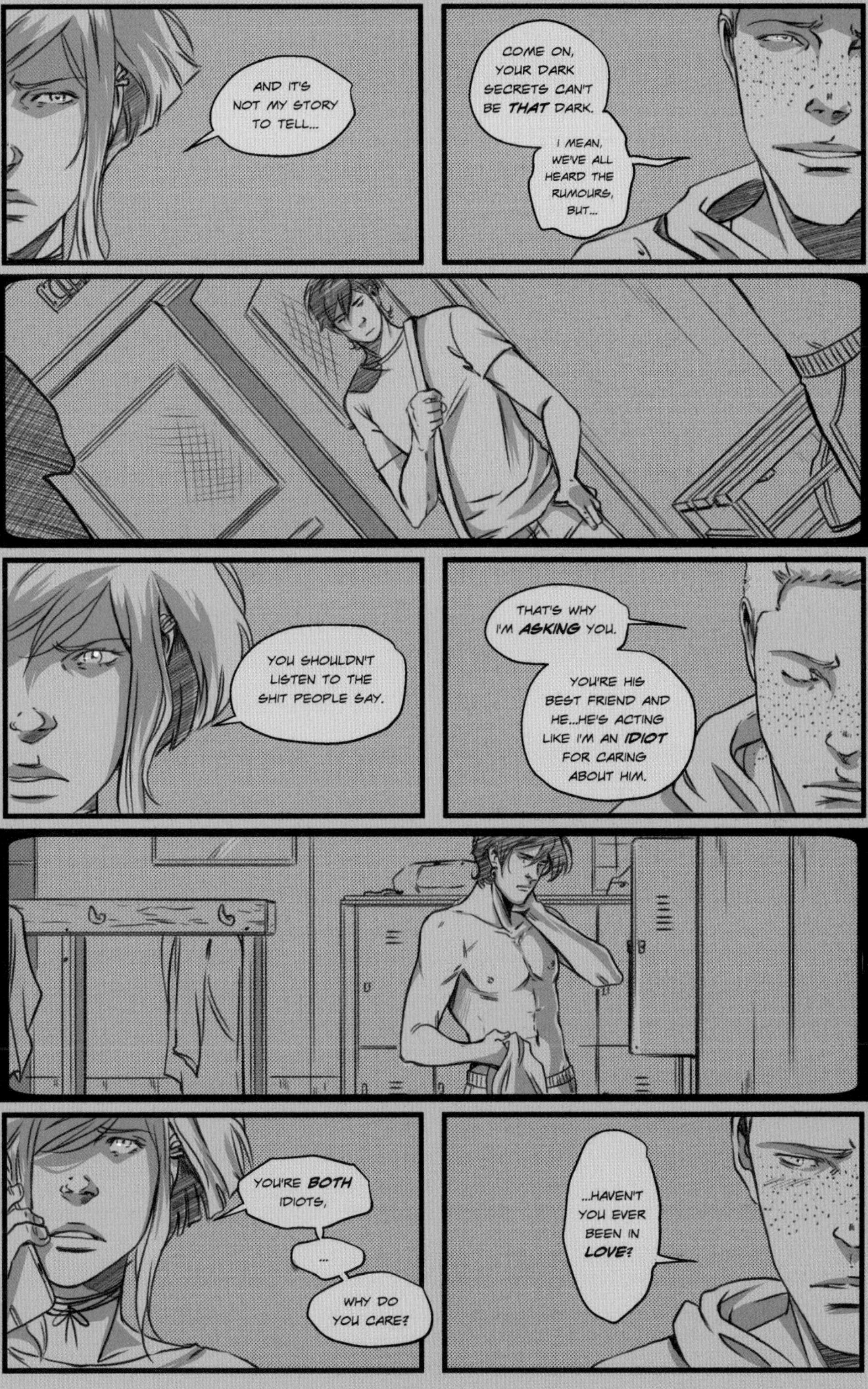
AND IT'S NOT MY STORY TO TELL...
COME ON, YOUR DARK SECRETS CAN'T BE **THAT** DARK.
I MEAN, WE'VE ALL HEARD THE RUMOURS, BUT...
YOU SHOULDN'T LISTEN TO THE SHIT PEOPLE SAY.
THAT'S WHY I'M **ASKING** YOU.
YOU'RE HIS BEST FRIEND AND HE...HE'S ACTING LIKE I'M AN **IDIOT** FOR CARING ABOUT HIM.
YOU'RE **BOTH** IDIOTS,
...
WHY DO YOU CARE?
...HAVEN'T YOU EVER BEEN IN **LOVE**?

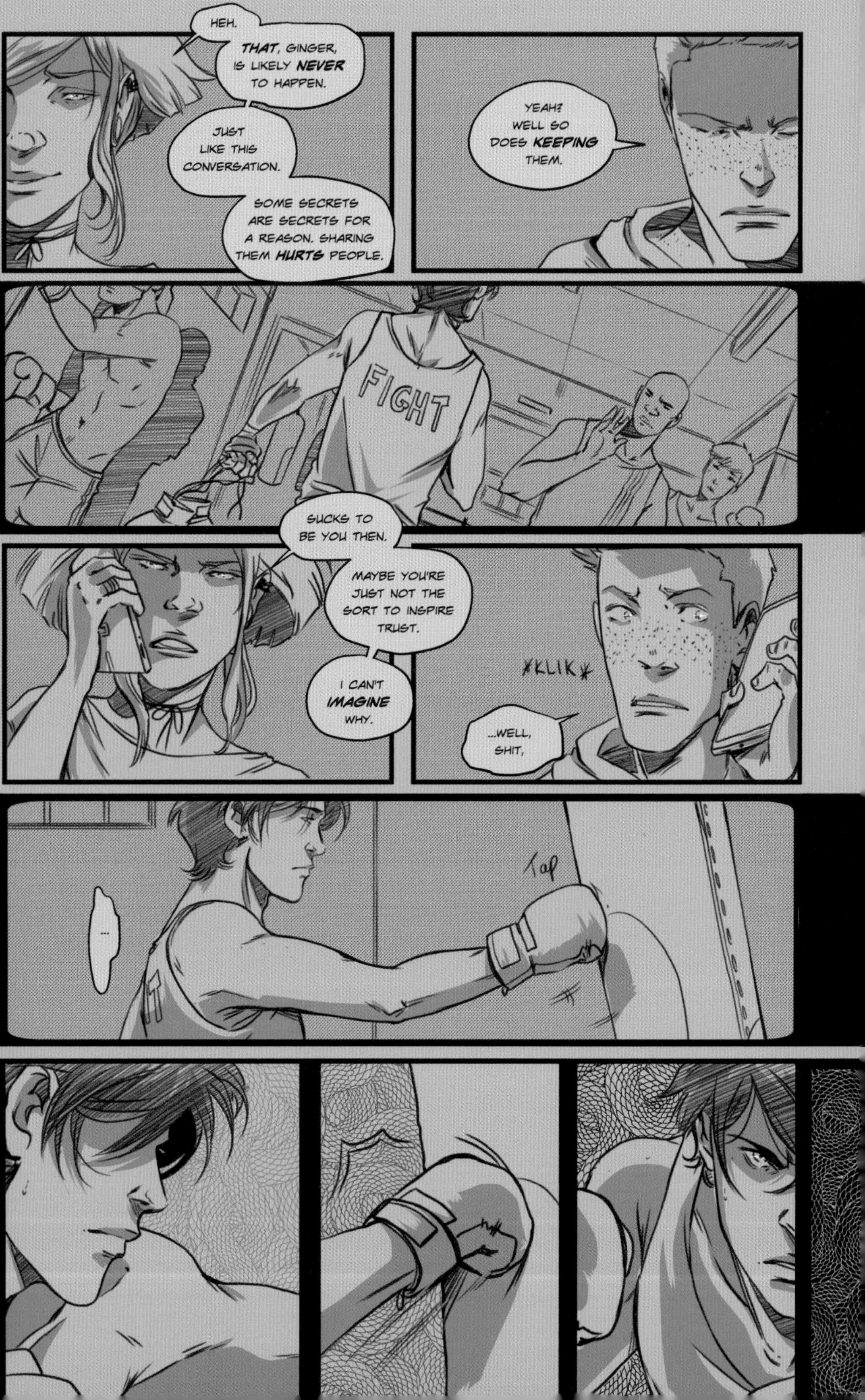
HEH.
THAT, GINGER, IS LIKELY NEVER TO HAPPEN.
JUST LIKE THIS CONVERSATION.
SOME SECRETS ARE SECRETS FOR A REASON. SHARING THEM HURTS PEOPLE.
YEAH? WELL SO DOES KEEPING THEM.
FIGHT
SUCKS TO BE YOU THEN.
MAYBE YOU'RE JUST NOT THE SORT TO INSPIRE TRUST.
I CAN'T IMAGINE WHY.
KLIK
...WELL, SHIT,
Tap
...

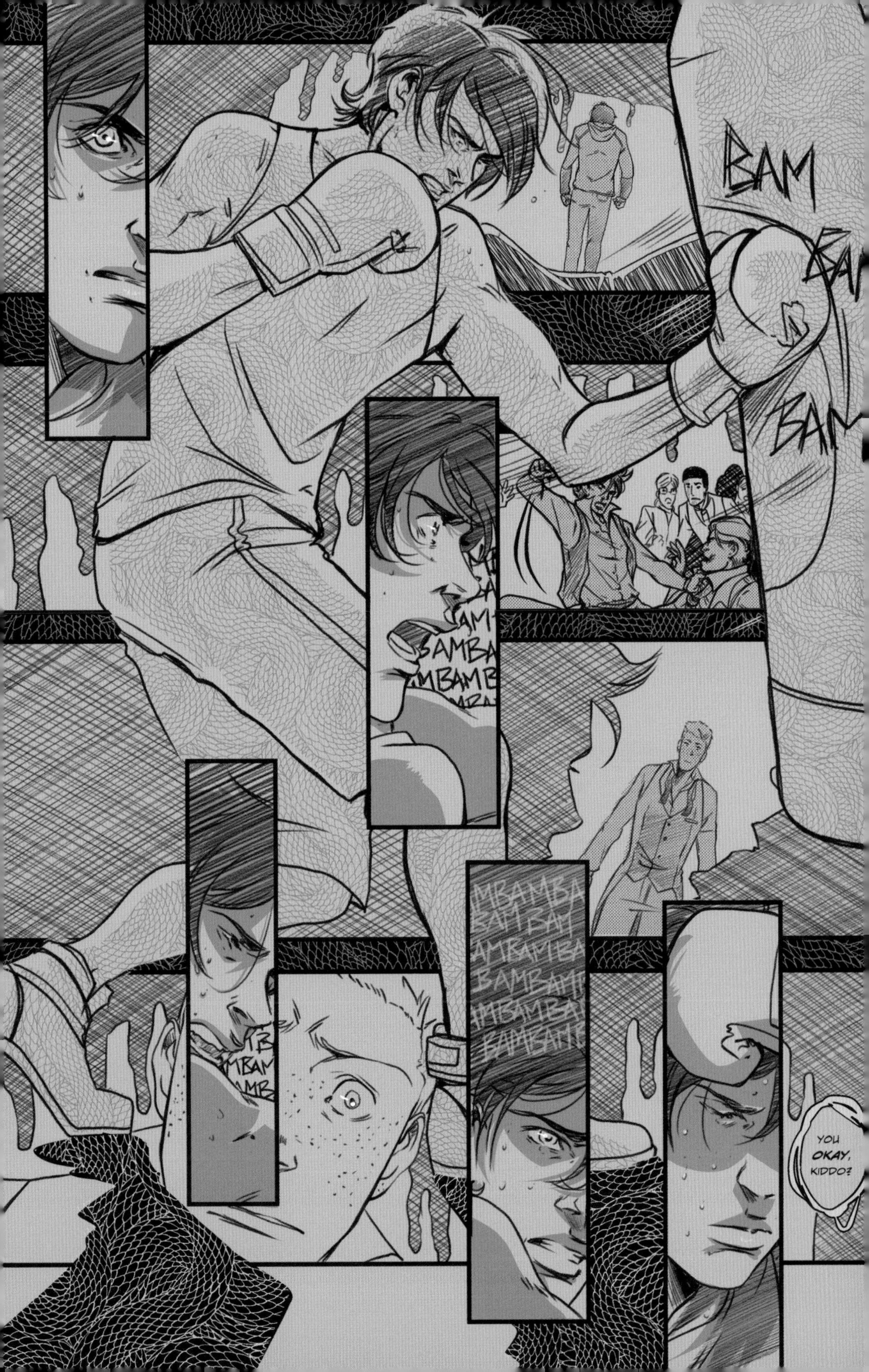
BAM
YOU OKAY, KIDDO?

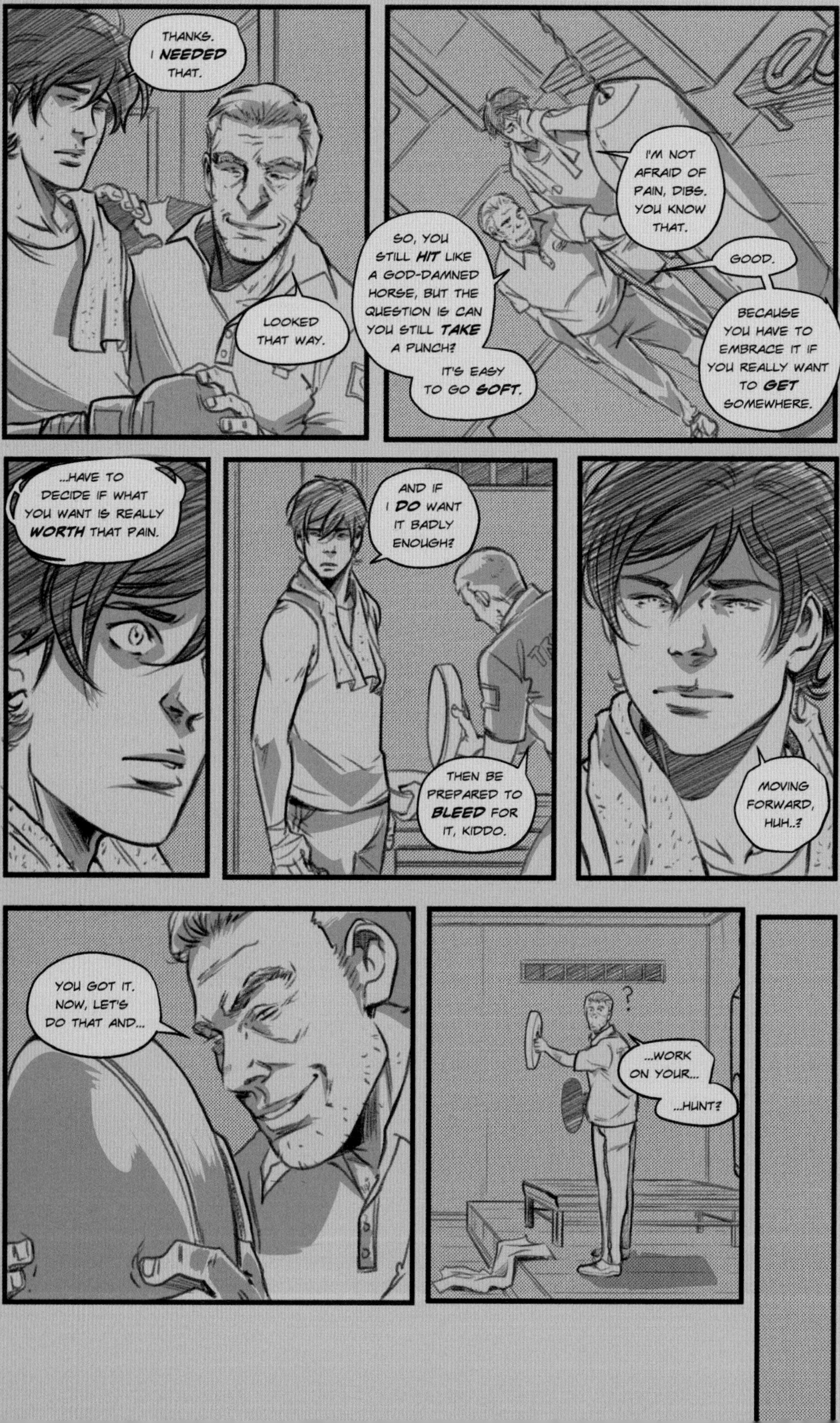
THANKS. I NEEDED THAT.
LOOKED THAT WAY.
SO, YOU STILL HIT LIKE A GOD-DAMNED HORSE, BUT THE QUESTION IS CAN YOU STILL TAKE A PUNCH?
IT'S EASY TO GO SOFT.
I'M NOT AFRAID OF PAIN, DIBS. YOU KNOW THAT.
GOOD.
BECAUSE YOU HAVE TO EMBRACE IT IF YOU REALLY WANT TO GET SOMEWHERE.
...HAVE TO DECIDE IF WHAT YOU WANT IS REALLY WORTH THAT PAIN.
AND IF I DO WANT IT BADLY ENOUGH?
THEN BE PREPARED TO BLEED FOR IT, KIDDO.
MOVING FORWARD, HUH..?
YOU GOT IT. NOW, LET'S DO THAT AND...
?
...WORK ON YOUR...
...HUNT?

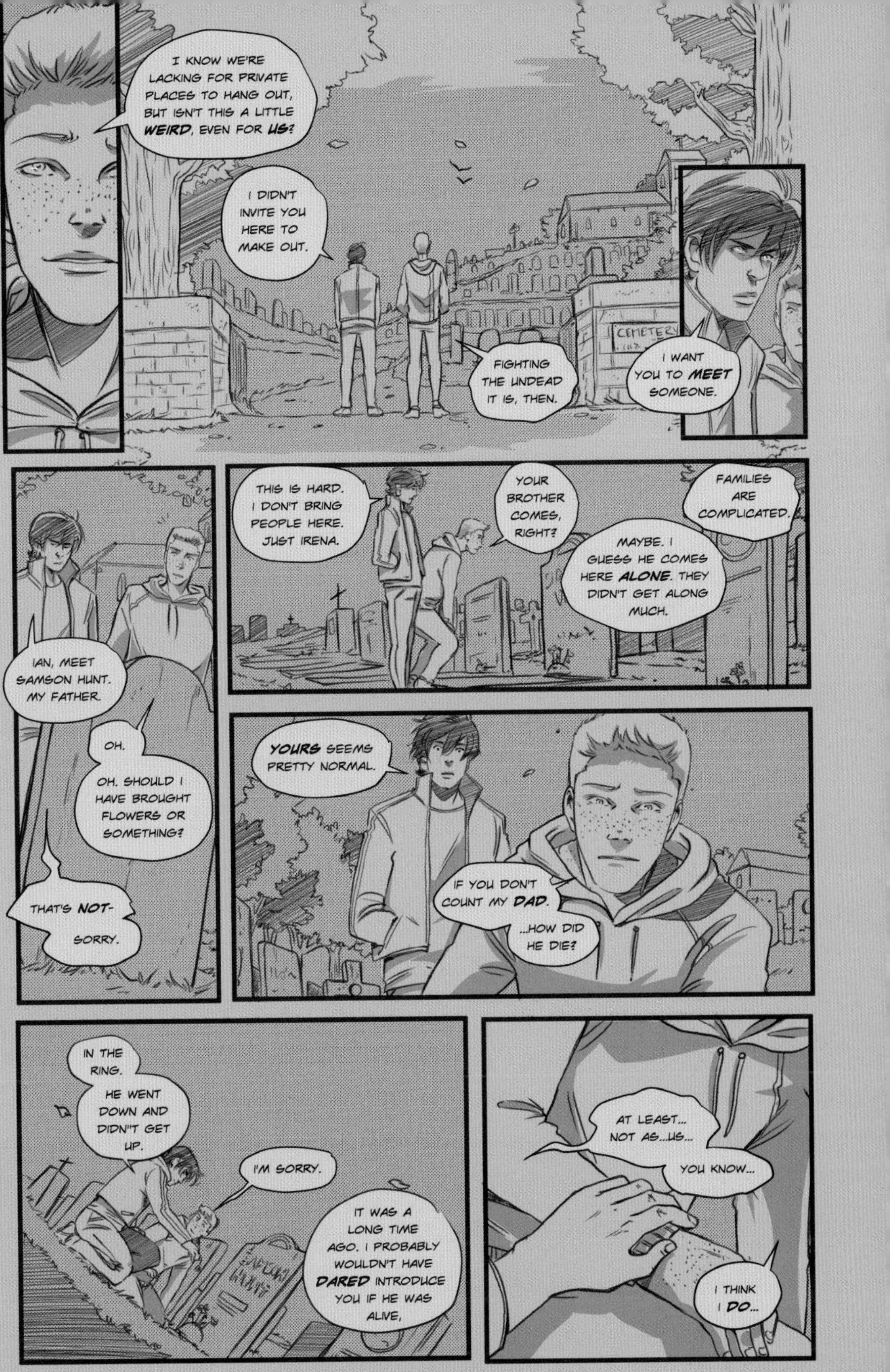
I KNOW WE'RE LACKING FOR PRIVATE PLACES TO HANG OUT, BUT ISN'T THIS A LITTLE **WEIRD**, EVEN FOR **US**?
I DIDN'T INVITE YOU HERE TO MAKE OUT.
FIGHTING THE UNDEAD IT IS, THEN.
CEMETERY
I WANT YOU TO **MEET** SOMEONE.
IAN, MEET SAMSON HUNT. MY FATHER.
OH.
OH. SHOULD I HAVE BROUGHT FLOWERS OR SOMETHING?
THAT'S **NOT**-
SORRY.
THIS IS HARD. I DON'T BRING PEOPLE HERE. JUST IRENA.
YOUR BROTHER COMES, RIGHT?
MAYBE. I GUESS HE COMES HERE **ALONE**. THEY DIDN'T GET ALONG MUCH.
FAMILIES ARE COMPLICATED.
YOURS SEEMS PRETTY NORMAL.
IF YOU DON'T COUNT MY **DAD**.
...HOW DID HE DIE?
IN THE RING.
HE WENT DOWN AND DIDN'T GET UP.
I'M SORRY.
IT WAS A LONG TIME AGO. I PROBABLY WOULDN'T HAVE **DARED** INTRODUCE YOU IF HE WAS ALIVE,
AT LEAST... NOT AS...US...
YOU KNOW...
I THINK I **DO**...

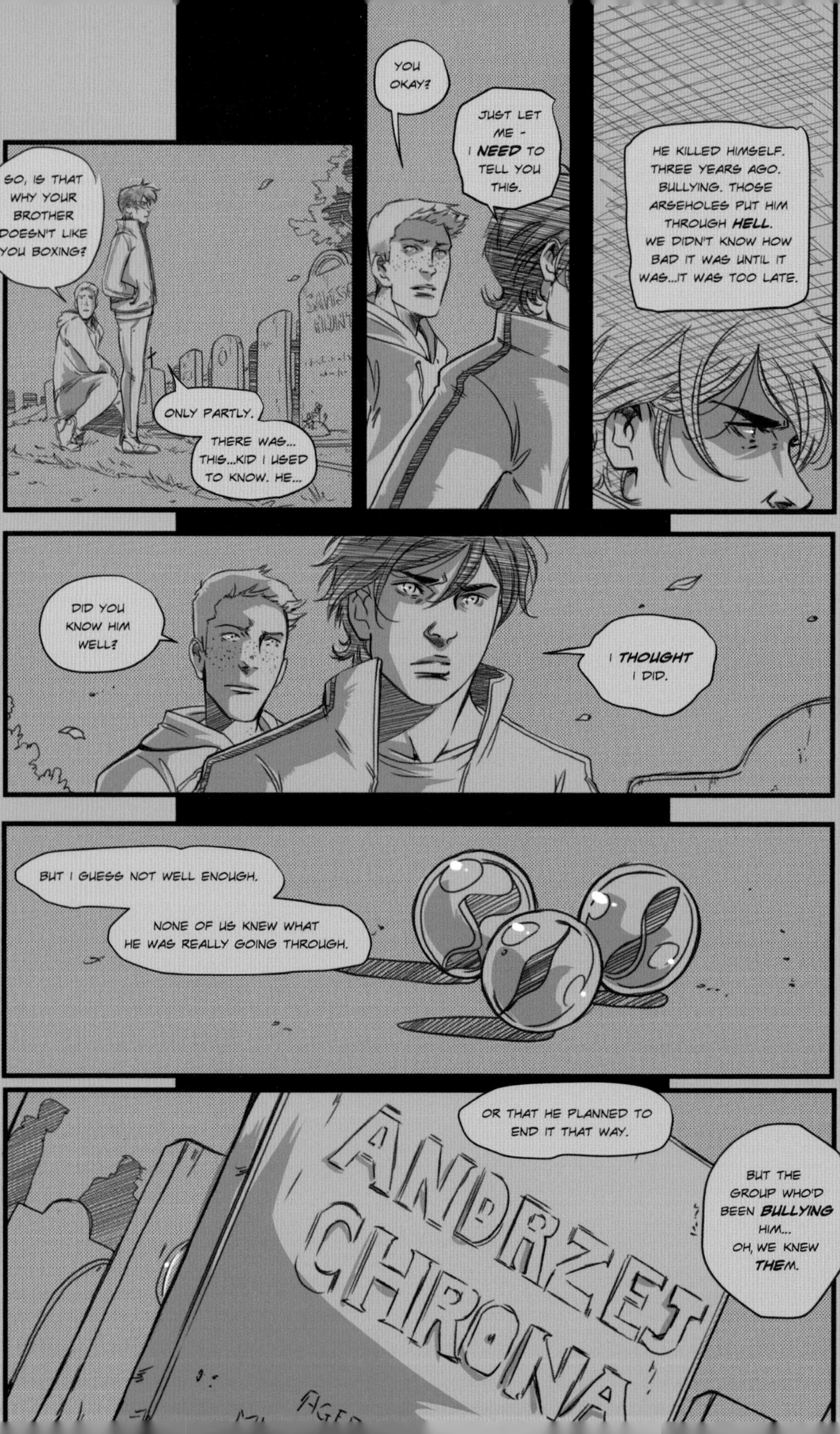
SO, IS THAT WHY YOUR BROTHER DOESN'T LIKE YOU BOXING?
ONLY PARTLY.
THERE WAS... THIS...KID I USED TO KNOW. HE...
YOU OKAY?
JUST LET ME - I NEED TO TELL YOU THIS.
HE KILLED HIMSELF. THREE YEARS AGO. BULLYING. THOSE ARSEHOLES PUT HIM THROUGH HELL. WE DIDN'T KNOW HOW BAD IT WAS UNTIL IT WAS...IT WAS TOO LATE.
DID YOU KNOW HIM WELL?
I THOUGHT I DID.
BUT I GUESS NOT WELL ENOUGH.
NONE OF US KNEW WHAT HE WAS REALLY GOING THROUGH.
OR THAT HE PLANNED TO END IT THAT WAY.
ANDRZEJ CHRONA
BUT THE GROUP WHO'D BEEN BULLYING HIM... OH, WE KNEW THEM.

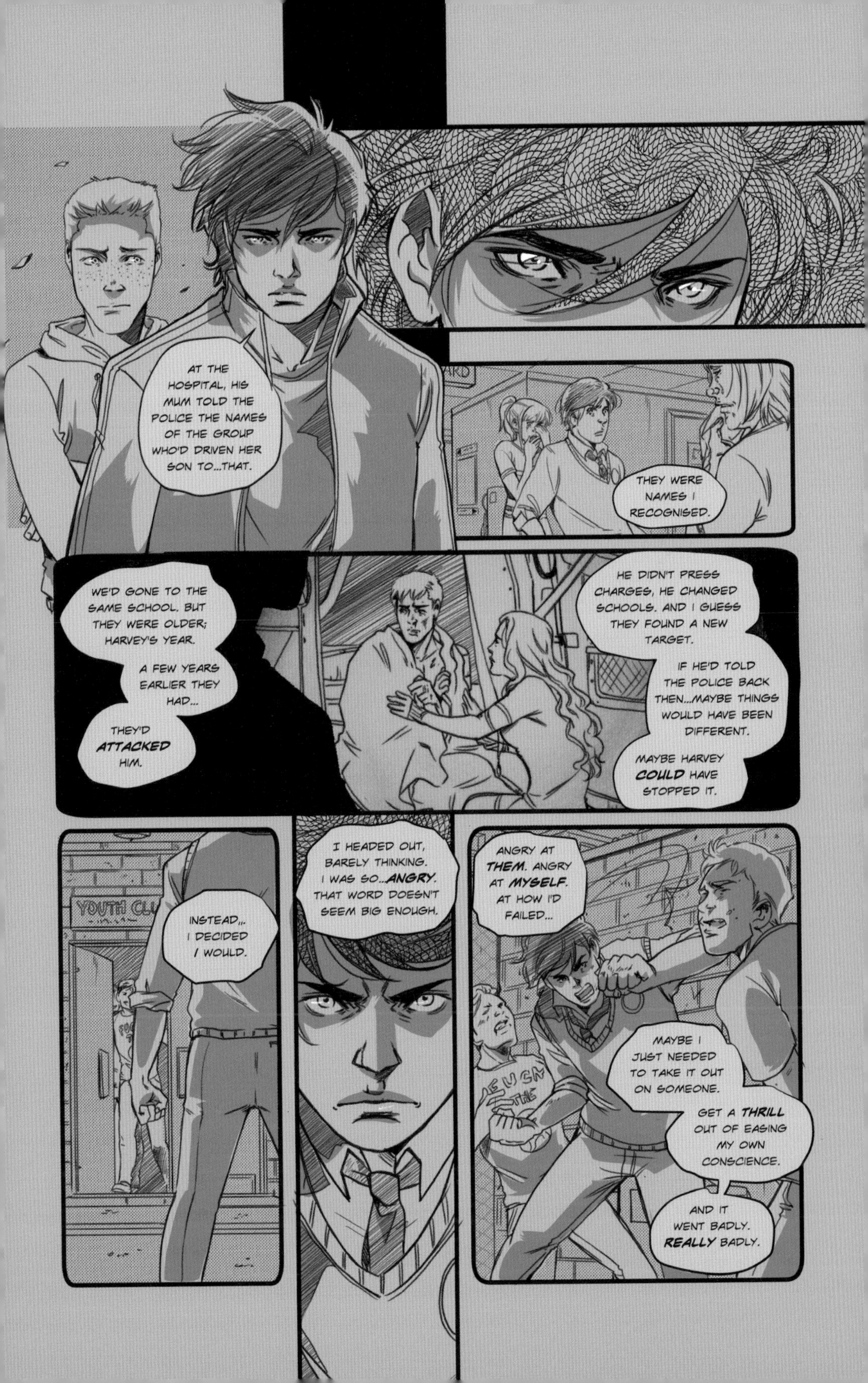
AT THE HOSPITAL, HIS MUM TOLD THE POLICE THE NAMES OF THE GROUP WHO'D DRIVEN HER SON TO...THAT.
THEY WERE NAMES I RECOGNISED.
WE'D GONE TO THE SAME SCHOOL. BUT THEY WERE OLDER; HARVEY'S YEAR.
A FEW YEARS EARLIER THEY HAD...
THEY'D ATTACKED HIM.
HE DIDN'T PRESS CHARGES, HE CHANGED SCHOOLS. AND I GUESS THEY FOUND A NEW TARGET.
IF HE'D TOLD THE POLICE BACK THEN...MAYBE THINGS WOULD HAVE BEEN DIFFERENT.
MAYBE HARVEY COULD HAVE STOPPED IT.
YOUTH CLU
INSTEAD... I DECIDED I WOULD.
I HEADED OUT, BARELY THINKING. I WAS SO...ANGRY. THAT WORD DOESN'T SEEM BIG ENOUGH.
ANGRY AT THEM. ANGRY AT MYSELF. AT HOW I'D FAILED...
MAYBE I JUST NEEDED TO TAKE IT OUT ON SOMEONE.
GET A THRILL OUT OF EASING MY OWN CONSCIENCE.
AND IT WENT BADLY. REALLY BADLY.

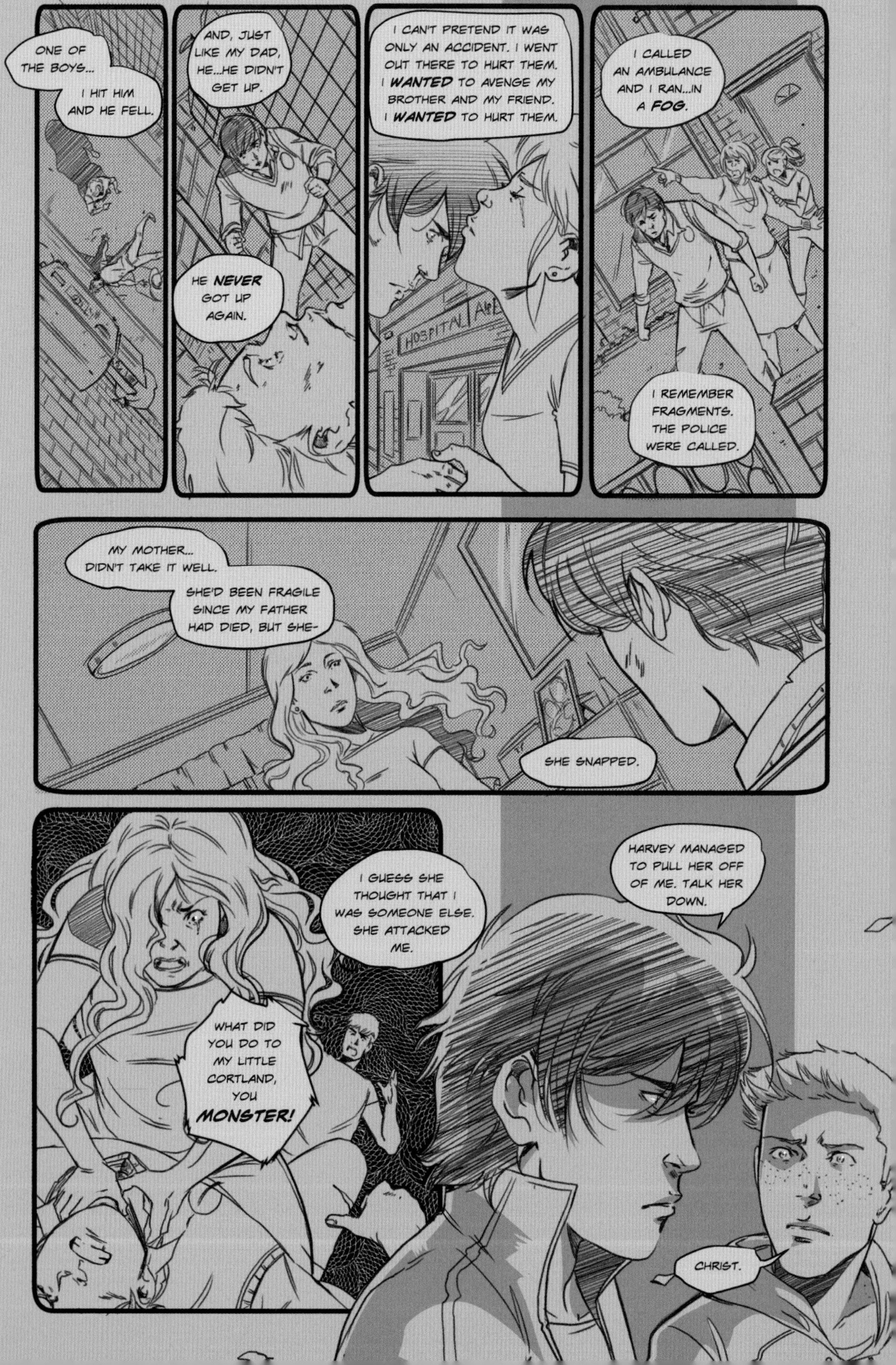
ONE OF THE BOYS...
I HIT HIM AND HE FELL.
AND, JUST LIKE MY DAD, HE...HE DIDN'T GET UP.
HE NEVER GOT UP AGAIN.
I CAN'T PRETEND IT WAS ONLY AN ACCIDENT. I WENT OUT THERE TO HURT THEM. I WANTED TO AVENGE MY BROTHER AND MY FRIEND. I WANTED TO HURT THEM.
HOSPITAL
I CALLED AN AMBULANCE AND I RAN...IN A FOG.
I REMEMBER FRAGMENTS. THE POLICE WERE CALLED.
MY MOTHER... DIDN'T TAKE IT WELL.
SHE'D BEEN FRAGILE SINCE MY FATHER HAD DIED, BUT SHE-
SHE SNAPPED.
I GUESS SHE THOUGHT THAT I WAS SOMEONE ELSE. SHE ATTACKED ME.
WHAT DID YOU DO TO MY LITTLE CORTLAND, YOU MONSTER!
HARVEY MANAGED TO PULL HER OFF OF ME. TALK HER DOWN.
CHRIST.

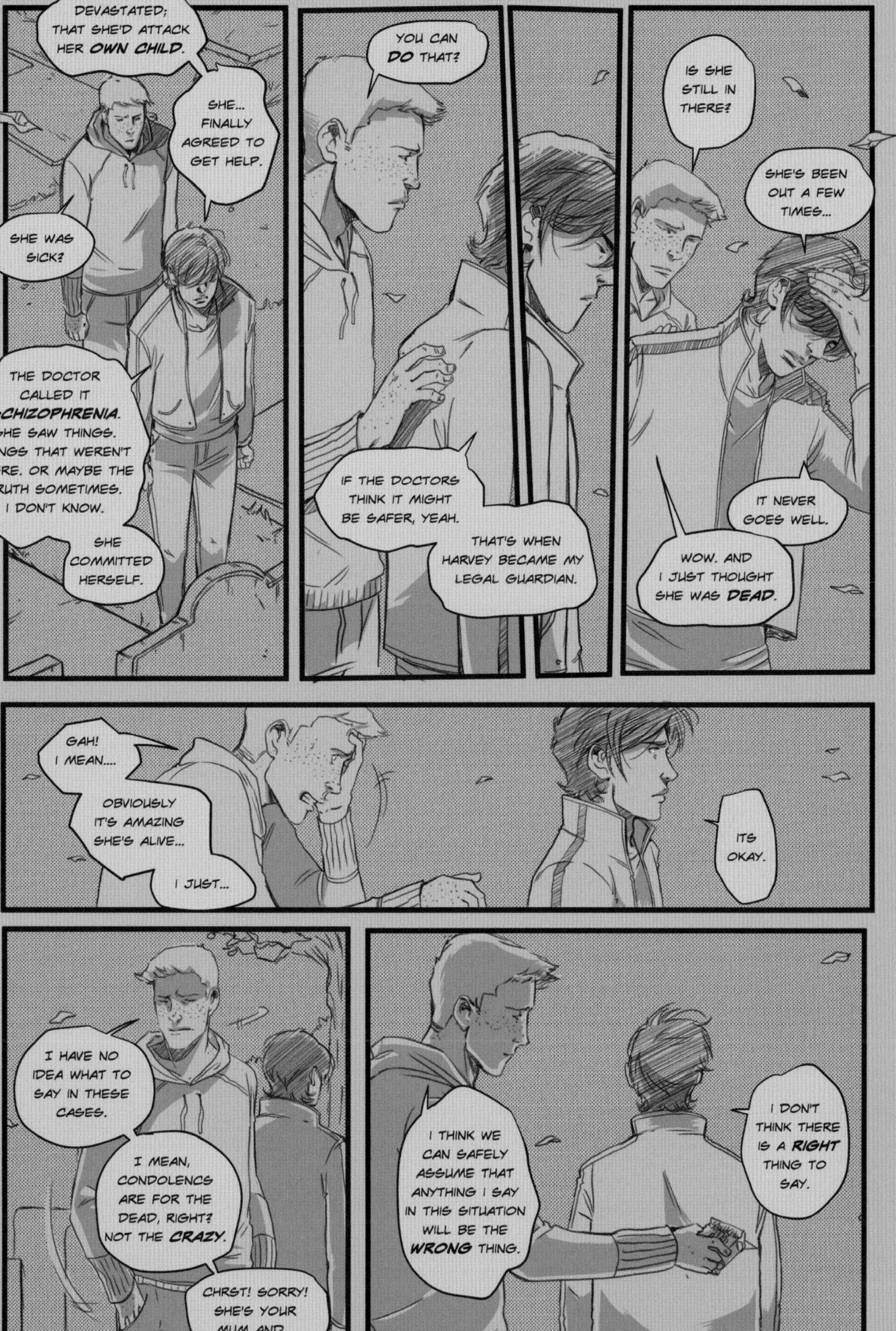
SHE WAS DEVASTATED; THAT SHE'D ATTACK HER OWN CHILD.
SHE... FINALLY AGREED TO GET HELP.
SHE WAS SICK?
THE DOCTOR CALLED IT SCHIZOPHRENIA. SHE SAW THINGS. THINGS THAT WEREN'T THERE. OR MAYBE THE TRUTH SOMETIMES. I DON'T KNOW.
SHE COMMITTED HERSELF.
YOU CAN DO THAT?
IF THE DOCTORS THINK IT MIGHT BE SAFER, YEAH.
THAT'S WHEN HARVEY BECAME MY LEGAL GUARDIAN.
IS SHE STILL IN THERE?
SHE'S BEEN OUT A FEW TIMES...
IT NEVER GOES WELL.
WOW. AND I JUST THOUGHT SHE WAS DEAD.
GAH! I MEAN....
OBVIOUSLY IT'S AMAZING SHE'S ALIVE...
I JUST...
ITS OKAY.
I HAVE NO IDEA WHAT TO SAY IN THESE CASES.
I MEAN, CONDOLENCS ARE FOR THE DEAD, RIGHT? NOT THE CRAZY.
CHRST! SORRY! SHE'S YOUR MUM AND...
I THINK WE CAN SAFELY ASSUME THAT ANYTHING I SAY IN THIS SITUATION WILL BE THE WRONG THING.
I DON'T THINK THERE IS A RIGHT THING TO SAY.

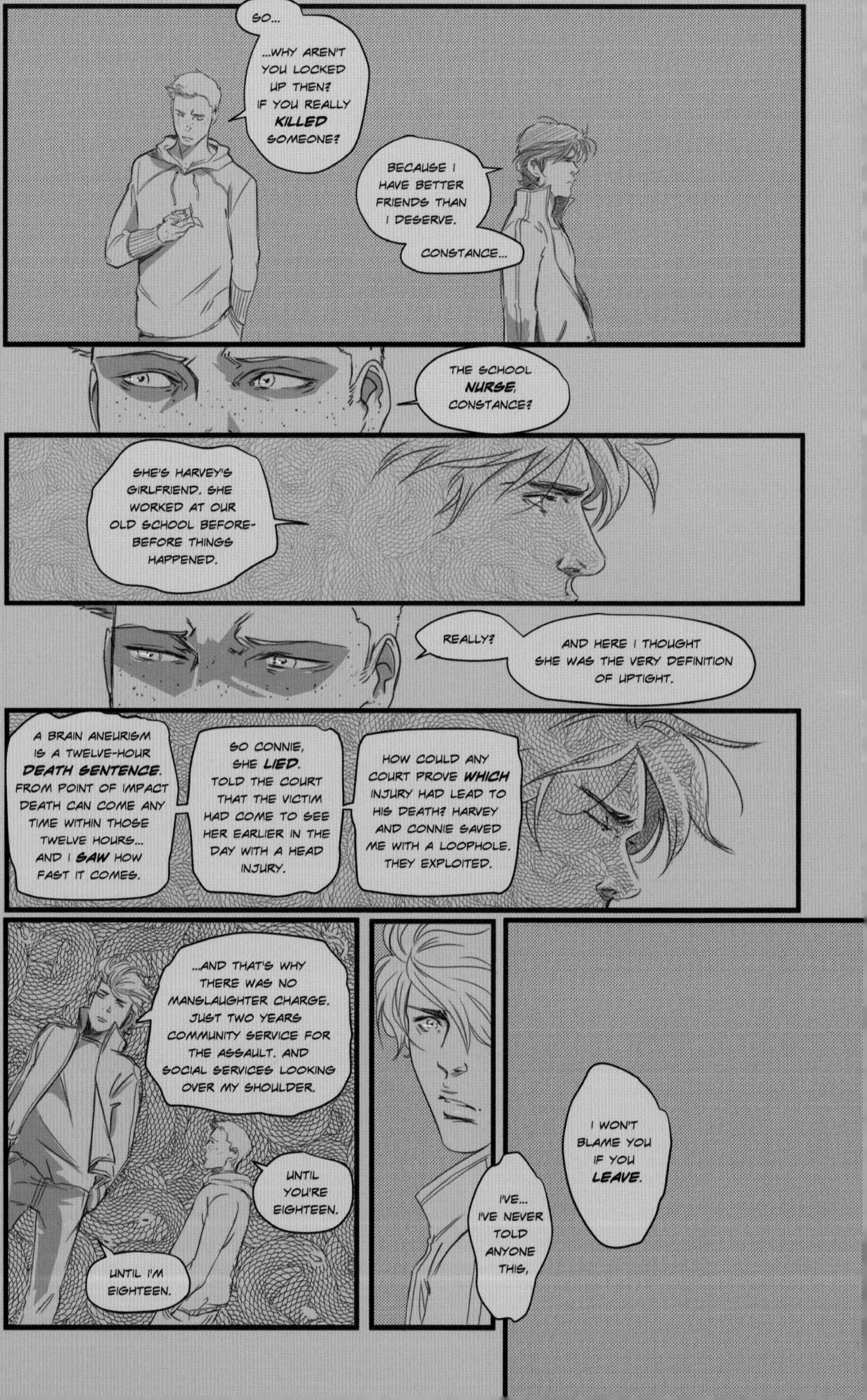
SO...
...WHY AREN'T YOU LOCKED UP THEN? IF YOU REALLY KILLED SOMEONE?
BECAUSE I HAVE BETTER FRIENDS THAN I DESERVE.
CONSTANCE...
THE SCHOOL NURSE, CONSTANCE?
SHE'S HARVEY'S GIRLFRIEND. SHE WORKED AT OUR OLD SCHOOL BEFORE- BEFORE THINGS HAPPENED.
REALLY?
AND HERE I THOUGHT SHE WAS THE VERY DEFINITION OF UPTIGHT.
A BRAIN ANEURISM IS A TWELVE-HOUR DEATH SENTENCE. FROM POINT OF IMPACT DEATH CAN COME ANY TIME WITHIN THOSE TWELVE HOURS... AND I SAW HOW FAST IT COMES.
SO CONNIE, SHE LIED. TOLD THE COURT THAT THE VICTIM HAD COME TO SEE HER EARLIER IN THE DAY WITH A HEAD INJURY.
HOW COULD ANY COURT PROVE WHICH INJURY HAD LEAD TO HIS DEATH? HARVEY AND CONNIE SAVED ME WITH A LOOPHOLE. THEY EXPLOITED.
...AND THAT'S WHY THERE WAS NO MANSLAUGHTER CHARGE. JUST TWO YEARS COMMUNITY SERVICE FOR THE ASSAULT. AND SOCIAL SERVICES LOOKING OVER MY SHOULDER.
UNTIL YOU'RE EIGHTEEN.
UNTIL I'M EIGHTEEN.
I'VE... I'VE NEVER TOLD ANYONE THIS,
I WON'T BLAME YOU IF YOU LEAVE.

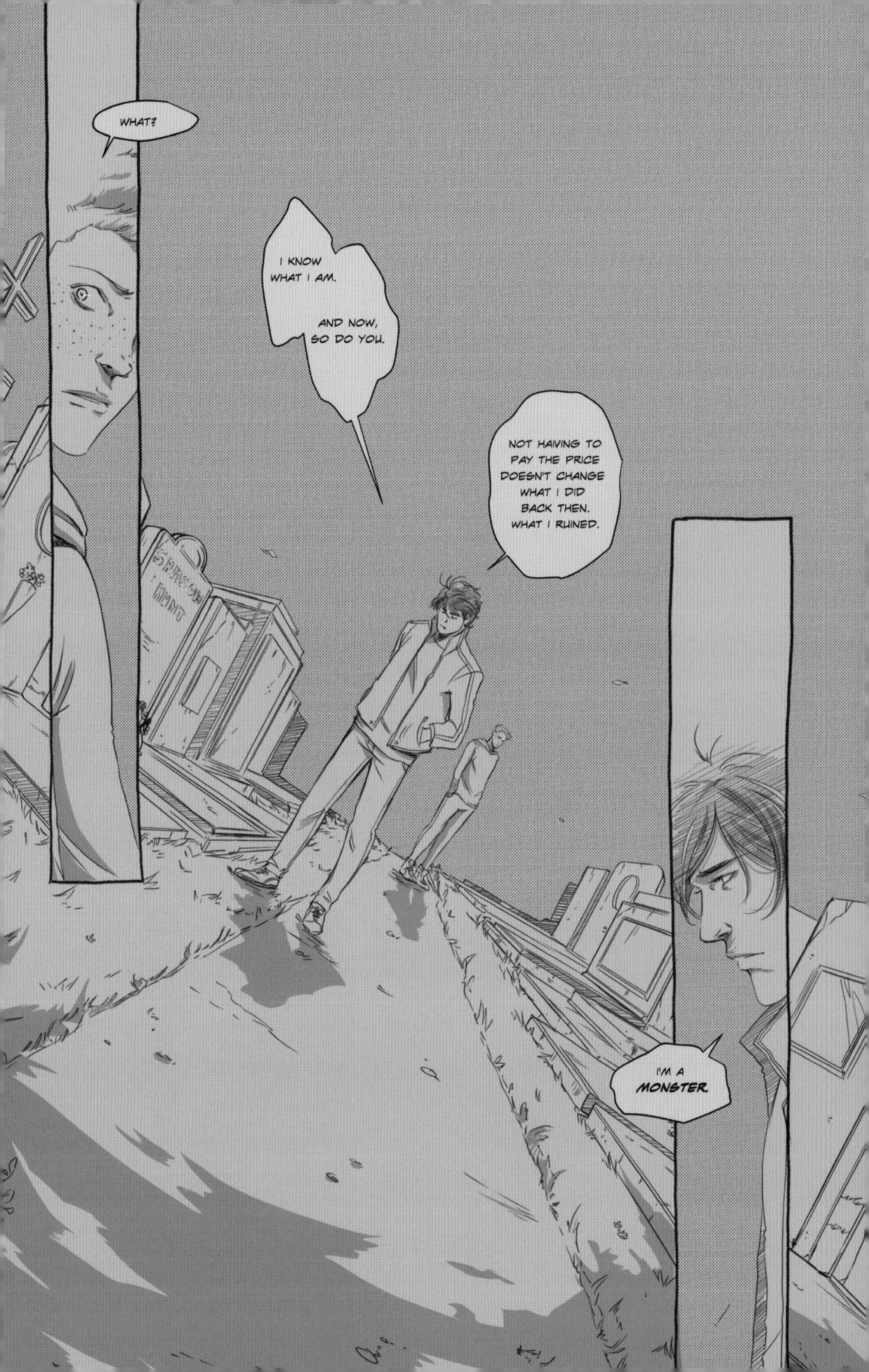
WHAT?
I KNOW WHAT I AM.
AND NOW, SO DO YOU.
NOT HAIVING TO PAY THE PRICE DOESN'T CHANGE WHAT I DID BACK THEN. WHAT I RUINED.
I'M A MONSTER.

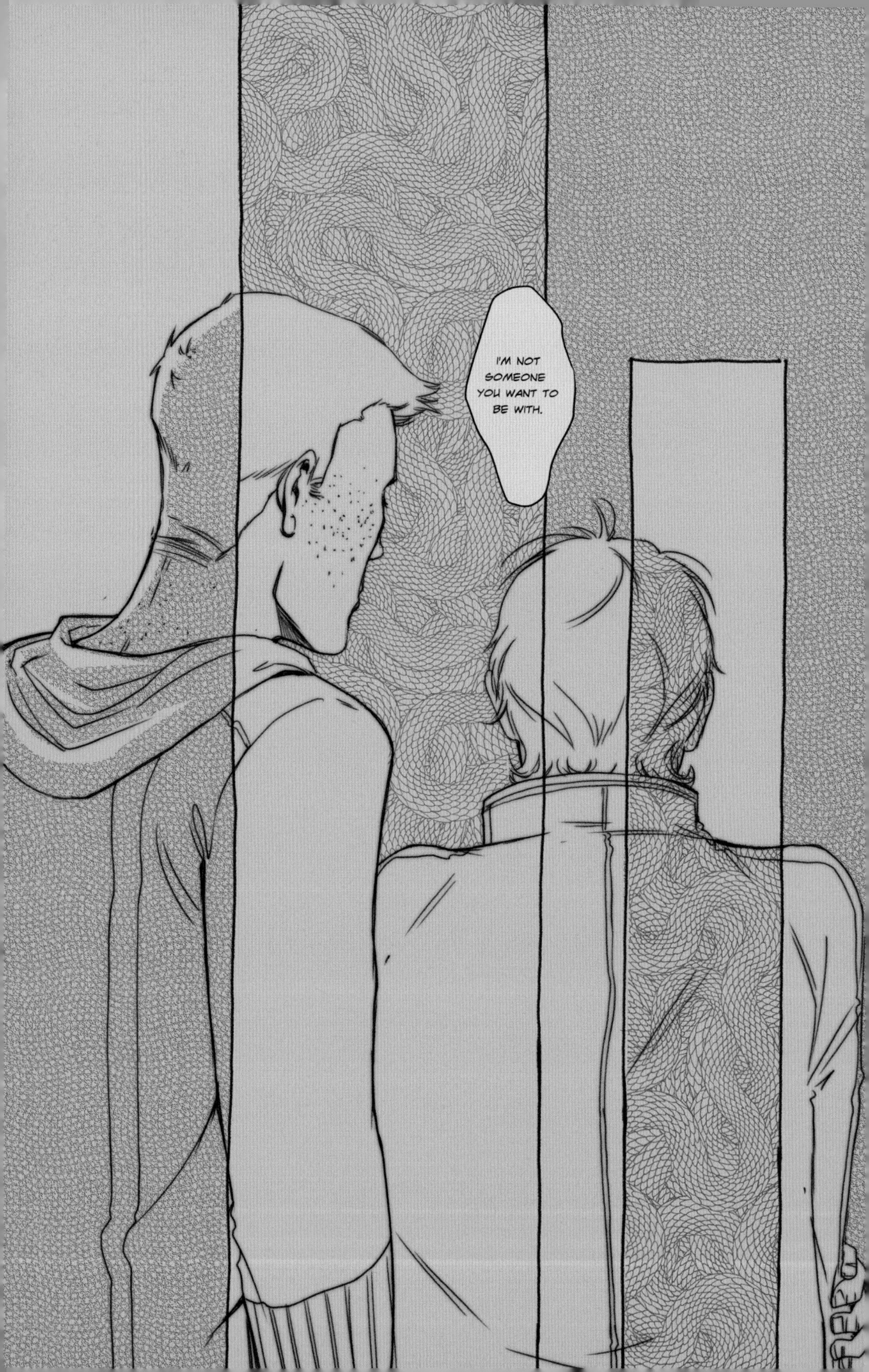
I'M NOT SOMEONE YOU WANT TO BE WITH.

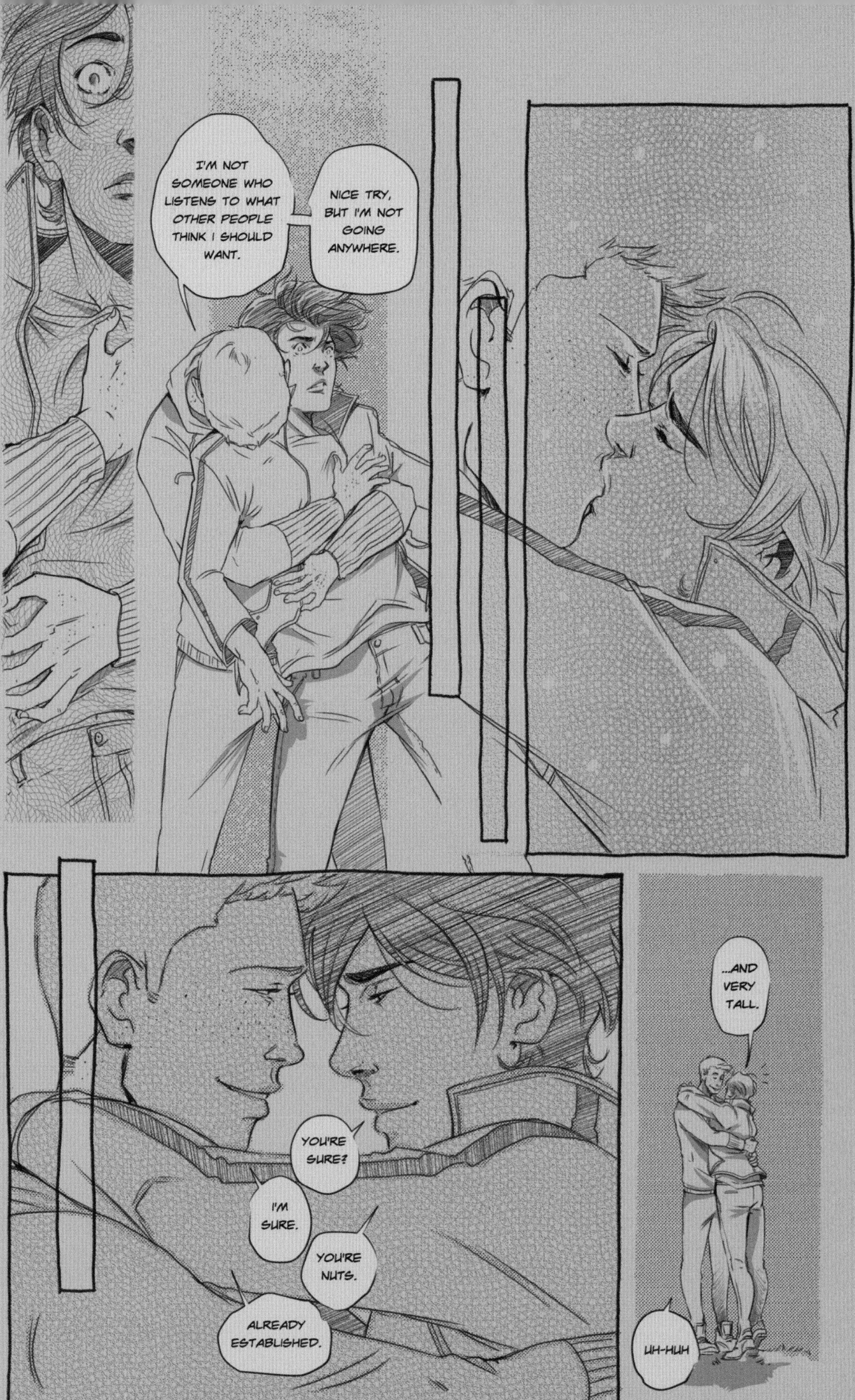
I'M NOT SOMEONE WHO LISTENS TO WHAT OTHER PEOPLE THINK I SHOULD WANT.
NICE TRY, BUT I'M NOT GOING ANYWHERE.
YOU'RE SURE?
I'M SURE.
YOU'RE NUTS.
ALREADY ESTABLISHED.
...AND VERY TALL.
UH-HUH

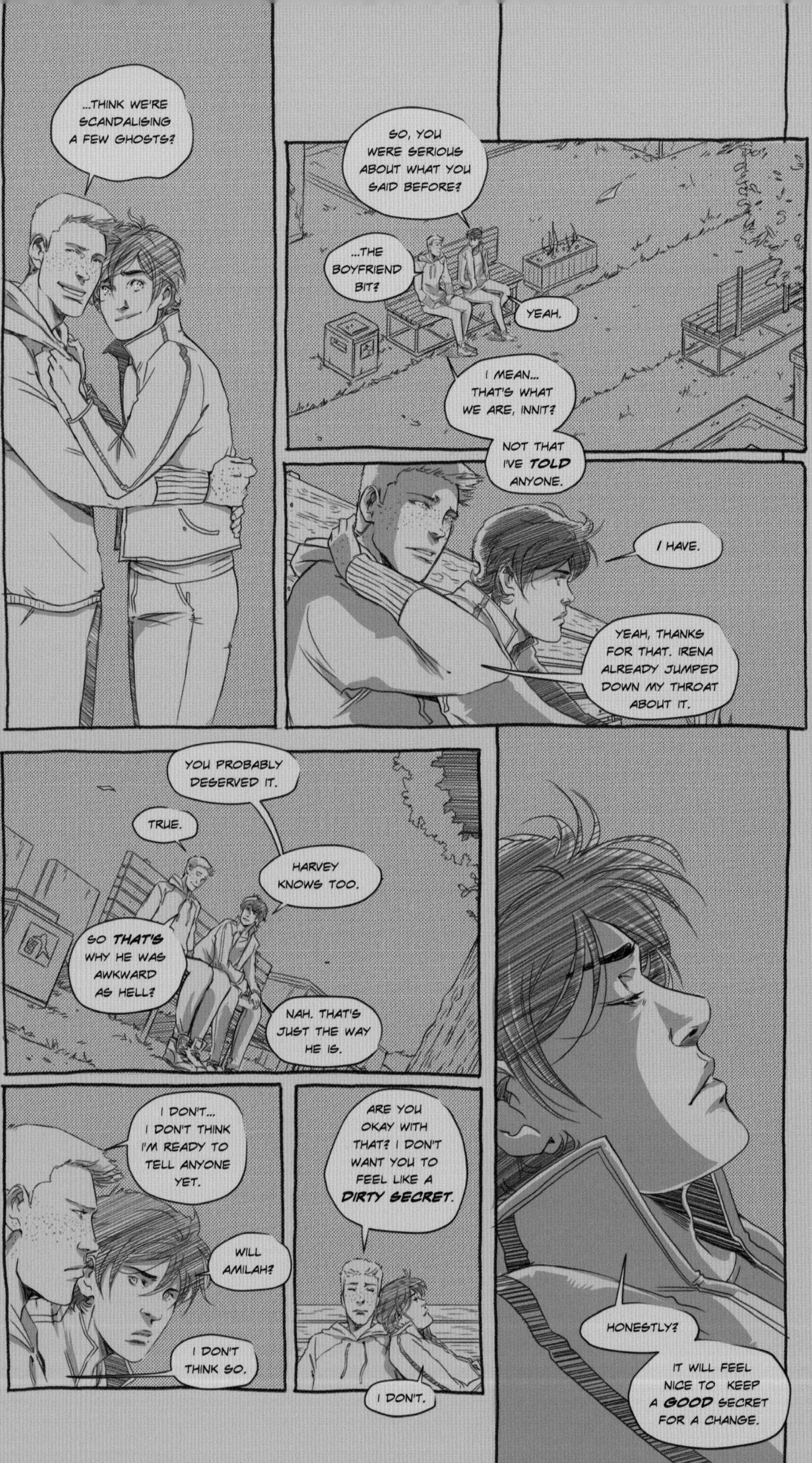
...THINK WE'RE SCANDALISING A FEW GHOSTS?
SO, YOU WERE SERIOUS ABOUT WHAT YOU SAID BEFORE?
...THE BOYFRIEND BIT?
YEAH.
I MEAN... THAT'S WHAT WE ARE, INNIT?
NOT THAT I'VE TOLD ANYONE.
I HAVE.
YEAH, THANKS FOR THAT. IRENA ALREADY JUMPED DOWN MY THROAT ABOUT IT.
YOU PROBABLY DESERVED IT.
TRUE.
HARVEY KNOWS TOO.
SO THAT'S WHY HE WAS AWKWARD AS HELL?
NAH. THAT'S JUST THE WAY HE IS.
I DON'T... I DON'T THINK I'M READY TO TELL ANYONE YET.
WILL AMILAH?
I DON'T THINK SO.
ARE YOU OKAY WITH THAT? I DON'T WANT YOU TO FEEL LIKE A DIRTY SECRET.
I DON'T.
HONESTLY?
IT WILL FEEL NICE TO KEEP A GOOD SECRET FOR A CHANGE.

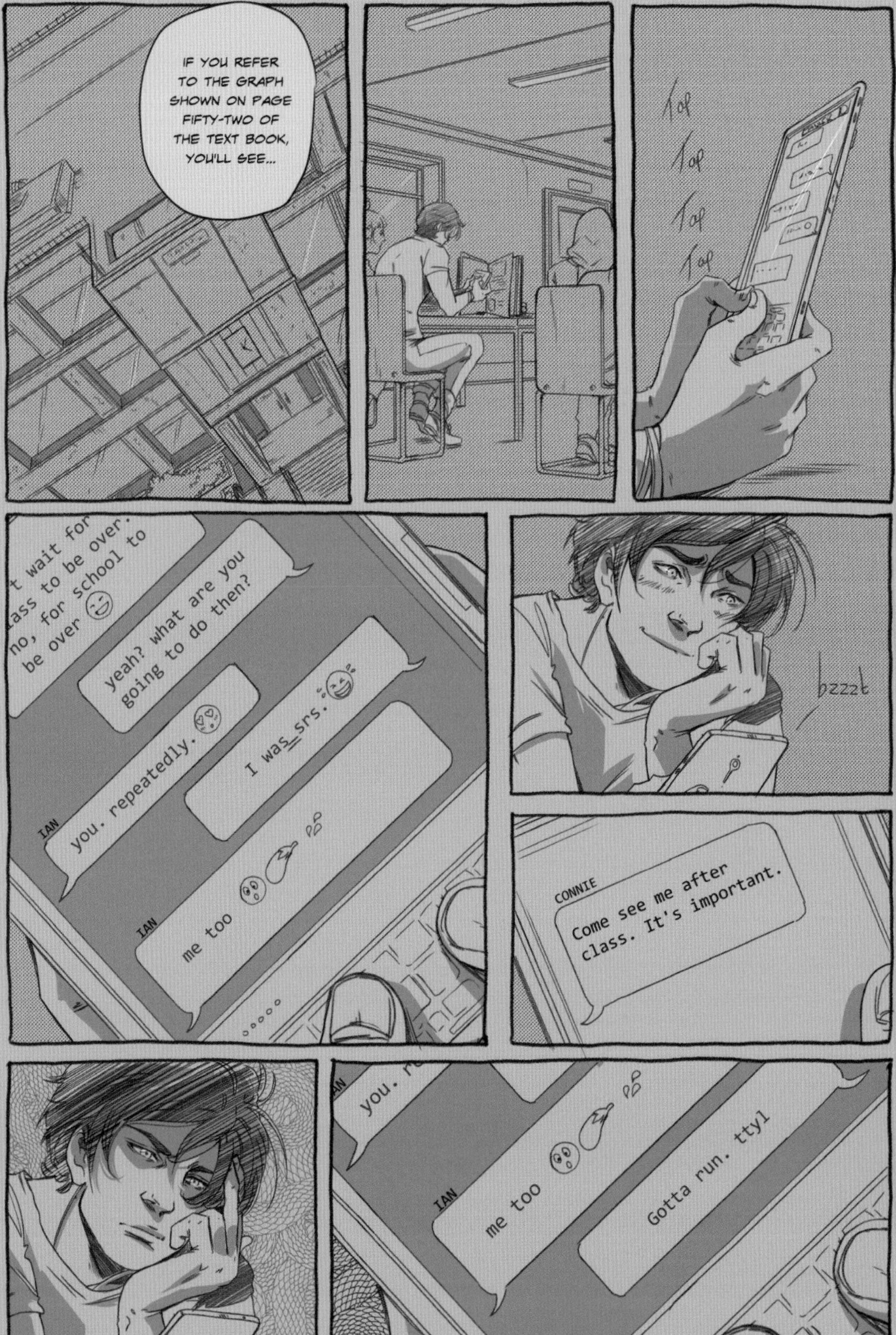
IF YOU REFER TO THE GRAPH SHOWN ON PAGE FIFTY-TWO OF THE TEXT BOOK, YOU'LL SEE...
Tap
Tap
Tap
Tap
t wait for
lass to be over.
no, for school to be over
yeah? what are you going to do then?
IAN
you. repeatedly.
I was srs.
IAN
me too
bzzzt
CONNIE
Come see me after class. It's important.
you. r
IAN
me too
Gotta run. ttyl

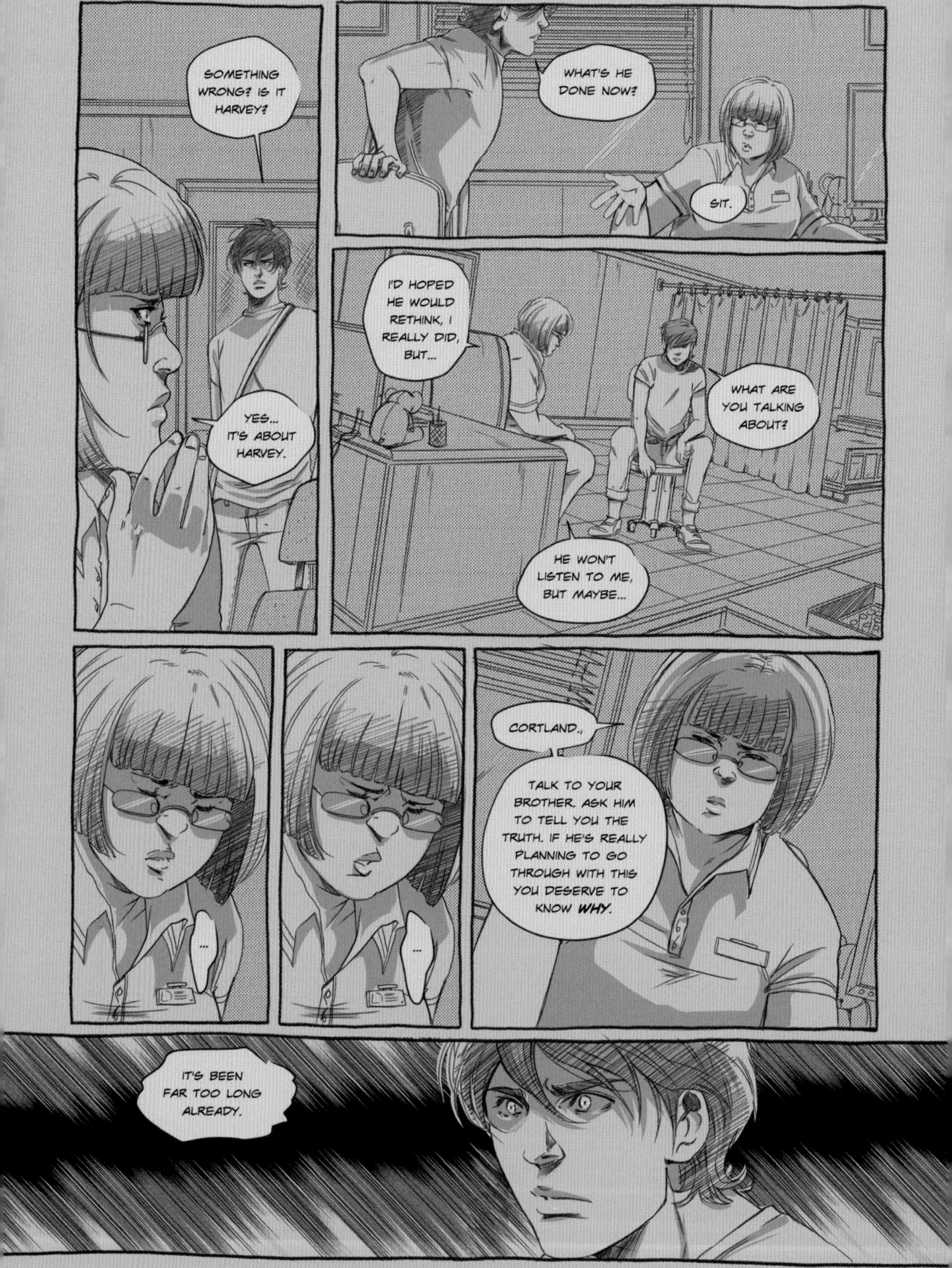
SOMETHING WRONG? IS IT HARVEY?
YES... IT'S ABOUT HARVEY.
WHAT'S HE DONE NOW?
SIT.
I'D HOPED HE WOULD RETHINK, I REALLY DID, BUT...
WHAT ARE YOU TALKING ABOUT?
HE WON'T LISTEN TO ME, BUT MAYBE...
...
...
CORTLAND..
TALK TO YOUR BROTHER. ASK HIM TO TELL YOU THE TRUTH. IF HE'S REALLY PLANNING TO GO THROUGH WITH THIS YOU DESERVE TO KNOW **WHY**.
IT'S BEEN FAR TOO LONG ALREADY.

ISSUE 11

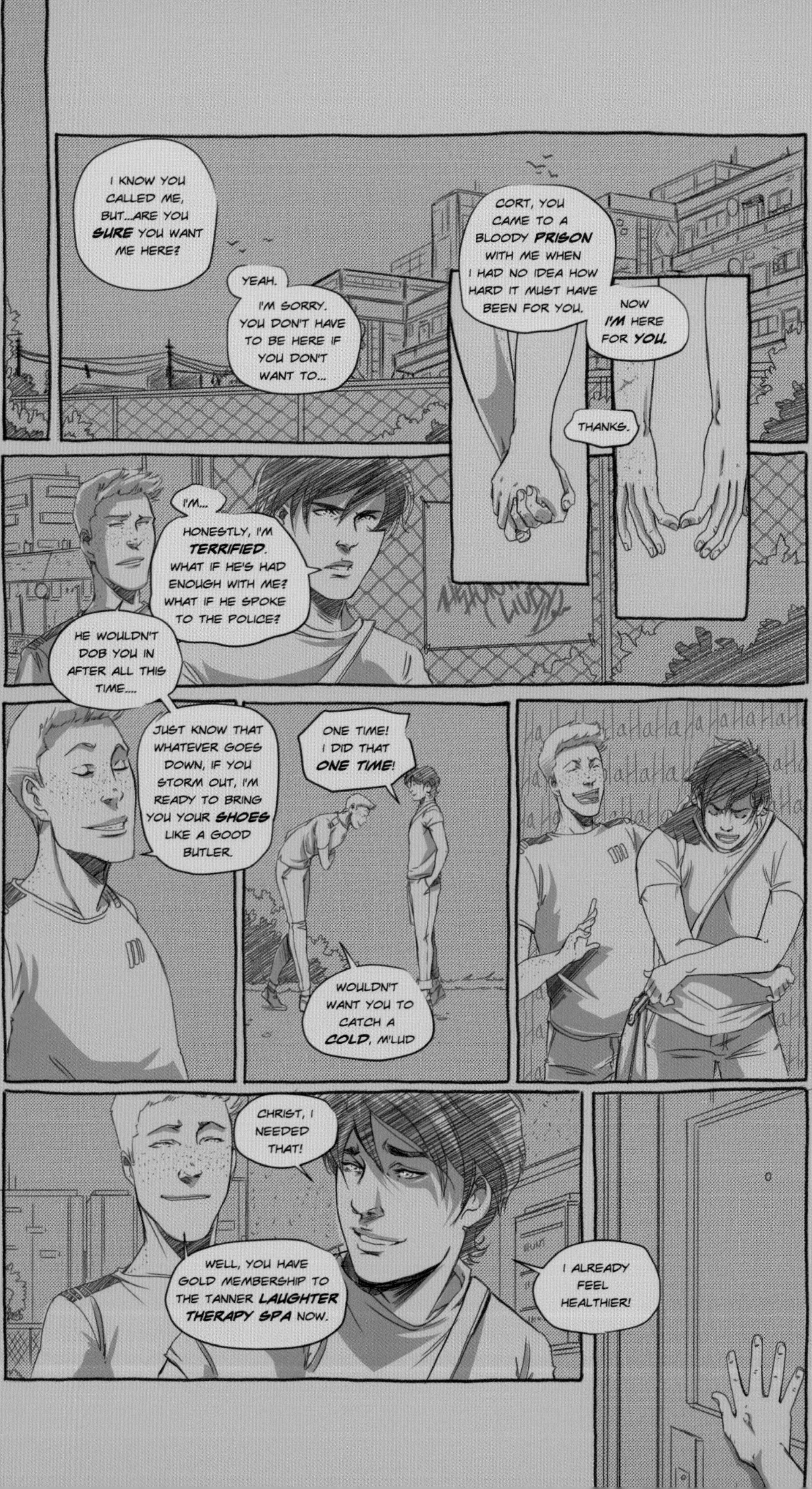
I KNOW YOU CALLED ME, BUT...ARE YOU SURE YOU WANT ME HERE?
YEAH.
I'M SORRY. YOU DON'T HAVE TO BE HERE IF YOU DON'T WANT TO...
CORT, YOU CAME TO A BLOODY PRISON WITH ME WHEN I HAD NO IDEA HOW HARD IT MUST HAVE BEEN FOR YOU.
NOW I'M HERE FOR YOU.
THANKS.
I'M...
HONESTLY, I'M TERRIFIED. WHAT IF HE'S HAD ENOUGH WITH ME? WHAT IF HE SPOKE TO THE POLICE?
HE WOULDN'T DOB YOU IN AFTER ALL THIS TIME...
JUST KNOW THAT WHATEVER GOES DOWN, IF YOU STORM OUT, I'M READY TO BRING YOU YOUR SHOES LIKE A GOOD BUTLER.
ONE TIME! I DID THAT ONE TIME!
WOULDN'T WANT YOU TO CATCH A COLD, M'LUD
CHRIST, I NEEDED THAT!
WELL, YOU HAVE GOLD MEMBERSHIP TO THE TANNER LAUGHTER THERAPY SPA NOW.
I ALREADY FEEL HEALTHIER!

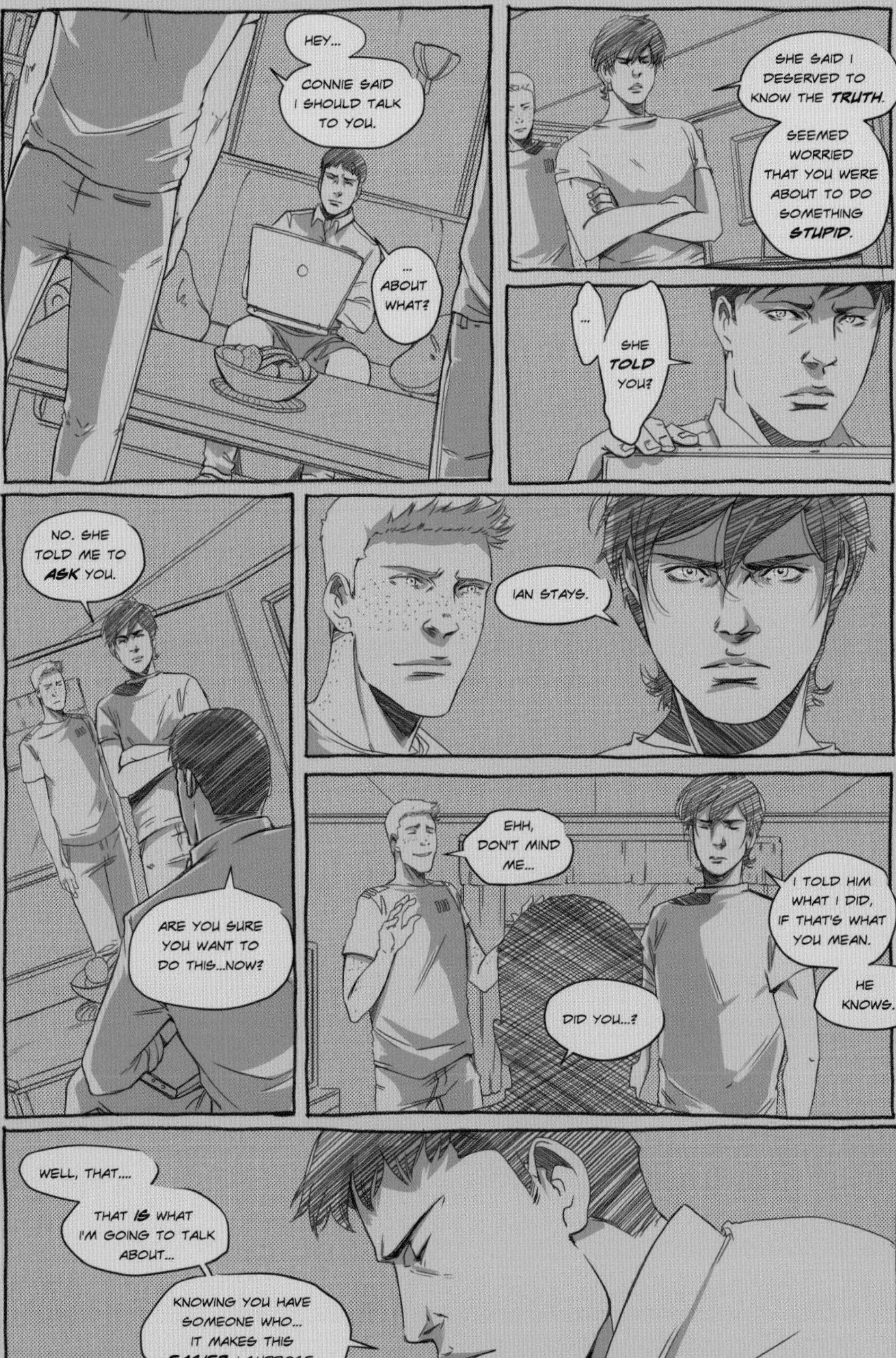
HEY...
CONNIE SAID I SHOULD TALK TO YOU.
... ABOUT WHAT?
SHE SAID I DESERVED TO KNOW THE TRUTH.
SEEMED WORRIED THAT YOU WERE ABOUT TO DO SOMETHING STUPID.
...
SHE TOLD YOU?
NO. SHE TOLD ME TO ASK YOU.
ARE YOU SURE YOU WANT TO DO THIS...NOW?
IAN STAYS.
EHH, DON'T MIND ME...
DID YOU...?
I TOLD HIM WHAT I DID, IF THAT'S WHAT YOU MEAN.
HE KNOWS.
WELL, THAT....
THAT IS WHAT I'M GOING TO TALK ABOUT...
KNOWING YOU HAVE SOMEONE WHO... IT MAKES THIS EASIER, I SUPPOSE.

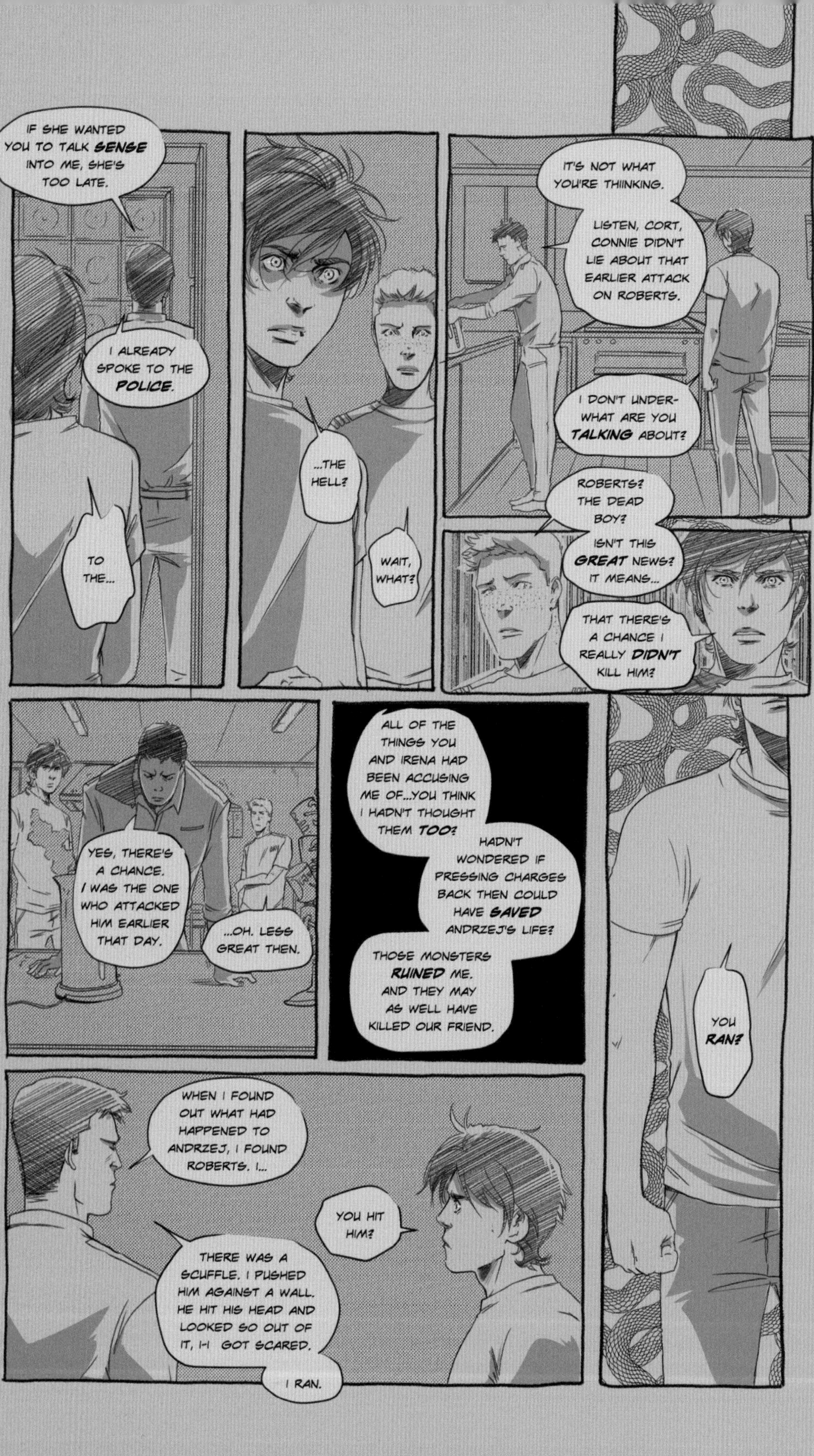
IF SHE WANTED YOU TO TALK SENSE INTO ME, SHE'S TOO LATE.
I ALREADY SPOKE TO THE POLICE.
TO THE...
...THE HELL?
WAIT, WHAT?
IT'S NOT WHAT YOU'RE THIINKING.
LISTEN, CORT, CONNIE DIDN'T LIE ABOUT THAT EARLIER ATTACK ON ROBERTS.
I DON'T UNDER- WHAT ARE YOU TALKING ABOUT?
ROBERTS? THE DEAD BOY?
ISN'T THIS GREAT NEWS? IT MEANS...
THAT THERE'S A CHANCE I REALLY DIDN'T KILL HIM?
YES, THERE'S A CHANCE. I WAS THE ONE WHO ATTACKED HIM EARLIER THAT DAY.
...OH. LESS GREAT THEN.
ALL OF THE THINGS YOU AND IRENA HAD BEEN ACCUSING ME OF...YOU THINK I HADN'T THOUGHT THEM TOO?
HADN'T WONDERED IF PRESSING CHARGES BACK THEN COULD HAVE SAVED ANDRZEJ'S LIFE?
THOSE MONSTERS RUINED ME. AND THEY MAY AS WELL HAVE KILLED OUR FRIEND.
WHEN I FOUND OUT WHAT HAD HAPPENED TO ANDRZEJ, I FOUND ROBERTS. I...
YOU HIT HIM?
THERE WAS A SCUFFLE. I PUSHED HIM AGAINST A WALL. HE HIT HIS HEAD AND LOOKED SO OUT OF IT, I-I GOT SCARED.
I RAN.
YOU RAN?

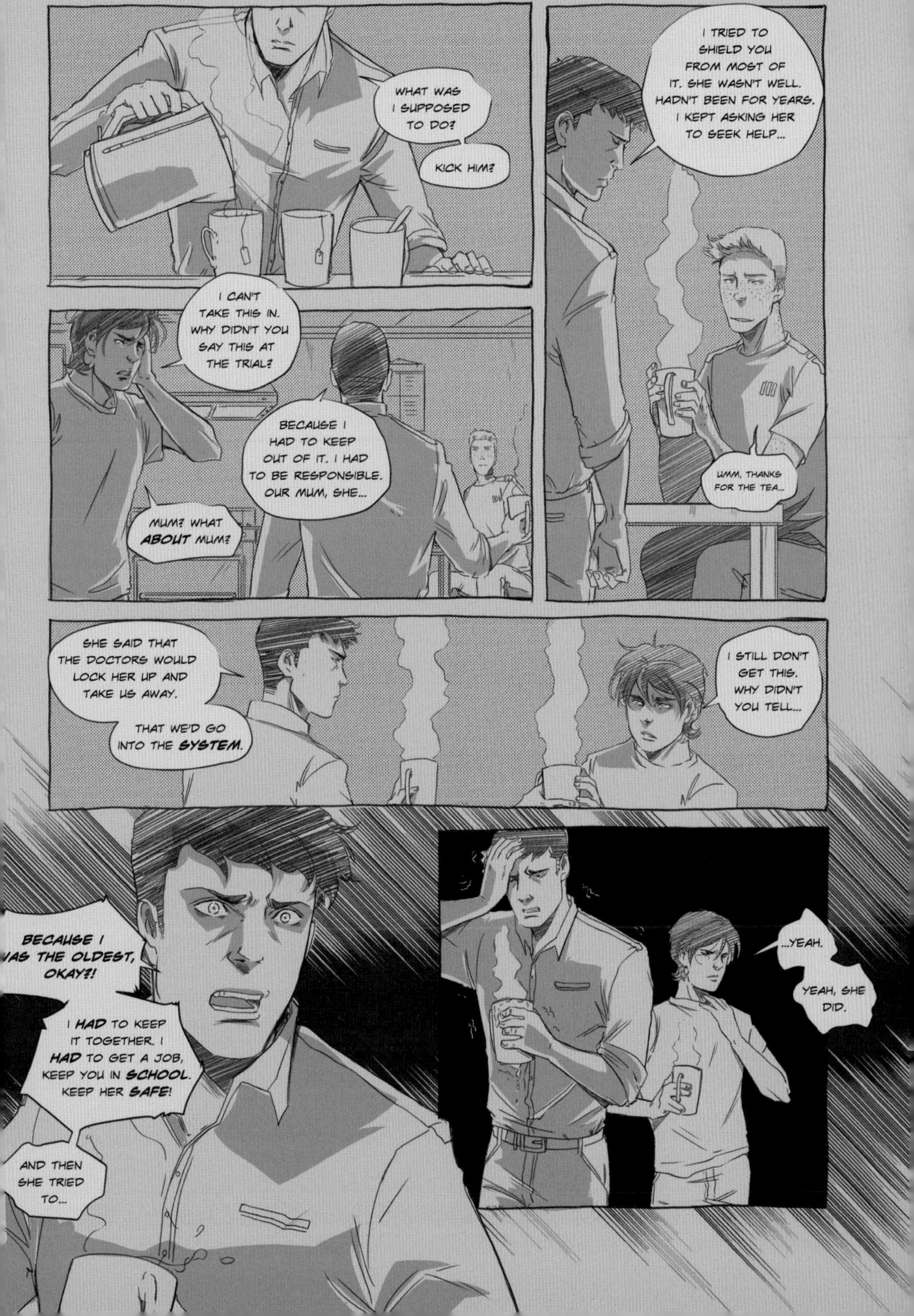
WHAT WAS I SUPPOSED TO DO?
KICK HIM?
I TRIED TO SHIELD YOU FROM MOST OF IT. SHE WASN'T WELL. HADN'T BEEN FOR YEARS. I KEPT ASKING HER TO SEEK HELP...
I CAN'T TAKE THIS IN. WHY DIDN'T YOU SAY THIS AT THE TRIAL?
BECAUSE I HAD TO KEEP OUT OF IT. I HAD TO BE RESPONSIBLE. OUR MUM, SHE...
MUM? WHAT ABOUT MUM?
UMM, THANKS FOR THE TEA...
SHE SAID THAT THE DOCTORS WOULD LOCK HER UP AND TAKE US AWAY.
THAT WE'D GO INTO THE SYSTEM.
I STILL DON'T GET THIS. WHY DIDN'T YOU TELL...
BECAUSE I WAS THE OLDEST, OKAY?!
I HAD TO KEEP IT TOGETHER. I HAD TO GET A JOB, KEEP YOU IN SCHOOL. KEEP HER SAFE!
AND THEN SHE TRIED TO...
...YEAH.
YEAH, SHE DID.

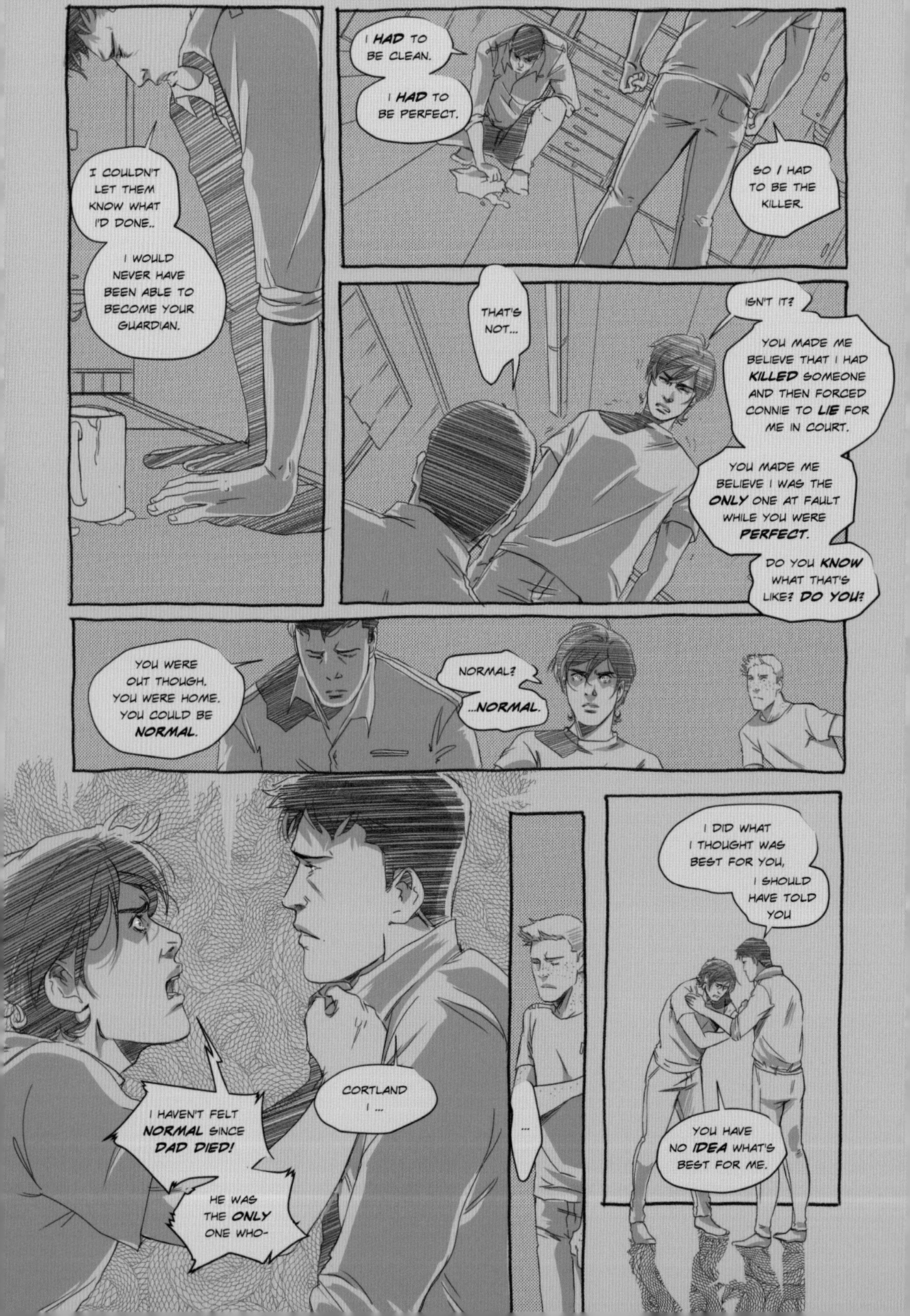
I COULDN'T LET THEM KNOW WHAT I'D DONE..
I WOULD NEVER HAVE BEEN ABLE TO BECOME YOUR GUARDIAN.
I HAD TO BE CLEAN.
I HAD TO BE PERFECT.
SO I HAD TO BE THE KILLER.
THAT'S NOT...
ISN'T IT?
YOU MADE ME BELIEVE THAT I HAD KILLED SOMEONE AND THEN FORCED CONNIE TO LIE FOR ME IN COURT.
YOU MADE ME BELIEVE I WAS THE ONLY ONE AT FAULT WHILE YOU WERE PERFECT.
DO YOU KNOW WHAT THAT'S LIKE? DO YOU?
YOU WERE OUT THOUGH. YOU WERE HOME. YOU COULD BE NORMAL.
NORMAL?
...NORMAL.
I HAVEN'T FELT NORMAL SINCE DAD DIED!
HE WAS THE ONLY ONE WHO-
CORTLAND I ...
...
I DID WHAT I THOUGHT WAS BEST FOR YOU, I SHOULD HAVE TOLD YOU
YOU HAVE NO IDEA WHAT'S BEST FOR ME.

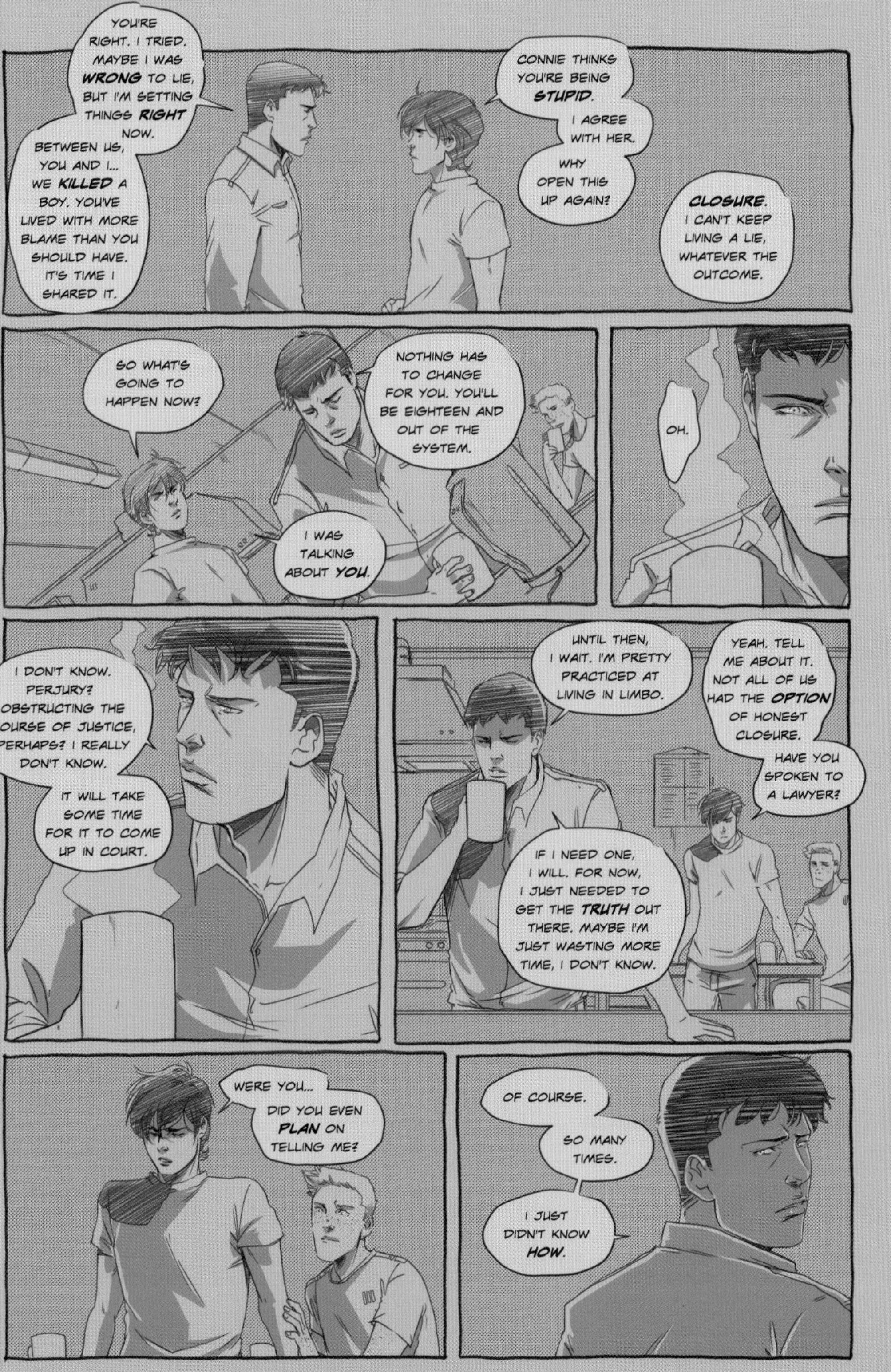
YOU'RE RIGHT. I TRIED. MAYBE I WAS WRONG TO LIE, BUT I'M SETTING THINGS RIGHT NOW.
BETWEEN US, YOU AND I... WE KILLED A BOY. YOU'VE LIVED WITH MORE BLAME THAN YOU SHOULD HAVE. IT'S TIME I SHARED IT.
CONNIE THINKS YOU'RE BEING STUPID.
I AGREE WITH HER.
WHY OPEN THIS UP AGAIN?
CLOSURE. I CAN'T KEEP LIVING A LIE, WHATEVER THE OUTCOME.
SO WHAT'S GOING TO HAPPEN NOW?
NOTHING HAS TO CHANGE FOR YOU. YOU'LL BE EIGHTEEN AND OUT OF THE SYSTEM.
I WAS TALKING ABOUT YOU.
OH.
I DON'T KNOW. PERJURY? OBSTRUCTING THE COURSE OF JUSTICE, PERHAPS? I REALLY DON'T KNOW.
IT WILL TAKE SOME TIME FOR IT TO COME UP IN COURT.
UNTIL THEN, I WAIT. I'M PRETTY PRACTICED AT LIVING IN LIMBO.
YEAH. TELL ME ABOUT IT. NOT ALL OF US HAD THE OPTION OF HONEST CLOSURE.
HAVE YOU SPOKEN TO A LAWYER?
IF I NEED ONE, I WILL. FOR NOW, I JUST NEEDED TO GET THE TRUTH OUT THERE. MAYBE I'M JUST WASTING MORE TIME, I DON'T KNOW.
WERE YOU...
DID YOU EVEN PLAN ON TELLING ME?
OF COURSE.
SO MANY TIMES.
I JUST DIDN'T KNOW HOW.

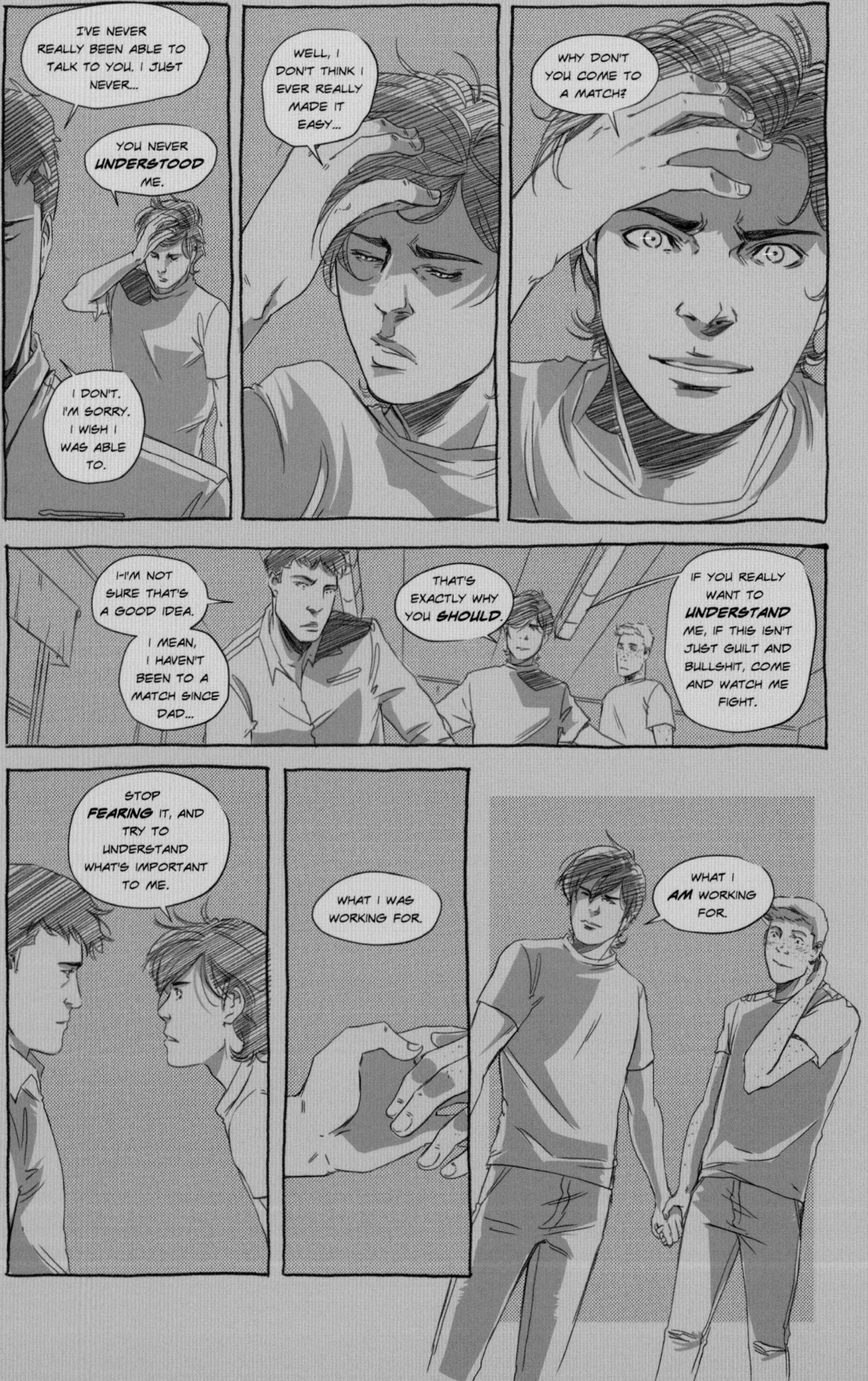
I'VE NEVER REALLY BEEN ABLE TO TALK TO YOU. I JUST NEVER...
YOU NEVER UNDERSTOOD ME.
I DON'T. I'M SORRY. I WISH I WAS ABLE TO.
WELL, I DON'T THINK I EVER REALLY MADE IT EASY...
WHY DON'T YOU COME TO A MATCH?
I-I'M NOT SURE THAT'S A GOOD IDEA.
I MEAN, I HAVEN'T BEEN TO A MATCH SINCE DAD...
THAT'S EXACTLY WHY YOU SHOULD.
IF YOU REALLY WANT TO UNDERSTAND ME, IF THIS ISN'T JUST GUILT AND BULLSHIT, COME AND WATCH ME FIGHT.
STOP FEARING IT, AND TRY TO UNDERSTAND WHAT'S IMPORTANT TO ME.
WHAT I WAS WORKING FOR.
WHAT I AM WORKING FOR.

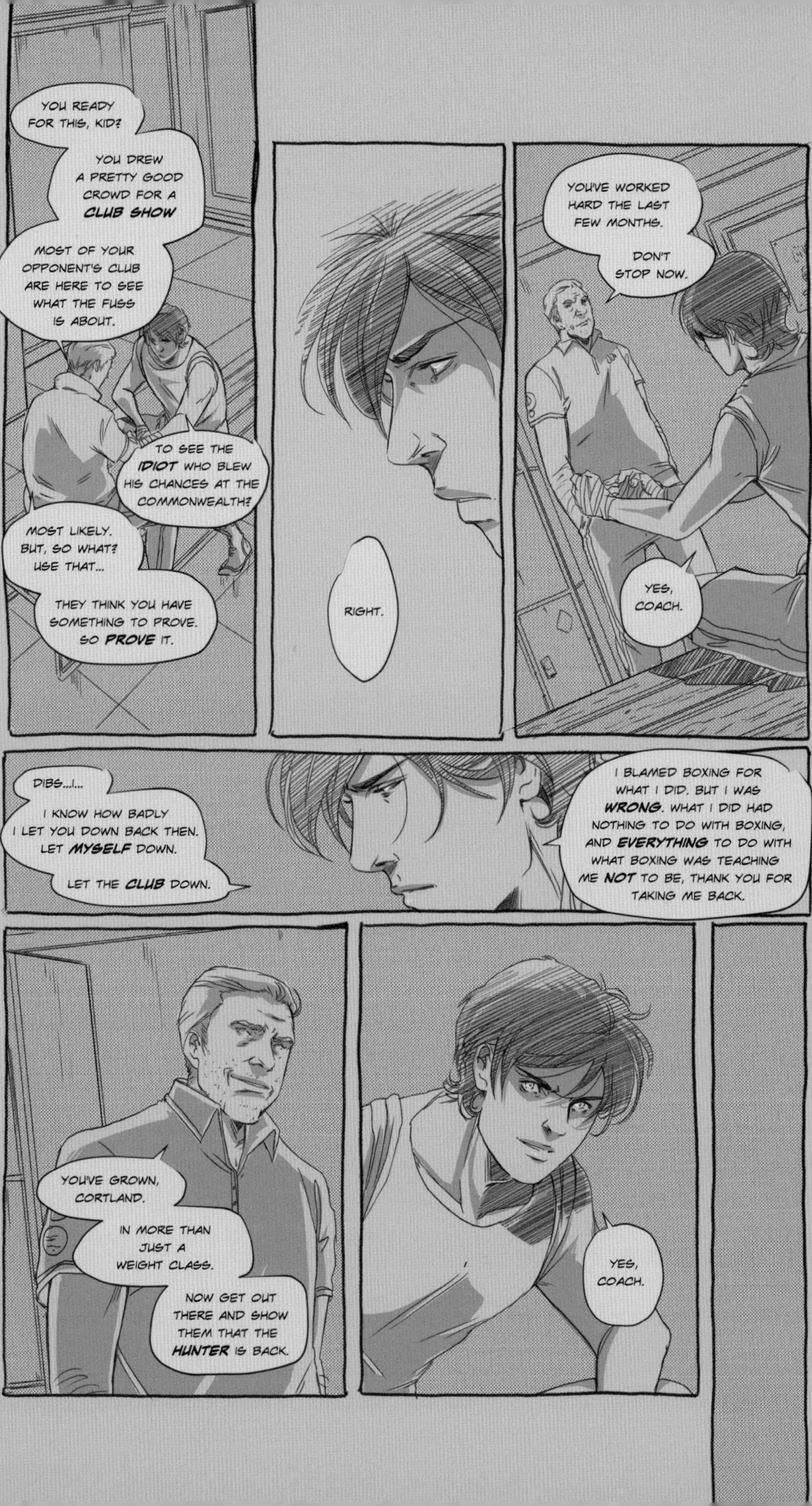
YOU READY FOR THIS, KID?
YOU DREW A PRETTY GOOD CROWD FOR A CLUB SHOW
MOST OF YOUR OPPONENT'S CLUB ARE HERE TO SEE WHAT THE FUSS IS ABOUT.
TO SEE THE IDIOT WHO BLEW HIS CHANCES AT THE COMMONWEALTH?
MOST LIKELY. BUT, SO WHAT? USE THAT...
THEY THINK YOU HAVE SOMETHING TO PROVE. SO PROVE IT.
RIGHT.
YOU'VE WORKED HARD THE LAST FEW MONTHS.
DON'T STOP NOW.
YES, COACH.
DIBS...I...
I KNOW HOW BADLY I LET YOU DOWN BACK THEN. LET MYSELF DOWN.
LET THE CLUB DOWN.
I BLAMED BOXING FOR WHAT I DID. BUT I WAS WRONG. WHAT I DID HAD NOTHING TO DO WITH BOXING, AND EVERYTHING TO DO WITH WHAT BOXING WAS TEACHING ME NOT TO BE, THANK YOU FOR TAKING ME BACK.
YOU'VE GROWN, CORTLAND.
IN MORE THAN JUST A WEIGHT CLASS.
NOW GET OUT THERE AND SHOW THEM THAT THE HUNTER IS BACK.
YES, COACH.

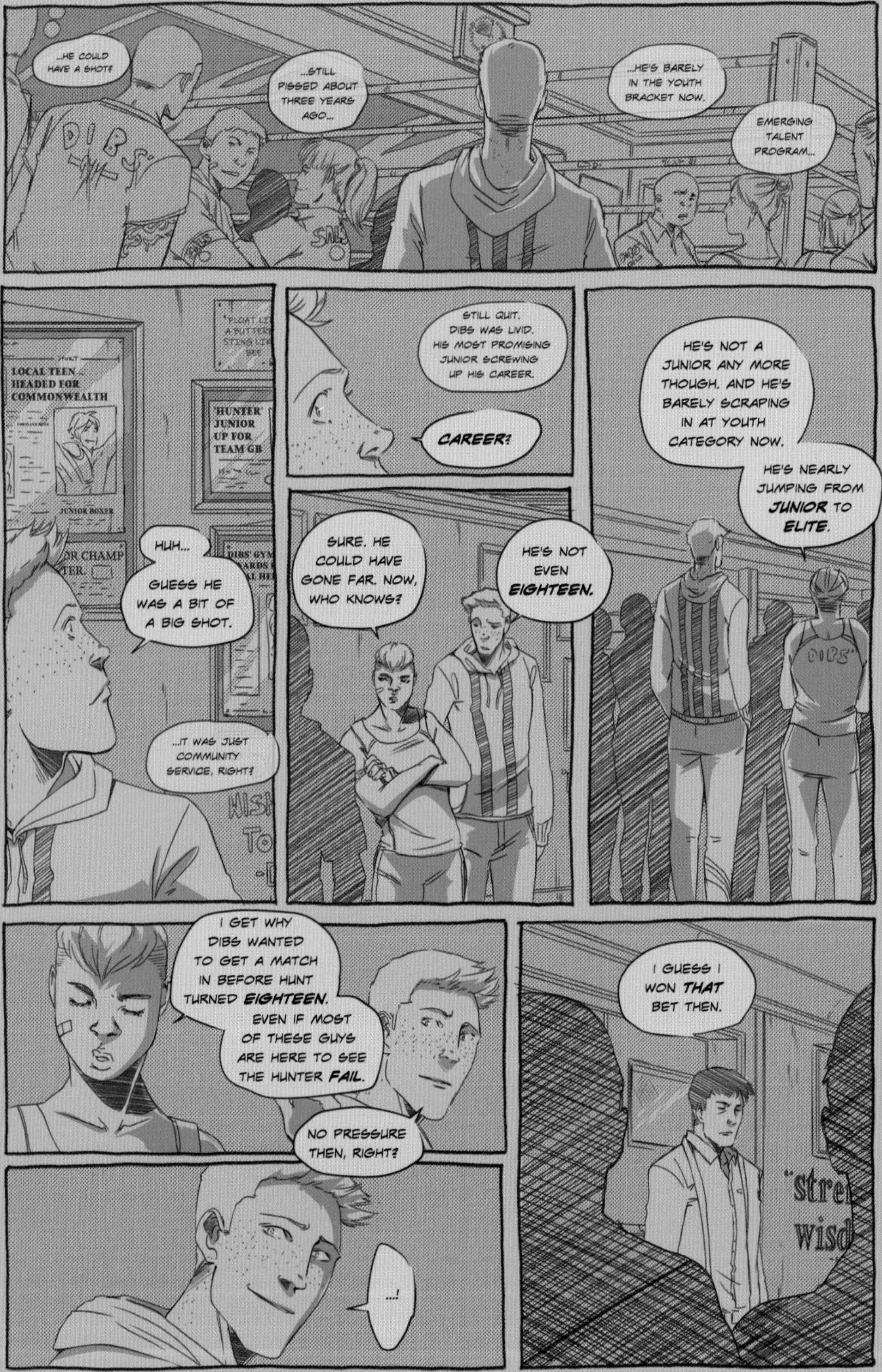
...HE COULD HAVE A SHOT?
...STILL PISSED ABOUT THREE YEARS AGO...
...HE'S BARELY IN THE YOUTH BRACKET NOW.
EMERGING TALENT PROGRAM...
LOCAL TEEN HEADED FOR COMMONWEALTH
'HUNTER' JUNIOR UP FOR TEAM GB
HUH...
GUESS HE WAS A BIT OF A BIG SHOT.
...IT WAS JUST COMMUNITY SERVICE, RIGHT?
STILL QUIT. DIBS WAS LIVID. HIS MOST PROMISING JUNIOR SCREWING UP HIS CAREER.
CAREER?
SURE. HE COULD HAVE GONE FAR. NOW, WHO KNOWS?
HE'S NOT EVEN EIGHTEEN.
HE'S NOT A JUNIOR ANY MORE THOUGH. AND HE'S BARELY SCRAPING IN AT YOUTH CATEGORY NOW.
HE'S NEARLY JUMPING FROM JUNIOR TO ELITE.
I GET WHY DIBS WANTED TO GET A MATCH IN BEFORE HUNT TURNED EIGHTEEN.
EVEN IF MOST OF THESE GUYS ARE HERE TO SEE THE HUNTER FAIL.
NO PRESSURE THEN, RIGHT?
...!
I GUESS I WON THAT BET THEN.

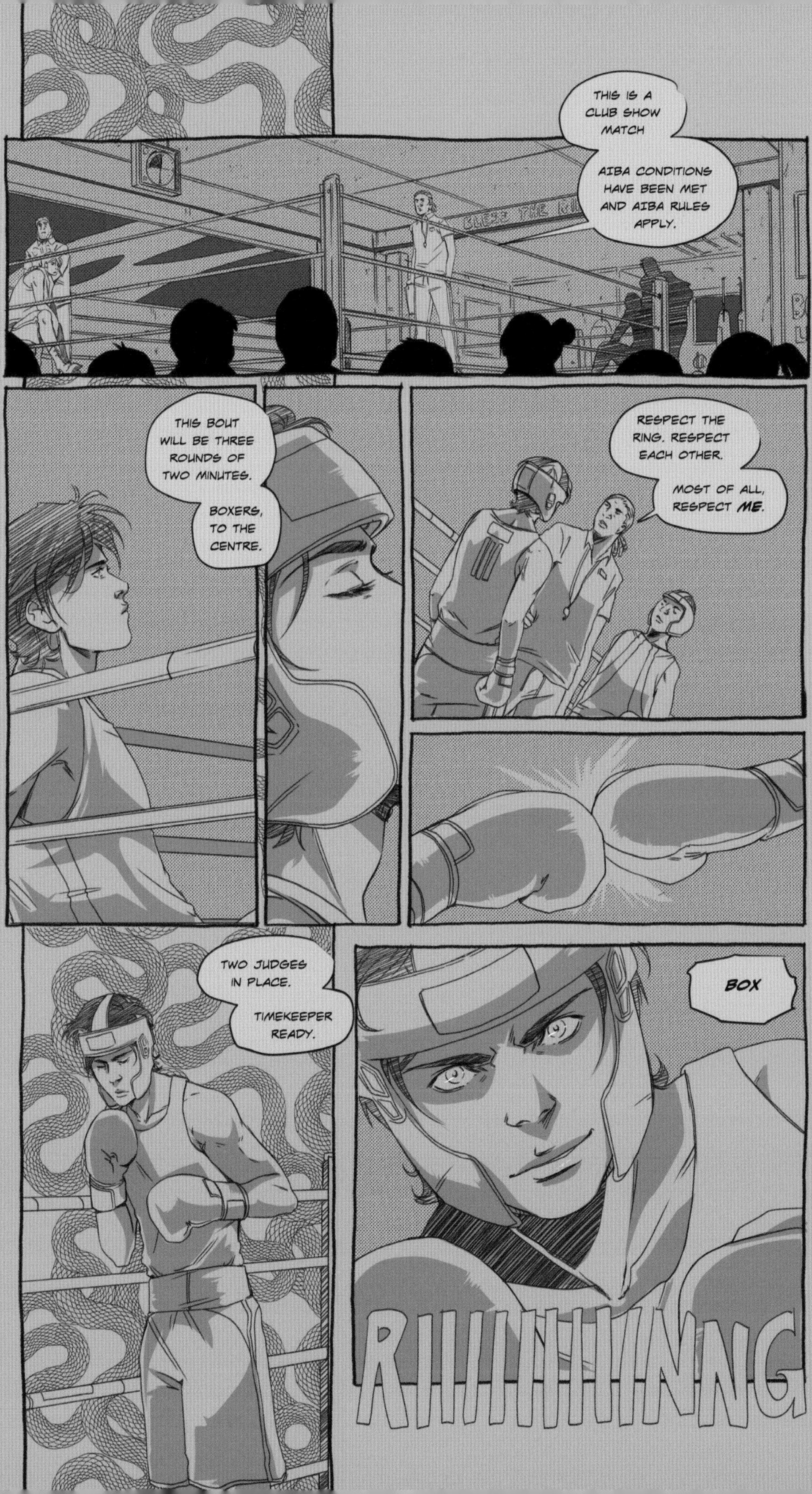
THIS IS A CLUB SHOW MATCH
AIBA CONDITIONS HAVE BEEN MET AND AIBA RULES APPLY.
THIS BOUT WILL BE THREE ROUNDS OF TWO MINUTES.
BOXERS, TO THE CENTRE.
RESPECT THE RING. RESPECT EACH OTHER.
MOST OF ALL, RESPECT ***ME***.
TWO JUDGES IN PLACE.
TIMEKEEPER READY.
BOX
RIIIIIIIINNG

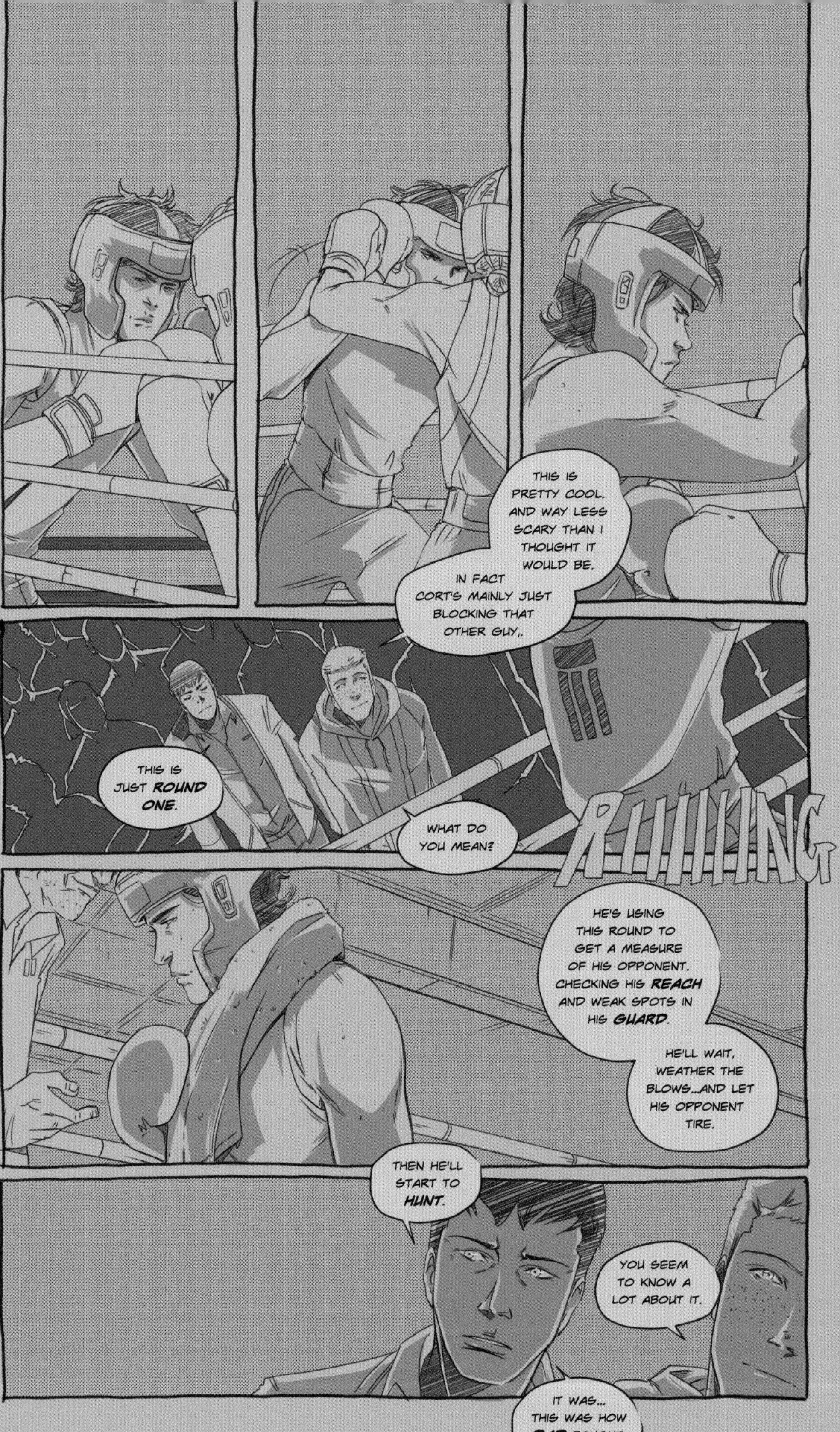
THIS IS PRETTY COOL. AND WAY LESS SCARY THAN I THOUGHT IT WOULD BE.
IN FACT CORT'S MAINLY JUST BLOCKING THAT OTHER GUY,.
THIS IS JUST **ROUND ONE**.
WHAT DO YOU MEAN?
RIIIIING
HE'S USING THIS ROUND TO GET A MEASURE OF HIS OPPONENT. CHECKING HIS **REACH** AND WEAK SPOTS IN HIS **GUARD**.
HE'LL WAIT, WEATHER THE BLOWS...AND LET HIS OPPONENT TIRE.
THEN HE'LL START TO **HUNT**.
YOU SEEM TO KNOW A LOT ABOUT IT.
IT WAS... THIS WAS HOW **DAD** FOUGHT.

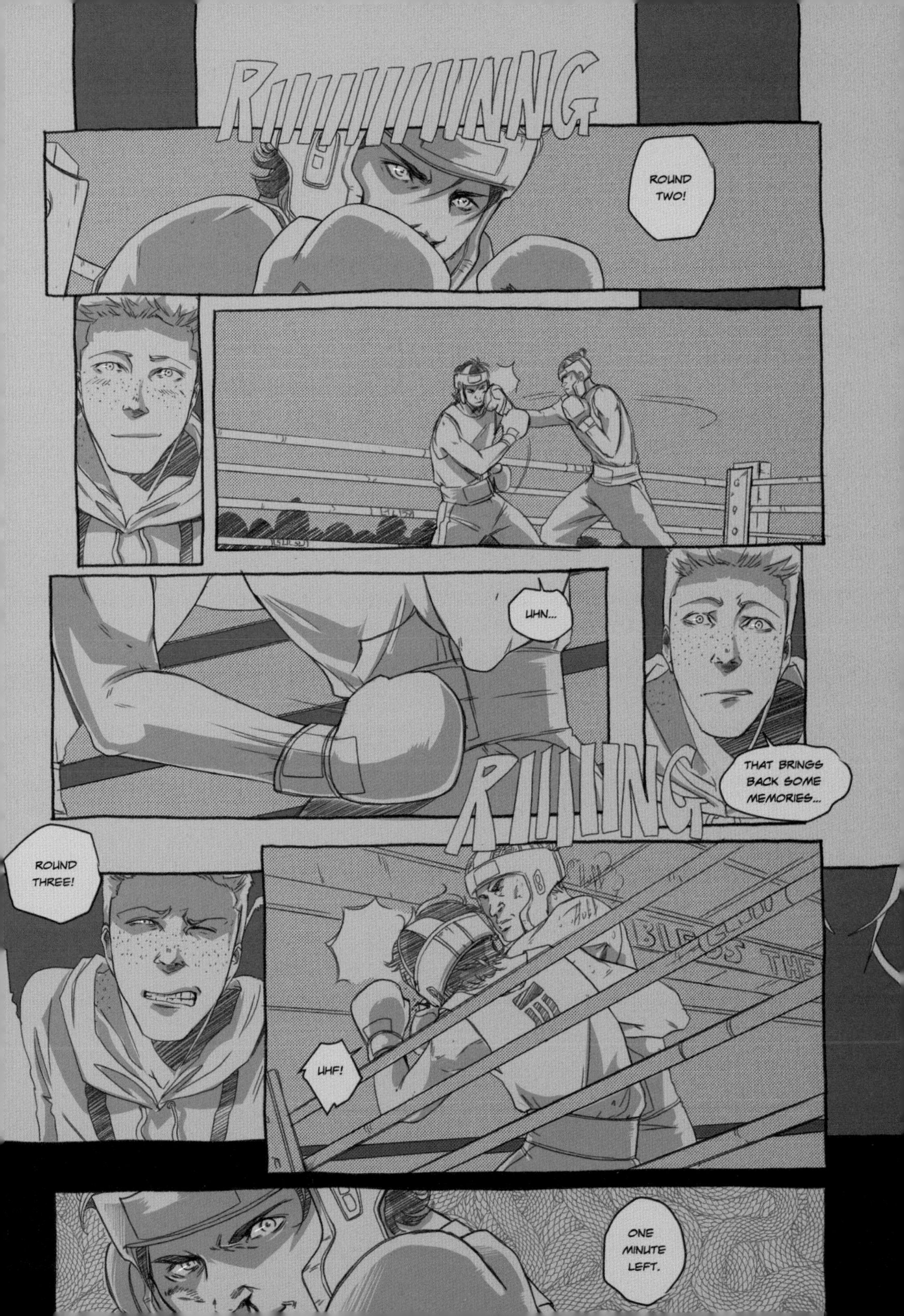
RIIIIIIIIIINNG
ROUND TWO!
UHN...
THAT BRINGS BACK SOME MEMORIES...
RIIIING
ROUND THREE!
UHF!
ONE MINUTE LEFT.

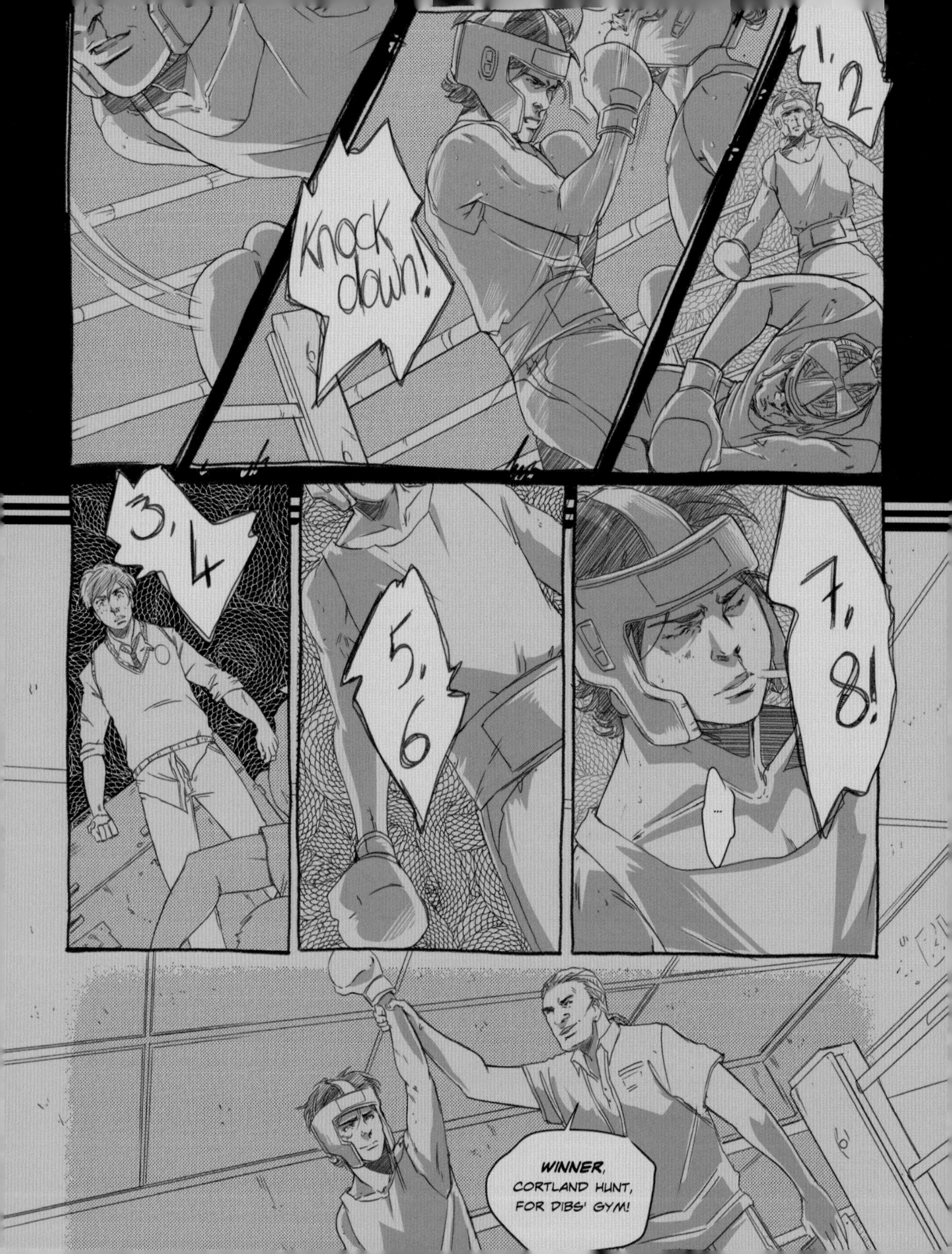
Knock down!
1, 2
3, 4
5, 6
7, 8!
...
WINNER, CORTLAND HUNT, FOR DIBS' GYM!

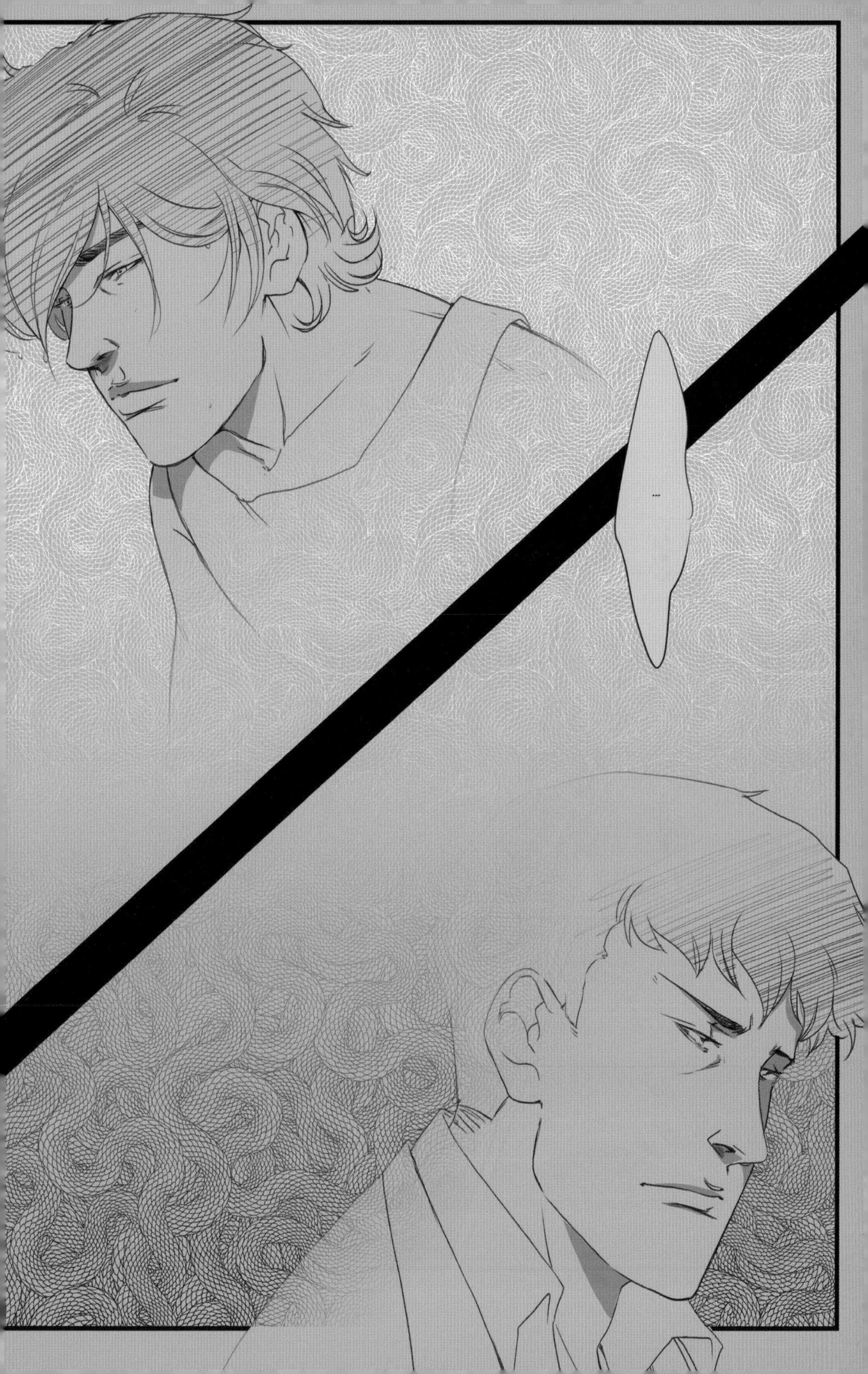
…

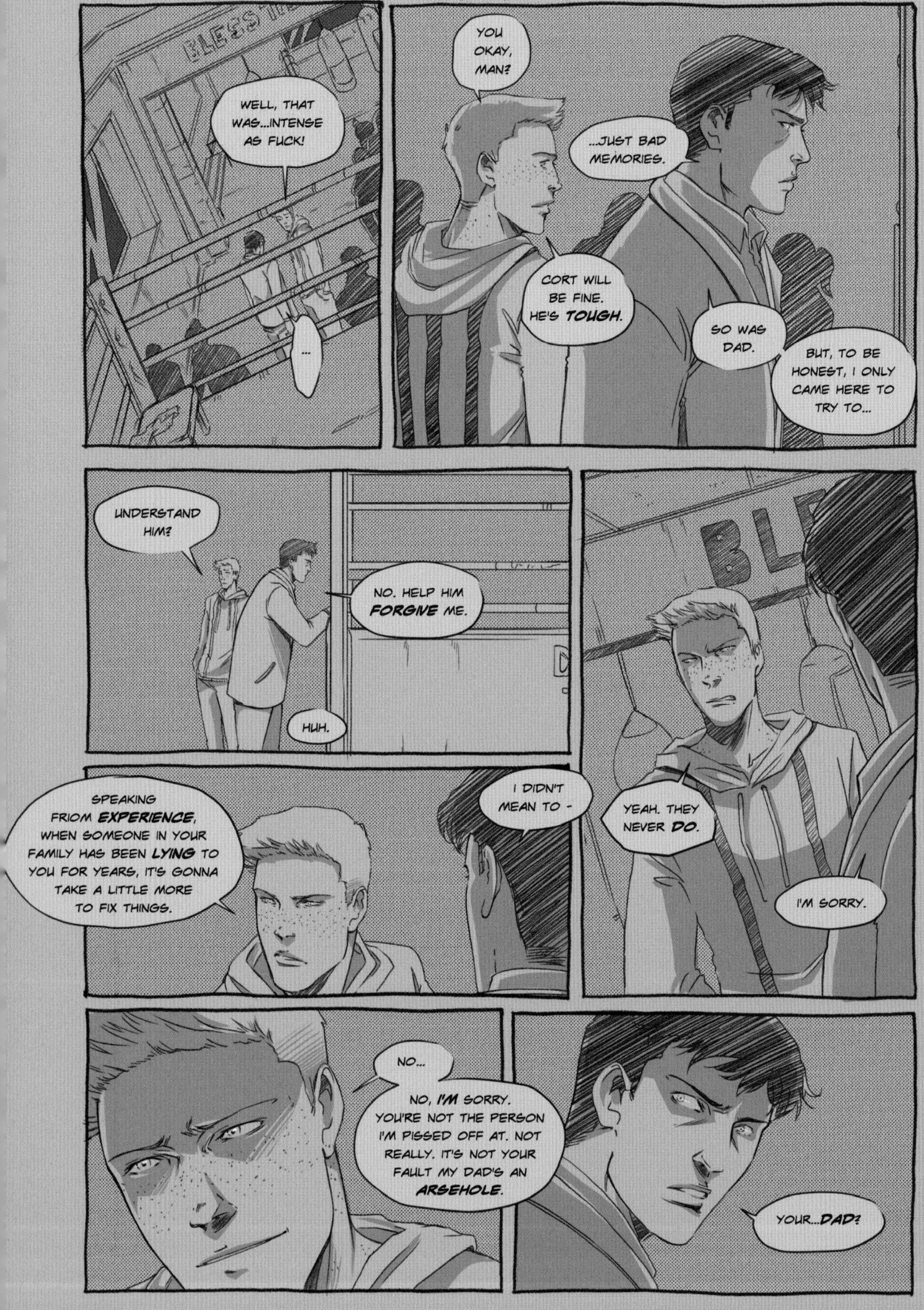
BLESS
WELL, THAT WAS...INTENSE AS FUCK!
...
YOU OKAY, MAN?
...JUST BAD MEMORIES.
CORT WILL BE FINE. HE'S TOUGH.
SO WAS DAD.
BUT, TO BE HONEST, I ONLY CAME HERE TO TRY TO...
UNDERSTAND HIM?
NO. HELP HIM FORGIVE ME.
HUH.
SPEAKING FRIOM EXPERIENCE, WHEN SOMEONE IN YOUR FAMILY HAS BEEN LYING TO YOU FOR YEARS, IT'S GONNA TAKE A LITTLE MORE TO FIX THINGS.
I DIDN'T MEAN TO -
YEAH. THEY NEVER DO.
I'M SORRY.
NO...
NO, I'M SORRY. YOU'RE NOT THE PERSON I'M PISSED OFF AT. NOT REALLY. IT'S NOT YOUR FAULT MY DAD'S AN ARSEHOLE.
YOUR...DAD?

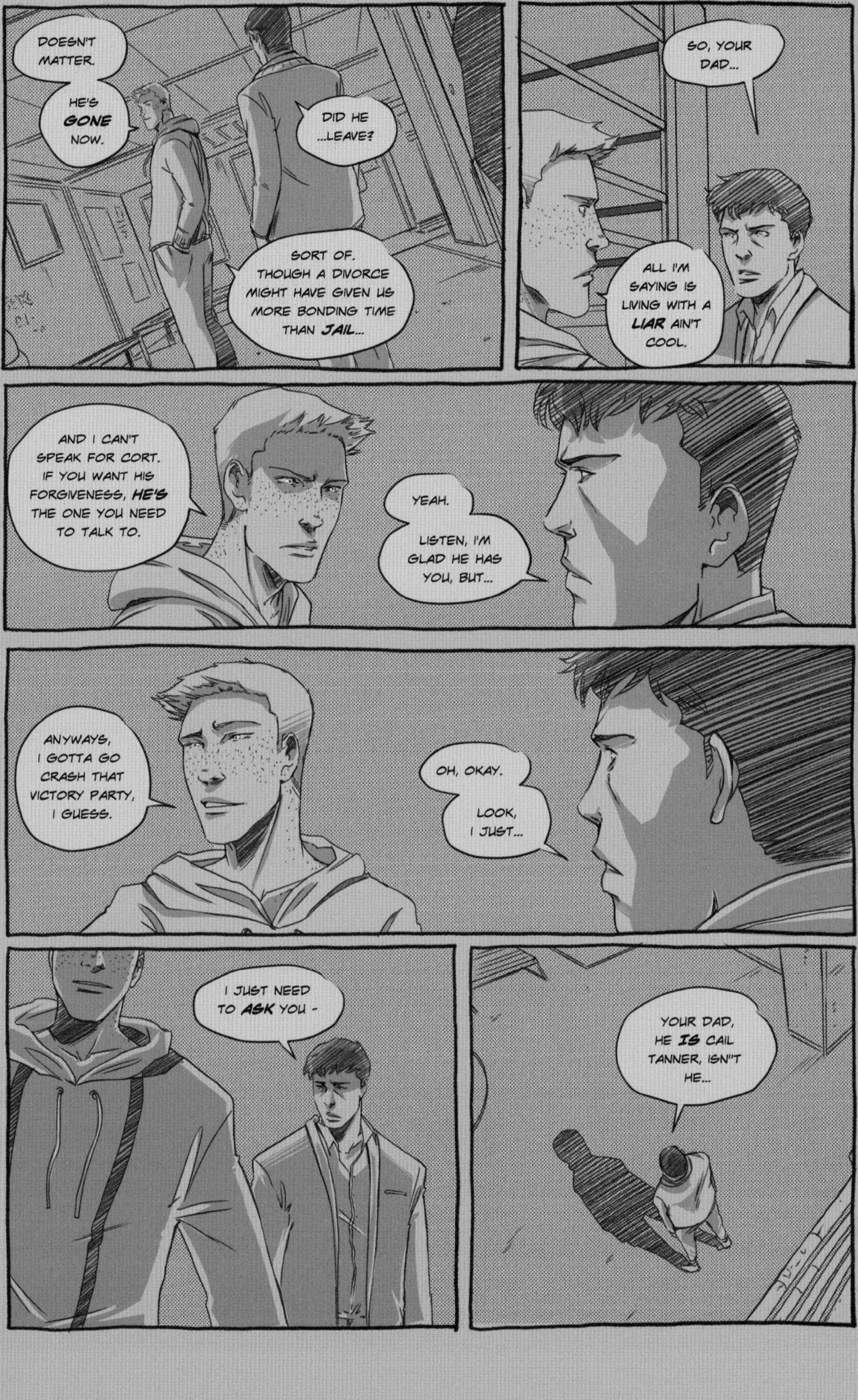
DOESN'T MATTER.
HE'S **GONE** NOW.
DID HE ...LEAVE?
SORT OF. THOUGH A DIVORCE MIGHT HAVE GIVEN US MORE BONDING TIME THAN **JAIL**...
SO, YOUR DAD...
ALL I'M SAYING IS LIVING WITH A **LIAR** AIN'T COOL.
AND I CAN'T SPEAK FOR CORT. IF YOU WANT HIS FORGIVENESS, **HE'S** THE ONE YOU NEED TO TALK TO.
YEAH.
LISTEN, I'M GLAD HE HAS YOU, BUT...
ANYWAYS, I GOTTA GO CRASH THAT VICTORY PARTY, I GUESS.
OH, OKAY.
LOOK, I JUST...
I JUST NEED TO **ASK** YOU -
YOUR DAD, HE **IS** CAIL TANNER, ISN'T HE...

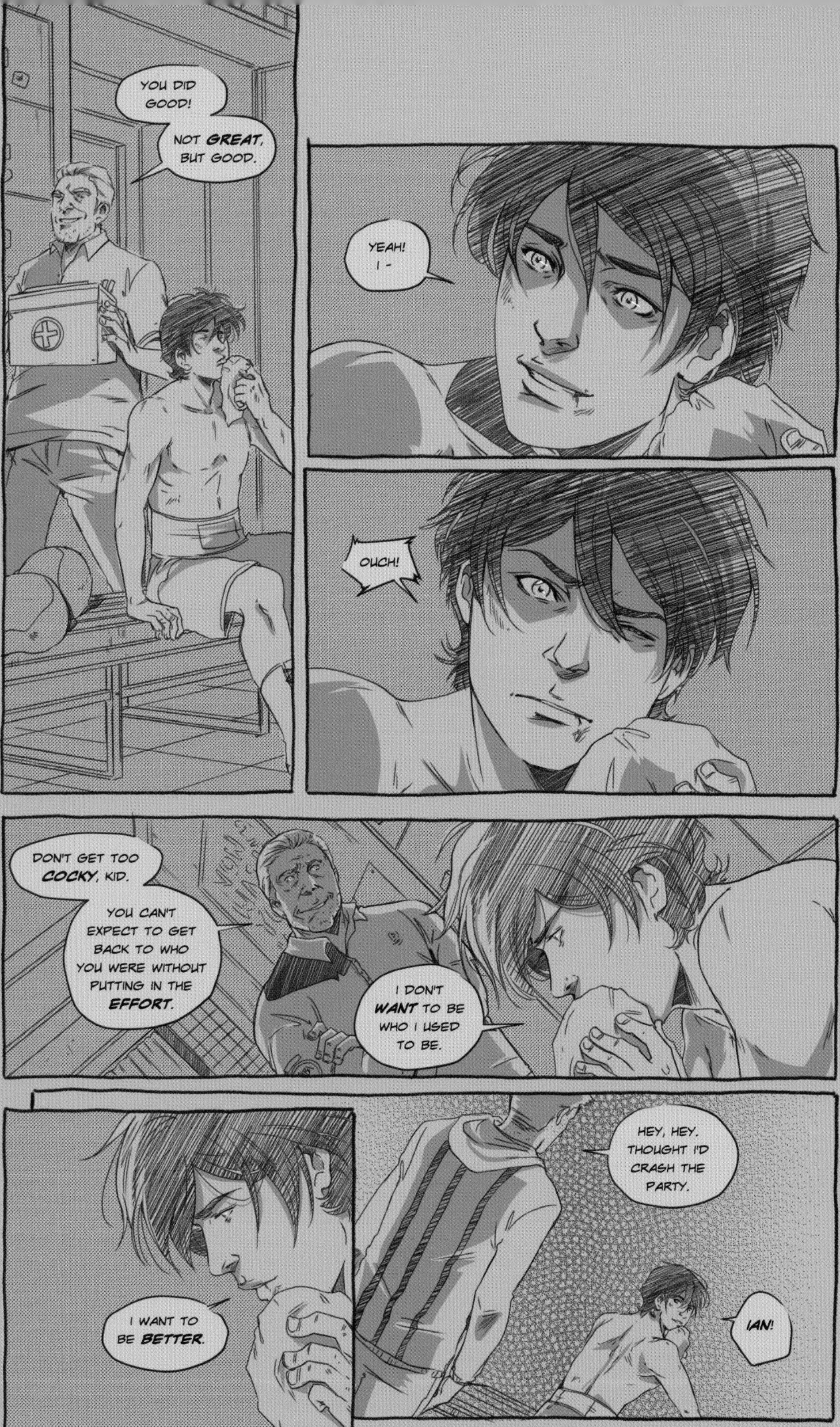
YOU DID GOOD!
NOT **GREAT**, BUT GOOD.
YEAH! I -
OUCH!
DON'T GET TOO **COCKY**, KID.
YOU CAN'T EXPECT TO GET BACK TO WHO YOU WERE WITHOUT PUTTING IN THE **EFFORT**.
I DON'T **WANT** TO BE WHO I USED TO BE.
I WANT TO BE **BETTER**.
HEY, HEY. THOUGHT I'D CRASH THE PARTY.
IAN!

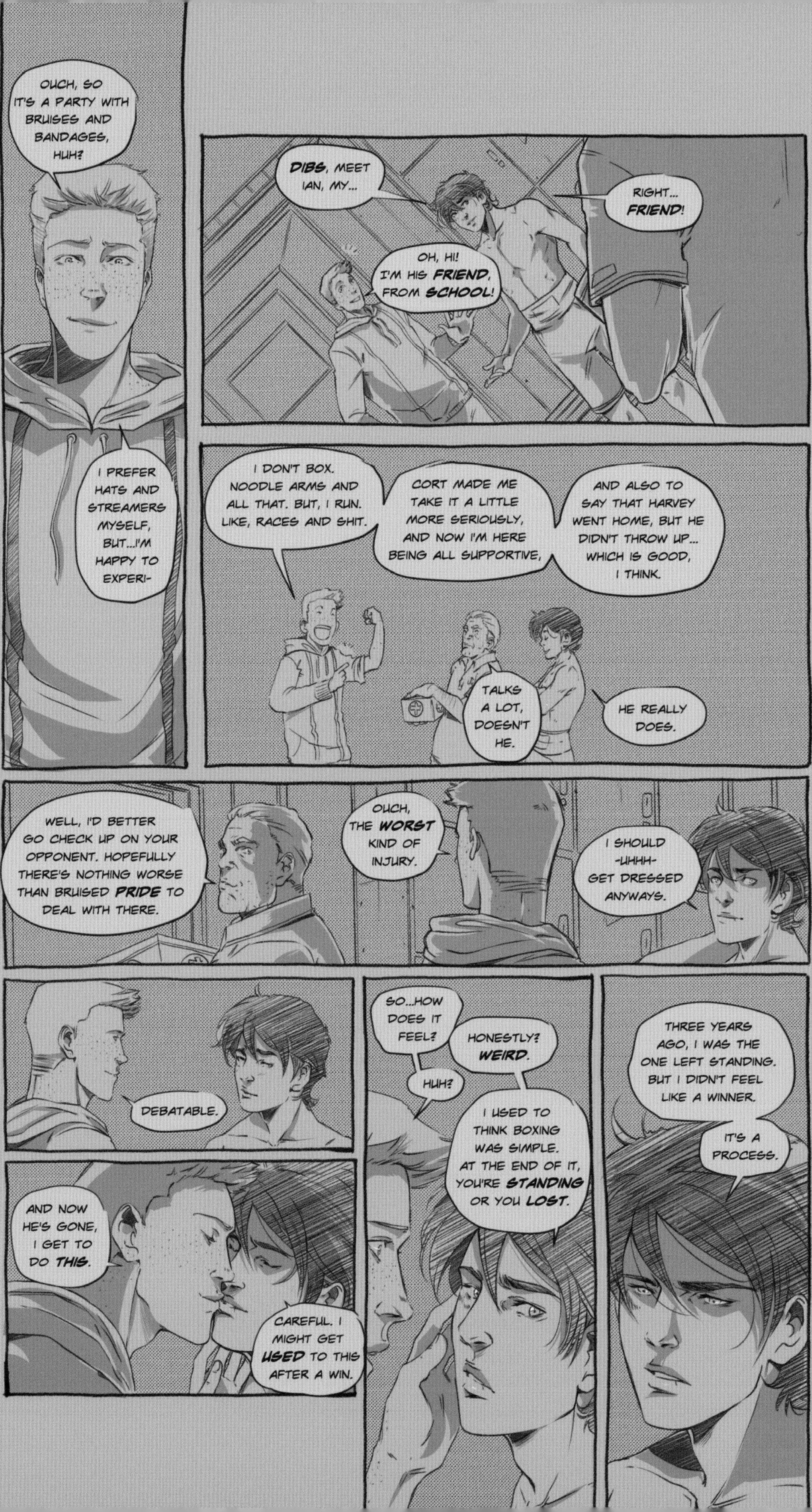
OUCH, SO IT'S A PARTY WITH BRUISES AND BANDAGES, HUH?
DIBS, MEET IAN, MY...
RIGHT... FRIEND!
OH, HI! I'M HIS FRIEND, FROM SCHOOL!
I PREFER HATS AND STREAMERS MYSELF, BUT...I'M HAPPY TO EXPERI-
I DON'T BOX. NOODLE ARMS AND ALL THAT. BUT, I RUN. LIKE, RACES AND SHIT.
CORT MADE ME TAKE IT A LITTLE MORE SERIOUSLY, AND NOW I'M HERE BEING ALL SUPPORTIVE,
AND ALSO TO SAY THAT HARVEY WENT HOME, BUT HE DIDN'T THROW UP... WHICH IS GOOD, I THINK.
TALKS A LOT, DOESN'T HE.
HE REALLY DOES.
WELL, I'D BETTER GO CHECK UP ON YOUR OPPONENT. HOPEFULLY THERE'S NOTHING WORSE THAN BRUISED PRIDE TO DEAL WITH THERE.
OUCH, THE WORST KIND OF INJURY.
I SHOULD -UHHH- GET DRESSED ANYWAYS.
DEBATABLE.
AND NOW HE'S GONE, I GET TO DO THIS.
CAREFUL. I MIGHT GET USED TO THIS AFTER A WIN.
SO...HOW DOES IT FEEL?
HONESTLY? WEIRD.
HUH?
I USED TO THINK BOXING WAS SIMPLE. AT THE END OF IT, YOU'RE STANDING OR YOU LOST.
THREE YEARS AGO, I WAS THE ONE LEFT STANDING. BUT I DIDN'T FEEL LIKE A WINNER.
IT'S A PROCESS.

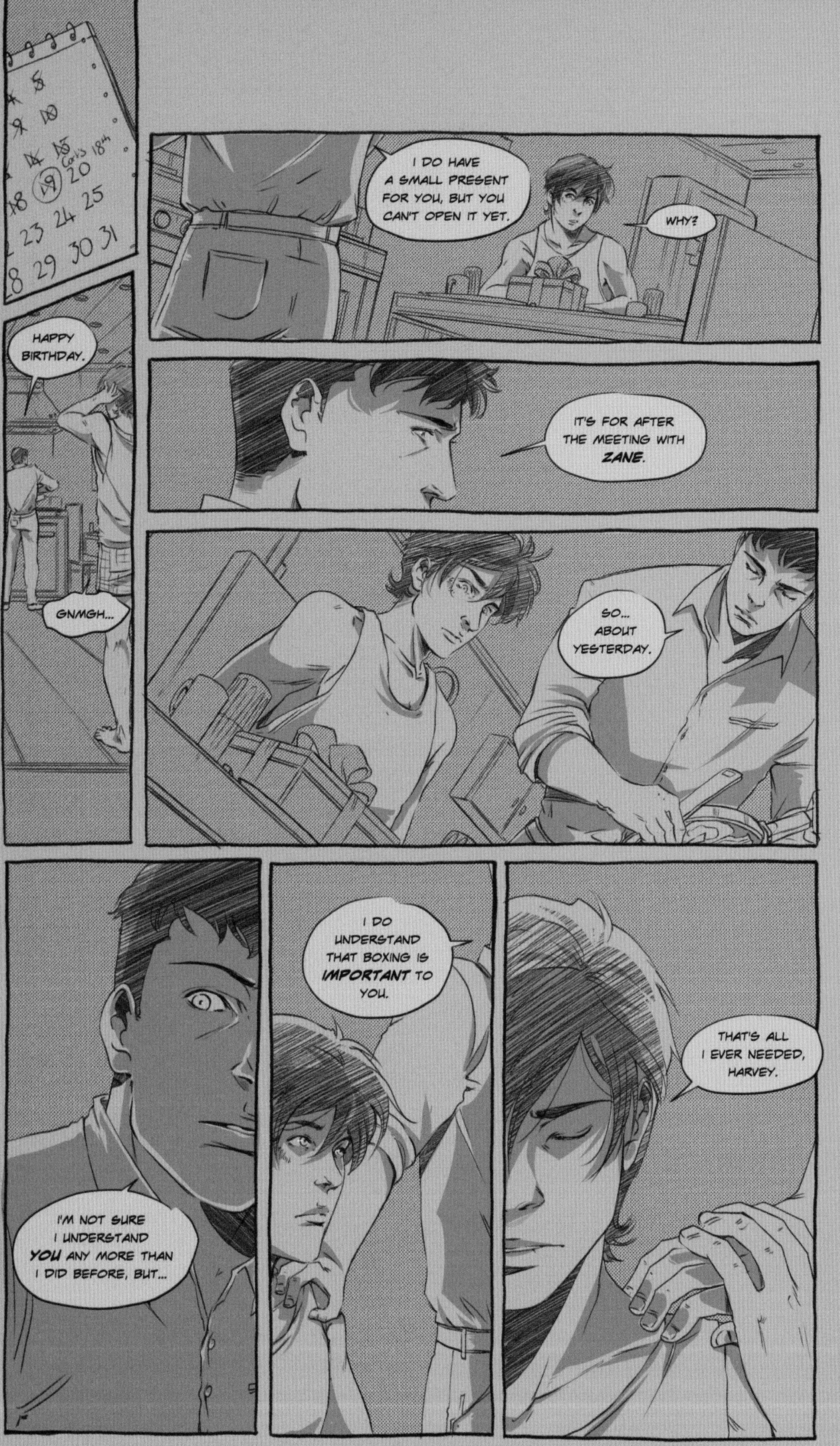
HAPPY BIRTHDAY.
GNMGH...
I DO HAVE A SMALL PRESENT FOR YOU, BUT YOU CAN'T OPEN IT YET.
WHY?
IT'S FOR AFTER THE MEETING WITH **ZANE**.
SO... ABOUT YESTERDAY.
I'M NOT SURE I UNDERSTAND **YOU** ANY MORE THAN I DID BEFORE, BUT...
I DO UNDERSTAND THAT BOXING IS **IMPORTANT** TO YOU.
THAT'S ALL I EVER NEEDED, HARVEY.

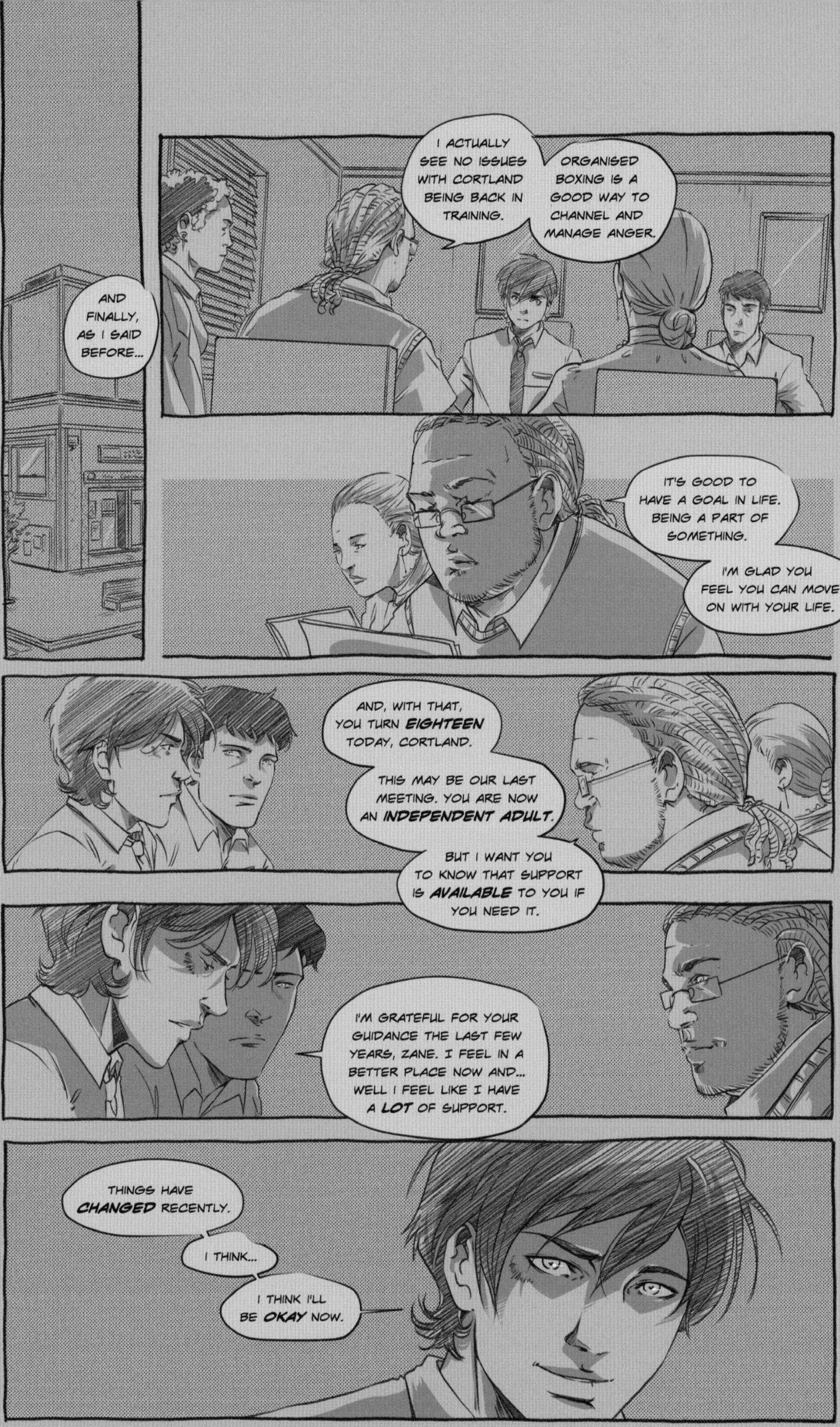
AND FINALLY, AS I SAID BEFORE...
I ACTUALLY SEE NO ISSUES WITH CORTLAND BEING BACK IN TRAINING.
ORGANISED BOXING IS A GOOD WAY TO CHANNEL AND MANAGE ANGER.
IT'S GOOD TO HAVE A GOAL IN LIFE. BEING A PART OF SOMETHING.
I'M GLAD YOU FEEL YOU CAN MOVE ON WITH YOUR LIFE.
AND, WITH THAT, YOU TURN EIGHTEEN TODAY, CORTLAND.
THIS MAY BE OUR LAST MEETING. YOU ARE NOW AN INDEPENDENT ADULT.
BUT I WANT YOU TO KNOW THAT SUPPORT IS AVAILABLE TO YOU IF YOU NEED IT.
I'M GRATEFUL FOR YOUR GUIDANCE THE LAST FEW YEARS, ZANE. I FEEL IN A BETTER PLACE NOW AND... WELL I FEEL LIKE I HAVE A LOT OF SUPPORT.
THINGS HAVE CHANGED RECENTLY.
I THINK...
I THINK I'LL BE OKAY NOW.

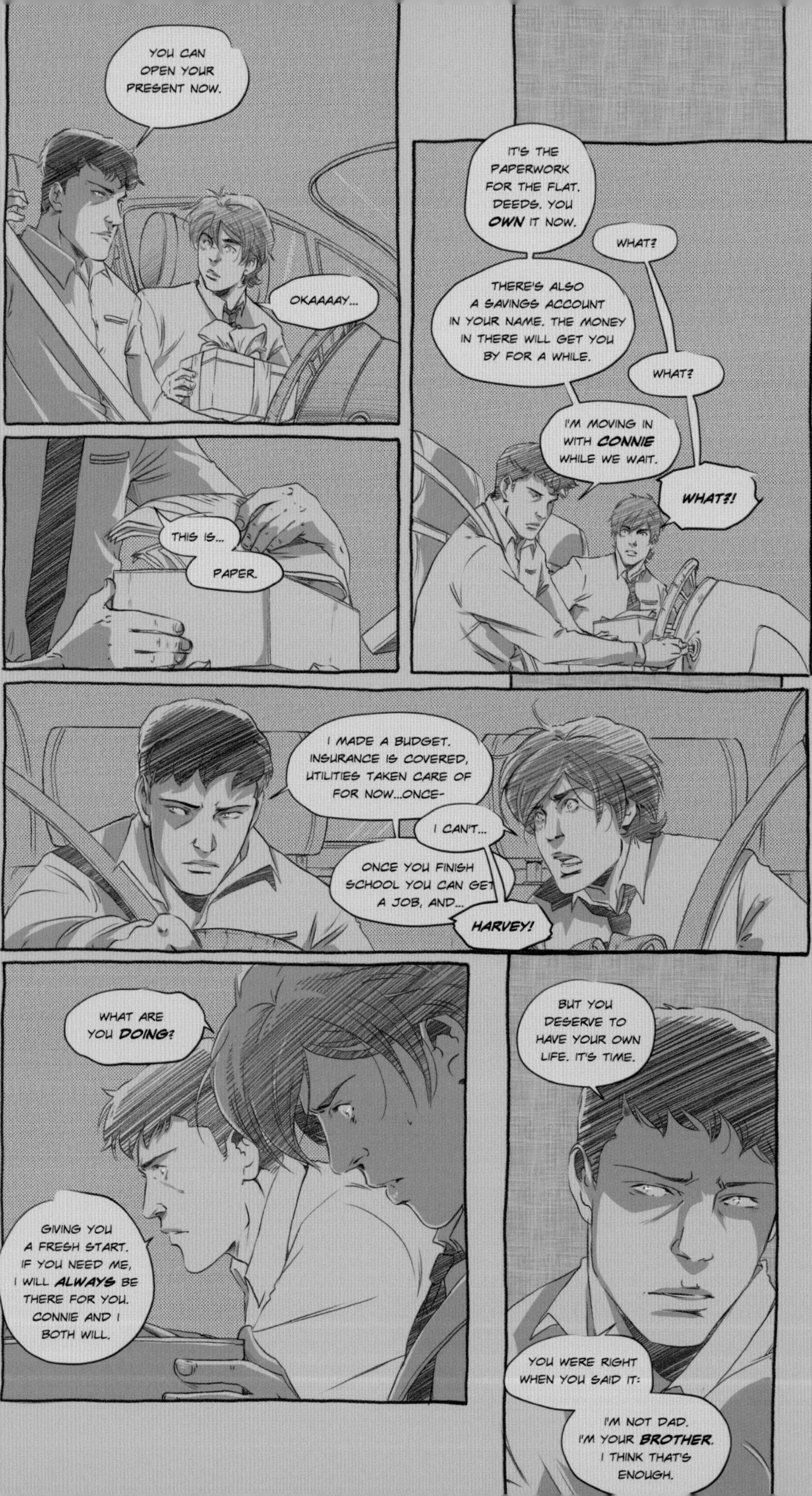
YOU CAN OPEN YOUR PRESENT NOW.
OKAAAAY...
IT'S THE PAPERWORK FOR THE FLAT. DEEDS. YOU OWN IT NOW.
WHAT?
THERE'S ALSO A SAVINGS ACCOUNT IN YOUR NAME. THE MONEY IN THERE WILL GET YOU BY FOR A WHILE.
WHAT?
I'M MOVING IN WITH CONNIE WHILE WE WAIT.
WHAT?!
THIS IS...
PAPER.
I MADE A BUDGET. INSURANCE IS COVERED, UTILITIES TAKEN CARE OF FOR NOW...ONCE-
I CAN'T...
ONCE YOU FINISH SCHOOL YOU CAN GET A JOB, AND...
HARVEY!
WHAT ARE YOU DOING?
GIVING YOU A FRESH START. IF YOU NEED ME, I WILL ALWAYS BE THERE FOR YOU. CONNIE AND I BOTH WILL.
BUT YOU DESERVE TO HAVE YOUR OWN LIFE. IT'S TIME.
YOU WERE RIGHT WHEN YOU SAID IT:
I'M NOT DAD. I'M YOUR BROTHER. I THINK THAT'S ENOUGH.

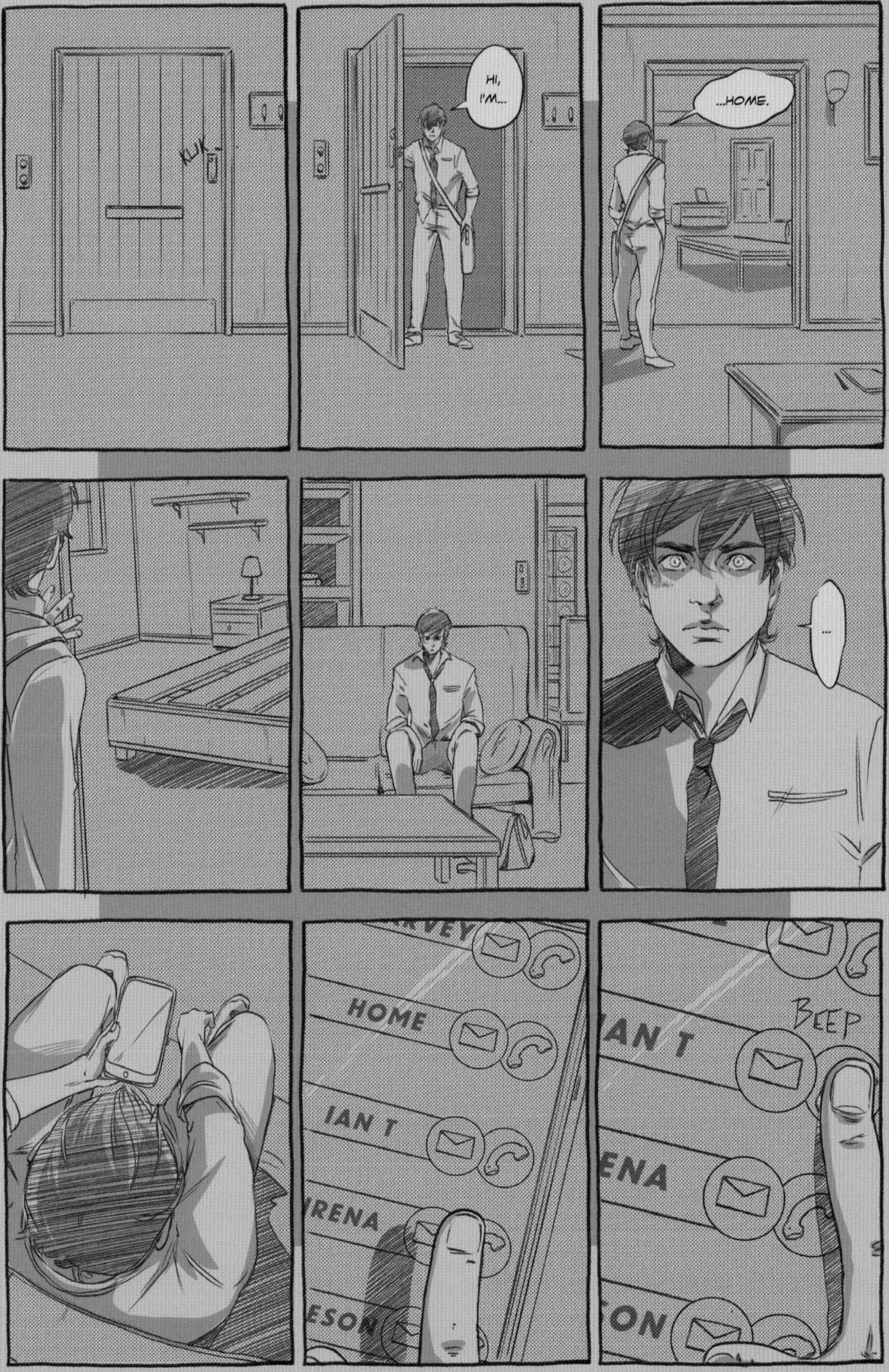
KLIK
HI, I'M...
...HOME.
...
HOME
IAN T
IRENA
BEEP
IAN T

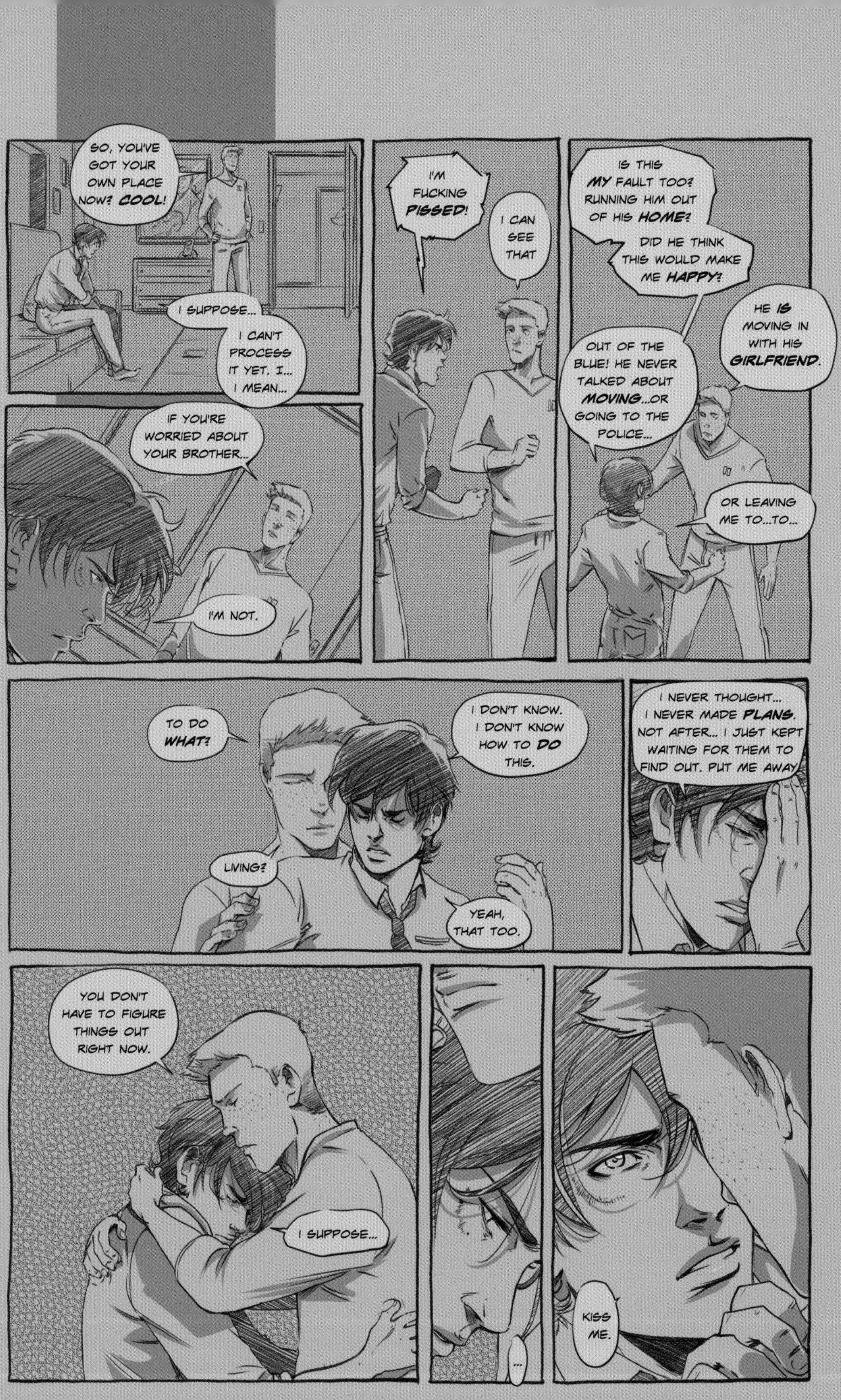
SO, YOU'VE GOT YOUR OWN PLACE NOW? COOL!
I SUPPOSE...
I CAN'T PROCESS IT YET. I... I MEAN...
IF YOU'RE WORRIED ABOUT YOUR BROTHER...
I'M NOT.
I'M FUCKING PISSED!
I CAN SEE THAT
IS THIS MY FAULT TOO? RUNNING HIM OUT OF HIS HOME?
DID HE THINK THIS WOULD MAKE ME HAPPY?
OUT OF THE BLUE! HE NEVER TALKED ABOUT MOVING...OR GOING TO THE POLICE...
HE IS MOVING IN WITH HIS GIRLFRIEND.
OR LEAVING ME TO...TO...
TO DO WHAT?
I DON'T KNOW. I DON'T KNOW HOW TO DO THIS.
LIVING?
YEAH, THAT TOO.
I NEVER THOUGHT... I NEVER MADE PLANS. NOT AFTER... I JUST KEPT WAITING FOR THEM TO FIND OUT. PUT ME AWAY.
YOU DON'T HAVE TO FIGURE THINGS OUT RIGHT NOW.
I SUPPOSE...
...
KISS ME.

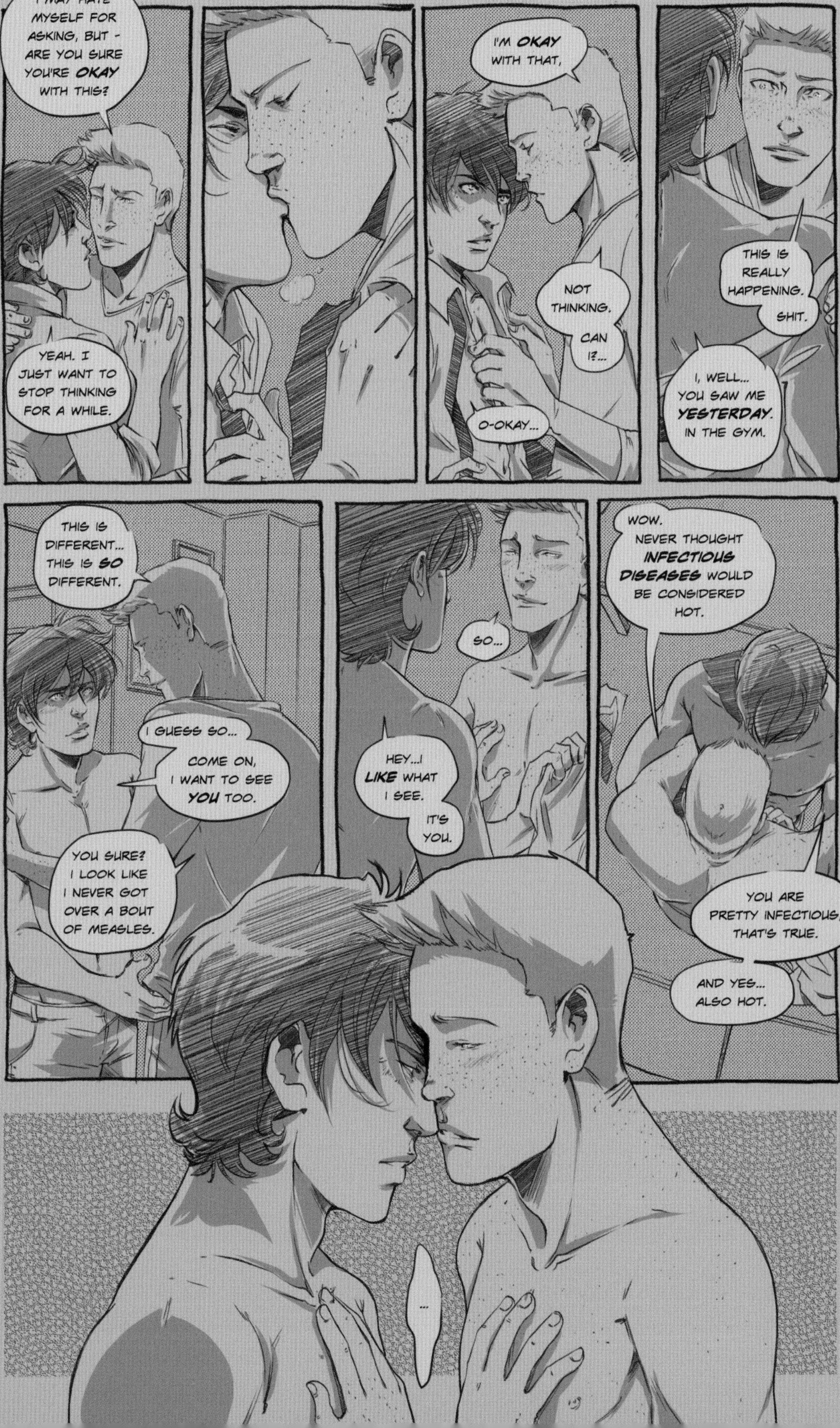
I MAY HATE MYSELF FOR ASKING, BUT - ARE YOU SURE YOU'RE **OKAY** WITH THIS?
YEAH. I JUST WANT TO STOP THINKING FOR A WHILE.
I'M **OKAY** WITH THAT.
NOT THINKING.
CAN I?...
O-OKAY...
THIS IS REALLY HAPPENING.
SHIT.
I, WELL... YOU SAW ME **YESTERDAY**. IN THE GYM.
THIS IS DIFFERENT... THIS IS **SO** DIFFERENT.
I GUESS SO...
COME ON, I WANT TO SEE **YOU** TOO.
YOU SURE? I LOOK LIKE I NEVER GOT OVER A BOUT OF MEASLES.
SO...
HEY...I **LIKE** WHAT I SEE.
IT'S YOU.
WOW. NEVER THOUGHT **INFECTIOUS DISEASES** WOULD BE CONSIDERED HOT.
YOU ARE PRETTY INFECTIOUS, THAT'S TRUE.
AND YES... ALSO HOT.
...

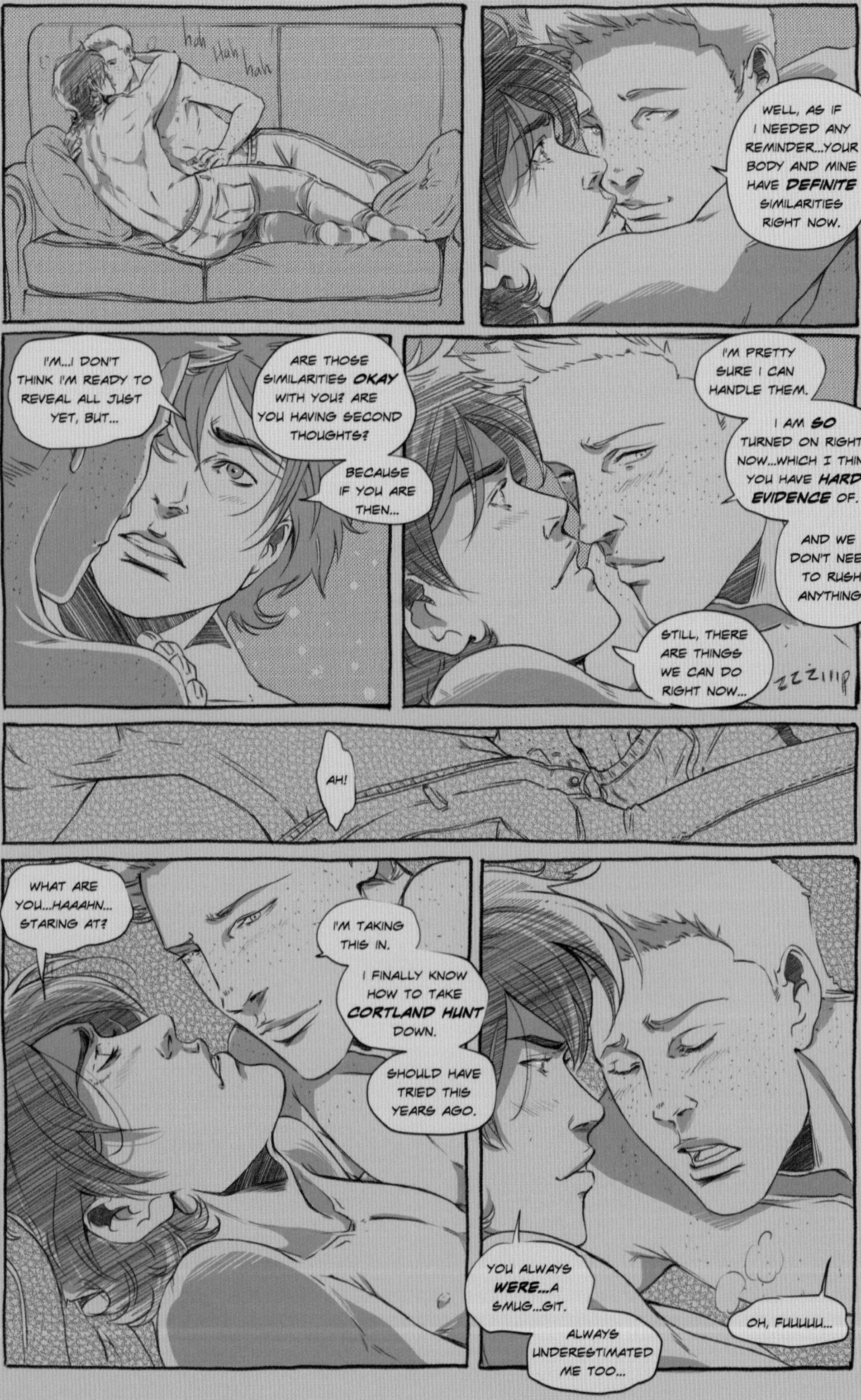

hah hah hah
WELL, AS IF I NEEDED ANY REMINDER...YOUR BODY AND MINE HAVE **DEFINITE** SIMILARITIES RIGHT NOW.
I'M...I DON'T THINK I'M READY TO REVEAL ALL JUST YET, BUT...
ARE THOSE SIMILARITIES **OKAY** WITH YOU? ARE YOU HAVING SECOND THOUGHTS?
BECAUSE IF YOU ARE THEN...
I'M PRETTY SURE I CAN HANDLE THEM.
I AM **SO** TURNED ON RIGHT NOW...WHICH I THINK YOU HAVE **HARD EVIDENCE** OF.
AND WE DON'T NEED TO RUSH ANYTHING.
STILL, THERE ARE THINGS WE CAN DO RIGHT NOW...
ZZZiiip
AH!
WHAT ARE YOU...HAAAHN... STARING AT?
I'M TAKING THIS IN.
I FINALLY KNOW HOW TO TAKE **CORTLAND HUNT** DOWN.
SHOULD HAVE TRIED THIS YEARS AGO.
YOU ALWAYS **WERE...** A SMUG...GIT.
ALWAYS UNDERESTIMATED ME TOO...
OH, FUUUUU...

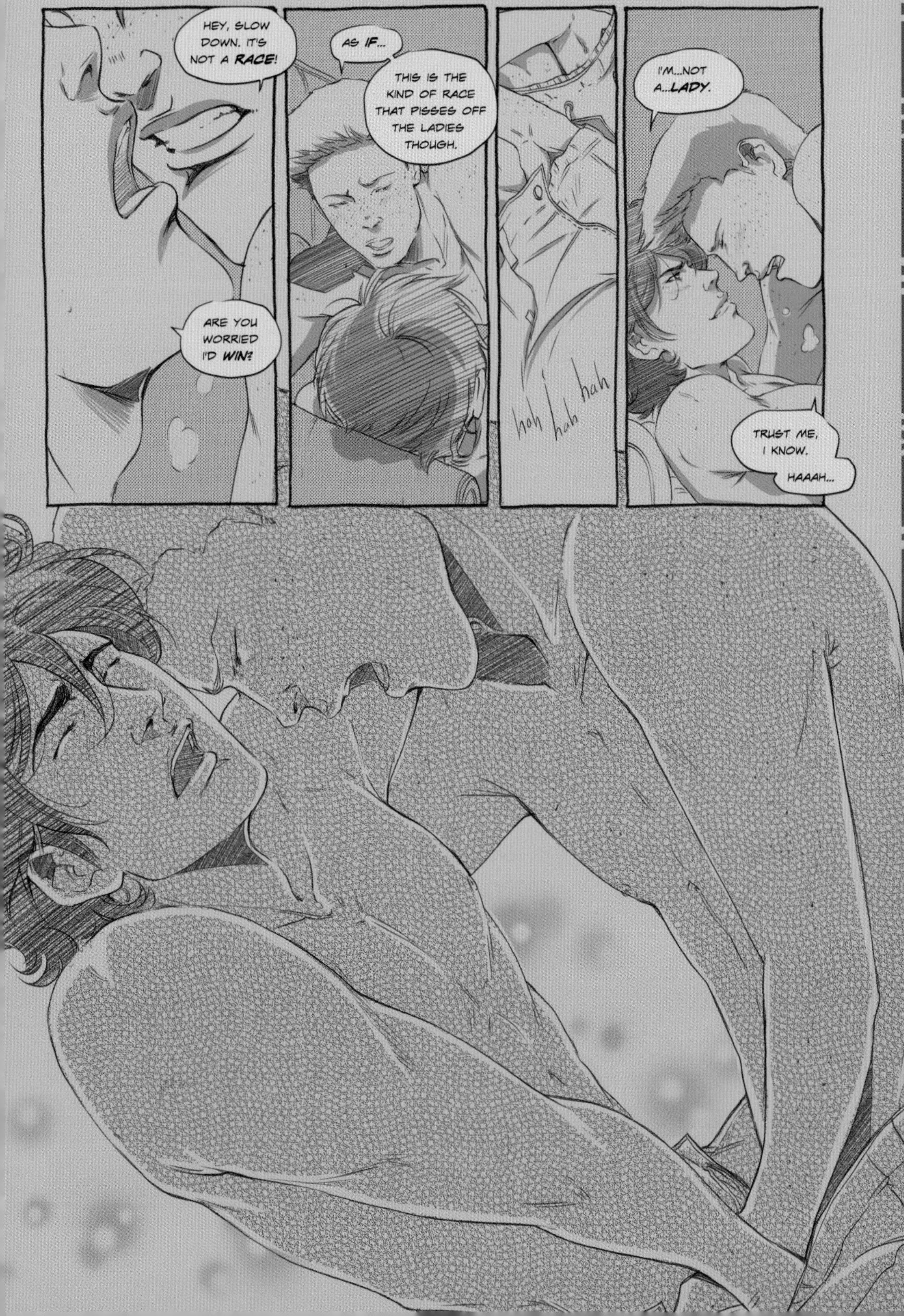
HEY, SLOW DOWN. IT'S NOT A RACE!
ARE YOU WORRIED I'D WIN?
AS IF...
THIS IS THE KIND OF RACE THAT PISSES OFF THE LADIES THOUGH.
hah hah hah
I'M...NOT A...LADY.
TRUST ME, I KNOW.
HAAAH...

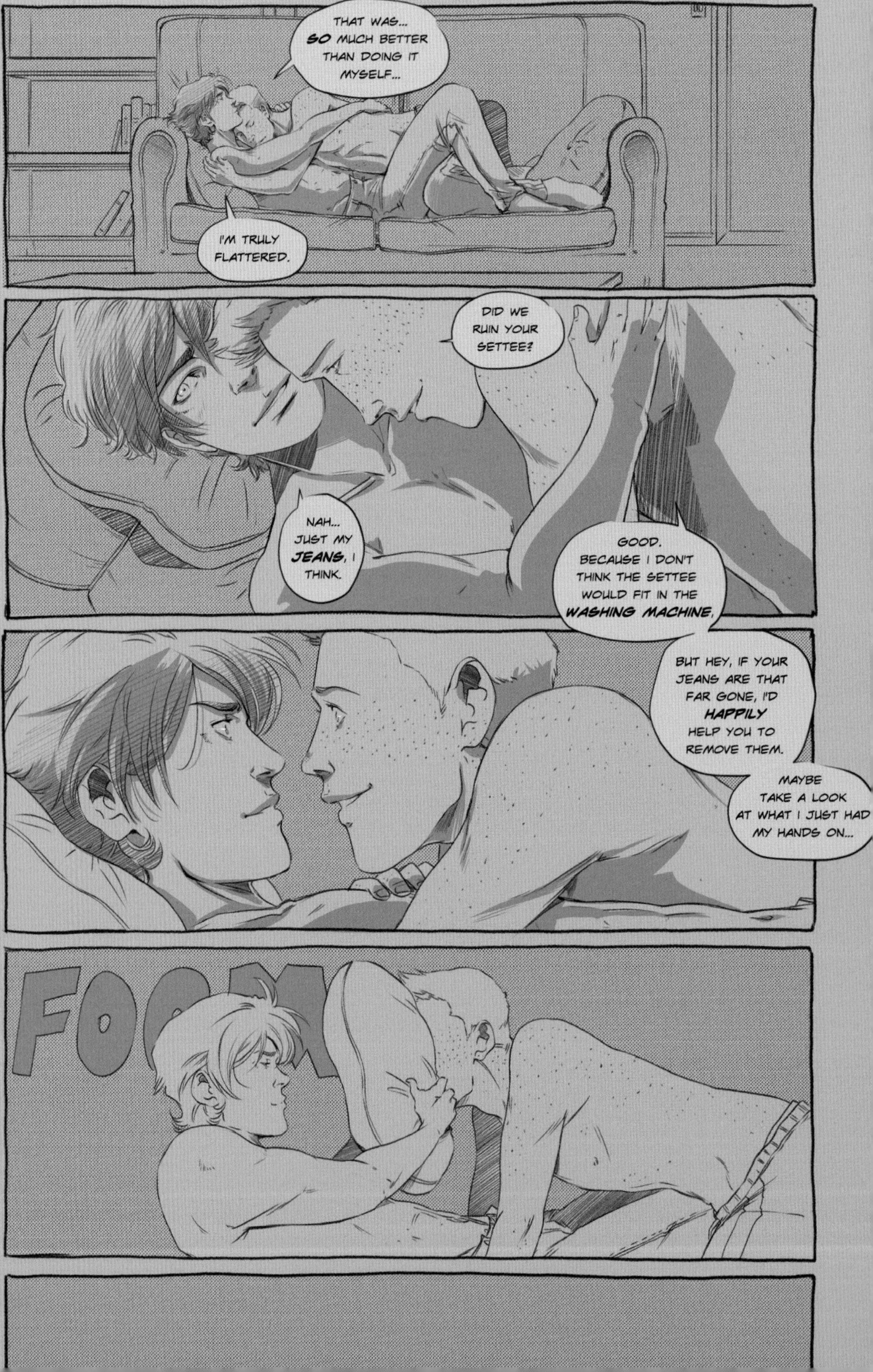
THAT WAS... **SO** MUCH BETTER THAN DOING IT MYSELF...
I'M TRULY FLATTERED.
DID WE RUIN YOUR SETTEE?
NAH... JUST MY **JEANS**, I THINK.
GOOD. BECAUSE I DON'T THINK THE SETTEE WOULD FIT IN THE **WASHING MACHINE**,
BUT HEY, IF YOUR JEANS ARE THAT FAR GONE, I'D **HAPPILY** HELP YOU TO REMOVE THEM.
MAYBE TAKE A LOOK AT WHAT I JUST HAD MY HANDS ON...
FOO

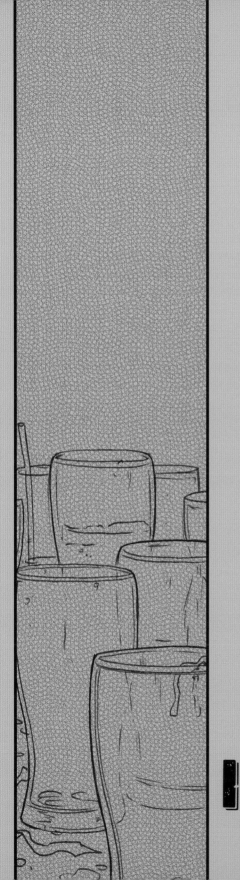

ISSUE 12

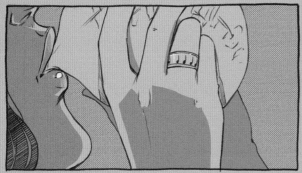

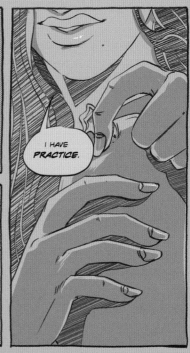

I HAVE *PRACTICE.*

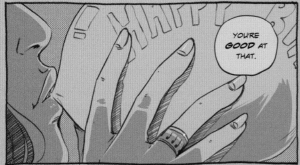

YOU'RE *GOOD* AT THAT.

DO YOU HAVE ANY IDEA HOW MUCH LIKE *HIM* YOU SOUND?

YOU MEAN HOW MUCH *HE* SOUNDS LIKE *ME?*

CHICKEN, EGG.

WHATEVER. LET'S GET THIS DONE WHILE THERE'S STILL *TIME.*

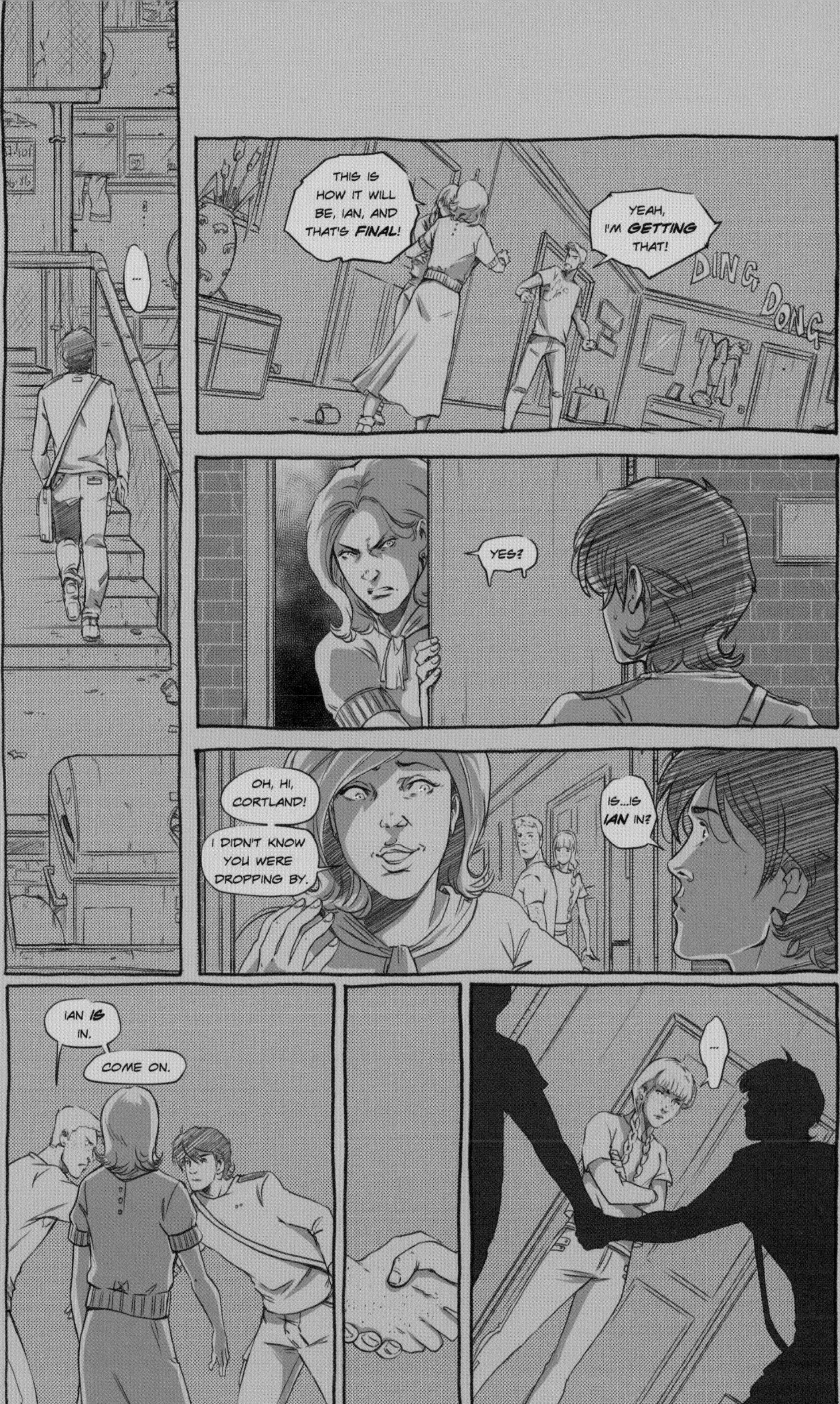
...
THIS IS HOW IT WILL BE, IAN, AND THAT'S FINAL!
YEAH, I'M GETTING THAT!
DING DONG
YES?
OH, HI, CORTLAND!
I DIDN'T KNOW YOU WERE DROPPING BY.
IS...IS IAN IN?
IAN IS IN.
COME ON.
...

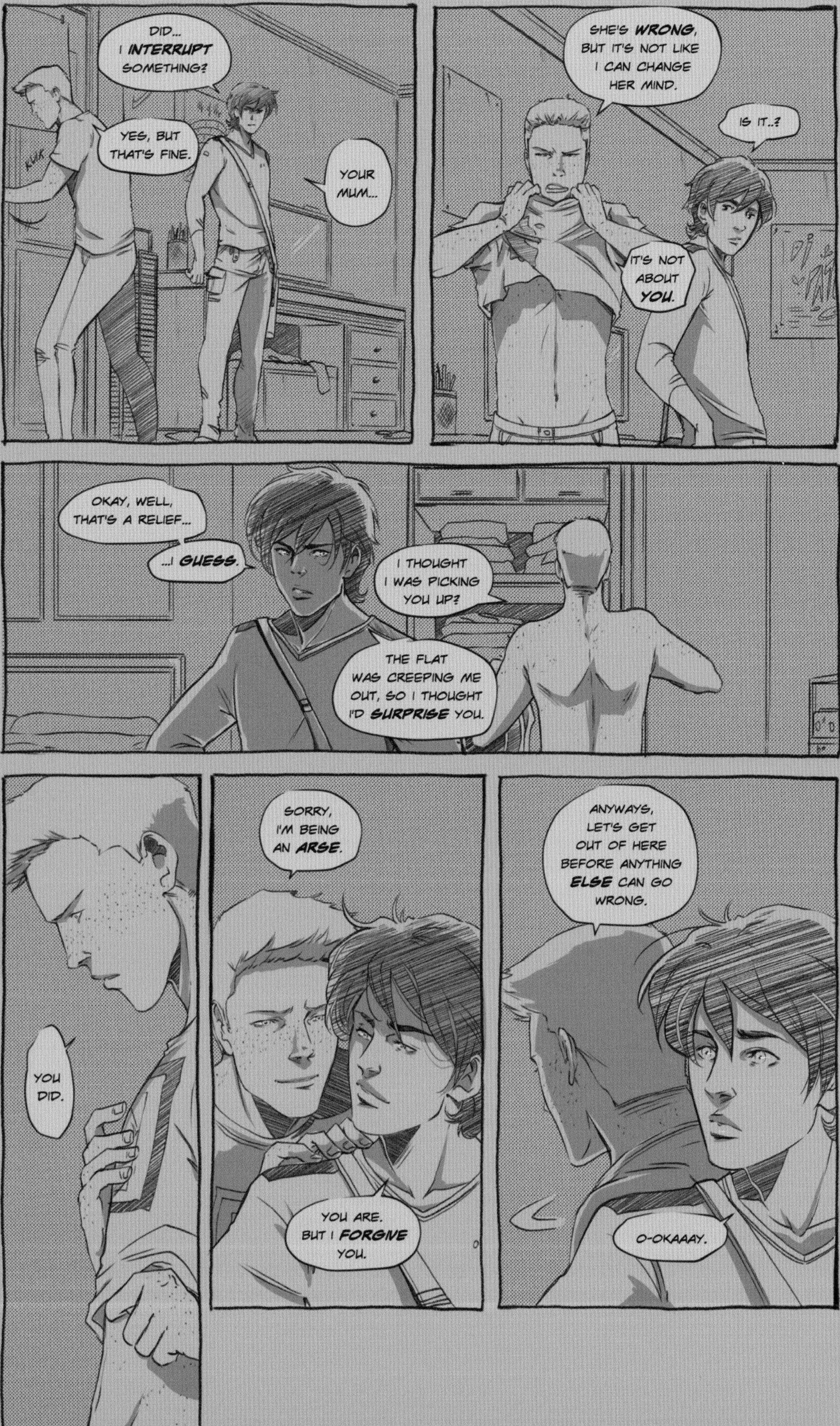
DID... I **INTERRUPT** SOMETHING?
YES, BUT THAT'S FINE.
YOUR MUM...
SHE'S **WRONG**, BUT IT'S NOT LIKE I CAN CHANGE HER MIND.
IS IT..?
IT'S NOT ABOUT **YOU**.
OKAY, WELL, THAT'S A RELIEF...
...I **GUESS**.
I THOUGHT I WAS PICKING YOU UP?
THE FLAT WAS CREEPING ME OUT, SO I THOUGHT I'D **SURPRISE** YOU.
YOU DID.
SORRY, I'M BEING AN **ARSE**.
YOU ARE. BUT I **FORGIVE** YOU.
ANYWAYS, LET'S GET OUT OF HERE BEFORE ANYTHING **ELSE** CAN GO WRONG.
O-OKAAAY.

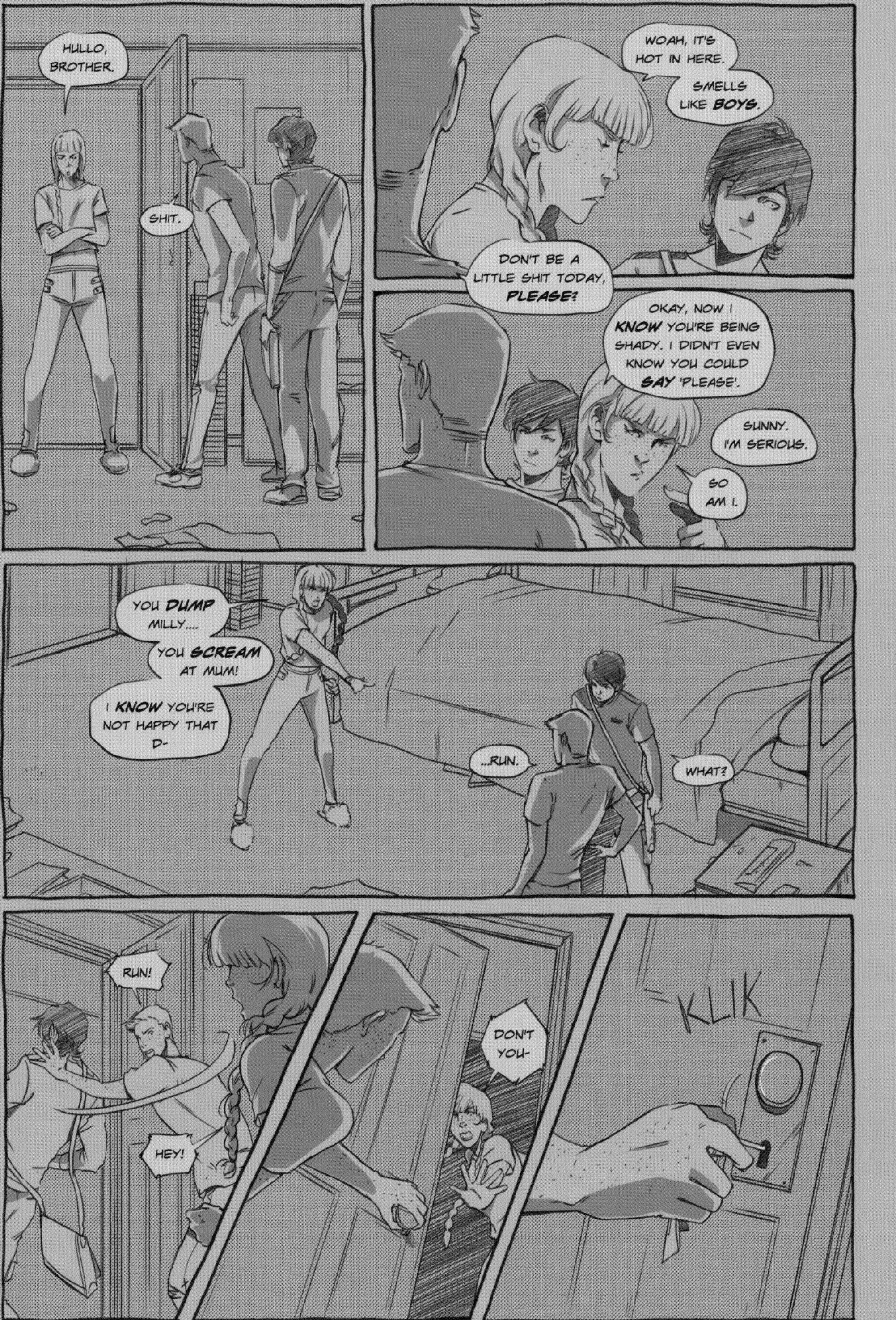

HULLO, BROTHER.
SHIT.
WOAH, IT'S HOT IN HERE.
SMELLS LIKE **BOYS**.
DON'T BE A LITTLE SHIT TODAY, **PLEASE?**
OKAY, NOW I **KNOW** YOU'RE BEING SHADY. I DIDN'T EVEN KNOW YOU COULD **SAY** 'PLEASE'.
SUNNY. I'M SERIOUS.
SO AM I.
YOU **DUMP** MILLY....
YOU **SCREAM** AT MUM!
I **KNOW** YOU'RE NOT HAPPY THAT D-
...RUN.
WHAT?
RUN!
HEY!
DON'T YOU-
KLIK

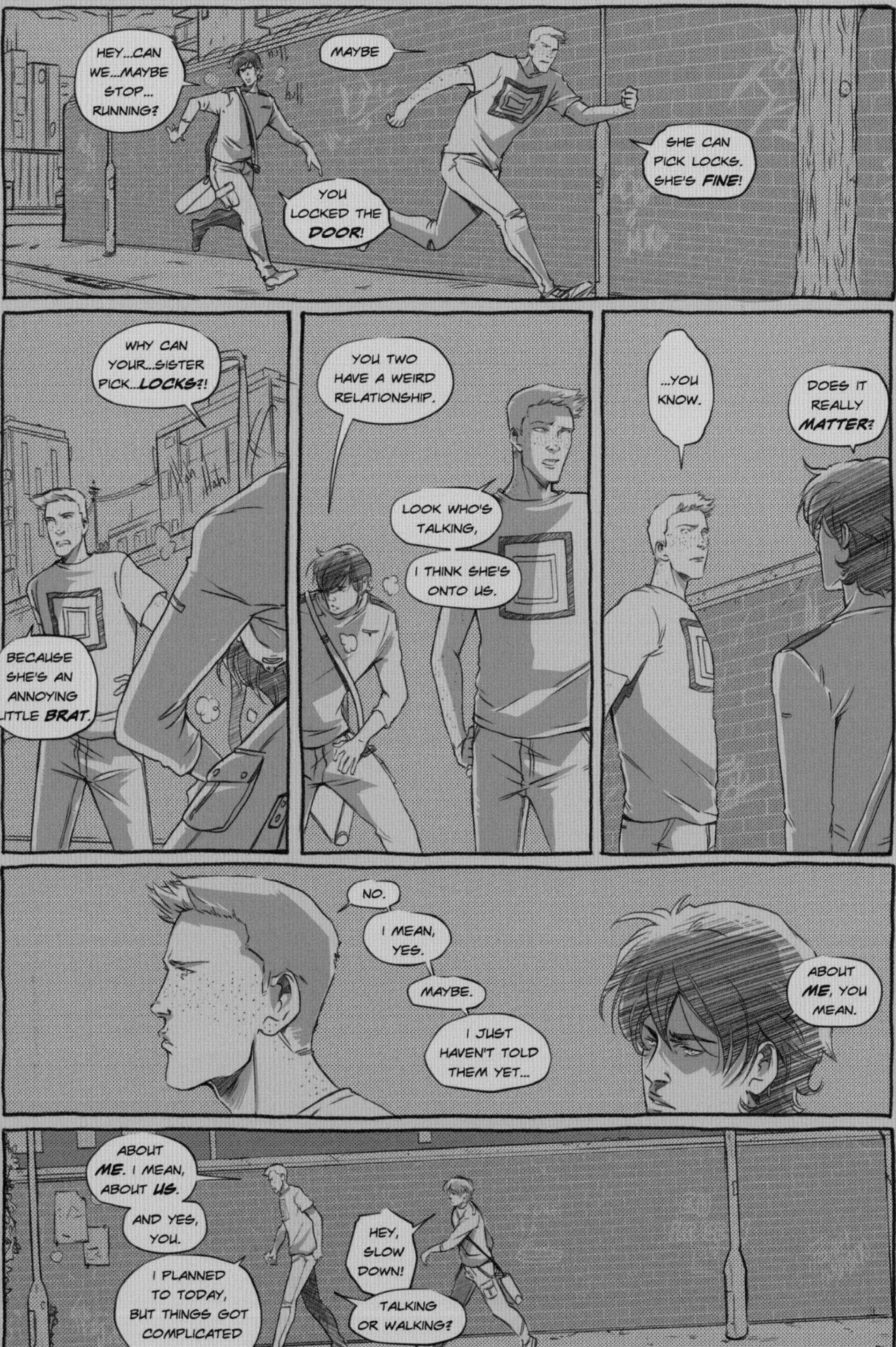
HEY...CAN WE...MAYBE STOP... RUNNING?
MAYBE
YOU LOCKED THE **DOOR**!
SHE CAN PICK LOCKS. SHE'S **FINE**!
WHY CAN YOUR...SISTER PICK...**LOCKS**?!
BECAUSE SHE'S AN ANNOYING LITTLE **BRAT**.
YOU TWO HAVE A WEIRD RELATIONSHIP.
LOOK WHO'S TALKING,
I THINK SHE'S ONTO US.
...YOU KNOW.
DOES IT REALLY **MATTER**?
NO.
I MEAN, YES.
MAYBE.
I JUST HAVEN'T TOLD THEM YET...
ABOUT **ME**, YOU MEAN.
ABOUT **ME**. I MEAN, ABOUT **US**.
AND YES, YOU.
I PLANNED TO TODAY, BUT THINGS GOT COMPLICATED AND NOW...
HEY, SLOW DOWN!
TALKING OR WALKING?

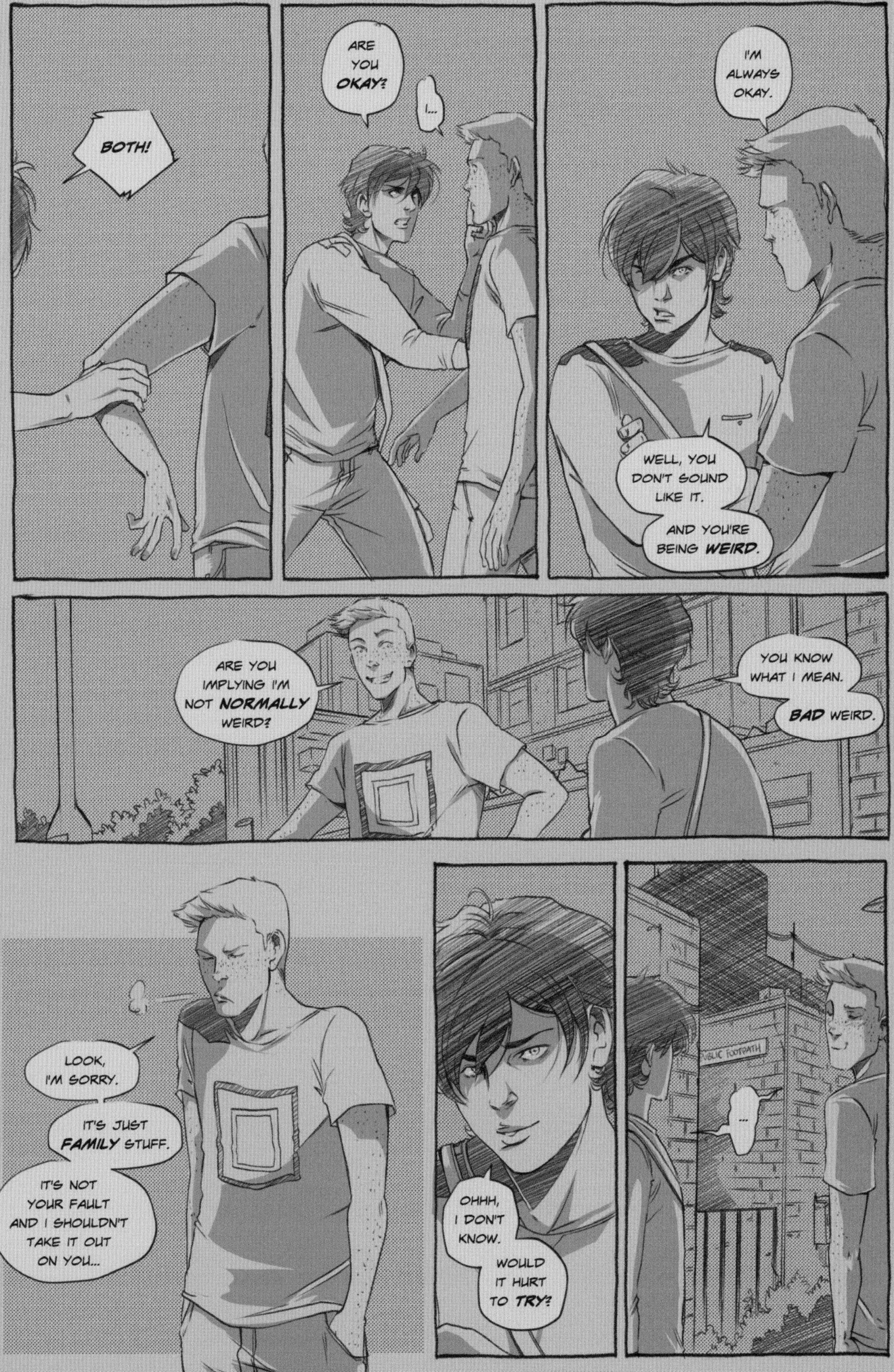
BOTH!
ARE YOU OKAY?
I...
I'M ALWAYS OKAY.
WELL, YOU DON'T SOUND LIKE IT.
AND YOU'RE BEING WEIRD.
ARE YOU IMPLYING I'M NOT NORMALLY WEIRD?
YOU KNOW WHAT I MEAN.
BAD WEIRD.
LOOK, I'M SORRY.
IT'S JUST FAMILY STUFF.
IT'S NOT YOUR FAULT AND I SHOULDN'T TAKE IT OUT ON YOU...
OHHH, I DON'T KNOW.
WOULD IT HURT TO TRY?
...
PUBLIC FOOTPATH

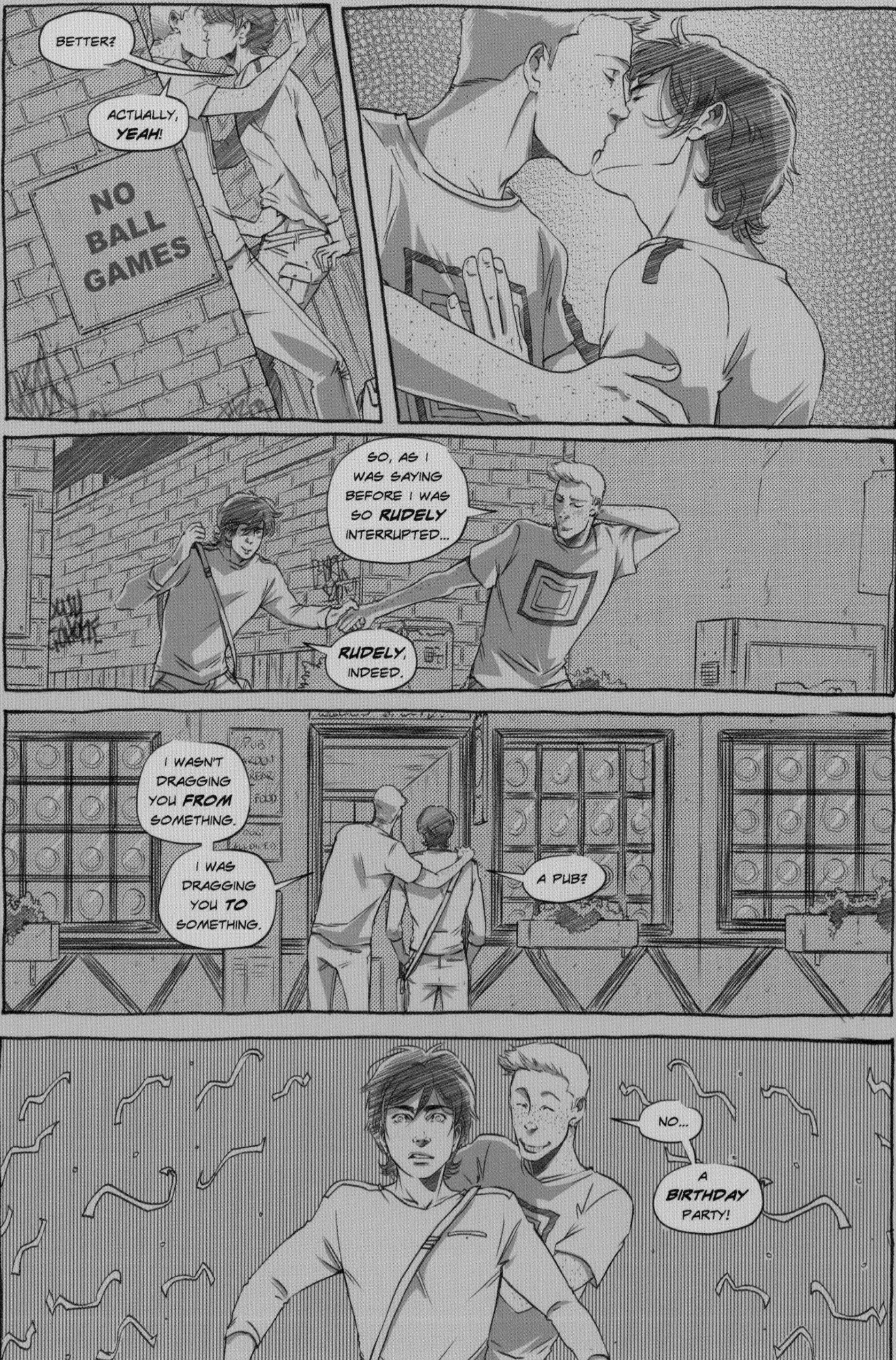
BETTER?
ACTUALLY, YEAH!
NO BALL GAMES
SO, AS I WAS SAYING BEFORE I WAS SO RUDELY INTERRUPTED...
RUDELY, INDEED.
I WASN'T DRAGGING YOU FROM SOMETHING.
I WAS DRAGGING YOU TO SOMETHING.
A PUB?
NO...
A BIRTHDAY PARTY!

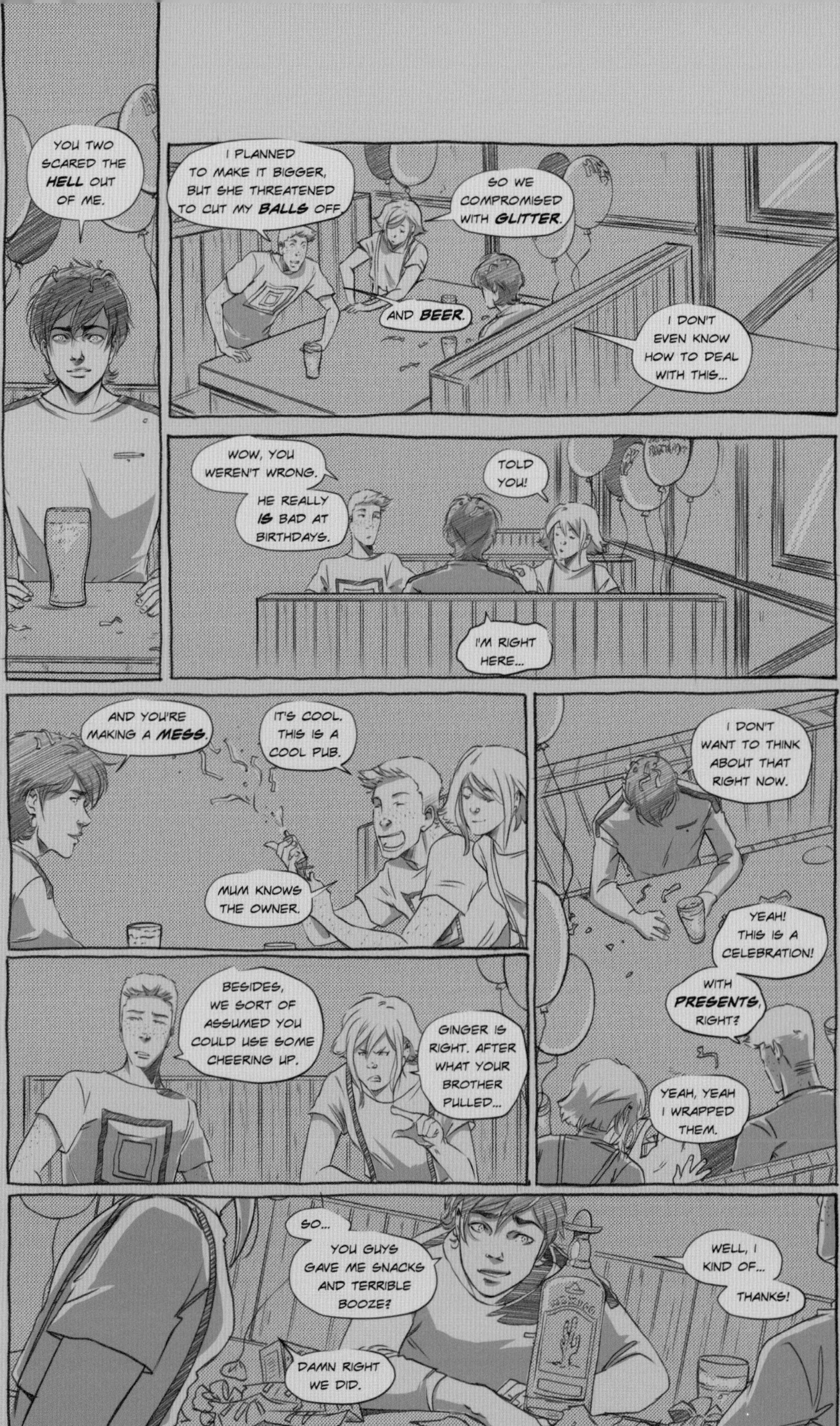
YOU TWO SCARED THE HELL OUT OF ME.
I PLANNED TO MAKE IT BIGGER, BUT SHE THREATENED TO CUT MY BALLS OFF.
SO WE COMPROMISED WITH GLITTER.
AND BEER.
I DON'T EVEN KNOW HOW TO DEAL WITH THIS...
WOW, YOU WEREN'T WRONG.
HE REALLY IS BAD AT BIRTHDAYS.
TOLD YOU!
I'M RIGHT HERE...
AND YOU'RE MAKING A MESS.
IT'S COOL. THIS IS A COOL PUB.
MUM KNOWS THE OWNER.
I DON'T WANT TO THINK ABOUT THAT RIGHT NOW.
BESIDES, WE SORT OF ASSUMED YOU COULD USE SOME CHEERING UP.
GINGER IS RIGHT. AFTER WHAT YOUR BROTHER PULLED...
YEAH! THIS IS A CELEBRATION!
WITH PRESENTS, RIGHT?
YEAH, YEAH I WRAPPED THEM.
SO...
YOU GUYS GAVE ME SNACKS AND TERRIBLE BOOZE?
DAMN RIGHT WE DID.
WELL, I KIND OF...
THANKS!

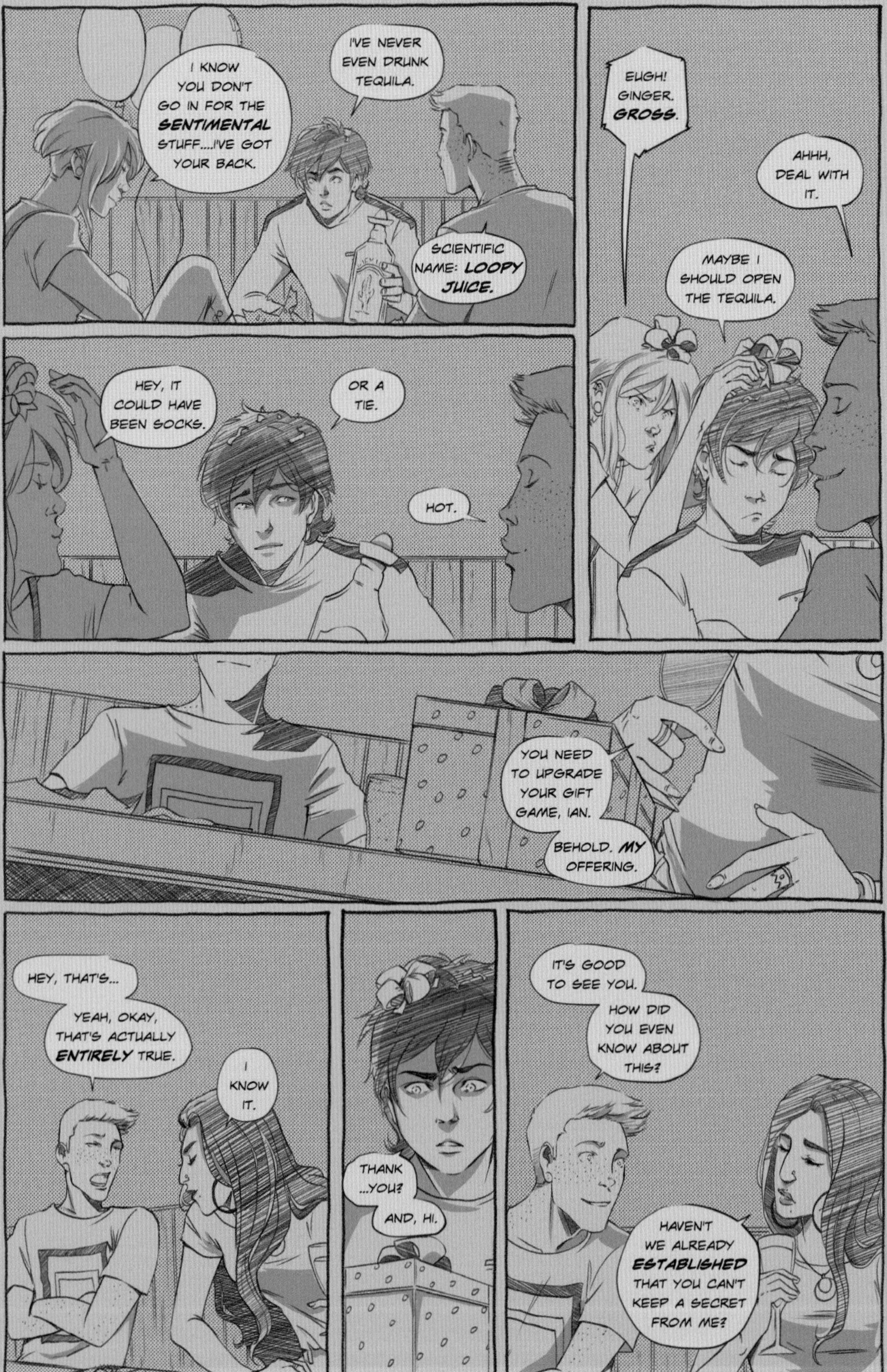
I KNOW YOU DON'T GO IN FOR THE **SENTIMENTAL** STUFF....I'VE GOT YOUR BACK.
I'VE NEVER EVEN DRUNK TEQUILA.
SCIENTIFIC NAME: **LOOPY JUICE.**
EUGH! GINGER. **GROSS**.
AHHH, DEAL WITH IT.
MAYBE I SHOULD OPEN THE TEQUILA.
HEY, IT COULD HAVE BEEN SOCKS.
OR A TIE.
HOT.
YOU NEED TO UPGRADE YOUR GIFT GAME, IAN.
BEHOLD. **MY** OFFERING.
HEY, THAT'S...
YEAH, OKAY, THAT'S ACTUALLY **ENTIRELY** TRUE.
I KNOW IT.
THANK ...YOU?
AND, HI.
IT'S GOOD TO SEE YOU.
HOW DID YOU EVEN KNOW ABOUT THIS?
HAVEN'T WE ALREADY **ESTABLISHED** THAT YOU CAN'T KEEP A SECRET FROM ME?

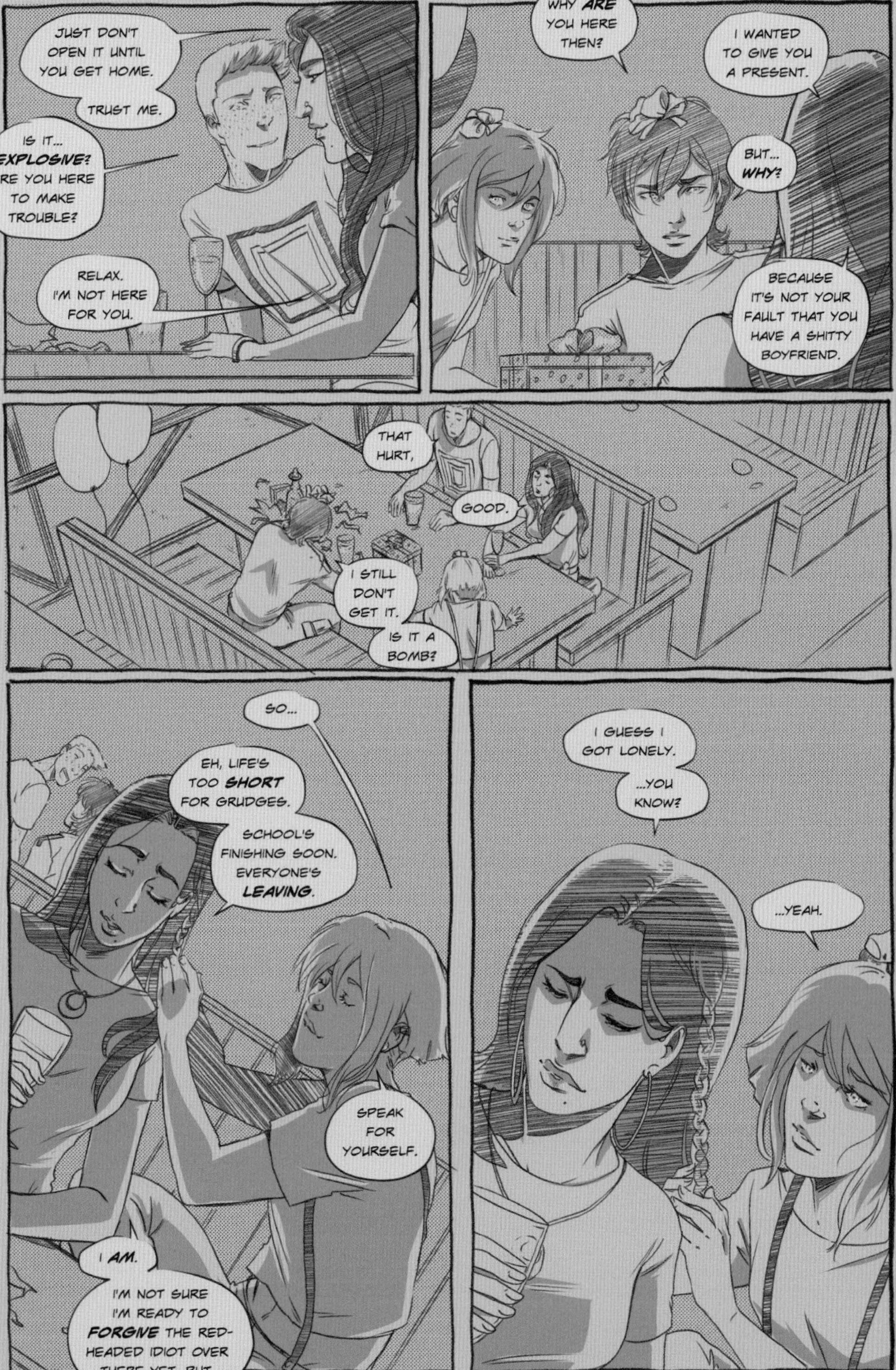

JUST DON'T OPEN IT UNTIL YOU GET HOME.
TRUST ME.
IS IT... EXPLOSIVE? ARE YOU HERE TO MAKE TROUBLE?
RELAX. I'M NOT HERE FOR YOU.
WHY ARE YOU HERE THEN?
I WANTED TO GIVE YOU A PRESENT.
BUT... WHY?
BECAUSE IT'S NOT YOUR FAULT THAT YOU HAVE A SHITTY BOYFRIEND.
THAT HURT,
GOOD.
I STILL DON'T GET IT.
IS IT A BOMB?
SO...
EH, LIFE'S TOO SHORT FOR GRUDGES.
SCHOOL'S FINISHING SOON. EVERYONE'S LEAVING.
SPEAK FOR YOURSELF.
I AM.
I'M NOT SURE I'M READY TO FORGIVE THE RED-HEADED IDIOT OVER THERE YET, BUT...
I GUESS I GOT LONELY.
...YOU KNOW?
...YEAH.

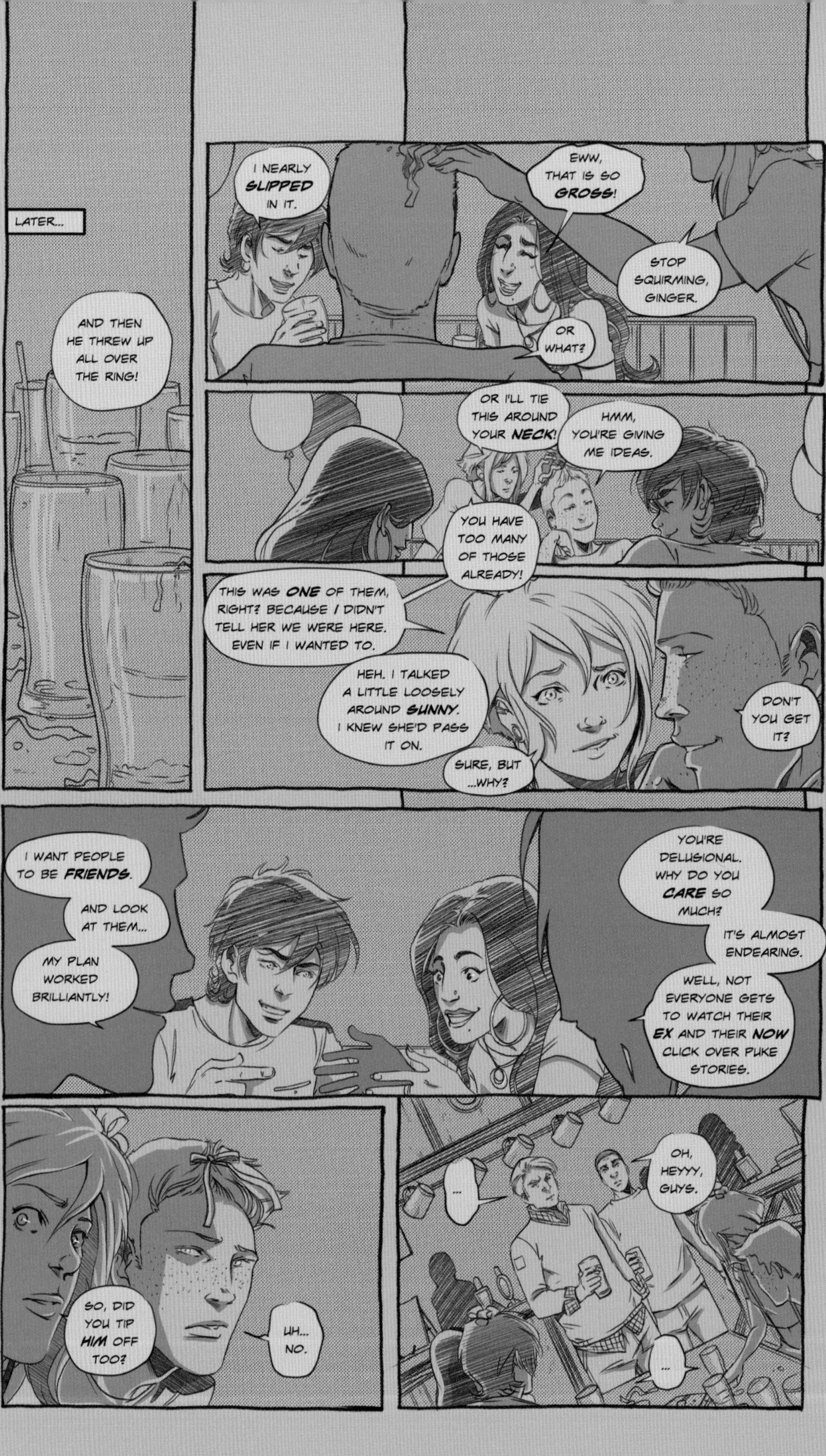
LATER...
AND THEN HE THREW UP ALL OVER THE RING!
I NEARLY SLIPPED IN IT.
EWW, THAT IS SO GROSS!
STOP SQUIRMING, GINGER.
OR WHAT?
OR I'LL TIE THIS AROUND YOUR NECK!
HMM, YOU'RE GIVING ME IDEAS.
YOU HAVE TOO MANY OF THOSE ALREADY!
THIS WAS ONE OF THEM, RIGHT? BECAUSE I DIDN'T TELL HER WE WERE HERE. EVEN IF I WANTED TO.
HEH. I TALKED A LITTLE LOOSELY AROUND SUNNY. I KNEW SHE'D PASS IT ON.
SURE, BUT ...WHY?
DON'T YOU GET IT?
I WANT PEOPLE TO BE FRIENDS.
AND LOOK AT THEM...
MY PLAN WORKED BRILLIANTLY!
YOU'RE DELUSIONAL. WHY DO YOU CARE SO MUCH?
IT'S ALMOST ENDEARING.
WELL, NOT EVERYONE GETS TO WATCH THEIR EX AND THEIR NOW CLICK OVER PUKE STORIES.
SO, DID YOU TIP HIM OFF TOO?
UH... NO.
...
OH, HEYYY, GUYS.
...

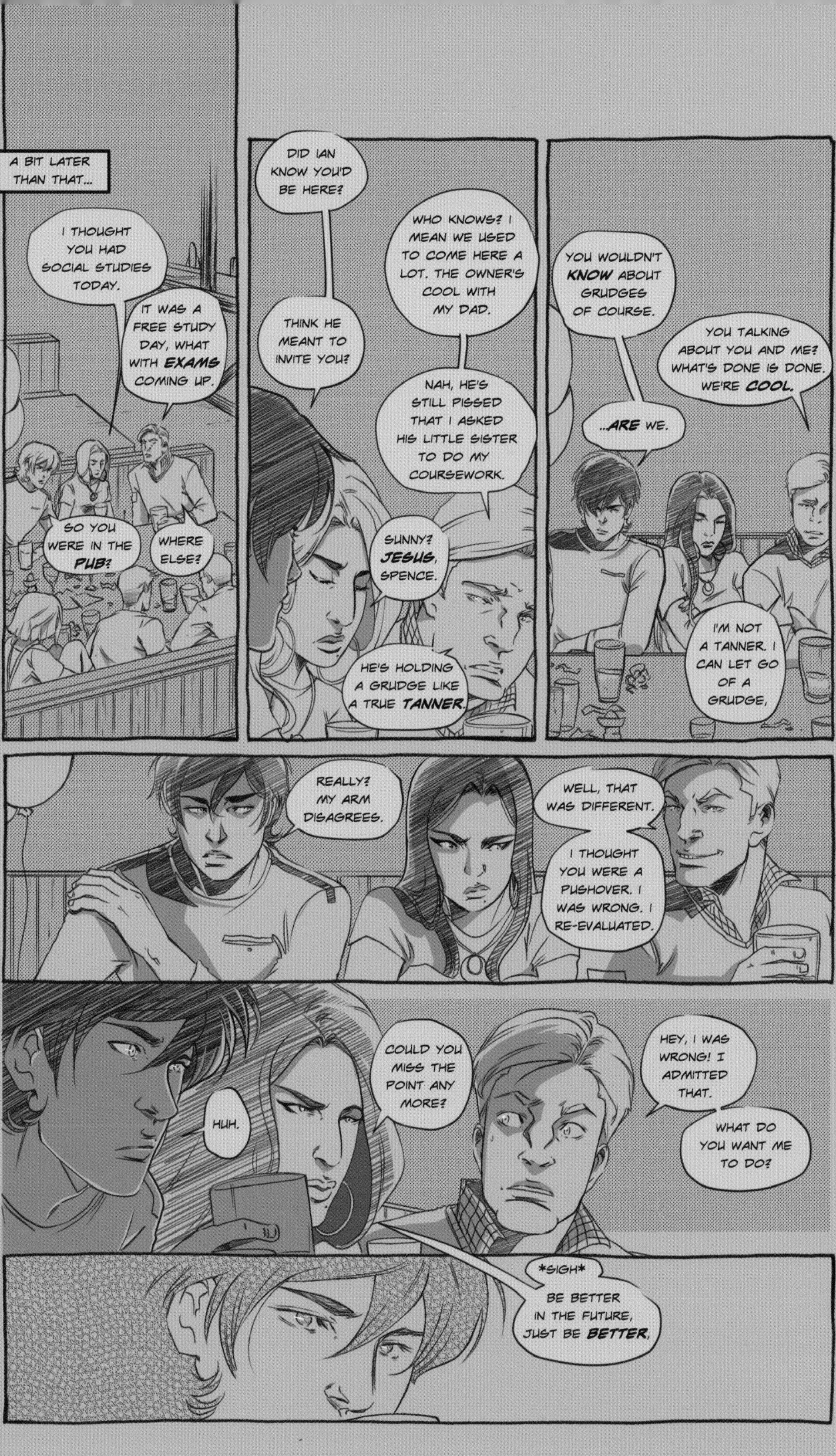

A BIT LATER THAN THAT...
I THOUGHT YOU HAD SOCIAL STUDIES TODAY.
IT WAS A FREE STUDY DAY, WHAT WITH **EXAMS** COMING UP.
SO YOU WERE IN THE **PUB**?
WHERE ELSE?
DID IAN KNOW YOU'D BE HERE?
THINK HE MEANT TO INVITE YOU?
WHO KNOWS? I MEAN WE USED TO COME HERE A LOT. THE OWNER'S COOL WITH MY DAD.
NAH, HE'S STILL PISSED THAT I ASKED HIS LITTLE SISTER TO DO MY COURSEWORK.
SUNNY? **JESUS**, SPENCE.
HE'S HOLDING A GRUDGE LIKE A TRUE **TANNER**.
YOU WOULDN'T **KNOW** ABOUT GRUDGES OF COURSE.
YOU TALKING ABOUT YOU AND ME? WHAT'S DONE IS DONE. WE'RE **COOL**.
...**ARE** WE.
I'M NOT A TANNER. I CAN LET GO OF A GRUDGE,
REALLY? MY ARM DISAGREES.
WELL, THAT WAS DIFFERENT.
I THOUGHT YOU WERE A PUSHOVER. I WAS WRONG. I RE-EVALUATED.
HUH.
COULD YOU MISS THE POINT ANY MORE?
HEY, I WAS WRONG! I ADMITTED THAT.
WHAT DO YOU WANT ME TO DO?
SIGH
BE BETTER IN THE FUTURE, JUST BE **BETTER**.

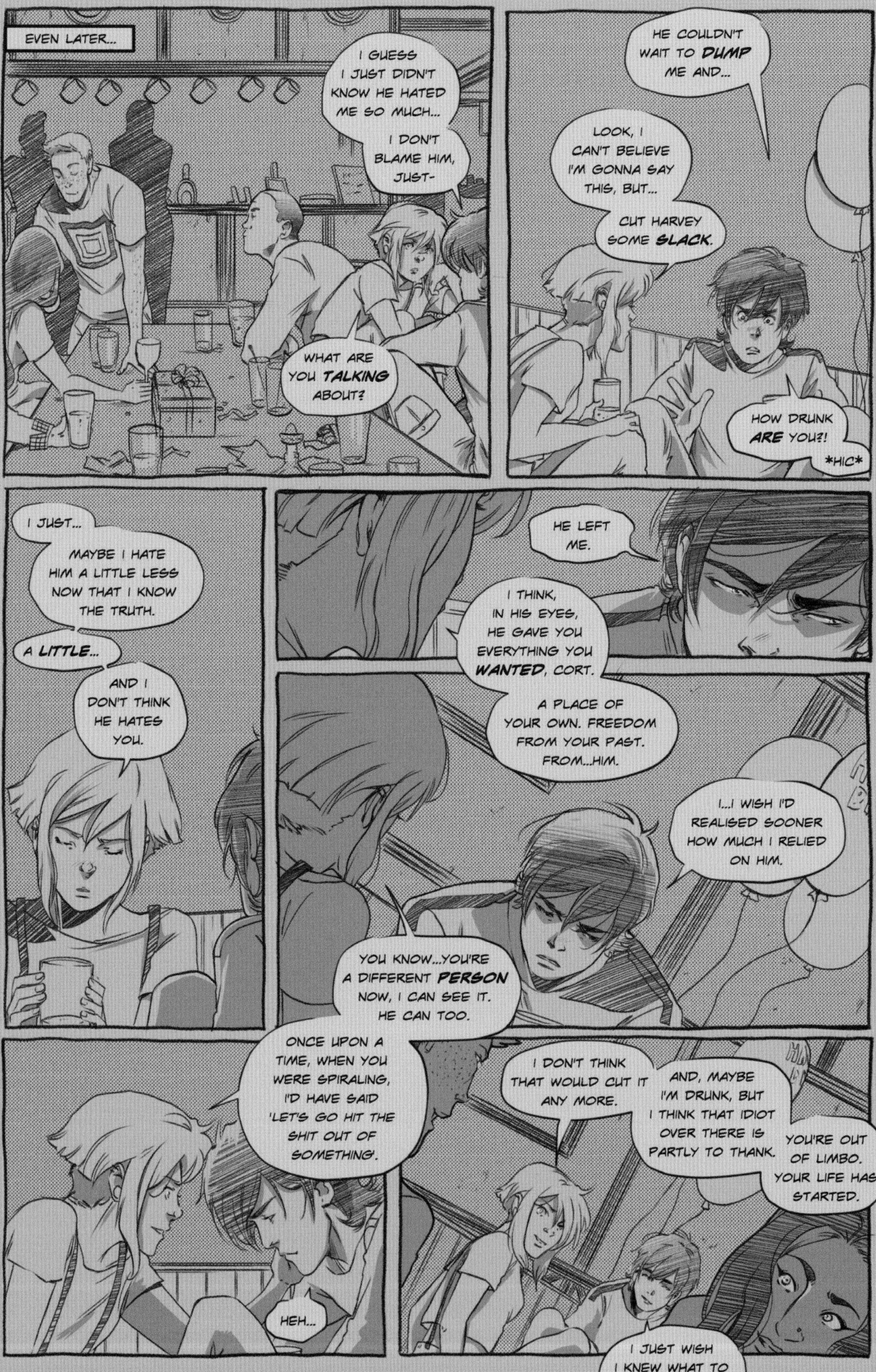

EVEN LATER...
I GUESS I JUST DIDN'T KNOW HE HATED ME SO MUCH...
I DON'T BLAME HIM, JUST-
WHAT ARE YOU TALKING ABOUT?
HE COULDN'T WAIT TO DUMP ME AND...
LOOK, I CAN'T BELIEVE I'M GONNA SAY THIS, BUT...
CUT HARVEY SOME SLACK.
HOW DRUNK ARE YOU?!
HIC
I JUST...
MAYBE I HATE HIM A LITTLE LESS NOW THAT I KNOW THE TRUTH.
A LITTLE...
AND I DON'T THINK HE HATES YOU.
HE LEFT ME.
I THINK, IN HIS EYES, HE GAVE YOU EVERYTHING YOU WANTED, CORT.
A PLACE OF YOUR OWN. FREEDOM FROM YOUR PAST. FROM...HIM.
I...I WISH I'D REALISED SOONER HOW MUCH I RELIED ON HIM.
YOU KNOW...YOU'RE A DIFFERENT PERSON NOW, I CAN SEE IT. HE CAN TOO.
ONCE UPON A TIME, WHEN YOU WERE SPIRALING, I'D HAVE SAID 'LET'S GO HIT THE SHIT OUT OF SOMETHING.
HEH...
I DON'T THINK THAT WOULD CUT IT ANY MORE.
AND, MAYBE I'M DRUNK, BUT I THINK THAT IDIOT OVER THERE IS PARTLY TO THANK.
YOU'RE OUT OF LIMBO. YOUR LIFE HAS STARTED.
I JUST WISH I KNEW WHAT TO DO WITH IT...
HIC

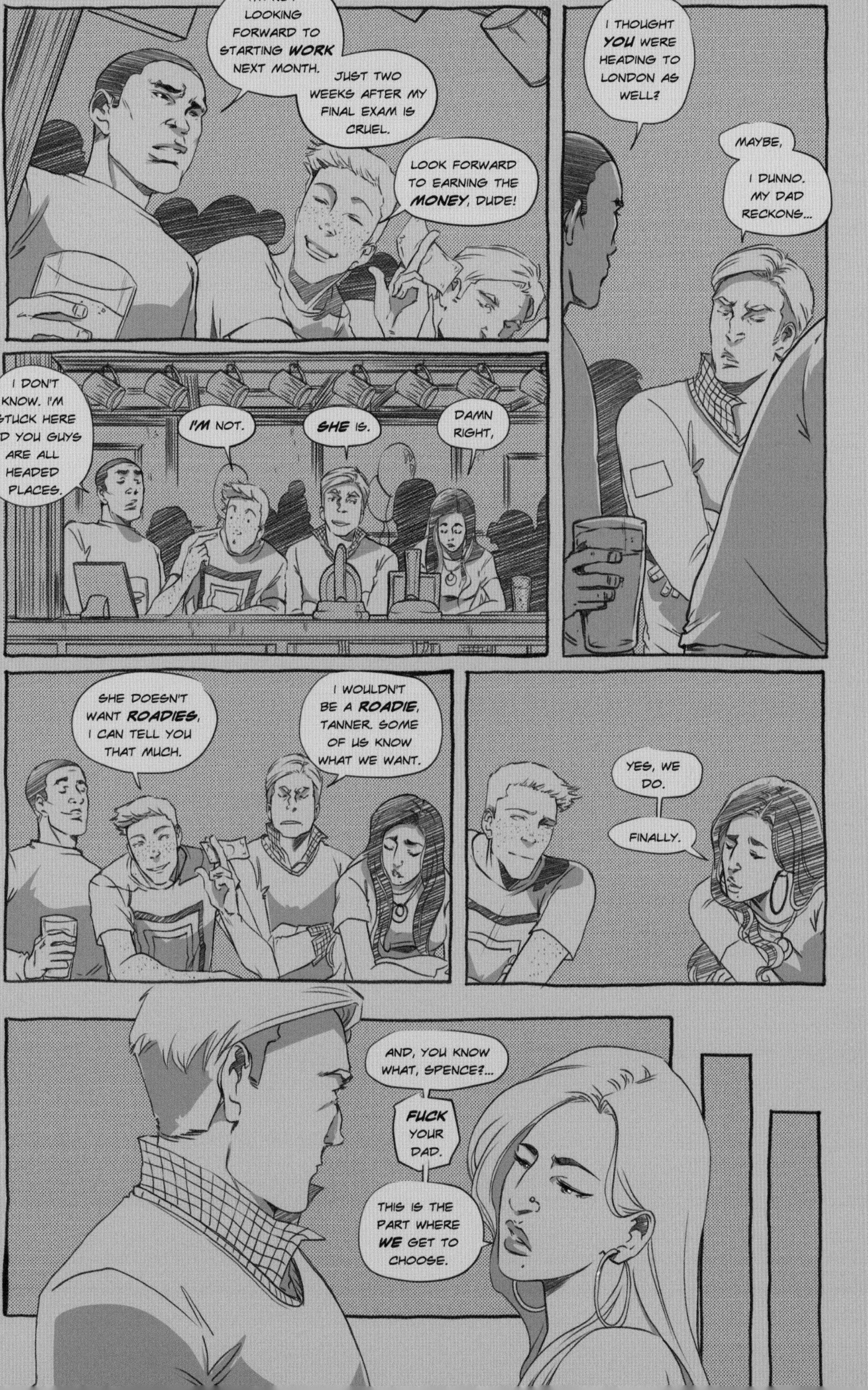
I'M NOT LOOKING FORWARD TO STARTING WORK NEXT MONTH.
JUST TWO WEEKS AFTER MY FINAL EXAM IS CRUEL.
LOOK FORWARD TO EARNING THE MONEY, DUDE!
I THOUGHT YOU WERE HEADING TO LONDON AS WELL?
MAYBE,
I DUNNO. MY DAD RECKONS...
I DON'T KNOW. I'M STUCK HERE AND YOU GUYS ARE ALL HEADED PLACES.
I'M NOT.
SHE IS.
DAMN RIGHT,
SHE DOESN'T WANT ROADIES, I CAN TELL YOU THAT MUCH.
I WOULDN'T BE A ROADIE, TANNER. SOME OF US KNOW WHAT WE WANT.
YES, WE DO.
FINALLY.
AND, YOU KNOW WHAT, SPENCE?...
FUCK YOUR DAD.
THIS IS THE PART WHERE WE GET TO CHOOSE.

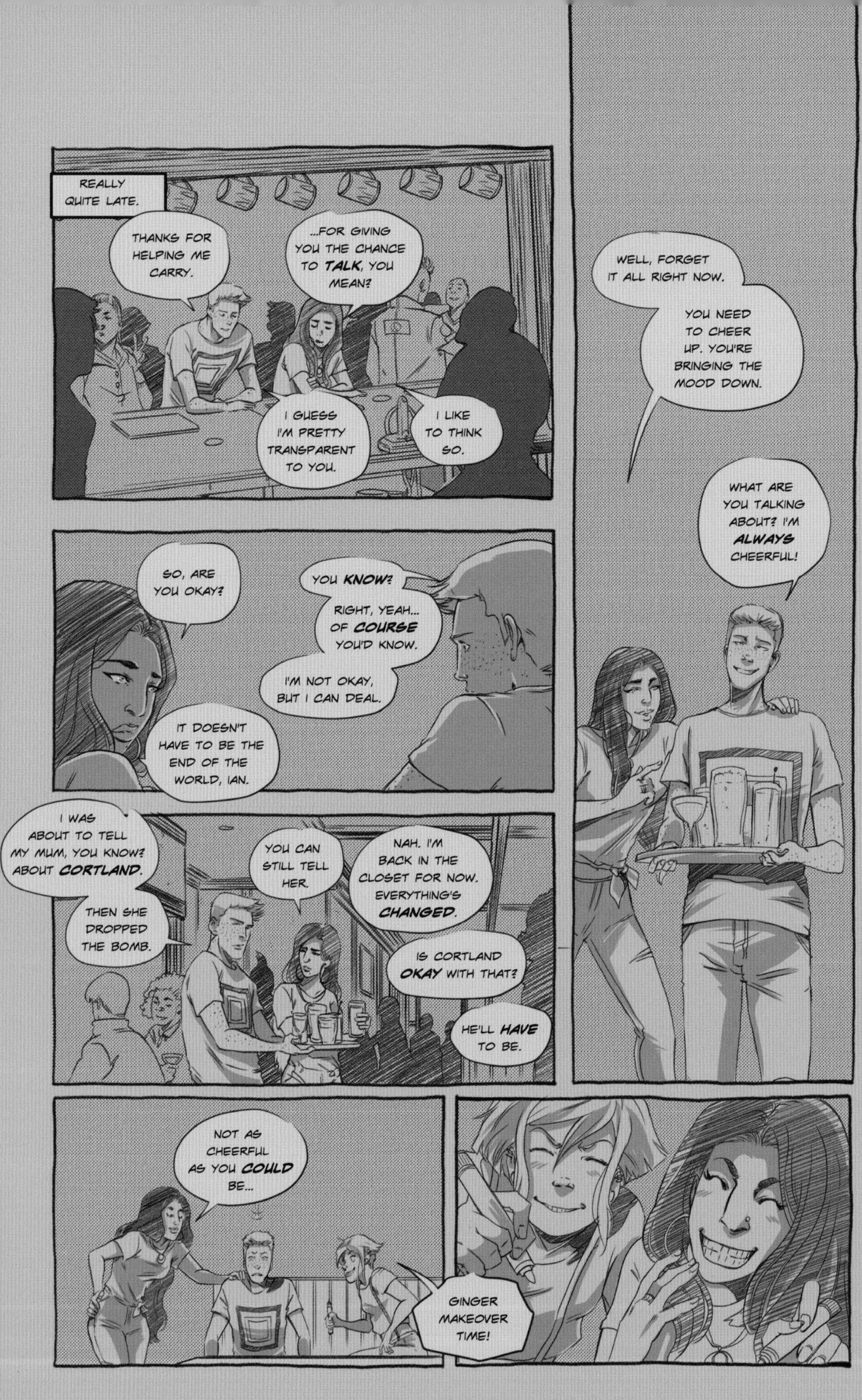

REALLY QUITE LATE.
THANKS FOR HELPING ME CARRY.
...FOR GIVING YOU THE CHANCE TO TALK, YOU MEAN?
I GUESS I'M PRETTY TRANSPARENT TO YOU.
I LIKE TO THINK SO.
SO, ARE YOU OKAY?
YOU KNOW?
RIGHT, YEAH... OF COURSE YOU'D KNOW.
I'M NOT OKAY, BUT I CAN DEAL.
IT DOESN'T HAVE TO BE THE END OF THE WORLD, IAN.
I WAS ABOUT TO TELL MY MUM, YOU KNOW? ABOUT CORTLAND.
THEN SHE DROPPED THE BOMB.
YOU CAN STILL TELL HER.
NAH. I'M BACK IN THE CLOSET FOR NOW. EVERYTHING'S CHANGED.
IS CORTLAND OKAY WITH THAT?
HE'LL HAVE TO BE.
WELL, FORGET IT ALL RIGHT NOW.
YOU NEED TO CHEER UP. YOU'RE BRINGING THE MOOD DOWN.
WHAT ARE YOU TALKING ABOUT? I'M ALWAYS CHEERFUL!
NOT AS CHEERFUL AS YOU COULD BE...
GINGER MAKEOVER TIME!

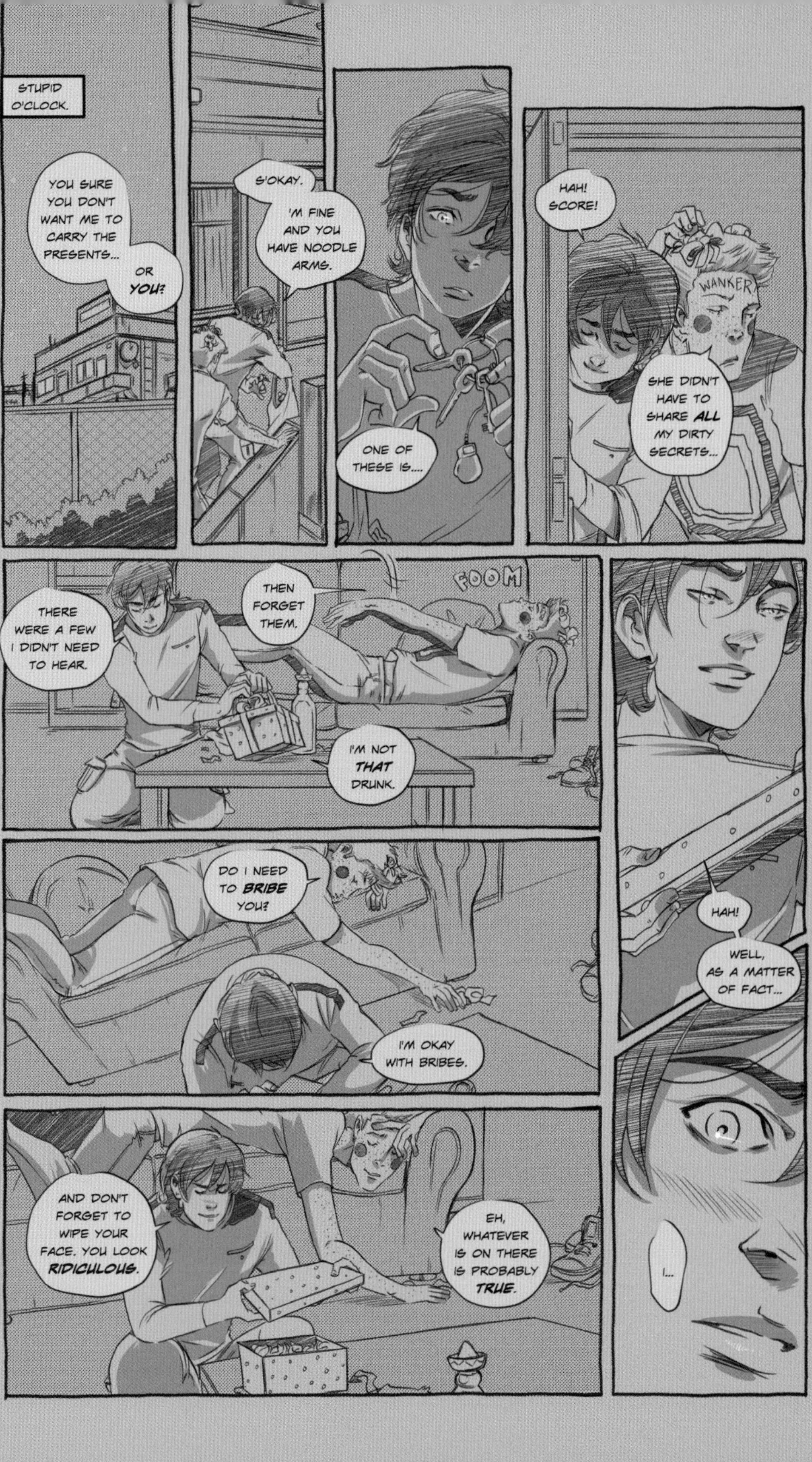
STUPID O'CLOCK.
YOU SURE YOU DON'T WANT ME TO CARRY THE PRESENTS...
OR YOU?
S'OKAY.
'M FINE AND YOU HAVE NOODLE ARMS.
ONE OF THESE IS....
HAH! SCORE!
WANKER
SHE DIDN'T HAVE TO SHARE ALL MY DIRTY SECRETS...
THERE WERE A FEW I DIDN'T NEED TO HEAR.
THEN FORGET THEM.
FOOM
I'M NOT THAT DRUNK.
HAH!
WELL, AS A MATTER OF FACT...
DO I NEED TO BRIBE YOU?
I'M OKAY WITH BRIBES.
AND DON'T FORGET TO WIPE YOUR FACE. YOU LOOK RIDICULOUS.
EH, WHATEVER IS ON THERE IS PROBABLY TRUE.
I...

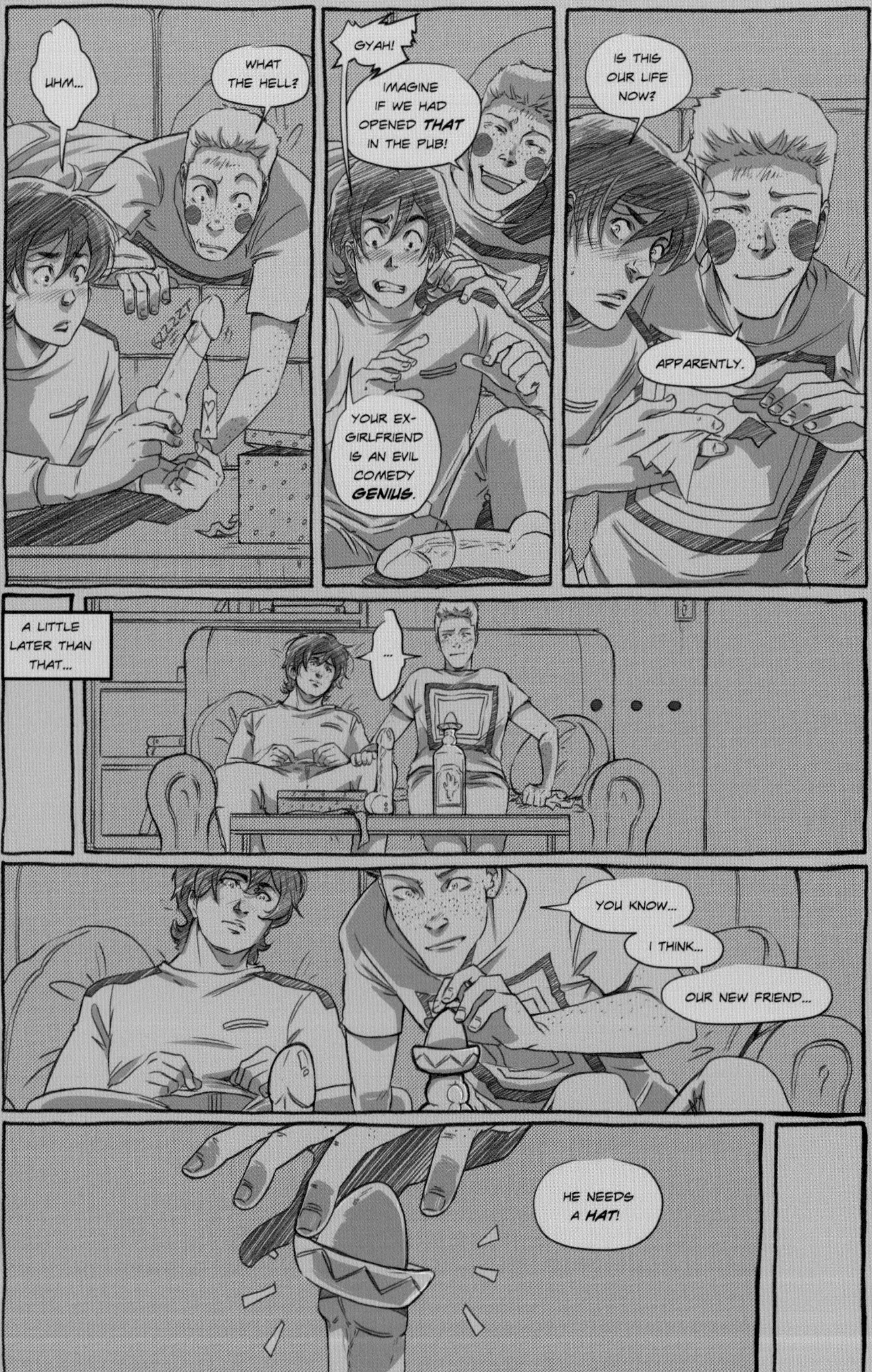
UHM...
WHAT THE HELL?
SZZZZT
GYAH!
IMAGINE IF WE HAD OPENED THAT IN THE PUB!
YOUR EX-GIRLFRIEND IS AN EVIL COMEDY GENIUS.
IS THIS OUR LIFE NOW?
APPARENTLY.
A LITTLE LATER THAN THAT...
...
YOU KNOW...
I THINK...
OUR NEW FRIEND...
HE NEEDS A HAT!

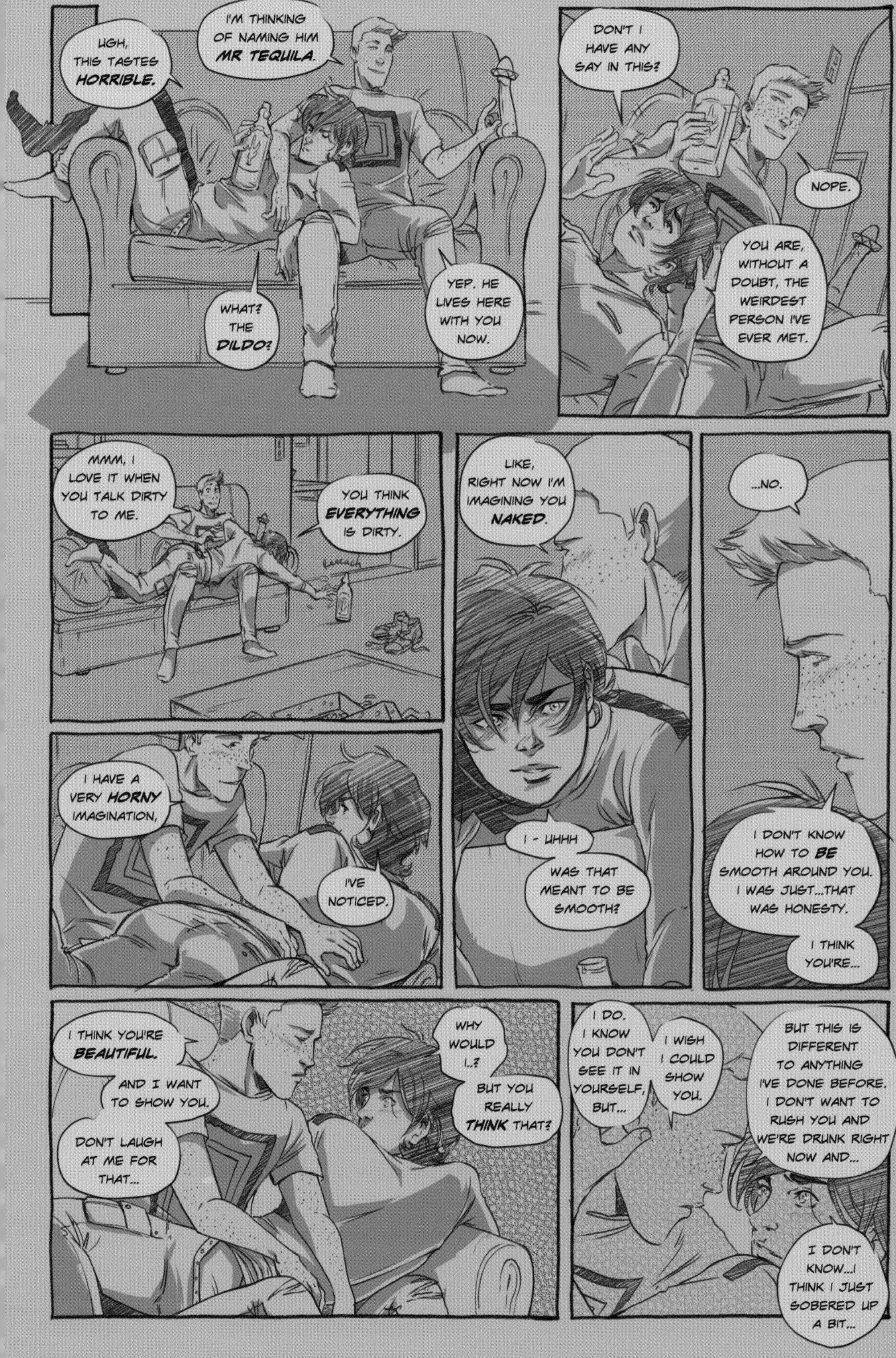
UGH, THIS TASTES HORRIBLE.
I'M THINKING OF NAMING HIM MR TEQUILA.
WHAT? THE DILDO?
YEP. HE LIVES HERE WITH YOU NOW.
DON'T I HAVE ANY SAY IN THIS?
NOPE.
YOU ARE, WITHOUT A DOUBT, THE WEIRDEST PERSON I'VE EVER MET.
MMM, I LOVE IT WHEN YOU TALK DIRTY TO ME.
YOU THINK EVERYTHING IS DIRTY.
LIKE, RIGHT NOW I'M IMAGINING YOU NAKED.
...NO.
I HAVE A VERY HORNY IMAGINATION,
I'VE NOTICED.
I - UHHH
WAS THAT MEANT TO BE SMOOTH?
I DON'T KNOW HOW TO BE SMOOTH AROUND YOU. I WAS JUST...THAT WAS HONESTY.
I THINK YOU'RE...
I THINK YOU'RE BEAUTIFUL.
AND I WANT TO SHOW YOU.
DON'T LAUGH AT ME FOR THAT...
WHY WOULD I..?
BUT YOU REALLY THINK THAT?
I DO. I KNOW YOU DON'T SEE IT IN YOURSELF, BUT...
I WISH I COULD SHOW YOU.
BUT THIS IS DIFFERENT TO ANYTHING I'VE DONE BEFORE. I DON'T WANT TO RUSH YOU AND WE'RE DRUNK RIGHT NOW AND...
I DON'T KNOW...I THINK I JUST SOBERED UP A BIT...

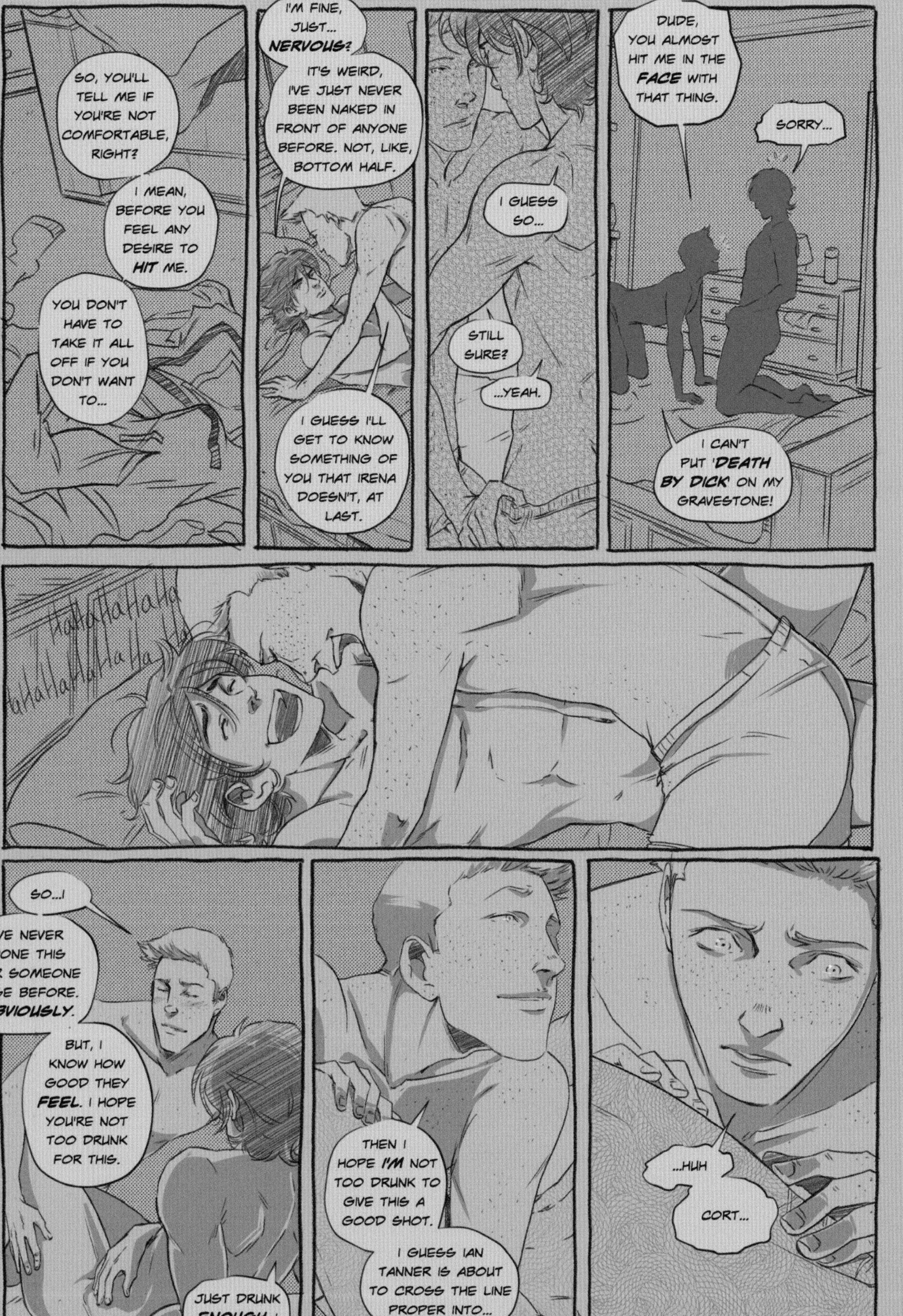
SO, YOU'LL TELL ME IF YOU'RE NOT COMFORTABLE, RIGHT?
I MEAN, BEFORE YOU FEEL ANY DESIRE TO **HIT** ME.
YOU DON'T HAVE TO TAKE IT ALL OFF IF YOU DON'T WANT TO...
I'M FINE, JUST... **NERVOUS?**
IT'S WEIRD, I'VE JUST NEVER BEEN NAKED IN FRONT OF ANYONE BEFORE. NOT, LIKE, BOTTOM HALF.
I GUESS I'LL GET TO KNOW SOMETHING OF YOU THAT IRENA DOESN'T, AT LAST.
I GUESS SO...
STILL SURE?
...YEAH.
DUDE, YOU ALMOST HIT ME IN THE **FACE** WITH THAT THING.
SORRY...
I CAN'T PUT '**DEATH BY DICK**' ON MY GRAVESTONE!
SO...I
I'VE NEVER DONE THIS FOR SOMEONE ELSE BEFORE. **OBVIOUSLY**.
BUT, I KNOW HOW GOOD THEY **FEEL**. I HOPE YOU'RE NOT TOO DRUNK FOR THIS.
JUST DRUNK **ENOUGH**, I THINK.
THEN I HOPE **I'M** NOT TOO DRUNK TO GIVE THIS A GOOD SHOT.
I GUESS IAN TANNER IS ABOUT TO CROSS THE LINE PROPER INTO...
...HUH
CORT...

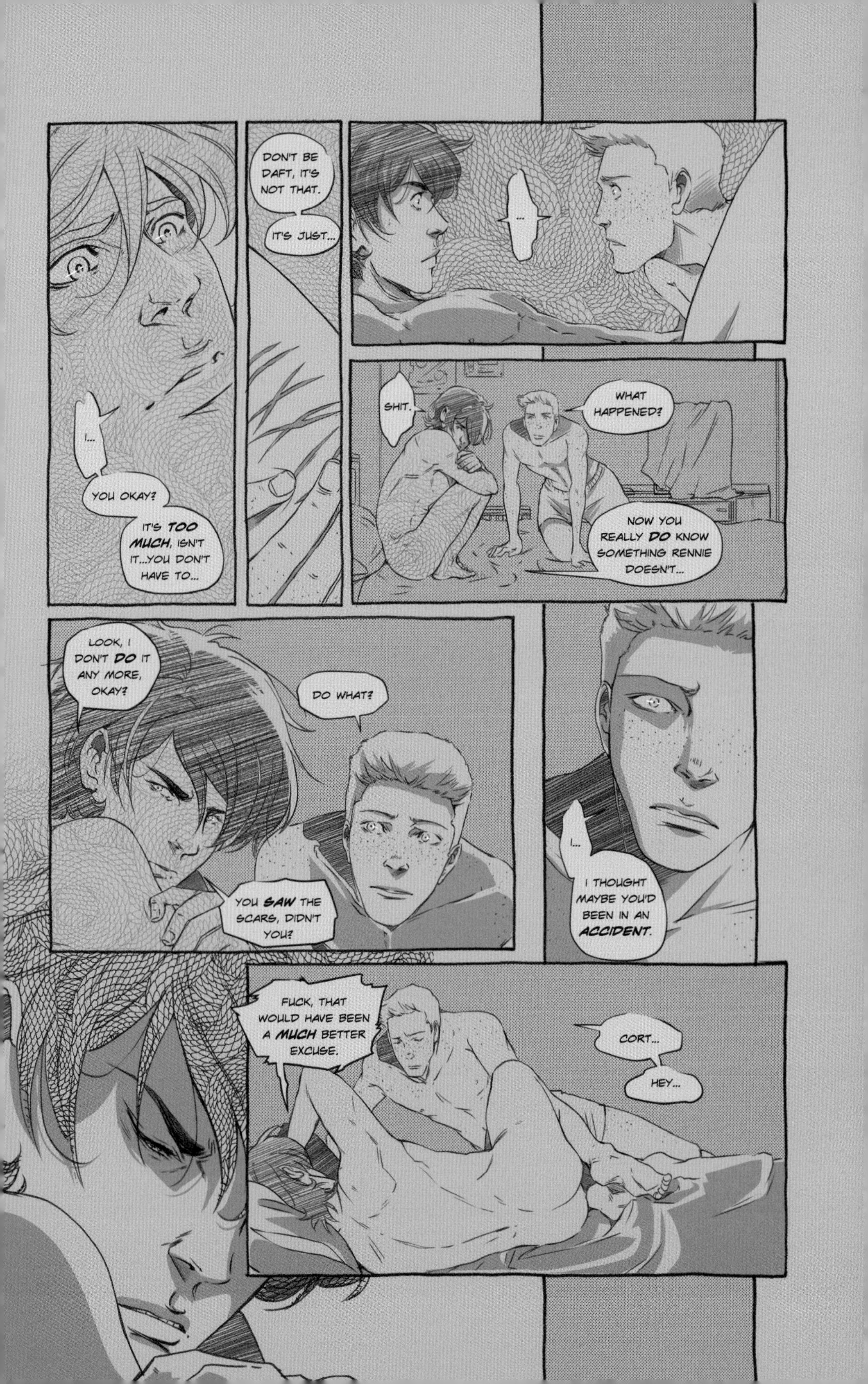
I...
YOU OKAY?
IT'S **TOO MUCH**, ISN'T IT...YOU DON'T HAVE TO...
DON'T BE DAFT, IT'S NOT THAT.
IT'S JUST...
...
SHIT.
WHAT HAPPENED?
NOW YOU REALLY **DO** KNOW SOMETHING RENNIE DOESN'T...
LOOK, I DON'T **DO** IT ANY MORE, OKAY?
DO WHAT?
YOU **SAW** THE SCARS, DIDN'T YOU?
I...
I THOUGHT MAYBE YOU'D BEEN IN AN **ACCIDENT**.
FUCK, THAT WOULD HAVE BEEN A **MUCH** BETTER EXCUSE.
CORT...
HEY...

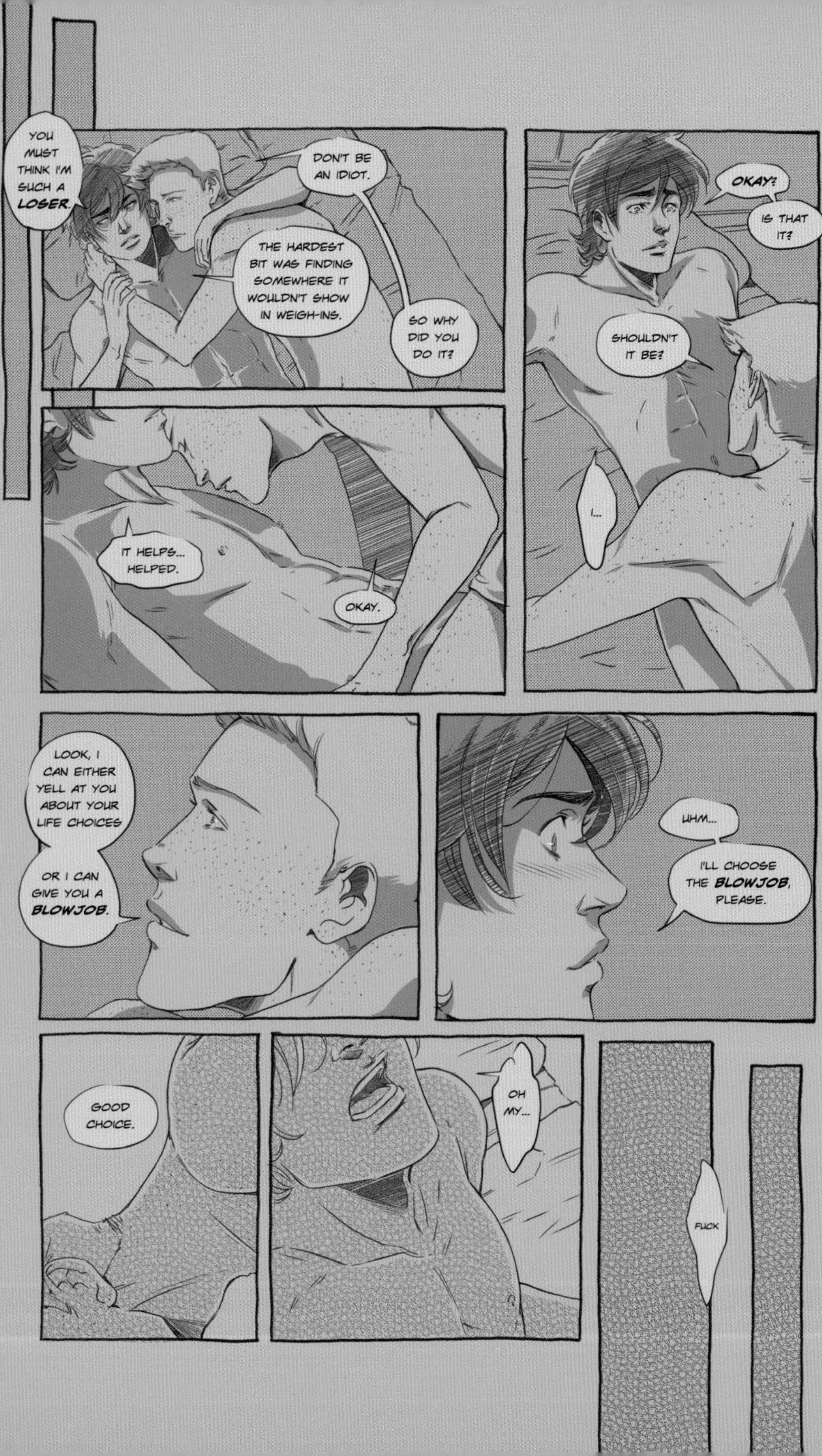
YOU MUST THINK I'M SUCH A **LOSER**.
DON'T BE AN IDIOT.
THE HARDEST BIT WAS FINDING SOMEWHERE IT WOULDN'T SHOW IN WEIGH-INS.
SO WHY DID YOU DO IT?
IT HELPS... HELPED.
OKAY.
OKAY?
IS THAT IT?
SHOULDN'T IT BE?
I...
LOOK, I CAN EITHER YELL AT YOU ABOUT YOUR LIFE CHOICES
OR I CAN GIVE YOU A **BLOWJOB**.
UHM...
I'LL CHOOSE THE **BLOWJOB**, PLEASE.
GOOD CHOICE.
OH MY...
FUCK

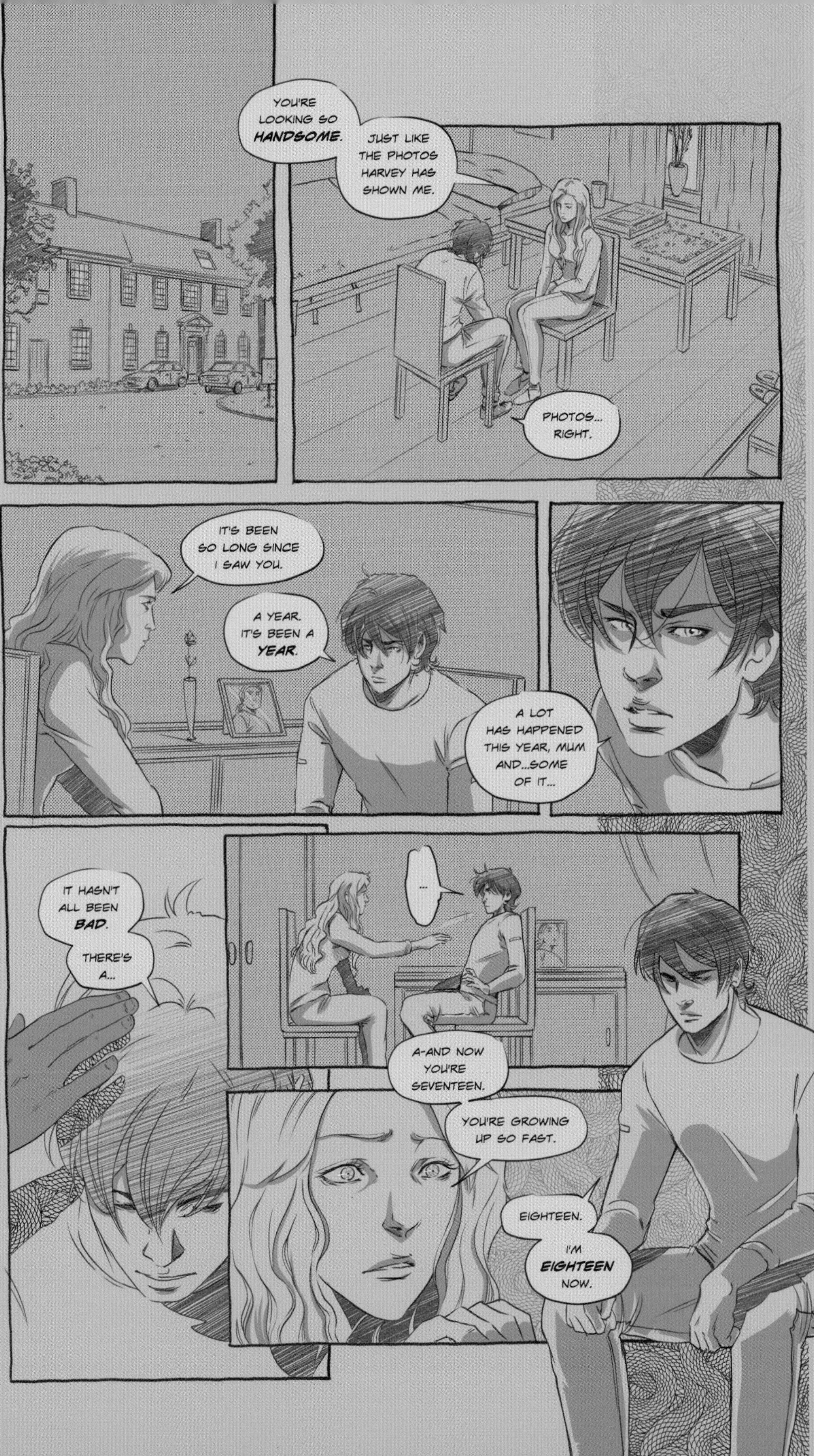
YOU'RE LOOKING SO HANDSOME.
JUST LIKE THE PHOTOS HARVEY HAS SHOWN ME.
PHOTOS... RIGHT.
IT'S BEEN SO LONG SINCE I SAW YOU.
A YEAR. IT'S BEEN A YEAR.
A LOT HAS HAPPENED THIS YEAR, MUM AND...SOME OF IT...
IT HASN'T ALL BEEN BAD.
THERE'S A...
...
A-AND NOW YOU'RE SEVENTEEN.
YOU'RE GROWING UP SO FAST.
EIGHTEEN.
I'M EIGHTEEN NOW.

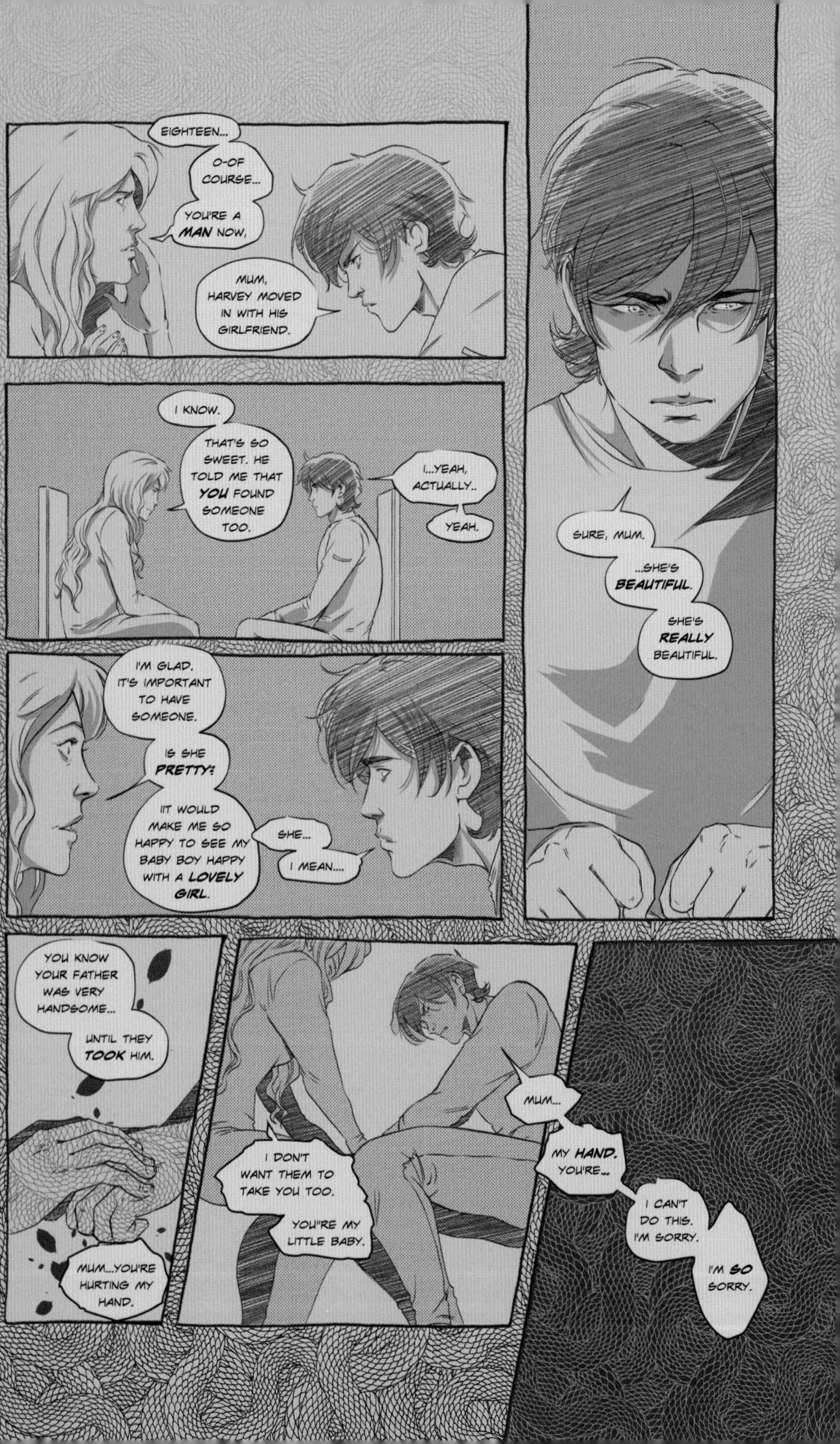
EIGHTEEN...
O-OF COURSE...
YOU'RE A MAN NOW,
MUM, HARVEY MOVED IN WITH HIS GIRLFRIEND.
I KNOW.
THAT'S SO SWEET. HE TOLD ME THAT YOU FOUND SOMEONE TOO.
I...YEAH, ACTUALLY..
YEAH.
I'M GLAD. IT'S IMPORTANT TO HAVE SOMEONE.
IS SHE PRETTY?
IIT WOULD MAKE ME SO HAPPY TO SEE MY BABY BOY HAPPY WITH A LOVELY GIRL.
SHE...
I MEAN....
SURE, MUM.
...SHE'S BEAUTIFUL.
SHE'S REALLY BEAUTIFUL.
YOU KNOW YOUR FATHER WAS VERY HANDSOME...
UNTIL THEY TOOK HIM.
MUM...YOU'RE HURTING MY HAND.
I DON'T WANT THEM TO TAKE YOU TOO.
YOU"RE MY LITTLE BABY.
MUM...
MY HAND. YOU'RE...
I CAN'T DO THIS. I'M SORRY.
I'M SO SORRY.

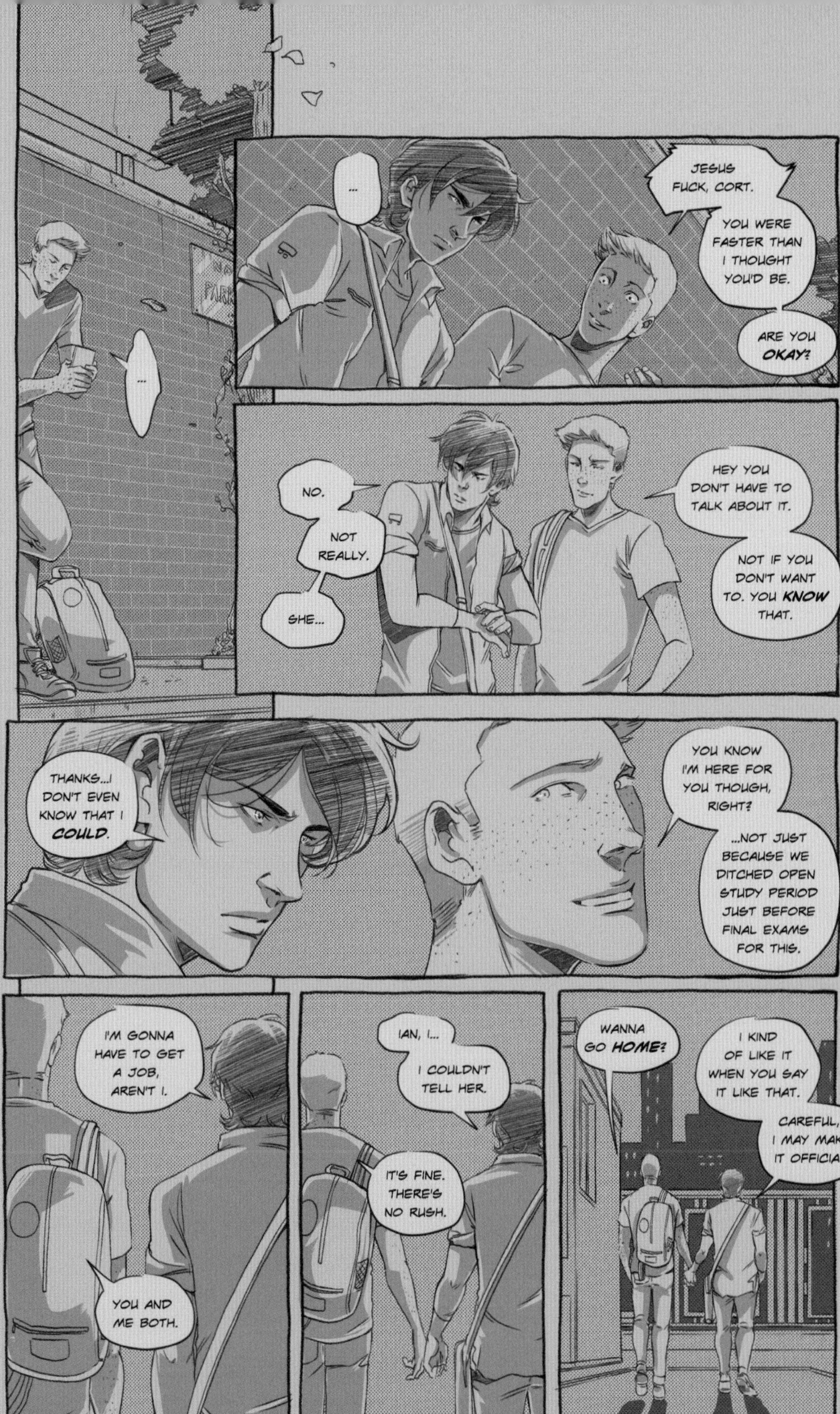
...
JESUS FUCK, CORT.
YOU WERE FASTER THAN I THOUGHT YOU'D BE.
ARE YOU OKAY?
...
NO.
NOT REALLY.
SHE...
HEY YOU DON'T HAVE TO TALK ABOUT IT.
NOT IF YOU DON'T WANT TO. YOU KNOW THAT.
THANKS...I DON'T EVEN KNOW THAT I COULD.
YOU KNOW I'M HERE FOR YOU THOUGH, RIGHT?
...NOT JUST BECAUSE WE DITCHED OPEN STUDY PERIOD JUST BEFORE FINAL EXAMS FOR THIS.
I'M GONNA HAVE TO GET A JOB, AREN'T I.
YOU AND ME BOTH.
IAN, I...
I COULDN'T TELL HER.
IT'S FINE. THERE'S NO RUSH.
WANNA GO HOME?
I KIND OF LIKE IT WHEN YOU SAY IT LIKE THAT.
CAREFUL, I MAY MAKE IT OFFICIAL.

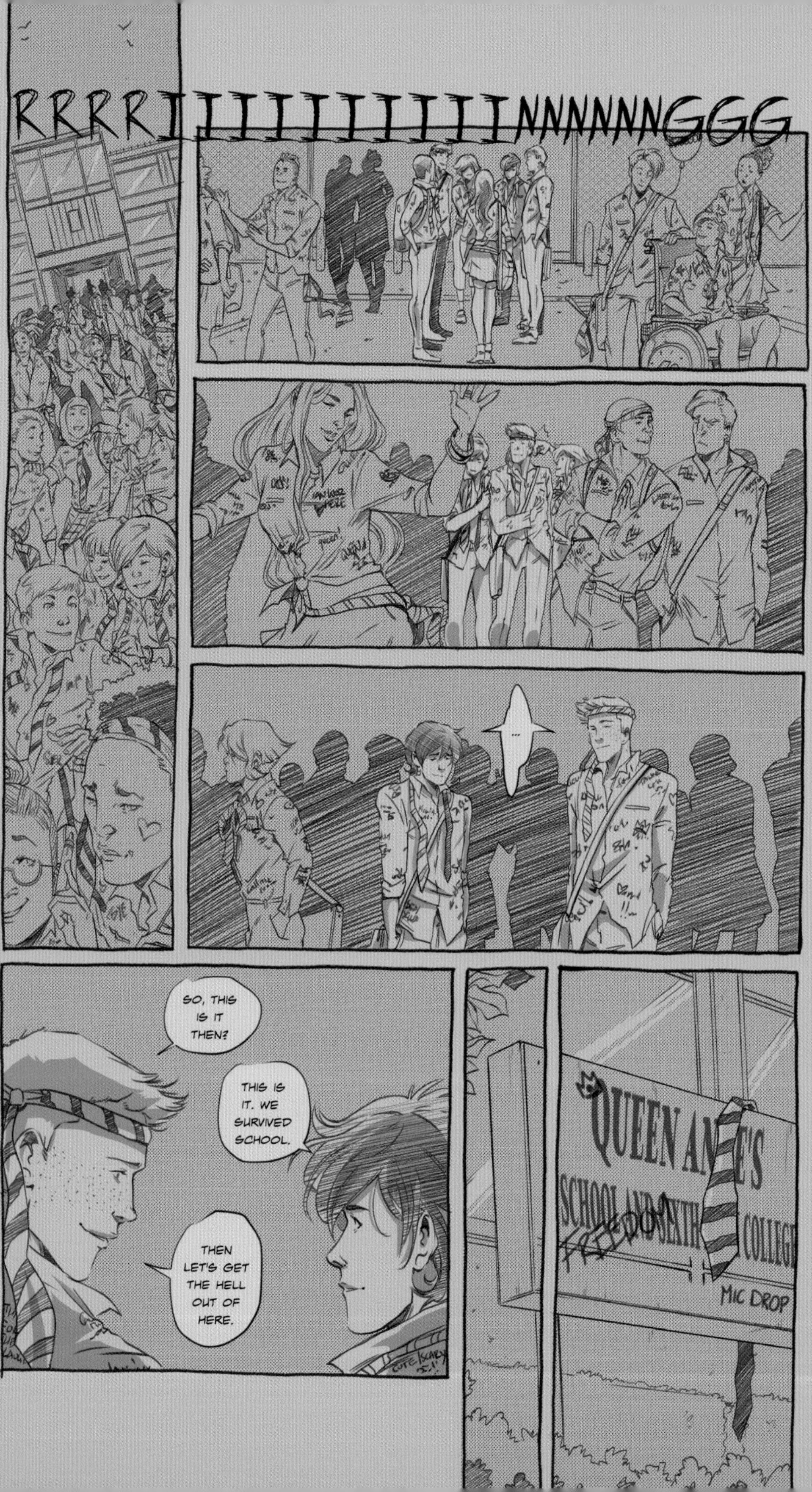
RRRRIIIIIIIIIIIIIINNNNNNGGG
...
SO, THIS IS IT THEN?
THIS IS IT. WE SURVIVED SCHOOL.
THEN LET'S GET THE HELL OUT OF HERE.
QUEEN ANNE'S SCHOOL AND SIXTH FORM COLLEGE
FREEDOM
MIC DROP

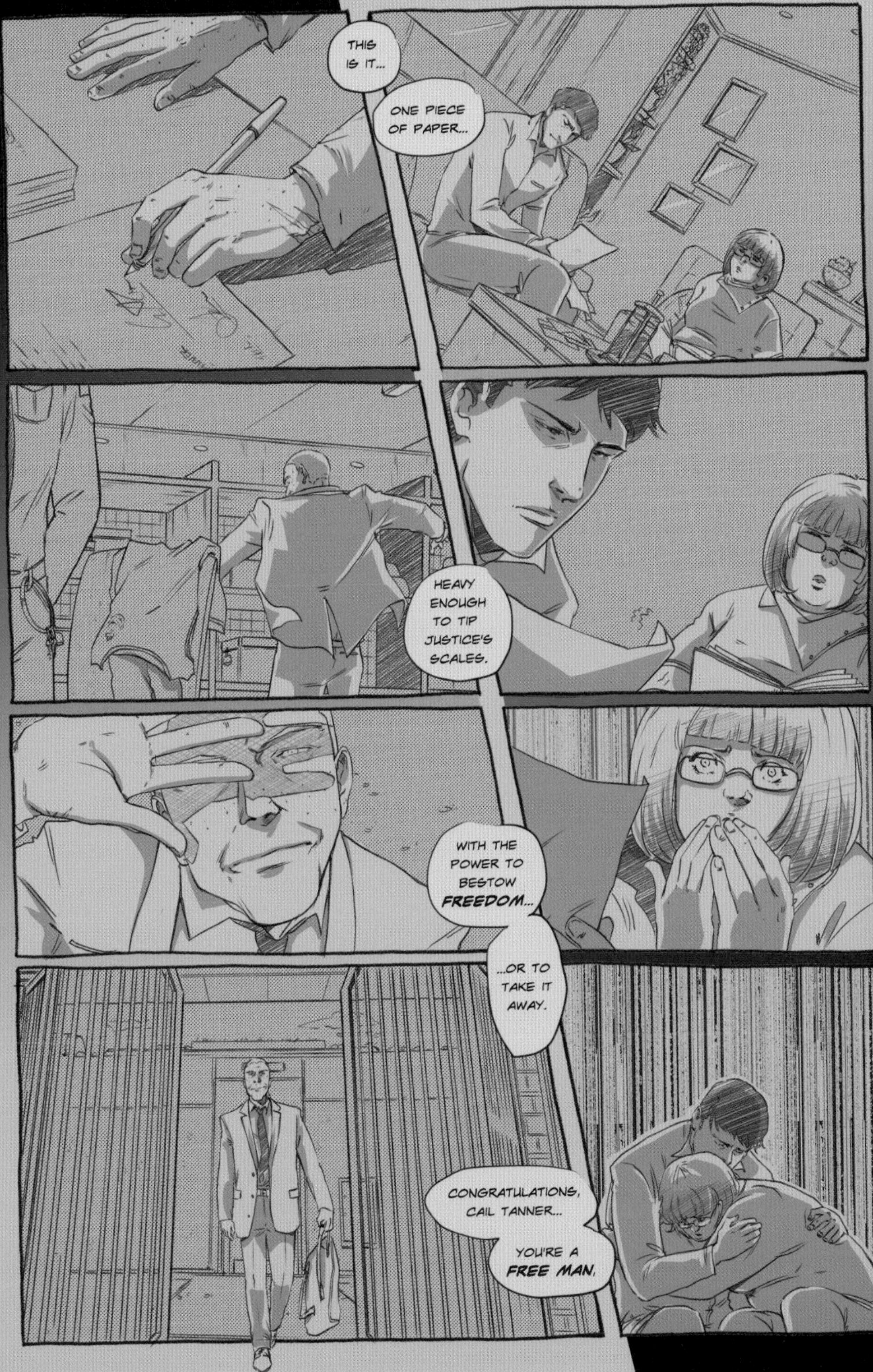
THIS IS IT...
ONE PIECE OF PAPER...
HEAVY ENOUGH TO TIP JUSTICE'S SCALES.
WITH THE POWER TO BESTOW FREEDOM...
...OR TO TAKE IT AWAY.
CONGRATULATIONS, CAIL TANNER...
YOU'RE A FREE MAN.

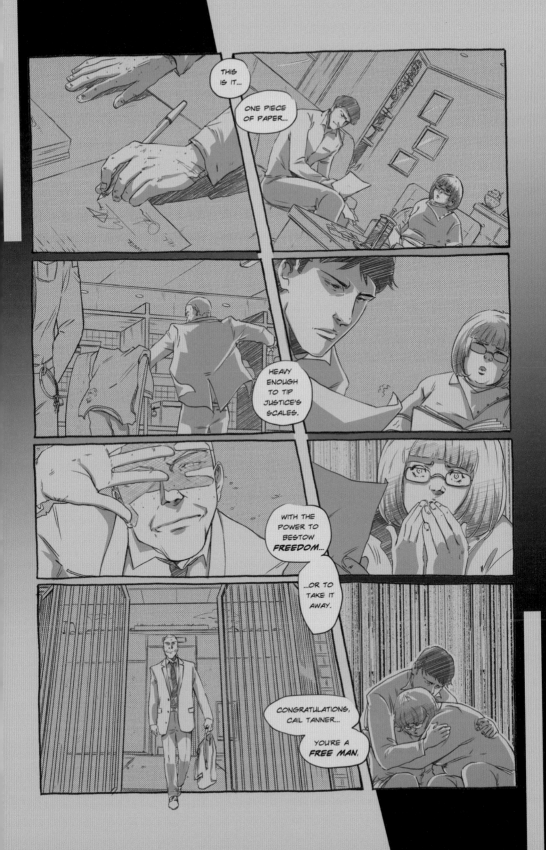